THE EMPIRE CHRONICLES

Children of the Anunnaki

by **MARK BARNETTE**

Bloomington, IN Milton Keynes, UK

authorHOUSE

AuthorHouse™
1663 Liberty Drive, Suite 200
Bloomington, IN 47403
www.authorhouse.com
Phone: 1-800-839-8640

AuthorHouse™ UK Ltd.
500 Avebury Boulevard
Central Milton Keynes, MK9 2BE
www.authorhouse.co.uk
Phone: 08001974150

This book is a work of fiction. People, places, events, and situations are the product of the author's imagination. Any resemblance to actual persons, living or dead, or historical events, is purely coincidental.

© 2006 Mark Barnette. All rights reserved.

No part of this book may be reproduced, stored in a retrieval system, or transmitted by any means without the written permission of the author.

First published by AuthorHouse 9/12/2006

ISBN: 1-4259-3016-6 (sc)
ISBN: 1-4259-3214-2 (dj)

Library of Congress Control Number: 2006906257

Printed in the United States of America
Bloomington, Indiana

This book is printed on acid-free paper.

To Jenny

My Muse
My Wife
My Life

1

THE CAR FLEW OUT of the night, taking aim at the stranger crossing the street; it didn't brake. In one horrible, grotesque instant, they met, the body bouncing up and rolling over the car's hood. The awful thud of impact was followed by a second, softer one, as the body landed on the roadway. The body's soft moans were interrupted only by the decreasing sound of squealing tires.

Dallas could do nothing but watch from the curb; his body frozen in the shadows, his mind screaming. All he could see was the crumpled form lying by the curb and the red of the car's taillights growing dim in the distance.

He roused himself to action and ran to the body, which lay on its side facing the curb.

"Listen ... to ... me ... "the body whispered up to him, between gasps of pain. "Beware ... they ... are ... watching ... the ... Order ... must ... find ... ."

"Beware who? Who's watching? What's the Order?"

"No ... my ... brief ... case? Where ... brief ... ?"

"Here, here it is," Dallas said, dragging it toward the stranger.

"Take ... take ... it. Look ... inside. They ... are ... watching. Find ... le gren ... find ... the ... fisherman. You ... must ... find ... them ... the ... Order ... beware ... " Then there came the sound of rushing air, like the opening of the valve on a tire, and then silence, as the body lay still.

With the briefcase still in his left hand, Dallas knelt over the body as a police car screeched to a stop mere feet away from him. Reflexively, he shielded his eyes against the car's bright lights with his right hand. In the newfound illumination, he glanced down at the lifeless body. Its dead eyes stared up at him, as intent in death as his last wish had been in life.

"Step back, please," one of the officers called out as he climbed out of the cruiser. "Step back, an ambulance is on the way."

Dallas responded immediately, instinctively clutching the briefcase as he retreated.

"Tell 'em to take their time," the other one said, leaning over the corpse. "This one's not in a rush; not anymore."

"Sir," the first officer said, matter-of-factly, as he turned to face Dallas, "is ... was this man a friend of yours?"

"No, I don't know him. I was just walking down this way," Dallas pointed down the road, "and this gentleman here was crossing the street ... and suddenly the car just came out of nowhere. He turned, just stood there like a deer in headlights, and the car drove right through him."

"Through him?" The officer repeated.

"Yeah. It didn't swerve or slow down. It just hit him and drove on."

"I see. Did he do anything before he died? Did he say anything ... did he give you anything?"

His shock subsiding, the scientist in Dallas began to assert itself. His mind filled with suspicion at such an odd question. His eyes darted between the two officers. One was shorter, white and with a waistline that hinted at too many donuts. The second, more senior officer was a large, wiry, black man. Dallas then shifted his gaze up and down the street and saw no one, no one at all. It was then he became aware that he was holding the briefcase as if it were his own.

"How did you get here so fast? Who called you?" Dallas asked finally.

"We got a call," the white officer said as his partner moved away. "Just let us ask the questions. Did he say anything?"

"No." Dallas paused, perhaps a moment too long. "He was dead when I got to him."

"I see." The officer's tone was full of skepticism. "May I see some ID?"

"ID? Sure," Dallas said, reaching for his wallet, "here."

"Dr. Dallas Roark?" The police officer showed the license to his partner; Dallas could have sworn the second officer cocked one eyebrow in recognition. He decided it was best to be friendly and engaging.

"Yes, that's right. I'm an archaeology professor at—"

"Still live at this address?" The officer asked, brushing aside the small talk.

"Yes."

The officer eventually finished the interview, after having tried several times unsuccessfully to trick the witness into contradicting himself. As Dallas stepped back slightly, the second officer walked over after inspecting the body and began whispering to the interrogator.

"It's not on him," the second one mumbled.

"What do you mean? It must be here. It must be around here somewhere."

The distracted officers began shining their flashlights around the area, as if searching for something; but what? Dallas suspected that what they were searching for must be in the briefcase.

"Am I free to go?" Dallas asked nervously. Receiving no reply, he slowly moved away with his hand tensed around the case's smooth leather handle.

He spun around and quickened his pace, trying not to act strangely as he crept off. He had withheld evidence, taken the briefcase; and yet, something about those two didn't feel right. There had been no one else around; who could have called? And how could they have arrived so quickly? Also, with all their questions, they never even asked if him to describe the car or if he had seen its license plate. What were they really looking for, and why?

Like any scientist, Dallas was an unusually curious and observant man, yet introspective by nature. His allies were the librarian, the bookkeeper, and the night watchman. He was typical of those in his profession, and until now, happy in the role of observer. This time, involvement had been thrust upon him.

Why had he not surrendered the case? He couldn't say; no more than he could answer his own questions about those "policemen." One thing was certain; those men now knew where he lived. If they didn't find what they were looking for, then they'd come for him. Sooner or later, they'd come.

All these thoughts only made Dallas quicken his pace. Arriving at his apartment building he sprinted across the lobby to the waiting elevator. Eleven floors up, he dashed out the still opening elevator door. He literally flung his six- foot-five-inch frame at the doorway, fumbling with his keys, and trying desperately to open his door. His agitated state only delayed him, and he scraped his knuckles on the latch. Once inside, he locked every bolt, tossed the keys on to a nearby table, and collapsed onto the couch, with the briefcase slapping heavily into his lap.

He stared at the case with growing curiosity. Dallas rubbed his hands briefly across the fine ostrich leather. It felt firm, yet supple, and obviously expensive. Slowly, his thumbs slid the latches. It was well-made; constructed of solid heavy brass fittings that yielded silently to his touch

At last he opened it; but simple answers were not forthcoming. Inside was an unsigned, typewritten manuscript, a supermarket tabloid, a small, daily diary, and a smooth, green, crystalline object about twice the size of a man's hand. That object caught Dallas's eye and his immediate attention.

It seemed at once translucent and solid; like tiger's eye, but without the bands of varying color, yet it shimmered through many levels. The object was tapered and faceted. Its triangular shape was without fault or flaw, totally unblemished, and smooth on one side. On the wide base of its isosceles shape, only a pair of small notches interrupted the otherwise straight lines.

The reverse contained many small rows of carefully etched symbols. Grabbing a magnifying glass, he studied the markings, which bore an uncanny similarity to hieratic script. There were also alternating rows of a cuneiform-style, script so small that their very presence amply demonstrated the abilities of its engraver. Its polished surface reminded him of a river stone, as if it had been worked by water since before man's ancestors had come down from the trees. Laying it aside, he continued to the other items.

He flipped through the diary and discovered the stranger's name: Dr. Montgomery Todd; then he wandered through the "F" section of the addresses, hoping he might find some clue about the fisherman; no luck.

The newspaper article was on the most recent in the long series of missing Martian space probes. The string had now run to six straight lost ships, and NASA was officially at a loss to explain the problem. The article hinted at several "unofficial" reasons, none of which made any more sense of the problem.

The manuscript appeared to be a report or academic paper on some obscure aspect of Mayan civilization. Dallas glanced at it briefly and found it vaguely interesting. The plentiful handmade corrections suggested that the stranger knew the author, or might be the author; Dallas wasn't sure which. He set it aside for later study.

The diary was, save one obscure entry, completely empty. That entry, an appointment for tomorrow, was noted in a code or shorthand that Dallas could not readily decipher. The day and time were plain enough, the diary's calendar format had seen to that, but the meeting's location and subject were nonsensical; a single cryptic notation, "CFatAker." What, he wondered, could it mean - "CFatAker"? All the letters ran together; was it an anagram? Did the capital letters stand for something? Or was it just sloppy writing?

His mind looked for natural combinations ... C Fat Aker; was that "see someone named Fat Aker"? ... CF at Aker; maybe someone's initials: CF. "Okay, meet CF, whoever CF might be, at ... Aker," He muttered, "What the hell's an Aker?" This seemed as meaningless as Fat Aker.

Dallas went back to the initials, CF. "The Fisherman," the dying man had said. "Find the fisherman." Was F for fisherman? Could CF mean "see fisherman"; "see fisherman at Aker?" His circular logic brought him back to Aker and his original question. Still, he could make no sense of the rest of the note; he must be on the right track, he thought to himself.

He moved to his computer and logged onto the Internet. If there was a word "Aker," he'd know in a moment. He stared at the search's response and realized it would take more than a moment. Let's see, he thought, there's an observatory in Arizona named after someone named Governor Aker. That might tie in with the article on Mars; or not. The first search engine offered some thirty sites. Some, like those directing one to Pooh's "100 Aker Wood", could be instantly eliminated.

Dallas tried to recall old man's dying words, was it, "Beware, find the Order?" Or was it, "Beware the Order?" He typed in the Order, and the results were less than exciting. The first hundred entries had something to do with Harry Potter; then on to various religious orders, book orders; in fact, just about any web site having something to do with the word, "order."

He entered "Aker" again, this time on a second search engine, and immediately hit an even bigger road block. This one offered over twenty-eight hundred different choices. Dallas let out a sigh and leaned back in his chair, absentmindedly, while his hand continued to work the mouse. The first choices seemed to be duplicates of the other search engine, so he clicked quickly past the first few pages. Suddenly an entry caught his eye.

Curiosity got the better of him and he rolled the cursor over the entry, "Egyptian God." When the screen popped up the subject, he sat upright. "Aker," Dallas finally remembered, was the Egyptian lion god, guardian of sunrise and sunset. Was that a link to the manuscript? Could the dead man have been talking in code? Was a lion somehow involved in the mystery? He bookmarked the page and moved on to other possibilities.

Several hours and pots of coffee later, Dallas had viewed almost a thousand entries, mostly personal web sites or Rotary club chapters or some other damned thing. He decided to return to his two most interesting possibilities: the observatory and the Egyptian god. Dallas considered the two options.

The observatory made more sense, logically, especially given the article. He could even stretch the argument to suggest that "fisherman" was code for Pisces, a constellation, as well as an astrological sign. That would mean he was going to Arizona to see the constellation Pisces from the observatory. It didn't seem like something worth dying for, though, and that "accident" was no accident. Besides, according to Dallas's research, the constellation would not be visible in Arizona until nine p.m. each night during the month of November. Seeing as it was only April, with the meeting seemingly just hours away and obviously during the day, the logic of stargazing fell short. Besides, Dallas thought to himself, trying to bring conclusion to the internal debate, the notation makes no mention of flight numbers or times, and there's no airline ticket in the briefcase.

He thought back to the other possibility; Aker the lion god. As he read the notes, he corrected himself; Aker was a double-lion god; a pair of lions sitting back-to-back ... A pair of lions! The museum had a pair of lions sitting in front of it. Could it be that simple? Was the dead man meeting the fisherman at the museum?

Well, Dallas thought to himself as he moved to look at his watch, tomorrow was Saturday and I'll find ... no, today is Saturday; where had the night gone? It was now early morning; the sun would be coming up sooner than he wanted. Still, Dallas had to admit this was the most exciting thing to happen to him in years. The last exciting thing, he reminded himself, had sent him into professional exile.

He sipped slowly on his coffee and gave an accounting of himself, to himself. It was a bad habit of his, especially late at night when he was tired and introspective. But he couldn't help it; this was a habit years in the making. He had an almost obsessive desire to examine himself, his life, and measure it against he own expectations. Not surprisingly he always came up short; a fact of which he was always quick to remind himself.

He was now, he thought, forty-five years old, and what had he accomplished? Nothing. He sensed his life had become small, his vision now myopic. It had once been otherwise. He found himself surrounded by fossilized trophies of decades' worth of work; careful, meticulous effort aimed at discovering some greater truth; a truth that had eluded him in his own soul. Like most people, when middle age forces them to begin facing their own mortality, Dallas darkly pondered his own accomplishments; measuring himself against the yardstick of eternity, and coming up short.

Dallas ran his left hand through his ample salt-and-pepper hair, and then slid the hand down his forehead, over his eyelids and hawkish nose. This ritualistic movement was Dallas's way of reminding himself he was tired and needn't have this mental conversation again. His mind was too weary to debate.

Dallas's body chose this moment to remind him just how tired he truly was. He rested his cup on the table and, using his palms as platforms, raised himself slowly to his tingling feet. He discarded his clothing as he stumbled to the bedroom and collapsed diagonally on top of his bedspread.

His sleep was troubled and restless. He dreamt repeatedly about the moment the car hit the old man, like a slow-motion, instant replay from a football game. In his dream, he seemed to take in more and more of the details of what had happened around him during those fateful moments. Each time it played, more of the puzzle's pieces fell into place, with some new detail remembered; or was it imagined? In his mind, it all seemed so real, so much a part of the experience.

By the time he awoke, Dallas had an even more vivid recollection of the event than when it happened, but he couldn't be sure how much of what he now remembered was fact, and how much was merely imagination There was something about the mystery car that keep pulling at him; a recollection which seemed somehow just out of reach. It haunted him.

Sitting in his kitchen, he played the scene over and over in his mind, with all the details he now seemed to remember. He saw the old man, he heard the squealing of tires and that terrible thump, and he saw the headlights of that car as it took its deadly aim. There was something still missing; what, he couldn't say, not yet.

At the appointed time, he set off to test his hypothesis. The walk to the museum was pleasant enough, only carrying the briefcase detracted from the stroll. It was an awkward, but necessary effort. Dallas reasoned that whoever he might be meeting just might recognize the case and want its contents. Initially, it was a desire he was anxious to satisfy, until it occurred to him that whoever killed the old man might also recognize it. With a sudden inspiration he detoured slightly, and entering his bank, went straight for his safety deposit box. He worked quickly, removing all of the case's contents and locking them away. Now if anyone approached, he felt he would have some measure of protection. They couldn't get what they wanted without keeping him alive. If, he reminded himself nervously, they stopped to ask him first.

Leaving the bank with the now-empty case, he glanced up and down the tree-lined streets. The sky was a deep blue, dotted with cotton-ball clouds. It was a beautiful, spring day with only a slight breeze to remind him that winter had not completely surrendered its grip. His left arm swung habitually under the unfamiliar weight of the black case.

Reaching the museum, Dallas sat on a nearby bench, anchored in the shadow of one of the building's pair of massive lions, opened the case, and stared at its empty insides. He slowly examined its interior – every seam, every snap, wondering if he'd missed anything. So engrossed had Dallas become that he failed to notice a young woman sit down on the bench facing opposite him.

She was properly and discreetly – even conservatively – dressed, with short, neatly cropped blonde hair. Her large, dark sunglasses covered the upper half of her face, giving her the ability to view the object of her attention with total anonymity; and at this moment, her attention was focused on Dallas.

Fifteen minutes past the appointed meeting time, he was having doubts about his library lion theory. He took note of only one man who had been waiting as long as himself: a large, wiry, black man with closely cropped silver hair loitering in line of trees just past the other side of the museum's massive steps. Dallas judged the distance between them to be about two hundred feet or so. The man leaned idly against one of the trees, his fingers rolling a freshly lit cigarette back and forth, its blue smoke drifting upward through the trees bare branches.

While the man was at too great a distance to make out his features, Dallas read from the man's body language only complete disinterest in his surroundings; he appeared lost in his own world. Dallas suddenly felt very foolish. Perhaps the police were really police; perhaps the old man was hallucinating; perhaps the last twelve hours had been a total waste.

Dallas was feeling very Walter Middy about the whole affair when the young woman left her bench and came over to him. He slapped the case closed as she approached. She stood before him, with her navy trench coat fluttering in the chilly spring breeze. He stared at her, absorbing the essence of what he saw; a work of art whose comprehension took less than a second. She stood straight and sure, with a posture that some might call cockiness, but that Dallas allowed to quiet confidence. She was not thin, but lean; well-muscled, yet lithe.

"Who are you?" the young woman demanded, destroying the moment. "Where is Dr. Todd?" She added, threateningly, "You have five seconds."

Dallas blinked in surprise, and then decided the personality most definitely fit. "Your Dr. Todd; was he an older gentleman, gray hair, balding, wears … wore … gold-colored, wire-rim glasses?"

"Yes." Her tone was simple and direct.

"Well, I'm sorry to tell you this but … he's, well, he's dead. Hit-and-run last night. He gave me this briefcase before he died, and he told me to find the Fisherman."

"He told you – a stranger – to meet me here?" Her tone was incredulous.

"No, not exactly. He had coded an entry in his diary. I deciphered its meaning and came here; I was beginning to think I had imagined the whole thing." Dallas added a chuckle. She, however, was not amused.

"I'll take that case now."

"Are you the Fisherman?"

"Let's just say I am."

"Let's just say you're not. Look, lady, I spent most of the night trying to figure out where to go, I lied to the police … "

The police!" She interrupted, with the first show of emotion he had seen. "You fool, if the police know about you, you'll have led them right to me." She shot glances over her shoulders in both directions. "Get up; we've got to go NOW!"

Her body language gave her away, and at that moment, Dallas, glancing around him, saw three pairs of neatly dressed, expressionless, plainclothesman, each about eighty yards away, starting to move toward them from different directions.

"Lady, what's going on?"

"You want to meet the Fisherman; fine. Looks like you'll get your chance." She looked at Dallas with barely concealed rage, "Let's go."

She quickly hustled him into a waiting SUV, parked a few feet away from the benches. One of her allies opened the door upon their approach, and the trio jumped inside. They had barely closed the doors behind them before the six men were at the car. The driver paid them no heed as he sped away, leaving the dark-suited men with clenched teeth. From the line of trees, the old black man watched all the activity with a bemused expression, his fingers rolling the cigarette back and forth absentmindedly.

Looking back from the SUV at the men in dark suits told Dallas all he wanted to know about not wanting to meet them. The question flashed through his mind: were they FBI, CIA, maybe Secret Service? If they were, then who was he with, terrorists? Reflexively, Dallas shook his head. What had he gotten himself into?

2

AS THEY PULLED AWAY from the museum, the six antagonists dashed for their own black SUVs. Dallas turned in his seat to face the woman. He was no longer amused. "Look, lady … " He interrupted himself. "Do you have a name?"

"Yes," she snapped, offering nothing further.

"Okay … Do you want me guess?"

"I want you to be quiet."

"Lady, I didn't want to be here, and I don't need to be here. I think I'm due a few answers."

"First, you insisted on meeting the Fisherman, and you brought them," she thrust her thumb toward the pursuing men, "so you *did* ask to be here. Second, I don't care what you want. Third, I don't think you're due anything; but lucky for you, I'm not the final answer. Fourth, if I put you out of this car now, you'll be dead before the sun sets. Last, please give me a reason to put you out." She spun around, leaving him to stare at the back of her head.

Dallas didn't know what he had done to this woman, but he was sure that trying to talk to her could only make it worse. He began to turn around when the SUV executed a series of sharp right turns, then slammed to a stop in a back alley.

The nameless driver of Dallas's car waited a moment then maneuvered a U-turn and drove calmly back from where they came; back to the museum. They passed the main entrance, instead entering the building's underground garage. The SUV didn't stop as it reached the gates blocking their path; rather, the gates rose by some unseen command. The vehicle finally reached an apparent dead end; only it wasn't. When they pulled up to the wall, an entire concrete section swung slowly out of the way. After they drove through the hidden passage, it returned to its former position, leaving anyone on the other side with no evidence that they had been there.

"Come on." The woman seemed to relax a bit, at least slightly, as the car pulled to a stop.

"Where?" Dallas's question was reflexive and rhetorical.

"Look, you can sit in the garage, or you can come with me," she muttered only barely, under her breath, "I don't have time for this."

Dallas slid across the seat and fell in behind her and the others as they walked to a nearby door. The driver waved a magnetic security card over a nearby, wall-mounted black plate, and the door popped open noiselessly. The contrast between the sterile concrete garage and the area beyond the door was extreme. Dallas had expected the ubiquitous dark, dank, urine-scented stairway which comes with every such structure. Instead, he entered immediately into a spectacularly decorated complex. The network of corridors, offices, and apartments was warm, inviting, and well-lit. So well-lit, in fact, that it didn't occur to Dallas until later that there were no windows; meaning that they were obviously deep underground.

Following his rescuer-captors, Dallas found himself entering a large, immaculately decorated room; was it an office, a lounge, or someone's living quarters? Dallas wasn't sure. There was only thing he was sure of; it was huge. This single room was larger than his entire apartment. Its high ceiling further exaggerated its spaciousness, if that were possible. Dallas felt like he'd entered a museum within a museum; every space decorated by works of art and archeological treasures.

The group of four stood there, silently, as if waiting for something dramatic to happen. Ambling over to the far wall, Dallas left his guards to study a massive Renaissance drawing in an incredible ornate frame. The lines, the depth, and the art seemed to leap off the ancient paper. He was convinced this sketch was not a reproduction; it had the classic lines and feel of a genuine Renaissance work. He stared in disbelief at the scene before him.

"Beautiful, isn't it?"

Dallas started at the sudden end to the silence. The voice boomed, deep and powerful, the words precise and even, with a tone that concealed any hint of its owner's birthplace. He spun to agree and was shocked once again. Before him had appeared a powerful man with dark hair and eyes. His jaw was strong and square. His even, expressionless, yet powerful, gaze seemed to freeze Dallas. It was then he realized the possessor of that voice sat confined to a wheelchair, although it was clearly unlike any such chair he had ever seen.

"Yes, yes, it is." Dallas said finally. "It must be worth a fortune."

"Oh, it is quite beyond any valuation, Dr. Roark. It is literally priceless."

"I don't recall ever seeing this specific piece, but it looks like a drawing for a panel from the Sistine Chapel."

"You wouldn't have seen it anywhere. As far as the world knows, this piece does not exist. What would the world say if an unknown Michelangelo panel were to appear out of nowhere?"

"Michelangelo! Just hanging here on the wall?"

"What would you have us do with it, Dr. Roark, hide it in a closet? Besides, it is not alone. Every item in this room, indeed in this entire complex, is equally genuine and equally unknown; I assure you, this Michelangelo is in excellent company."

"I must admit, sir, you have me at a disadvantage, Mister ... Mister—" Dallas asked, suddenly conscious that this stranger had been addressing him by name.

"Fisher, Dr. Joshua Fisher. Welcome to our humble home."

"How do you know me? Have we met?"

"Come, Dr. Roark, such modesty. You are, or were, a linguist and archeologist of some note, I recognized you at once. I make it a point to keep track of such things. Now, I believe you have something for me."

"Not exactly. I have the case, as you can see, but I have taken the precaution of retaining its contents for the present."

"I do see," Fisher's expression didn't change; his tone remained strong and thoughtful. "It would appear you don't trust us, Dr. Roark."

"I have no doubt you understand my caution, sir. After all, it has been a strange past twenty-four hours, I'm sure you'll agree. I mean, that poor old man was intentionally run down by that car; and then the police appearing out of nowhere … Something about them didn't … well, it just didn't seem right, so I kept the existence of the case to myself."

"Quite, quite." Fisher's face revealed for the first time any hint of humanity. "I imagine I would have taken similar precautions were I in your shoes. I compliment you on your insight regarding the police; you were quite correct not to trust them. So, Dr. Roark, how would you propose we resolve this little impasse?"

"A test. Dr. Todd told me to beware an organization. What organization?"

Fisher's absence of expression turned to a slight frown. He brought his hands together, interlocking his fingers with his indexed fingers raised to a point. He rested his chin on that point for a long moment, his eyes staring into space. There was no anger in his expression; rather, he seemed to be calculating the dangers of revealing things yet unspoken.

"If he knew what he hinted he knew; the information which required our scheduled meeting, then the correct answer would be 'the Order'."

"And what … or who is the Order? I must admit, I searched the Internet and found nothing but links to Harry Potter."

"Ah, and thereby hangs the tale." Turning to the rest of the group, he continued, "Gentlemen, I appreciate your help, but I believe I can handle everything from here. Please return to your duties in the museum. Miranda, you may stay if you wish. Perhaps you can help me fill in the blanks."

"You're not really going to—" she began. Dr. Fisher cut her off.

"That must be his choice." Turning back, he locked eyes with Dallas. "Before I continue, I must ask you one question; did you examine the contents of the case? Did you find a flat, triangular green stone?"

"Yes, I did. Why?"

Joshua brushed aside Dallas's question. "Did you thoroughly examine it?"

"Yes, I spent most of the night on it."

"And did you discover anything odd?"

"Only if you consider that it's covered in almost microscopic engravings of cuneiform and hieratic text odd."

"I see," Joshua intoned softly, "were you able to read any of it?"

"No, no, I wasn't. Perhaps, if I had more time, I might; but that really wasn't the center of my attention at that particular moment."

Joshua continued, giving no explanation for his questions. "I must warn you that, if I answer your question, your future will forever be altered; it fact, it may already be so. But if I fully answer you, then the die, as they say, will be cast. You may want to ponder that for a moment. If you leave now, my men will return with you, collect the doctor's materials, then take you to your home and will keep you under surveillance until we believe the danger has passed. Even so, you may have to move to another apartment, possibly another city. For your help to this point, we'll assist you, if you wish; even find you another teaching position if need be. But if I answer you, then you will never be able to return to your home or your life. For your own safety you will have to stay here, with us; join us, in effect. That is your choice, but you must make it alone, and you must make it now."

"Hell," Dallas said finally, "like you say, I'm already halfway in this mess now. Even if you don't tell me another thing, those goons will think you did. Besides, that tease has too much temptation for anyone to pass up."

"Quite."

"If I stay, what happens next? What about my job, my friends, my family?"

"What you will do is both simple and difficult; you will assist us. That will become your life's work; work for which you will be well rewarded both financially and emotionally. As for your job, they'll receive a vague letter of immediate resignation; we'll send someone to collect your belongings. I'm not concerned about your friends; I'm betting you haven't got any. And as for your family, you'll disappear while on a dig in some obscure part of the world. You will never be able to contact them directly again. For their safety as well as your own, you must leave them behind, forever."

"With all due respect, aren't you being a tad melodramatic," Dallas interjected. "You make it sound like I'm joining the witness protection program."

"As to whether I'm being 'melodramatic,' ask Dr. Todd. He chose to stay *outside,* and we ultimately proved incapable of protecting him; that is why I cannot, in good conscience, let you simply walk away. As to your comparison to the witness protection program, it is most apt. You will understand better, if and when you wish me to explain."

"Ah, what the hell. I've got nothing better to do this afternoon."

"I caution you, you are taking this far too lightly. Perhaps it is best you leave … as soon as we arrange for you to give us the items."

"But you haven't answered my question."

"To do that, I must give you too much information to allow you to just walk away; you have, in fact, already seen far too much. Your choices are simple. Give us the tablet and walk away, or have your archaeologist's curiosity satisfied; join us, and become part of the most important quest in history."

Dallas stared at Joshua Fisher for a long time, then turned and paced the around the room in silence. In doing so, he mentally took stock of his life. His hair was in the midst of turning gray, and his recent accomplishments could be counted on one hand; with fingers to spare. He recalled his thoughts of the night before; that he had become a nondescript teacher of a nondescript discipline in a nondescript college.

He had abandoned a once-promising future, and in so doing, found the anonymity he had craved. Now he saw himself as one small, insignificant cog in an immensely larger organism, whose sole purpose was to assist in the creation of additional nondescript cogs for future consumption. Perhaps, he thought, this was the moment he could shed himself of his myopic life. What this man in front of him offered was more than he could have imagined or hoped for; to once again be a part of something meaningful, and thereby find some meaning for himself.

"All right," Dallas said finally, and for the first time, seriously, "I'm in."

"Wonderful." Fisher motioned for Dallas to be seated, and then moved his wheelchair to face him, almost within whispering distance. He studied Dallas's face for a moment as a stern faced Miranda lowered herself in the chair opposite. "What I am about to tell you is part fact, part conjecture, part legend, and perhaps part fantasy. As you are a man of learning, I must ask you to set aside your training for a time, to take a leap of faith in all that I am about to tell you—"

"I'm honored," Dallas interrupted, "by your assessment of my background, but I assure you I would hardly qualify as a learned man in my profession."

"Perhaps, perhaps not. Our information suggests otherwise. You might possibly offer more than you give yourself credit for." Fisher continued, with a look that suggested he knew more about that subject than he wished to volunteer, "At any rate, you know of the so-called 'Dark Ages'?"

"Of course, the five-hundred-year period from the fall of Roman to the end of the first Christian Millennium; roughly 476 AD to around 1000 AD."

"What if I told you that this time period was not the true Dark Age, at least not all of it? What if I told you that, comparatively speaking, we are still in a 'Dark Age,' a period that began perhaps thirteen thousand, five hundred years ago. What if I were to tell you that the commonly accepted Dark Age was nothing more than an extremely minor setback in an extremely long, extremely slow climb back to our species' former greatness? Greatness, I might add, which we have not, despite our current technological advances, even come close to attaining."

"Well," Dallas said finally, "I'd have to say you've been reading too many comic books, or watching too much bad TV."

"Dr. Roark, are you familiar with the 'alternative' works of Charles Hapgood, Zecharia Sitchin, Richard Hoagland, Graham Hancock, Robert Bauval, Alan Alford, and especially James Marrs, to name just of few?"

"Not really; I know the names, of course, but even associate professors know enough to stay away from pseudo-science."

"Pseudo-science? I guess to you it might seem like that. Remember, I told you that you must set aside your preconceptions. Oh, I'll grant that, separately, none of them have it quite right, but when put together, they're far closer to the truth than traditional 'scientists' care to accept, or admit."

"Really? And you telling me that Dr. Todd was killed by little green men from Mars?"

"Actually, they're flesh-toned. In fact, 'they' are 'us.'"

3

"THE STORY BEGINS TENS of thousands of years ago; at a time when our solar system was the seat of power for a vast galactic empire ruled by a race who called themselves the Anunnaki. It stretched for untold hundreds of light years in all directions. This empire was extremely advanced technically, but legend has it, brutal and vicious. Its rulers were an ancient race possessing abilities that would dwarf the human race today. They maintained their power for millennia through an enormous star fleet and weapons supposedly powerful enough to destroy planets, and they subjugated thousands of races through these weapons. To us, today, with their technology, they would seem godlike.

"Then there came a time, so the tales say, that after many thousands of years of domination, the oppressed star systems of the empire rose up. A civil war broke out, fought on a scale so vast that we cannot even begin to comprehend it. The fighting went on for centuries. The ancient myths tell of whole races being wiped from existence. The rebels fought on, against overwhelming odds, until one day they came into possession of a weapon to rival that of the oppressive rulers.

"They found a way to get past the empire's defenses and laid waste to the empire's home world with that weapon; a device so terrible that it stripped the planet of most of its atmosphere and threatened to split the planet in two. Up until thirteen thousand, five hundred years ago, it was known throughout the known galaxy as Nibiru. That world … is the planet we know today as Mars.

"The weapon developed by the rebels was, we believe, a directed energy pulse converter. It's far too complicated for me to explain its construction, but the science upon which it is based is simple enough. You are, of course, familiar with Einstein's $E=mc^2$?"

"I know what the letters mean." Dallas offered in response to a clearly rhetorical question, "As to the rest, I'm an archeologist not a physicist."

"Well, the concept is simple, really. In essence, Einstein stated that energy and matter are really the same thing and; therefore, are convertible from one state to the other, in theory. The atomic bomb is one crude application of converting matter to energy. The theory works in both directions; energy can also be converted into matter. In 1933, in Paris, two French scientists, Irène and Frédéric Joliot-Curie, demonstrated this principle on the atomic level using light rays.

"We think the rebels found a way of creating matter on a massive scale. Possibly, they were able to harness the radiated energy of a star, in this case the sun, and convert it into matter, and then direct that matter into a collision course with the empire's home. Our scientists speculate that they created an asteroid-sized body and sent it to impact Nibiru – Mars; with catastrophic results. They believe such an impact formed the Hellas Basin at the point of the collision and a canyon on the opposite side of the planet, known to astronomers today as Valles Marineris; a gash some 1,875 miles long, and five miles deep. The colliding mass, due to its unstable nature, converted back to energy, resulting in a secondary explosion that would dwarf a simultaneous detonation of all the nuclear weapons of Earth. Our scientists have calculated that such a combination of explosions ripped away most of the atmosphere and also reduced the planet's mass by perhaps as much as thirty percent. We believe Mars' two moons, Phobos and Deimos, are the remnants of these events. These moons, and all the space debris, which we refer to as near-Earth Asteroids, including meteorite fragments found here on

Earth that geologists have proven as coming from Mars, are almost all that remains of that vast empire."

"*Almost* all?"

"Almost, but not quite. When the empire realized all was lost, and as the rebels were preparing to their final assault, the emperor prepared for one last stand. Legend tells of the emperor began hiding great stores of weapons and technology in huge vaults here on Earth in the time before the final invasion. At the very last moment, some of his subjects on Nibiru, perhaps vainly hoping to avoid total annihilation, betrayed him to the rebels. After the final battle, the betrayers were brought to Earth and were given the responsibility of overseeing the growth of the new Neolithic human culture. We were to wipe out the evil past and begin our race anew."

"We," continued Josh, pausing a moment for emphasis, "are the descendants of those traitors, and we have served the role of guardian ever since; hence our name, the Guardians. Also, and this is fact, not myth, the emperor had also prepared a great ship – an ark, if you will, to be filled with people and equipment. As it turned out, a group of subjects loyal to the emperor did manage to escape in the emperor's ark and made it to Earth. They and their descendants perceived themselves as the rightful architects of the planet's future, and thus was the conflict borne that has continued until today. Today, they call themselves the Order. We are two groups, equally powerful and equally determined to steer the destiny of the Earth.

"We have struggled to a standoff: the Guardians and the Order, neither able to dominate the other, and neither willing to concede to the other. During all this time, the Order has searched in vain for the emperor's secret weapons vaults."

"But," quizzed Dallas, "if the Order were loyal supporters of the emperor then why don't they already know where the vaults are?"

"Obviously we can't speak to their history but we know the vaults were already in place and secreted away before they made good their escape. Perhaps the emperor didn't have time to tell them before they fled, or perhaps they were never told. All we know is that our tales tell us that, rather than find them, the vaults must remain forever buried. Over the centuries, the Guardians came to believe these vaults to be nothing more than myth; the product of wishful thinking produced by a humbled group of people who longed to rebuild the former empire. Then, a year ago, I discovered the first tablet —"

"You have another tablet?" interrupted Dallas.

"Yes, I found it quite by accident while excavating a Pleistocene epoch burial chamber; it dated to the Older Dryas stadial. Its discovery resulted in a cave-in that confined me to this damnable chair. Anyway, once we understood what we had found, we realized that the vaults might not a legend, but may in fact be very real, and potentially very dangerous."

"But why," Dallas asked, "did the tablets make you suddenly believe in the vaults if you are unable to read them?"

"The myths of the vaults also tell of four tablets, such as these, that are somehow combined to unlock the entrance to their secret location. Without them, so the story goes, one could never find vaults. Within the Guardians, opinion had long been split between those who believed the tablets never really existed, and others who felt that, if they had existed at one time, that they had long since vanished. We have reluctantly had to accept the possibility that if the tablets exist, then the vaults must also exist.

"We now find ourselves in a race with the Order to solve this puzzle. They have always wished to use the contents of the vaults in an attempt to restore the empire; that is something our legends say we must prevent at all costs. Now, it would appear that we must find them, if only to keep them from falling into the hands of the Order. We would use their contents to better the lives of the human race, and hopefully lead us into a new era of enlightenment. While we assume from what we do know of the hidden chambers that they contain weapons, it is also possible that other technology exists, as well as some history of our ancestors, the Anunnaki. Such a revelation would fundamentally alter mankind's cosmic view."

"I suppose you know what I'm thinking," Dallas said finally, thinking to himself that he'd fallen in with a group stranger than the People's Temple and Heaven's Gate put together.

"Would you like me read your mind?" Joshua's statement had the tone of a challenge rather than a joke.

Dallas finally spoke up, "But all the geologists say Mars has been dead, frozen planet for over three billion years. I remember reading the latest study in the journal *Science*; they stated unequivocally three and a half billion years, not ten thousand."

"So they say ... so they believe. We know a different truth."

"For the sake of argument, let's say I accept everything you've told me so far; so what? We're descended from a race of super-brained, bad-tempered, sadistic, galactic rulers who got vaporized. This is not a message people on Earth would welcome, even if they believed you. But you've got no archeological proof: no ruins, no death ray, and no spaceships. Besides some cute green triangular stones that could be from anywhere, or anytime, you haven't got squat."

"Actually, that isn't ... exactly correct."

"Excuse me?"

"Yes, that's part of what Dr. Todd's research was all about."

"I think I need a —"

"Drink? I don't need to read your mind for that one. Actually, our ancestors really could read minds, and much more. Legends tell of tremendous mental powers: teleportation, projection, telekinesis; and they would have done it with no more effort than breathing.

"These abilities were bred out of Earth's human race long ago for reasons I will also explain later; but those of us of more pure blood still retain some small portion of their mental abilities."

"And what's Miranda's gift," Dallas laughed, "her good manners?"

The woman glared; a low, threatening guttural growl was her only reply.

"Don't be too hard on her, Dr. Roark. She is in constant danger from our enemies and she carries a difficult burden. As my daughter it is her responsibility to one day replace me."

"Your daughter? I apologize, I was just—"

Fisher dismissed it with a wave of his hand. "Let's just say that's not an original observation. Now, where was I? Oh, yes, I have leapt ahead. Let me digress a bit. Now, the Anunnaki, before their own destruction, used Earth in much the same was we used Alcatraz; or so the stories say. Long before the fall of the empire, when they wanted to exile individuals or groups of people, they would send them here. While we can't prove it, we believe the Anunnaki were a tall, slender people owing to the lesser gravity of their home world. Logically, anyone sent here from Nibiru would have weighed twice what they were used to on the own planet. They were brought here, dropped off with only the clothes on their backs, and left on their own to live or die. After many, many generations of this type of exile the Anunnaki realized that the resources of this planet could be better utilized, so we they organized the descendants of the exiles into forced labor camps. Independent of that group, the planet was evolving its own primate life, the primitive hominins, whose skeletons have been found around the world. The ancient Australopithecus, the more recent Homo Erectus, even Neanderthal; all of them were the proper evolutionary line of this planet; but not us, not what we now call Homo Sapiens Sapiens.

"Over the generations, the Anunnaki experimented with genetics to merge the awareness and intelligence of the exiles with the more robust local species. Today's human race, absent the vast mental powers, is the result."

Joshua stopped to pour himself a glass of water. Dallas felt like a freshman getting his first archaeology lecture. He had to confess that regardless of its truthfulness, it made a fascinating tale. He found himself waiting eagerly for Joshua to continue; which, in due course, he did.

"This story," Joshua began again, "is told in surprisingly specific detail in the ancient Sumerian creation legends; though today these tales are relegated to mere myth by 'modern' science. Genetic research has hinted at the truthfulness of them, through the discrepancies of the genetic record – we know the genetic Eve appeared approximately two hundred thousand ago, but the genetic Adam appeared many thousands of years later. It is an interesting genetic fact is that all the greater apes from which we are supposedly descended, even the Neanderthals, had twenty-four pairs of chromosomes. Humans have twenty-three pairs. Scientists today explain the discrepancy away through something they refer to as chromosome fusion; but at the same time, failing to explain how such a mutation could be passed on without having at least one breeding pair of mutants. They also conveniently ignore the corollary question; how such a random mutation could have spontaneously occurred in given population in numbers sufficient to allow for the creation of future generations. In short, they would have us believe we evolved from a species with whom we are not genetically compatible."

"This story is truly fascinating, truly it is, but it sounds insane. Do you really believe this tale?" Dallas could only shake his head.

"Insane? No. Believe? Most definitely. Remember your Bible: after Cain slew Abel, he fled to another city where he married a woman native to that land, and together they had many children. It's there, in Genesis, 'there were giants on Earth in those days, the Nephilim' – they weren't creating fantasy, they were speaking what to them was a simple truth. They knew from the ancient stories that the sons of the gods married the daughters of men. The descendants of the Anunnaki were indeed giants, figuratively and literally. Those people were giants mentally, aside from being physically taller. Before the end of the empire, with their advanced science and technology, they would indeed have seemed like gods.

"Did you know," Joshua continued, "that among the ancient Kurdish cultures, there are legends of a tall, pale skinned, golden-haired superhuman race that lived apart from other men? They were a race feared and worshipped for their powers, but who were destroyed in a global flood. One Kurdish legend even tells of one of these super-humans saving a live by performing a medical procedure that today we recognize as a cesarean section. The legend has been traditionally dated loosely to sometime before 3,000 BCE. In fact, it is much, much older."

"I grant that is interesting, even thought-provoking, but I still don't understand how the Anunnaki could just lose track of their past. How could there not be any intervening written records?"

"Remember," Miranda jumped in, "those exiled here in the end times, while relatively few in number, were of pure blood. The planet was almost completely populated with the hybrids. These hybrids feared the powers of our ancestors. And clearly, whether Kurdish, Hebrew, or Sumerian; the legends tell of a massive break with the past, due to a massive worldwide flood."

"But everything you've told me is couched as legend, myth or rumor. If your group has over thirteen millennia of unbroken history, there must be some firsthand record. Oral traditions may be quite interesting, maybe even meaningful, but they are hardly proof of—"

"We can't give something that doesn't exist," interrupted Joshua. "Let me give you a simple example. Objectively, we can't even prove today that Jesus ever really existed; yet there are over one billion people who call themselves Christians. Despite the Roman penchant for recording everything, there are no contemporaneous independent written accounts supporting Christ's existence. There are references to a him, made years later – Roman historian, Flavius Josephus, for example, but he borrowed what little he wrote on the subject from the Gospel of Luke. Then of course there are the writings of Roman historian Tacitus, who called Jesus by the name Christus; and Lucian, the second century Greek satirist who ridiculed Christian traditions; and the letters of Pliny the Younger to the emperor Trajan. Yet, all these things were written years after the crucifixion, all relying on hearsay; not one single shred of objective eye witness evidence exists. Even the Gospels themselves were apparently written anonymously long afterward. If I wanted to be a cynic I could say that everything we think we know about Christ comes from unknown sources who apparently had a vested interest in maintaining the myth; and that was only two thousand years ago. We're talking about a period over six times as long. I am sometimes amazed that any knowledge survived at all."

"Dr. Fisher ... " Dallas paused, "the matter of Christ existence is one of faith, one I choose to accept. Of course I understand the implications of the story you tell. What you say is fascinating, intriguing – all those adjectives; but talk, as they say, is cheap. If you want me to believe you show me something, anything, which proves what you say."

"Very well." Turning to his daughter, Fisher pointed toward the door on the far wall. "Miranda, do be so kind as to ask our geologist, Dr. Carbonara, to bring me some items from the lab. Tell him I wish to show them to Dr. Roark." Turing back to Dallas, Fisher continued, "These few items are by no means all we possess. Two of them we keep in the laboratory safe because they are dangerous; the third, frankly because it's a puzzlement."

Miranda returned shortly, with both a tray containing four items and a protective scientist in tow; a cloud of continued angry defiance still hanging around her head. She laid the tray carefully on the coffee table and withdrew silently to her seat. Dallas reached for the object nearest to him. It one of a pair of what appeared to be futuristic derringers; a pistol-like grip and delicate barrel. Unlike a firearm, however, the barrel tapered to a smooth point. It was light to the touch, with a matte, almost pewter, finish. It could be ten minutes old or ten thousand years old for all he knew. There was nothing that suggested its age or purpose. Next to those pieces was a triangular-shaped piece of unknown metal, adorned on one side with an engraving of a figure vaguely reminiscent of Baphomet, and on the reverse with a hieroglyph of an eye – the "All-Seeing Eye." He supposed the object was a medallion or amulet, but its symbols were mythologically inconsistent, at least in the conventional context. Joshua let Dallas continue his examination for a few moments longer before continuing.

"That is a type of weapon, electrical in nature, like a stun gun but with no wires and vastly more sophisticated," he explained as he gestured for the scientist, "as to the amulet, the engraving suggests a connection with the Knights Templar, although it predates that group by millennia. I'm sure you recognize Baphomet; and its shape recalls the amulet of King Solomon, which he used to control evil spirits. Legend has it that we must have it when we find the vaults. Now, Dr. Dallas Roark, may I present Dr. Jorge Carbonara. Dr. Carbonara is both a geologist and member of the Guardians. Jorge, tell our guest about the stone tablet."

"Well, it isn't merely stone," he began casually, as he lifted a piece of suede from the tray to reveal a green translucent, triangular material. The geologist spoke in a soft Spanish accent, reminiscent of Antonio Banderas.

Dallas's eyes moved from Jorge's face, to his hand and back; he held a large, triangular section of smooth green translucent stone tablet without fault or flaw, totally unblemished, and flat on the reverse; almost exactly the same as the thing in the briefcase. The sole difference was that this piece, unlike the one in the safety deposit box, did not have any notches extending from its widest base. It did, however, contain matching raised and faceted notches on what Dallas supposed were its left and right sides.

Dr. Carbonara continued, "Although it does look and feel like stone, it is really beryllium aluminum silicate, better known as an emerald; and it's artificially made. It's the most perfect example of synthetic gem I've ever seen; we couldn't come close creating something like this specimen. Something else interesting; its crystalline matrix was created in this shape. There's absolutely no evidence of cutting, grinding, shaping or polishing. It's a thing of beauty under an electron microscope.

"Look at these notches on the sides and the faceted edges," he went on, pointing to the sides, "these clearly fit into the corresponding parts of the pyramidal shape. That suggests this piece goes into a particular place, a specific place in a larger object."

Dallas liked the man at once; he had a charming, disheveled air about him. Jorge seemed a man totally without motive or pretense; a disposition that Dallas had long ago determined as being extremely rare for a scientist. Upon a closer examination of the item, Dallas saw that, like the other piece, this one was covered with tiny rows of ancient script, alternating with cuneiform style writing. Once again, the writing was so small that, to the untrained eye, it might be casually dismissed.

"This script is also in the style of hieratic, just like the one I have," Dallas mused aloud as he returned the piece to Jorge, "and yet its language form and structure is different from ancient Egyptian; much older, I would think."

"Yes, Dr. Roark, that is correct." Turning to Dr. Carbonara, Joshua gestured toward the door, "Thank you, Jorge, that will be all." As the geologist left, Joshua turned back toward Dallas and continued, "Hieratic, as you know, was the ancient Egyptian writing style for governmental purposes; the better known hieroglyphs were reserved for use on buildings and the like. There is one important difference, however. Hieratic is thought to have come into wide use in ancient Egypt about forty-seven hundred years ago as a refinement of the hieroglyphic form. In fact, this tablet is three times that old. It is not Egyptian; at least not Egyptian in the sense that today's archeologists would use the term."

"And the cuneiform?"

"While the symbols are cuneiform, it isn't classic Sumerian," the older scientist offered, "and we haven't been able to translate it. Given the level of technology required for its creation, we are confident the tablets must come from a time at or just before the end of the empire."

"But it's a stone; you can't date it, so how do you know how old it really is?"

"We don't know how it was created, but, as I said earlier, we do know is that it was found in an obscure grave beneath a body that was carbon dated to 11,500 BCE, approximately thirteen thousand, five hundred years ago."

"But that's impossible! There must be some other explanation. Perhaps it was placed there much latter; or the test results were wrong; or –"

"You have eyes yet you refuse to see." Fisher interrupted as if quoting scripture. "Do you not know the Law of Parsimony?"

"You mean Ockham's Razor?"

"Indeed; but Aristotle stated the principle first. In essence, you can look at this tablet in one of two ways. The first and simplest solution, is that it was buried with the body we found; or the second, and more complex solution, is that someone broke into the tomb ten thousand years after it was sealed, left the other artifacts alone and went the trouble of carefully planting the tablet under the skeleton. Ockham would tell us 'if two theories explain the facts equally well, then the simpler theory is to be preferred'."

"Okay, fine, it's as old as you say, but I still don't understand; if you have all this information how can neither you or the Order know where the vaults are? And, if you have a continuity of existence of thirteen millennia, why can't you read them?"

"Dallas," Joshua said softly, "remember who was exiled here. They were left in primitive conditions, without the luxury of technology of any sort; and that includes such basics as pencil and paper. And let's not forget the flood. How long could we today maintain our own level of culture if we were to be dropped en masse in the jungles of Africa or the rainforests of Brazil without tools, without electricity, without medicine, without metals, and without the knowledge to produce it? I am afraid it is a truism that the veneer of civilization is indeed quite thin. As to the vaults, like I said earlier, we didn't even know there was anything that might prove the rumors true until this piece of the tablet turned up.

"Our ancestors were careful to conceal their knowledge by embellishing the oral histories but always, at the center of each tale, a kernel of truth remained. They were only partly successful, though, because in time, the true meaning and hidden messages were lost. Over the thousands of years that followed, they eventually relearned the basics of civilization-building. By the time they began using writing again, the ancient fables became exactly that; fables. Now, we are all that remain, and our knowledge is comparatively scant. If it weren't for the few artifacts and these tablets that the ancients were able to conceal, we wouldn't have any proof about our past; our true history"

"As you say," Dallas interrupted, "if these are genuine artifacts, then their creation must have predated the empire's destruction. But if they were defeated, how did the ancients preserve any artifacts at all?"

"Obviously, they concealed what they could, and they kept their secrets. Perhaps most important, they left their clues in a form that the conquerors didn't grasp. They constructed messages in stone, in monuments, in symbols and in signs, and I can only assume, prayed that when the time came, that their progeny could decipher them."

"Okay, setting aside the history you've told me for a moment. Who exactly are you?"

"As I said, we've always referred to ourselves the Guardians, but over the millennia, we have gone by many public names, as suited our purpose at the time. In ancient times, we were known to some as the Guardians of Osiris; and before that, as the high priests of Ur, and even earlier by other names. At other times, we have used different names as the needs required.

"Under whatever guise we use, we have layers of membership with many outsiders who do not even know our true mission. In that sense, perhaps we are like any other secret society. Only to those whom we deem worthy are the Guardian's true secrets revealed."

"So, now you're telling me you're Freemasons?"

"Well, yes and no. We use them, and other groups, as our eyes and ears, our hands and feet, but they do not know of us. We have created a convoluted series of nonsense rituals as we gradually indoctrinate them."

"Which begs the question," Dallas asked, "why do I qualify? Why have I, a mere hybrid, moved to the head of this class?"

"The answer should be obvious. You have something we desperately need, and there was no other way to get it. Dr. Todd had told us he found another piece of the pyramid tablet, one virtually identical to this one here. We think there were originally four pieces; we have one, the Order has one, Dr. Todd had one, and there is one still missing. You now are in possession of Dr. Todd's piece.

"That, as you might guess, is part of the reason for my daughter's animosity. I don't think I'm putting words in her mouth when I say that she feels you haven't earned the right to possess so valuable and important an artifact as that. However, I am getting old, and I don't have time to bring you along slowly. I must admit, your background did help me in coming to my decision. By sheer coincidence, your training and skills will prove invaluable to us in our quest to find that fourth piece."

Dallas sat, utterly speechless, his mind trying and failing to absorb what he heard. His reason rebelled against this fantasy; and yet a man had died, someone had been following him, and he was sitting in this elaborately furnished underground headquarters. His reason demanded that he disregard his curiosity; but his curiosity would not be denied.

4

DALLAS ROLLED OVER SLOWLY, stretching as he moved, trying to focus on his surroundings. The fuzziness cleared, and he bolted upright, remembering all he had heard the night before. Miranda and Joshua had continued the history lesson for many hours before Dallas finally told them he needed sleep.

Lying in the bed, he looked around the bedroom with an odd sense of déjà vu. All his personal belongings were around him, but it wasn't his room. Getting out of bed, Dallas stumbled to the closet and found his entire wardrobe. Dull and threadbare as it was, its presence comforted him.

As his brain cleared, Dallas followed his nose into what was obviously the kitchen. His coffeemaker sat on the counter brewing his morning pot, just like always. His belongings, his clothes, his coffee; all this had an unreal feel about it. The surroundings were his, but they weren't. He felt disoriented; among familiar surroundings that were somehow unfamiliar.

Reaching for the coffee pot, Dallas noticed a small envelope with his first name on it. It wasn't sealed; the flap merely being informally tucked in. Absentmindedly, he reached for his favorite mug, and found it exactly where it should be. He poured a cup and then turned the envelope over in his hands, studying it for clues. Seeing none, he opened it and slid out a small folded piece of paper.

It was from Fisher, inviting him for brunch and giving him directions. Dallas flashed back to the previous night when his new colleagues escorted him to his quarters. There was a post-modern architectural sameness to the seemingly endless, winding, windowless corridors. It all had an otherworldly feel to it, like a space station or sci-fi starship. Dallas had to remind himself that he was well below ground, beneath a museum full of antiquities. He found the incongruity strangely amusing.

He wandered back into the bedroom, checking a few drawers and cabinets along the way. Dallas found it simply amazing. While he slept, these people obviously had cleaned out his apartment, brought his belongings to his new quarters, and managed to place everything in exactly the same location. He felt simultaneously grateful and bothered. They had come into his quarters while he slept, not to mention violating his former space. On the one hand, they clearly cared enough about his comfort that they went to a great deal of trouble; but they were just as clearly signaling both their total control and their seriousness in not letting him return to his former life. He wondered what would happen if he should decide to leave anyway. Belatedly, his mind turned to the question of why he hadn't awakened with all the apparent late night activity. Had they drugged him?

Like everything else he did, Fisher's directions were clear, precise and concise. Dallas arrived at the appointed place at the appointed time; the door slid silently to one side as he approached. Fisher sat inside, his wheelchair pulled up to the table, sipping a cup of coffee while studying some papers. On the table in front of him sat a neatly organized stack of what appeared to be maps, reports and pamphlets. Beside this stack sat a formally set dining table, awaiting only the food. Looking up, he greeted Dallas warmly and motioned for him to take the seat next to him.

"Good morning, Dr. Roark," Fisher said with a smile, "slept well, I trust."

"Yes, thank you, Dr. Fisher," Dallas paused, "and my complements to your decorators."

"Please, call me Joshua. So your belongings arrived safely, then?"

"Arrived? Except for the lack of windows I'd swear I was still in my own apartment. I admit to being truly amazed. And, please, call me Dallas."

"Well, Dallas, I must admit to having a flare for the dramatic. Moving you was an uncommon challenge; we don't do that often, almost never, in fact. Usually it's to bring in one of our operatives whose cover has been compromised. I do hope you feel at home."

"To be honest, I'm not sure how I feel. The quarters you provided are quite comfortable, and undeniably familiar, but it all feels … strange. I have to ask you – would you really stop me from leaving?"

"It is for your own safety that you must stay here; your safety and our security. You now know our location, our mission, and even our very existence. The people we oppose, the Order, would love to get their hands on you and your piece of the puzzle; and that is something we cannot allow."

"So, I am a prisoner then?"

"Think of yourself as an honored guest in a very private little war."

"I won't lie to you," Dallas responded, "I agreed to help; I didn't bargain for being a hostage —"

"A guest —"

"Whatever—"

"I can't say that I blame you; I admit you've been sorely used. I can only assure you that if we had any other choice, we would have taken it; we didn't. In time, as you learn more, perhaps you'll come to understand that."

"And one more thing, I didn't sign up to live like a mole."

"Oh. Don't worry about that. We get out, but never alone, and never without taking precautions. And you'll have plenty to do; research, study, and, as you get more familiar with everything, field work."

"Field work?"

"Your type of field work; archaeology. Don't forget we have vaults to find. We're counting on your skills as a linguist to decipher the tablets. You'll be making history."

"Pity, no one will know if I succeed."

"We'll know. The rest of the world may only know if you … if we, fail." Joshua's tone became soft and serious. "But let's not think such negative thoughts, Dallas, come join me for some food and insightful conversation about your new life's work."

The new arrival could not help but respond to Joshua's soothing humor.

"Very well, Joshua, where do we begin?"

"After brunch I want to introduce you to the research team we've begun assembling; now that we have two tablets, we must begin in earnest. Also, I'll give you a tour of the rest of the facilities, as well as the reference library; it contains English translations of the collected oral history of the Guardians. Of course, we do have a museum above us with truly comprehensive resources. You'll need to read the popular texts of today; most hold no more than a grain of fact, but they do serve a purpose. Of course, there are also the more serious works on various ancient cultures. I'm sure you've read most of them. Then there are numerous geological papers you'll need to study—"

"I assume," Dallas interrupted, "that you'll want me to find the vault in *this* lifetime."

"Well, yes, that would be my first choice."

"In that case, I think it best if I learn on the job. The rest of the team can brief me as we go; at least I could get started."

"I have been considering that option. There is one person at this facility that is academically qualified to assist you – holds two PhDs, in fact; but I'm not sure if you're compatible."

"Don't worry Joshua; I can get along with anybody —"

"It's my daughter, Miranda."

"Oh," Dallas mused for a moment. "Well, if you'll just tell her not to kill me, I'm sure we can work it out. If you'll forgive my asking, why is she so hostile?"

"I guess it's a combination of things. Her mother died when she was young, and she's been raised with the knowledge of our mission. She carries more burdens than anyone her age should have to carry. She never could run and play like other children, growing up in blissful ignorance of what horrors the world might really hold. She knew, she's always known. For a little child, it's as if the imaginary monster under the bed were real. That is my fault, I suppose, but I felt she had to understand, to be prepared."

Joshua's face took on a sad, far away look; a shadow of regret passed over him only to me immediately replaced by his normally implacable expression. Finally, he added, "I'll be sure to tell her not to kill you. Now, let's get down to business."

Dallas let his observation pass in silence. "Okay, so tell me about the team."

"Yes, that's the other reason I wanted to talk with you privately. We have people from a variety of scientific specialties: geology, archeology, anthropology, and physics —"

"Physics?"

"Assuming we are successful, we'll need people on the team who can evaluate the science behind what we discover. For example, we know they traveled between the stars. We'll need someone who can understand the physics behind it. We'll also need someone from the medical sciences of course, and perhaps a biologist or zoologist, and certainly an astronomer. Of course you'll also be assigned a security team."

"A security team?"

"I would have thought the need for a security team would have been obvious to you by now. At any rate, we'll aim for a permanent team of twelve people, counting a support person or two. In addition, we'll bring in such specialists as we may from time to time require. While I'll be directing the entire operation – the CEO for lack of a better term – I'd like you to serve as the chief operating officer, organizing the group as you see fit to accomplish the task—"

"Won't that cause some hard feelings?"

"No, I don't believe so. We all know the importance of our mission, and what you can contribute to it. Since your arrival I've circulated your background with the others; I wanted to let them know you're highly thought of in linguistic circles. With a reputation like yours, acceptance shouldn't be a problem; we have no egos to bruise here."

"Not even your daughter's?"

"Well, no one's perfect, but she'll come around. As to our budget, it is, shall we say, open-ended. Our resources are more than adequate for our needs."

"Looking around here, I rather assumed that. Just where does all the money come from?"

"We've been around for quite a while," Josh said, smiling, "we've made some good investments, started a few companies, and generally just spread the wealth around to a variety of business sectors. Financially, I can tell you this much: we're financially larger than most third-world countries, even the Catholic Church."

"How could you be that big and be anonymous?"

"Anonymous is easy; it's the paperwork that's difficult. Seriously, we're very quiet, normally, and very patient. Now, let's eat, you'll find the food excellent; one of the nicer perks."

They settled into a pleasant meal, filled with idle chatter that seemed deliberately scripted to contain nothing more than small talk. There was no more conversation about the facilities, the team, the organization, or the mission. For the balance of their private session, the hottest topics were the weather, sports, and the stock market. Finally, Joshua signaled the end of brunch and their social interlude with a glance at his watch.

"Now, shall we go meet the others?" Joshua pointed to the door at the opposite end of the room. Dallas fell in behind his mysterious host, wondering how much of what he'd been told about the Guardians he could believe. One thing was also very clear: he'd never be told the whole truth, about anything. He found himself wondering if they even knew the whole truth.

The door flung open before Joshua's wheelchair, simultaneously shutting the door on Dallas's thoughts. He peered through the doorway and found it filled with people, some standing, and a dozen seated around a large, ornate conference table. Like everything else in this complex, the elegant decoration felt out of place in the sterile architecture of the tunnels.

Moving his chair to the empty space at the head of the table, Joshua motioned for Dallas to join him in the seat to his immediate right. To Joshua's left, facing Dallas across the table, sat a stern-faced Miranda; Joshua took no notice of her.

"Ladies and gentlemen, may I present Dr. Dallas Roark," he began, with an air of formality. "First, Dallas, I'd like to introduce the other members of the team. They have all had a chance to become familiar with your background. Now it is time for you to begin to get to know them."

Gesturing to his left, Joshua began in rapid-fire order. "You're already met my daughter, Miranda, more properly Dr. Miranda Fisher. As I mentioned earlier, Miranda holds two doctorates; in paleobiology and archaeology. Next to her is Dr. Hakeem Abu Saad. Dr. Saad is an expert in ancient Sumerian myths, legends, and culture. Next to Hakeem is Dr. Rajeev Singala. Dr. Singala is also an archaeologist, specializing in ancient Hindu and Indian myths and legends. Next to Rajeev is our geologist, Dr. Jorge Carbonara, who you've already met. Moving on, we have Dr. Jonathan Hardy as the team physicist. Next to Dr. Hardy we have Dr. Nancy Graham, the team anthropologist; her specialties include biblical and ancient Iranian cultures, among others.

"At the other end of the table is Dr. Karen Pollard; she's a real medical doctor. She helps on the pure science side of things, as well as deal with cuts and bruises. Now, coming up your side of the table we have Dr. Stefan Ostrowski, the team's astronomer, and, finally, seated next to you is Stephen 'Rocky' Hutchinson.

"Rocky is the head of security for the team. As I told you earlier, the organization's policy is that no one goes outside alone; the risk is simply too great. Whenever you are outside any of the organization's permanent facilities you will have someone, we call them security associates, protecting you at all times. Everyone else here already has their security associate assigned to them. Dallas, for the time being Rocky will work with you when he doesn't have to be with me. I want you protected by the best.

"The remaining people here function as assistants to the other members of the team, or are members of Rocky's team. As a safety precaution for the project, every member of each of team's research is backed up, both on a computer, and with an assistant who can bring the rest of the team up to speed if something unforeseen should happen to that department head. Now, Dallas, any questions?"

"Joshua, how do you maintain any secrecy?" Dallas whispered, gesturing around the room. "No offense, but you must be two dozen people here. How do you keep the world out?"

"Well, first we are really more of an extended family; we've grown up inside this close-knit group and have hundreds of generations together. Second, we share the same goal, and we understand the seriousness of our mission. Third, the security policy limits anyone's opportunity to break our code. Finally, if someone did try to reveal the inner workings of the organization the vast majority of the world would label them as kooks."

"I do see your point. ... " Dallas added finally.

"Okay," Joshua said, somewhat too loudly, "I'd like to thank everyone for joining us here today. I believe we may, with Dr. Roark's assistance, be on the verge of accomplishing the goal before us. I have asked him to assume day-to-day responsibility for operations on this project, I'm sure you'll all join me in welcoming him into our little group. Now, I would like everyone but the team leaders to go back to there stations. Dallas, I'll turn this meeting over to you."

"Uh, thanks ... I think," Dallas cleared his throat uncomfortably. The awkwardness of the situation brought a nervous chuckle from the group. Finally, he began again.

"I think the first step is for me to try to get to speed with a working knowledge of where the team stands – in terms of artifacts, traditions, languages, et cetera—"

"Dallas," Joshua interrupted, "Miranda can take you to the safe where the artifacts are. As to the traditions, that could take some time."

"Very well." Dallas hoped the heat he felt in his cheeks didn't show. "Okay, then, how about some housekeeping issues; with your permission, Dr. Fisher."

"By all means."

"Right. Now, do we have a central work space?"

"No, not yet," Miranda jumped in, "we've only just brought this group together."

"Then I would suggest a central nexus with each branch represented. I would prefer we be within easy access of one another. Obviously we'll need networking and Internet support."

"Okay." Miranda made notes as Dallas spoke.

"Also, obviously, since I'm not up to speed yet," Dallas concluded, "and since it would take a long time to go through all the information I need to discuss your roles intelligently, I suggest that each of you go to your offices, quarters, whatever, and prepare to relocate to the team headquarters. Finally, I would appreciate it if each of you could provide a hardcopy of whatever background information that you feel is most relevant to the project; I can't stand reading computer screens. Now, at the risk of sounding somewhat juvenile, let's go around the table so each of you can tell me all about yourselves."

That seemingly simple request took the better part of an hour to complete; but Dallas was happy he had asked, it put him more at ease. Finally, rising to leave, he looked at Rocky, "I guess you need to go with me to the bank."

5

THE WALK TO THE bank that day had been a pleasant one, somehow the air seemed fresher, the sky bluer than Dallas could ever remember. Rocky proved to be an amiable companion, but there was an underlying tenseness about him; his dark eyes were a constant blur, scanning everything and everyone.

Dallas watched Rocky and Rocky watched everything else. He was the kind of man who gave the impression of massiveness; a larger than life quality that would have intimidated Dallas if they had met in a dark alley. Rocky was shorter than Dallas by several inches, but the guard's shoulders were broader, his waist narrower, and his jaw firmer than the archaeologist's. His jet-black hair and rugged features gave no hint of his age; Dallas decided it best not to ask.

Having retrieved the artifact, Dallas set to work over the next week examining it, as well as the other one stored at the complex. His analysis of the notches proved correct. His piece and the Guardian's fit together like pieces of a three dimensional puzzle; and a puzzle it was, too. He was no further along with understanding the symbols than when this whole adventure began.

Still he persevered, trying to make some sense of the myriad of oddly shaped symbols etched into the two surfaces. He had the two triangular pieces photographed in minute detail, and then blown up to the height

of a full-grown man; at least he wouldn't lose his eyesight over the endeavor. His first impression of the markings had been correct; they did have the appearance of Sumerian and hieratic. Dallas quickly realized he would have to work exclusively on only one of the languages and decided to focus his attention on the cuneiform symbols.

While the symbols bore a superficial similarity, the language structure made no sense whatsoever. In that sense they were nothing like the tablets he'd worked on so many years ago, during his time at the British Museum. In comparison, it was like using "Dick and Jane" to translate "War and Peace." Surely, Dallas thought to himself, anyone creating these items had intended them to be understood. If they were left behind as a message, then the key to translating them must have been made as well.

He rubbed his eyes wearily. During the past seven days, he probably hadn't slept more than a handful of hours. He'd worked around the clock on the translation; he imagined everyone's eyes on him, watching to see if he was worth the trust Joshua had shown in him. When he wasn't working on translations, Dallas visited the facility's library. He was trying, and not really succeeding, to get his hands around the enormity of the task handed him.

Wearily, he leaned back in his chair, pondering again the short visit Dr. Carbonara had paid him days earlier, just after Dallas had settled into his research. Dallas had rambled on about how fascinating everything was and how it could change the face of humanity. Jorge didn't respond aloud, but merely smiled with the same smile that a parent might offer an eager child who had just discovered some obvious fact of life. The archaeologist became inwardly frustrated by the geologist's seeming lack of enthusiasm; he seemed more interested in the opportunity to do geological research than rediscover some lost history.

"I'll let you get back to it," Jorge had said casually when he rose to leave, "but don't lose too much sleep over changing the world. Personally, between you and me, I think this is going to turn out to be either a huge hoax or fairy tale. Anyway, the rest of us are going out for dinner, you're certainly welcome to come along. Only rule is you can't talk shop."

"Thanks, but ... some other time." Dallas didn't intend to sound so distant, but he suddenly felt like the class dunce. He knew he had to catch up, fast. Jorge shrugged and left Dallas alone.

He hadn't seen much of Jorge, or the rest of the group, for that matter, since that visit. Rubbing his eyes again and bringing his thoughts to the present, he decided it was up to him to mend any fences.

Joshua had passed by infrequently during this first week, always pleasant and diverting. It had been Joshua who arranged for the light table Dallas requested, as well as the photographic enlargements of the emerald tablets. As was his habit of many years, Dallas would stare at these life-sized color transparencies for hours, hoping for inspiration in translating the cuneiform script; but this time he found none.

On his visits, Joshua encouraged Dallas to get more rest, but that was not his way; not when he was ensnared in a scientific mystery. This one was a doozy. He could not deny the truth of what he had been told, but his scientific mind kept rebelling against what his heart told him was true. He found himself hoping he would discover something that made all of Joshua's claims false; but he couldn't.

Joshua finally ordered him to eat, to make his mind switch gears; but always, eventually, his mind returned to his mystery. Dallas began to finally comprehend this enormous undertaking. He certainly grasped it initially, but only in the academic sense; now the emotional reality set in. Forget the larger goal, he thought, I could spend a life just developing the nuance of this language. It could be the culmination of a life's work, working from what was known to be true Sumerian backward to a time eight thousand years earlier, when it was obviously a much richer and more complex language. In essence, it had not evolved, but rather devolved. To make it worse, there was no intermediate step. The language appeared to have been abandoned for millennia, and when it was eventually resurrected, it was in an almost juvenile form. Dallas began his attempt at reconstructing it but the work was painfully slow, the symbols made no sense.

Finally, after this week of self-imposed confinement, Dallas reluctantly concluded that he must call the team together. They needed direction, or at least he believed they did, and it was his responsibility to provide that direction.

Before he gathered them in one room, he knew there was one person he had to meet with first, if for no other reason than he had been avoiding it whenever possible over the past seven days. Their few interactions during that time had all been about as pleasant as a root canal, without Novocaine. He pressed the intercom button and left a message. A few minutes later his intercom buzzed loudly in response.

"You wanted to see me?" Miranda asked, with a mixture of surprise and irritation.

"Hello, Miranda, please come by when you get a chance." Dallas had decided not to let her bait him; a decision he was already regretting.

Moments later, she strolled in with an unmistakable look of curiosity on her face and took a seat opposite him. The organization had provided Dallas with a spacious office, but all the books, papers, and research items still made things look cramped. He had to shift a box of clay tablets to have a clear look at her.

"Miranda, I would like to get the team together … and I felt we should talk before we met with the others."

"Fine. What would you like to talk about?"

"First, I'm still not sure why I was put in charge, but I'd like you to be my number one, my second-in-command, so to speak."

"I thought that was a given."

This, thought Dallas, is not going well.

"Oh, well, yes; but we've never really discussed it. I wanted you to know I'll be counting heavily on you. Now, I'd like to put a regular schedule together; meetings, data review sessions, planning, and coordination for digs —"

"I see," she interrupted, "and you define second-in-command as, what, your secretary? You've got one, you know; tell all this to her."

"I thought you could contribute something to my concept of how to organize things."

"Did it occur to you that 'we' are already organized? You might want to see what we've been doing this past week before you waste everyone's time."

"Then why haven't you told me already what has been organized?"

"I assumed you'd think to ask, sooner or later; a big scientific mind like you."

"Look," Dallas said finally, "I'm not sure why I am the recipient of this continued hostility, and frankly, I don't care anymore. I've accepted this assignment, and I intend to see it through. Of all of us here, you know best the importance of our mission. Now, I'd like to work in as pleasant an atmosphere as possible. I have no desire to embarrass either you or Joshua by asking that you be removed from the team; but that doesn't mean I won't. It's your call; you either adopt a better attitude, now, or you WILL be replaced. Which will it be?"

Dallas wasn't one for confrontations, and he prayed it didn't show now. His throat tightened as he spoke; his heart pounded. He felt beads of sweat on his scalp and only hoped they wouldn't start rolling down his face, lest it reveal his self-perceived weakness. He kept his eyes fixed on her face, not daring to look away. He felt she was testing him, probing for weakness.

"You've had your say, now I'll have mine. My father placed you, placed us, in this position; I, for one, am committed to making the best of it. Remember this, just because I agreed to follow your orders doesn't mean I agreed to like it – or you. Now, if it is your wish, master, I'll gather the group together," she said, stonily. "Do you have an agenda you'd like me to distribute?"

Dallas chose for the moment not to push the subject further.

"No. I wanted to try and get a handle on my part of the research effort, but I've come to the conclusion I could remain locked in here for decades –"

"I'll be happy to keep the key," she interrupted again, wearing an expression that could have been either a smile or a sneer; Dallas couldn't tell which.

"As I was saying," he continued, "I could remain here for decades and not get any closer to a solution on my own. I am convinced that what is on these emerald tablets, fascinating as it is, will not give us all the answers we seek, but I am also convinced they hold the key. At this point, I figured it would be best to pool our thoughts and explore different possibilities."

"In other words," Miranda noted with an unmistakably gleeful tone, "you haven't got a clue about what to do next."

"In other words, I haven't got a clue; yes. What are your thoughts?"

"Well," she began, in a more scholarly tone, "let's start with the obvious. We know the basics of human settlements in the Middle East from roughly 7000 BCE forward."

"You're referring to Jericho?" interrupted Dallas.

"Yes and some other settlements from that time period in the vicinity of Lake Van in southeastern Turkey. Then, of course, there is Sumer, as well as the Harappan ruins in the Indus Valley region of Pakistan; and the Jomon culture in Japan; its relics date back to 11000 BCE. Beyond that, we don't know much. Raj will tell you the Hindu believe that there was an older civilization, which was destroyed. In fact, they believe that civilization rose and fell several times, each time less pure than the last."

"And, of course, there are the common flood myths," replied Dallas, picking up the litany, "all the ancient cultures have antediluvian myths and legends. We need a working hypothesis. What we need is to get all the facts that we have on the table and see what they suggest."

"Hence the meeting?" Miranda asked.

"Hence the meeting. Now, let's get the rest of the team together."

"Right." Miranda rose to leave.

"Oh, by the way," Dallas said as she opened the door, "you never gave me an answer."

"Oh, but I did; you're still alive." And then she was gone.

Dallas chuckled reflexively at the intense expression Miranda wore as she delivered that line. He couldn't decide whether she was serious, or if he had just experienced her sense of humor for the first time. He was determined to watch his back, just in case it was the former rather than the later.

6

LATER THAT DAY, DALLAS entered the conference room to find his colleagues chatting comfortably. It was clear that this group had used the past week to become well acquainted with one another. Dallas tried not to feel like an outsider, but the sensation was overwhelming. He did his best to feel at home, and hoped the awkward feelings didn't show. He smiled broadly at everyone in a forced, nonchalant manner and slid into his seat.

"George," he began, "how are you? I haven't seen you in a couple of days."

Jorge nodded politely in reply, barely wincing at the Anglicization of his proud name.

"So," Dallas said to the assembly, "I hope everyone is doing well. I'd like to apologize to all of you for being so solitary since our last meeting. I've been trying to get myself up to speed, but after a week, I've come to the realization that I could spend my whole life trying to catch up. So I thought it best to jump into the deep end of the pool, as it were, and just see where we are."

The other members of the team stared at him in bemused silence; making Dallas's first reaction a mixture of embarrassment and regret at speaking his mind. Finally, Jorge spoke up.

"Amigo, we were beginning to wonder if you were still alive," he said with an infectious grin. "We are most relieved that you came out of your room."

"I … see. Well, here I am. So, who would like to start?"

"Perhaps, we should start at the beginning," offered a very humble Dr. Hakeem Abu Saad. "We – Rajeev, Nancy and I – have been working on combining and comparing the world's most ancient myths. Now this has been done before, but always from the point of view that it was mere myth. We've been treating it more like a detective story."

"A detective story?"

"Well, yes. We agreed on a few assumptions. To begin with, we agreed that the myths contained elements of truth. Next, that they were designed to conceal that truth from those for whom it was not intended. Also, the creators wished to pass on these truths clandestinely to successive generations. Finally, that a proper analysis the myths will direct us toward our goal."

"This is science?"

"It is around here," Dr. Saad, replied, sounding wounded by the implication. "Dr. Roark, you must understand, we are all working on uncharted ground, with questions about subjects that other scientists refuse to acknowledge even exist. And, as you so rightly pointed out, we could all spend entire academic careers on the materials here, preparing papers that would never be published, without ever getting any closer to the vaults. We don't have time to do things strictly by the book; we have to take a leap of faith. This troubles you?"

"No," Dallas said thoughtfully, "it's just strange hearing those words from a scientist."

"Ah, but we all have faith," Dr. Saad smiled. "It's just that you western scientists put yours in different things. You believe in what you feel you can prove; but can you really? Where does gravity come from? We know it exists, but can your science explain it?"

"Really, Hakeem, we've had this discussion before." The booming voice came from the far end of the table, from a man who looked more like a Hemingway character than the team's physicist. Dallas tried to guess the accent, Scottish or Irish, he wasn't sure which; but with his thick, blonde beard and broad smile, Jonathan Hardy appeared unlike any scientist Dallas had ever met.

"It's quite an exaggeration to compare one's belief in a mythical supreme being with the eventually certainty of determining gravity's exact causality. Surely you can see the logic in gravity being a byproduct of the warping of space-time as proposed by Einstein, which—"

"Excuse me, gentlemen," Dallas interrupted, "I'm sure this is a fascinating philosophical debate, but right now, I feel we have more concrete items to discuss."

"Ah, but that was my point exactly," Hakeem continued, "Just how much of what we actually know is concrete. Until you joined us, you would have denied the scientific possibly of our very existence. Yet here we sit; rather concretely, I might add."

"Don't mind him," Jonathan said to Dallas, "he just likes to argue."

"Right." Dallas could think of nothing further to add on that score. "Now, it seems to me we must begin to identify areas to explore."

"And that," Hakeem chimed in again, "brings us back to our detective story. We have been analyzing the world's various flood myths. We've looked at them all, from all parts of the world; did you know that even the American Indians had their own Noah?"

"If I may," Jorge interrupted, "I think that what Hakeem is trying to suggest, in his own meandering way, is the hypothesis of the melting of the ice caps at the end of the last ice age being the cause for the flood myths."

"Yes," Dallas said, "That notion has been around since at least the late 1800s. Joshua gave me a relatively recent book on the subject by Graham Hancock; sounds interesting, impossible to prove; purely speculative. The irony is that he doesn't propose aliens, just the possibility of much more ancient civilizations."

"Yes, we've read his work," Hakeem came back. "We believe Hancock was right — that at the end of the Younger Dryas Ice Age the human population was forced to flee existing cities and seek higher ground. At any rate, we know the end of the ice age would account for a rapid rise in sea levels."

"Which would mean," Jorge continued, "that the most promising sites are —"

"Underwater." Dallas finished the sentence. "Okay, fine. Does anyone here know how to scuba dive?" Only Miranda and Rocky raised their hands. The rest of the assembly was a chorus of mutters, whispered denials, or sideways glances.

"Miranda, would you please arrange for the team to become certified divers as soon as possible, myself included," Dallas instructed. Turning back to the group, he added, "Does anyone have any other ideas?"

"Well, we could sacrifice a virgin at a Mayan temple, just for kicks." Jon beamed as he spoke. "Of course, we'd have to find a virgin first; that could prove difficult."

"Jon," Miranda interjected, "are you volunteering?"

Dallas just shook his head, and then rested his face in the palms of his hands. Slowly he straightened up, pulling his hands down past his eyes and bringing them to rest under his chin. "Aliens, spaceships, galactic empires, super weapons," he recited to himself, "what's next – the abominable snowman and the Loch Ness monster?"

"As a matter of fact —" Miranda whispered.

Dallas shot her a glance.

"Just kidding."

"It's a big planet," Jorge replied, bringing a serious tone back to the discussion, "and our secrecy works against us as well as for us. There are many rumors, silly ones that may take up our time; and others, which have the smell of truth. It is extremely difficult to separate fact from fiction."

"But George," retorted Dallas, "as broad as your organization is, surely you have eyes and ears everywhere."

"Si, but we must work from the shadows, in secret. We research in the margins, making sure never to call attention to ourselves."

"Yes," Miranda enjoined, "we do not allow ourselves to be placed in positions of public leadership. The attention one of might attract from that level of exposure is unacceptable."

The debate continued for what seemed like hours, mostly covering differing philosophical views about the best way to proceed, and with what degree of secrecy. None of it was concrete; none of it moved them closer to their goal.

"All of this is quite academic," Dallas interjected finally. "We need to lay out a concrete plan of action. We'll have plenty of time to discuss all these things. Dr. Graham, do you have any suggestions?"

His question caught her by surprise; she had become so absorbed in the dialogue that she jumped at the sound of her name.

"Well," she began, regaining her composure, "as Rajeev was saying, if we begin with the flood myths and pick up Graham Hancock's theme, then the obvious place to begin would be in searching for possible underwater sights. The Bible and related ancient writings are replete with such tales. We also have several other possibilities: the suspected sunken pyramid ruins off the coast of Japan, the supposed ruins found off the western coast of India in the Gulf of Cambay, several sites in the Black Sea, and a newly discovered site off the western coast of Cuba. Of course, we could organize our own search to hunt for other potential sites."

"Yes, Miranda and I were discussing those choices earlier. Japan's Jomon culture has the oldest relics, and that might connect with the Jonaguni Pyramids; the Harappan culture is certainly mysterious enough, and that might have a tie in with the Cambay site. I've read about the sonar findings off the Cuban coast ... "

"And don't forget the prehistoric petroglyphs in the caves at Punta del Este on the Isla de la Junventud," interrupted Rajeev. "They're only located about a hundred miles from the underwater Cuban site."

"Granted," continued Dallas, "but both are within Cuban territory, and I can't see Castro's government letting us go there. The Black Sea theory is compelling, but access could also be a problem there as well. I think we all agree that access is a necessary precondition. Of course, on a lighter side, there's always the Edgar Cayce and his mysterious lost Atlantean Halls of Record. Jorge, do you have any maps of the world's coastline thirteen thousand years ago?"

"Yes, Dallas; of course, it's just a best guess. We've done some rather detailed studies, but there are an almost an infinite number of variables for any local area—"

"I'm not looking for perfection," Dallas interrupted, "just following a hunch." He studied the charts for a moment, and then looked back up at the group. "I'd like to digest everything we've talked about, and, more importantly, I'm hungry. Let's break for now and reconvene in the morning. Hopefully, I'll have an epiphany between now and then. Miranda, you're with me."

With that, Dallas rose and left the room, with a clearly stunned Miranda following close behind. They walked a short distance down the corridor in total silence. Only when Dallas was sure they were out of earshot did he turn to Miranda.

"Sorry about the dramatic exit, but I want to discuss the possibilities with your father first. I got a hunch I'd like to follow, and I know he says I'm in charge, but I figure he's got more of a right than any of us to have the final say. At the same time, I don't think he should be forced to have that say in front of a crowd; he has a position to protect."

"I understand … that's thoughtful of you." In spite of herself, Miranda appreciated Dallas's insight in seeking her father's counsel and the self-confidence that his actions displayed.

"Why, Miranda, you surprise me," Dallas intoned. "Does that mean I'm starting to grow on you?"

"Perhaps," she said defensively as she turned away, "but then, the same can also be said for several types of fungus."

Dallas stood openmouthed as she made an abrupt retreat. Recovering, he turned the corner into the dining room and found Joshua right where he expected him, enjoying afternoon tea. For the next hour, the two men plotted their course of action over egg salad and cucumber finger sandwiches, after which Joshua made what to Dallas seemed an odd request. While they were agreed on the destination, the director told Dallas, in no uncertain terms, that it was not to be discussed with the remainder of the team; at least not yet.

"But," Dallas challenged, "how can they prepare if they don't know where they're headed?"

"Well, they know it's underwater. We can begin with such preparations as are common to any underwater dig. Of course, you have translations and ancient languages to consider; and there are still plenty of books to read, both scholarly and popular."

"As you say, it's underwater," countered Dallas, "that means we'll need a ship."

"Just let me take care of that, and we'll need a marine archaeologist. We have a great one in the organization: Sam Layne."

"So what do I tell Miranda? What do I tell the rest of the team?"

"Tell Miranda, of course. As for the others, tell them only that we're considering our options. Have everyone redouble their research into their areas of specialization, handle it however you wish, but do not disclose our plans to anyone else at this time."

With that, Joshua abruptly shifted his chair into gear and left the dining room, leaving a puzzled archaeologist in his wake.

In the few days that followed, Dallas, Miranda, and the team continued their planning sessions in preparation for the mission. At this morning's meeting, they were supposed to meet the marine archaeologist that Joshua had assigned to the team; Jorge was slated to give a presentation on the geology of several areas which the team believed were under consideration, even though none of them was the actual choice. Jorge would also review equipment recommendations for these sites. Dallas hated having to put his new friend through this wasted exercise, but Joshua's instructions had left him little choice. Then Hakeem and Raj would give the latest update on their continuing research into Sumerian and Hindu myths, in the hope that there might be some clue buried within them. Finally, Rocky would cover various continuing security questions, not the least among them being how to get everyone out of, and back into, the country. Adding in the usual banter would probably double the meeting's planned two hour schedule.

Of course, if Joshua showed up, the entire agenda would be tossed out the window. No matter; Dallas realized that at the Center, as he had come to call his new home, the one commodity everyone had was time.

As much as he enjoyed it, however, he looked forward to a change of scene. In this environment, he found it increasingly difficult of keep track of the days and nights, and he found himself working through the night on more than one occasion; this particular morning being one such occasion.

While Dallas had formed good working relationships with just about everyone, it was Jorge, Hakeem, and Raj who were his most frequent companions. On the opposite end of that spectrum sat Nancy Graham, a typical anthropologist who insisted on seeing the ancient world through a twenty-first century lens.

As to Miranda, Dallas could only confess puzzlement. They were together as much as professional needs required, and true to her word, she worked without further complaint. There were periods when they were together for so long that he began to tease her about being his work wife; a title she accepted with a pained smile. But there seemed to be a barrier she wouldn't cross; it was not spoken of, and Dallas never raised the subject himself.

He found himself considering all these things in the cafeteria over a cup or rapidly chilling coffee, and suddenly, he realized how different things had been in the almost two months he had been with Joshua, Miranda and the others. He sensed a comfort and belonging that had been absent up until this point in his life. It was as if all that went before was a distant memory, a mere prologue to the here and now. A wave of giddiness washed over him; an excitement of what adventures lay before him; it was an adrenaline rush.

"Amigo," Jorge's voiced boomed from behind him, "why are you sitting alone so early in the morning?"

"I'm not alone now," Dallas smiled back, "join me for a cup of coffee?"

"Si, of course. So, have you met the treasure hunter yet?"

"No, not yet; you?"

"Si, Jon and I did, last night when she arrived." He shook is head slowly. "Espero que sea una nave grande — I hope it is a big ship."

"Oh, come on, George, it can't be that bad."

"Si, it can."

"Say," Dallas offered, changing the subject, "have you seen Jon?"

"No. I guess he is sitting somewhere in the dark, pondering the fundamental forces of nature."

"Now, George, he is a physicist; he doesn't know any better."

"I heard that," Dr. Jonathan Hardy called out good-naturedly as he entered the room, "but I'll forgive you. I know you're only an archaeologist and can't help yourself."

"So, mi amigo, how goes the search for the grand unifying theory?" Jorge slapped him on the back as he asked his favorite question.

"I must admit, I'm looking forward to getting started with *our* little scavenger hunt. I'm convinced that our ancestors solved the mystery of a grand unifying theory. They must have if they truly did all the things that Joshua claims. I wish I could read the ancient tongues for myself."

Dallas laughed out loud. "I'll be glad to teach you, if you've got ten years or so. It's not just reading the symbols; it's the culture and the context."

"Oh, I know. I just keep fantasizing about us finding an old clay tablet with all the answers to the mysteries of the universe pressed into it."

"More likely, if we find any tablets they'll tell about grain or livestock sales, or someone buying this or that piece of land."

"Tell me again why we're doing this." Jonathan shook his head in mock confusion.

"We're trying to track them backward in time. We already know where people were five thousand years ago, and that's not the answer. If we can find some older settlements, then maybe we can find clues about where they were in the earliest times. Frankly, I'd be happy with some pot shards or stone tools with unique geological clues, made from clay or rocky native to somewhere else."

"But how does that help us?"

"Jonathan, wherever we're looking hasn't been above water in ten thousand years. IF we find something, it'll likely be something that no reputable archaeologist would be able to accept. We will have found a village that modern science says doesn't exist."

"And you tease me about the unifying theory. Tell us, honestly, what do you think the odds are of us finding anything?"

"Unofficially, based on all my years of training, I'd have to say we haven't got a rat's chance in hell. Officially, I've got no idea. It's a very big planet, and this whole exercise is an absolute shot in the dark, but like we said before, we have to start somewhere. If this one doesn't pan out, we'll keep looking. We can't afford not to. "

"Right you are," Joshua intoned, entering both the room and the conversation, Rocky in tow behind him. "If we all keep wandering in here, they'll be no need for the meeting. So, Jorge, Jonathan, what did you think of the newest member?"

The two men exchanged glances, but said nothing. The rolling eyes and slightly raised eyebrows spoke for them.

"Give Sam a chance," Joshua continued, turning to Dallas, "Sam's just out of sorts right now after being pulled off another project; it'll be okay. Now, a change of subject: We've had to move the schedule up. I'll explain later, but we must postpone breakfast. I need you all to gather up what items you might need and report to the conference room in fifteen minutes. Rocky here will assist you two."

With a dismissive nod of his head, Joshua turned his chair – and his back – on the two.

"You wait here for a moment, Dallas. We should talk."

"What's wrong?" Dallas said in a tone halfway between concern and anger, "You practically sent them out under armed guard. I've never seen you treat anyone that way."

"True … but then you haven't known me very long." Seeing no reaction, Joshua added more softly, "Just a little humor. Seriously, we have a problem. I believe we have a spy from the Order in our midst, someone who has managed to infiltrate the organization and the team. The problem is that we don't know who it is."

"But who ... how?" Dallas sputtered.

"I've received reliable intelligence that leaves me no doubt. For the moment, that's all I can say."

"But we're nowhere near ready to go. Last thing you told me, the ship wouldn't be ready for months. And all our equipment ... "

"I lied." Joshua's interruption was direct and honest. "As to the equipment, everything's on board already. We just duplicated everything so that no one would be the wiser. We've loaded everything but the team's computers, personal effects, and any research materials you might need."

"You lied?" Dallas couldn't get past the first part of the answer to consider the second. "You lied to me?"

"Sorry, Dallas, call it an occupational hazard. The fact is we had to check you out again, and first, before the others. Regardless of any personal opinions, you are, or were, the most likely suspect; if only because you are such a recent addition to our group. Remember, everyone else has practically grown up with the Guardians, they're hereditary members."

"So, what finally cleared me, if I may be so bold as to ask?"

"Well, we double-checked everything, but, honesty, it was Miranda. She finally convinced me that you weren't the one."

"Thanks for the vote of confidence!" Dallas's tone dripping with serrated sarcasm.

"Dallas, understand, I didn't want it to be you, I didn't really believe it was you, but I had to make sure."

"What about the others?"

"We're still checking them. They're harder to research in a way. Even though we've known about their backgrounds since they were children, one of them could have been turned years ago. For all we know one of them could be a sleeper agent waiting for the right moment."

"Miranda believed in me?" The rest of what Joshua said finally sunk in.

"Yep, hard to believe but for some reason she seems to have taken a certain liking to you. Can't really explain it; maybe you remind her of a lost puppy."

"So, who do you think is the spy?"

"Can't say, yet. That's why we had 'Plan B' in operation; the boat's ready. The team will be shipped out tonight without any further communication with anyone. Even the other members of this headquarters won't know where we've gone. All this is the real reason why I didn't want to tell the team our destination until we finalized preparations to get everyone onboard."

"I understand, but what if the spy isn't a member of the team? What if it's someone else here?"

"That is a possibility, but the information I've received could have only have been revealed by a team member. Besides, no one has tried to kidnap you – yet. However, our source says they know about you and your mission. No, they must think it's worth it to give you some space. They could only do that if they knew that whoever the spy is would be with you at the critical time; hence someone on the team."

"I can't argue with the logic, but then that means your headquarters location is compromised."

"I know, but within a few days after we leave, it won't exist anymore. We'll take the important research with us, the equipment and furnishings will be farmed out rather circuitously to various other locations, and we'll seal this one off. It may sit empty for a year, a generation, or maybe forever."

"So, where exactly is the ship now?" Dallas asking, then catching himself, added, "never mind, I don't need to know."

Fifteen minutes later, the team had assembled in the conference room. The standing–room-only crowd listened intently as the director began his briefing with a simple clearing of his throat.

"I'm sorry to surprise all of you like this, but certain factors necessitate advancing our departure. We will be leaving immediately. I'm sure you're all eager to get started so, if there are no questions, I'd like to make one final announcement before turning the meeting over to Rocky, who'll brief you on travel and security matters, but first — "

"Excuse me, Dr. Fisher." It was the team's anthropologist; a fact which surprised Dallas not at all. "Dr. Fisher, I personally find this most disturbing; and I'm sure that at least some other members of the team do as well. May we please have more of an explanation as to why, after weeks of careful planning, we are suddenly acting so impulsively?"

"I'm sorry, but I will not be providing any more information at this time," Joshua replied in a tone of finality, adding after a pause, "I am told that all necessary research materials – except your personal papers – have been packed and are ready to move. If that is incorrect, please speak up."

"I'm afraid I must insist." Dr. Graham wouldn't be so easily dismissed.

"Dr. Graham," Joshua responded evenly, with only the glare of his eyes reflecting his growing irritation, "your objections are noted, but your insistence changes nothing. I am not disposed to discuss my reasons at this time. You may, of course, resign your position. If you wish to do so, do it now and leave, so that we may continue."

Hearing no response, he began again, "Now, as I was about to say, before I turn the meeting over to Rocky, I'd like to introduce the newest member of the team: Samantha Layne, late of the Florida Keys, and formerly with the University of London. For the past several years, she has worked with some of the top marine treasure hunters in the US, and until now, has been working on the most recent attempts to salvage the Antocha."

At the words 'treasure hunter,' the archaeologists in the room rolled their eyes as one. She represented to their science what bounty hunters were to the police; interlopers who cared less for how they did their job than for short-term results. Joshua continued, taking no outward note of the team's reaction.

"By the way, Sam also holds dual PhDs in Archaeology and Ocean-ography; but prefers not to use the honorific of doctor. She has volun-teered to rejoin the fraternity for this venture—"

"Volunteered?" Sam muttered just above a whisper, "that's a laugh. I was shanghaied."

The group fixed its eyes on her as Joshua spoke; she fixed her eyes right back. They were the hard, dark eyes of someone who had already experienced more of life than any of the others would care to face. Her short, red hair had the texture of a steel-wool pad, and her skin, though richly tanned, showed the early effects of prolonged exposure to sun and ocean. One by one, all the team members looked away under the weight of her withering stare, all but Miranda, Dallas, and Nancy Graham.

"I hope it's a really big ship," Jonathan whispered softly to Jorge.

7

HOURS LATER, DALLAS FOUND himself sitting next to his duffle bag at the takeoff point. He surveyed the halls around him, thinking back over the weeks since he'd first arrived, about how much his life had changed, how much he had changed in that short space of time. The almost military sense of discipline surrounding him brought his thoughts back to the present. The others had all been moved out separately and at random times. They would proceed via different routes to an undisclosed destination, where they would be loaded in situ onto the ship. Only then would they be removed from their vehicles and allowed to make themselves comfortable in the new surroundings.

Most were amused by cloak-and-dagger approach, but a few, most notably Nancy Graham, complained endlessly about the inconvenience and obvious lack of trust. Joshua would only say in reply was that all would be explained on board the ship. Finally, after several hours of waiting and wandering the now-empty corridors, there was only Dallas, Miranda, and Joshua left to take their paneled van ride.

As they loaded up their belongings, Dallas turned to Joshua with a question that had been gnawing at him.

"Why bring in a treasure hunter? You're an archaeologist; you know the type of person she represents: Indiana Jones, grave robbers; all the worst."

"I know, Dallas, I know. But we are in a race, and we don't have the luxury of conducting a proper field expedition. We are after our own type of treasure, and she's what we need right now."

Dallas couldn't argue with Joshua's logic, distasteful as it was, and let the matter drop. Instead he focused on the journey to the ship which he found interesting, if exceedingly strange. There were starts and stops, lefts and rights, ups and downs, but he couldn't tell if any of it was part of a false trail. He had tried to count the turns, but finally gave up; it simply became too complicated. Joshua kept chattering away with uncharacteristically inane conversation, a tactic Dallas felt sure was designed to distract more than entertain.

Eventually, after what seemed like hours, the van came to an abrupt and bumpy halt. There had been the unmistakable sensation of driving up a slight incline and then leveling off. Suddenly, even though it was parked, the vehicle lurched. There was a sensation of upward movement, like riding in an elevator; the van was being lifted up. This was accompanied with a slight, but distressing, swaying. Dallas looked over at Joshua with a look of queasy astonishment that brought a wry smile to the elder man's face.

"You really don't trust us," Dallas finally said.

"Dallas, what good would it do to drive everyone around in blacked-out vans if I let everyone out at dockside; security must be complete, or it's pointless. Don't you agree?"

"Yes, but everyone knows we're leaving by ship and, as you say, they know we're dockside."

"Ah, but which dock? Which city?"

Dallas could see his point, but it also suggested that, despite all the driving, if the team had been let out dockside, then they would have been able to tell where they were. This, in turn suggested ways for any worthwhile spy to narrow down the list of possible locations. He also pondered how Joshua knew whether the drivers could be trusted.

For that matter, since any spy would have passed on the fact that the team planned to do its search by ship, it should be a simple thing to track all the ships that put out to sea; if, of course, they could identify the group's departure window. His thoughts were distracted by an abrupt thud as the van came to rest in what Dallas could only assume was the ship's hold. The van's rear doors opened, rather unceremoniously, to reveal the balance of the team. Their facial expressions ranged from benign amusement to frustration.

Joshua took no notice of anyone's reaction to their little drive, directing everyone toward their respective apartments. As in the headquarters, the quarters proved comfortable in the extreme. This may become a gilded cage, Dallas thought, but it was a very nice gilded cage.

Only scant directions were necessary to everyone as to where their particular work space was located, as well as other crucial areas, such as the dining hall and conference room. It quickly became clear to everyone that the place in which they found themselves bore an uncanny resemblance to their former surroundings beneath the museum. The director then summarily announced that, owing to the hour, which was by now late afternoon, the team should unpack and get some rest before the dinner meeting. As Joshua released everyone to their rooms, he reminded them not to be late for the meeting, when, as he put it, in Hercule Poirot fashion, "All would be revealed." With that, he wheeled off to leave the rest of the group standing in the narrow corridor.

"Well, I don't know about the rest of you," the team's anthropologist began, "but I've had enough of this nonsense. What about the rest of you?"

"Dr. Graham," Dallas replied wearily, "Joshua obviously had a reason to go to these extremes, and I, for one, am more than willing to give him the benefit of the doubt. I suggest we all get some rest; I'm sure he'll make clear his reasons when we gather."

There was grumbling agreement, which, if not overly enthusiastic, was at least sufficient to bring the conversation to a temporary close as everyone wandered away toward their separate quarters.

After a much needed nap, Dallas joined Miranda, and Joshua in the dining room. He sat sipping coffee as the team straggled into the conference room in ones and twos. They shuffled in, taking their customary seats in relation to one another. This left Sam, the group's newest member, standing awkwardly to one side.

"Come on, people make room." Joshua's request was silently obeyed, but one got the sense that the new member was taking note of who didn't offer her a space. "First, allow me, somewhat belatedly I'm afraid, to welcome you aboard the *Habibti*, our research vessel and home for the next few months. She's a converted oil tanker with plenty of space for our needs and the mission. In short, Jorge, you got your wish; a very big ship. Now, people, I'm sure you'd like to know what the hell is going on. Am I right?" Not waiting for an answer, he continued. "It seems that someone in this group isn't who he – or she – appears to be. It seems that we have a double agent in our midst."

The entire room, save Sam, Dallas, Miranda, Joshua, and Rocky sat bolt upright, eyes darting back and forth from colleague to colleague. Dallas sat silently, observing the others and looking for some sign that might give him a clue. None was forthcoming.

"Joshua, this is preposterous," Jorge began, only to be interrupted by everyone else's seconding of that option.

"Listen, I know it would seem so, but our 'sources' tell us that we have definitely been infiltrated. It would appear that the Order has taken an interest in our little treasure hunt. They obviously believe we are on the right track."

"So," Nancy intoned sarcastically, "our spies told us about their spies. Is it just me or is there something wrong with this picture?"

"Dr. Graham," he began, "all of you; you all know the importance of the mission and what the Order represents. They obviously believe this effort is important enough to bother with; whether it truly turns out to be or not. We can't allow them even the remotest possibility of success in disrupting us."

"Joshua," Raj interjected, "what do we know about this 'spy?' Obviously we don't know who it is, or we wouldn't be going through all this drama. What do you want us to do?"

"The best thing is just to do your work, and leave the rest to Rocky and me. If there is anything good about this, it's that the spy is trapped here now. We've left port and are now far out to sea."

"Joshua, how much longer until we can go topside?" Jorge sighed.

"We'll discuss that later. I think one of the first orders of business is for everyone to unpack their labs. Your belongings will be brought to you once they've been screened. Once that's done and we're settled in, then we'll take a tour of our new home. Now, I think it's time for us to discuss our destination – Dallas, it's your show."

"Thank God for that," Dr. Graham piped up, "at least now we'll know where we're being kidnapped to."

While her sarcasm didn't go unnoticed, it did go without retort. Everyone left her statement hang there in uncomfortable silence. It was Dallas who finally put her embarrassment out of its misery.

"Okay," he said finally, after draining his own coffee mug, "Here goes nothing … I'm thinking the Persian Gulf region is the place to start."

Before anyone could respond, Dallas continued, he thoughts now crystallized by the intervening weeks of introspection on the subject. "Let me detail my thoughts. To begin with, the language on the pieces of emerald is clearly some form of cuneiform writing. That script was based in this region; it is quite unlike the Jomon or Harappan writing styles. Next, in examining the charts provided me several weeks ago by George here, it is clear that before the end of the last ice age, thirteen thousand years ago, the Gulf didn't exist. He notes the possibility of a river, an extension of the merged Euphrates and Tigris Rivers, today called the Shat el Arab, which would have extended all the way to the Indian Ocean. Finally, the earliest Sumerian myths of creation place this region as their point of origin; their Eden, if you will."

"But," Rajeev interjected, "the Sumerian culture was demonstrably almost eight millennia removed from the time of the conquest. Surely it's a leap —"

"Of faith, Raj?" Dallas finished the thought, "You surprise me; isn't that what you wanted?"

"One question," Nancy Graham interrupted, "What does any of this have to do with Eden, the biblical Eden?"

"Well, that's the question, isn't it?" Raj couldn't resist the interjection.

"Look, forget Sumer for a moment. The biblical stories of Eden are quite specific; it was a land – the operative word here being land - from whence four rivers flowed; Genesis, chapter two, verses ten through fourteen: 'And a river went out of Eden to water the garden; and from thence it was parted, and became four heads. The name of the first is Pishon; that is it which compasseth the whole land of Havilah, where there is gold; and the gold of that land is good; there is bdellium and the onyx stone. And the name of the second river is Gihon; the same is it that compasseth the whole land of Cush. And the name of the third river is Tigris; that is it which goeth toward the east of Asshur. And the fourth river is the Euphrates.'"

"I'm impressed, you know your Bible."

"Torah; but thanks."

"Obviously, no location in existence today fits those coordinates. But it is clear that an ancient river channel still exists on the bed of the Persian Gulf. Perhaps it forked out and became the basis of that passage. There are even some Biblical scholars who claim that Bahrain was the original Eden."

"We'll let that one go for a moment," she replied wearily, "where exactly are we going?"

"Here," Dallas said, turning a map toward her, "Jazireh-ye Qeys."

"Dallas, that's part of Iran."

"And?"

"But there are many small islands in the area. Why specifically Jazireh-ye Qeys?"

"I can answer that," Jorge spoke up, passing down some charts, "examine the bathymetry chart, and this chart of the gulf seabed. It's not very precise, I'll grant you, but as you can see, what data there is suggests that while the average depth of the gulf is about one hundred and sixty feet, the depth around Jazireh-ye Qeys," he pointed at the chart as he spoke, "drops rapidly to two hundred and ninety feet. Notice the several shapes and their position relative to the island. I'm guessing Dallas's thinking – Dallas, correct me if I'm wrong – is that those would have been two, perhaps three ancient, huge, freshwater lakes, each a hundred miles long and maybe one hundred and thirty feet deep, laying on a broad plain. That would be the perfect place for an ancient settlement."

Sam, who'd thus far listened quietly to the exchange, felt the need to jump in; she did it with both feet. "Right idea, wrong location."

"Excuse me?" stammered Dallas as he struggled to retain his composure.

"Well, last night, Joshua here was kind enough to provide me with the information you gave him, and I've been studying your plan. I can see why you've chosen the gulf, but I think I've identified a better starting point. Sorry, Joshua, but with our abrupt departure I didn't have time to discuss this with you."

"Oh, so where exactly should we be headed?" Dallas's inquiry seemed a bit too pointed.

"As I said," she continued, "your basic premise is sound; however, I reviewed the recommendation and the charts and feel we should head to an area about sixty miles southwest your location, just west of a small island called Jazireh-ye Forur. I analyzed the entire gulf seabed, and, as you say, there is evidence of antediluvian chain of lakes with a broad river channel connecting them, rather like a string of pearls. However, I feel that this particular lake bed is the one we should test first." She pointed at the chart as she continued. "What the chart reflects is a smaller lake in the chain, approximately five miles wide and maybe twenty miles long. That would still have been a substantial body of fresh water; to the tune of about fifteen billion cubic feet. In conjunction with the river both above and below, it would represent an ideal settlement spot. A broad, flat plain; plenty of water, and moderate temperatures, given the ice age."

"That does follow with my basic premise." Dallas responded while trying his best not to sound wounded.

"Yes, it does. And this site has one thing your original site didn't have; and that you couldn't have known about."

"What's that?"

"Look here." Sam produced another chart as she spoke. "An unidentifiable magnetic anomaly sitting at exactly the same site as the shoreline of the ancient lake."

"What do you think it is?"

"Could be a natural occurrence," she said thoughtfully, "like an extremely large outcrop of iron ore; but I don't think so. The nearest iron ore deposits are in the Lagos Mountains of northern Iran; hundreds of miles away. There are no reported iron-ore deposits elsewhere in the region, except on the western border of Saudi Arabia, near the Red Sea, so it would seem strange to have one there, yet the magnetic deflection is ten degrees; that's substantial."

"But how does that help us?" Joshua questioned.

"I've got an idea. Back in the late 1980s, the U.S. Department of Interior published a paper concerning its ability to locate historic shipwrecks in the Gulf of Mexico by detecting much smaller magnetic anomalies. I know it works; I've used that technique myself. Now, there is an outside chance that this is also just a sunken cargo ship, but I don't think that's likely; first, because it such a strong anomaly, and second, if it were, it'd be reflected as such on the charts, as this area is so heavily traveled. At any rate, even if it isn't the vaults, the legends tell about the last emperor sending a ship to Earth—"

"You think it's a spaceship?"

"I think it's possible. Any ship he would send would have to have been massive. It's worth investigating."

"Okay," Dallas agreed finally, "I agree that this is as good a first start as any, but exactly how will we be investigating the location. Wherever we dive, we'll also need some type of remote viewing equipment or a pressurized submersible that can handle extended dives to depths of a hundred and sixty feet."

"Dallas is correct," agreed Sam, "the maximum depth we can go with no decompression stops is one hundred and forty feet. Even at that depth we would only have ten minutes of bottom time, and only two dives; or twenty minutes total per day with no decompression time. We're planning on going beyond that, which would require long decompression stops. At that rate, just locating potential sites could take months, if not years."

"I have a little surprise for you." Joshua responded as he steered his wheelchair over to a switch on his desk. Flicking it, the wall beyond opened like a pair of sliding-glass doors. Each segment moved silently out of the way, revealing another hallway decorated exactly like all the others.

At his encouragement, the team rose, en masse, and began moving down the mysterious hallway, twisting left, then right, and then left again. Finally they came to a well-lit cavernous chamber that seemed to be the size of a small airplane hanger. Looking back over his shoulder, Joshua smiled the broadest smile Dallas had ever seen. "Join me," he asked as he rolled into the huge space.

Sam moved forward without hesitation while Dallas and the others could only stand and stare. Before them sat a massive laboratory and workshop, combined into one cluttered whole. The arcing light and sparks of welders flickered throughout the space. On both sides stood banks of equipment; computers and other impressive electronics, some operating, and others silent. Above it all hung girders and high-powered halogen lights that gave him the sense of being inside a factory. One of the workers inside dropped a tool, and the distant clang echoed loudly.

"Joshua —" Dallas stopped momentarily, finding himself at a loss for words. "Just how big is this ship?"

"Oh, it's just your run-of-the-mill super-tanker, just under a thousand feet long and almost one hundred and seventy feet wide; that's about the size of four football fields, and as tall as a twenty-story building. In simplest terms – about the same size as aircraft carrier," Joshua replied as he brought them to his latest invention, and his pride and joy. "Everyone, let me present the answer to Dr. Layne's problem, and our home for the coming exploration. I call it the Seahab."

Everyone starred in disbelief at the massive series of objects before them. Before the group stood four huge cigar-shaped tubes the size of large yachts. Atop each one, about a third of the way behind the bow, sat a massive, clear bubble. Dallas felt as if he'd just walked into a shipyard. After waiting a moment to let the sight sink in, Joshua continued.

"As you can see, there are actually four sections; each a hundred and fifty feet long and thirty feet in diameter, not counting the command bridge – that's the bubble shape up top. Each section is self-propelled and independently controlled. When connected, it will have the shape of a boxy letter *A*, or an *H* with a top on it. There's a model of it over here, as it will look once fully operational on the seabed."

At his gesture, everyone walked over to their right and circled around a beautiful, intricately detailed scale model of the Seahab. Pointing at the model's components, Joshua began a more detailed description of their future underwater home.

"Two of the four sections are divided into two stories. The first section here serves as our living quarters. The second sits at a right angle to the first, and has our labs and conference rooms, as well as our dining and recreational facilities. The third joins the second, also at right angles, and houses the main wet area; our front door, if you will. It also serves as storage for all scuba and underwater excavation equipment. The fourth is the center section. It connects between sections one and three and houses the facilities' power and waste-management plants. As we prepare to position the sections with each other on the seabed, they will each extend three pairs of hydraulic supports and will securely anchor it to the bottom. In addition, each segment has a docking port topside. When we launch each section will have its own DSRV – short for deep submergence rescue vehicle. These DSRVs can carry 20 people to the surface and are for emergency evacuation, should that become necessary."

Gesturing to his left, Joshua pointed out two identical orange and white contraptions, submarine-looking devices with a single large, bubble-shaped, forward-facing observation window. They looked rather lonely, sitting off to one side, being completely ignored.

"Over there," he said, "we have two Nuytco Aquarius research submersibles; each carries one pilot and two passengers. They'll be piloted down separately from Seahab and docked on retractable docking chambers extending from the sides of sections one and three. We'll pilot the four separate sections to the bottom very much like submarines. Once there the computers will take over, positioning the segments together and connecting the entire facility. This will give us a fully functioning facility at the dig site. Actually, I got this whole idea from an old James Bond movie."

"But how will you get them out of the tanker?" Dallas stammered, still staring at the cigar-shaped pods.

"See these tracks that lead into that compartment there? We'll wheel each of them into that cavity, which is only slightly larger than these sections. They're sealed in, the chamber is pressurized, and then flooded. Once the chamber is full, we open the sea doors, and down they go. Of course, the ship will have to stop for the entire operation. First, the two Aquarius —"

"Aquarii?" Dallas quipped.

"Whatever – the two research subs will launch, while we're getting the Seahab in place. They'll begin looking for a good site, based on whatever data we have at that time. Then they'll be joined by the four Seahab segments. When we find a promising site, we'll set down, complete the docking sequence and begin exploration. Once the sections have been joined and Seahab is operational the tanker will continue on its way."

"How is it powered?" Sam asked approvingly.

"Basically, nuclear —"

"Nuclear!" interrupted Dallas.

"Yes, but it's really a combination of various technologies. The extremely small nuclear reactor superheats a closed line of coolant gas, in our case, CO_2, which loops through a tank of water, converting it into steam. The resulting steam drives a turbine, which is attached to a generator. That generator produces electricity which is used to power both the station and the electrolyzer. We use that device to separate oxygen and hydrogen from the sea water. From here, we divert some of the O_2 for breathing or diving; the rest we send into the regenerative hydrogen fuel cells. There, we recombine it with the hydrogen to produce a secondary supply of electricity for the station and to charge our backup batteries, as well as producing drinking water and heat. Actually, due to the depth, we'll really be breathing a compound called TriOx, a mixture of O_2, helium, and nitrogen. In fact, if we could figure out how to produce helium, we could stay submerged almost indefinitely. As it is we'll be using scrubbers to recycle both oxygen and helium, while removing the CO_2. We even have our own waste treatment plant; that's where we reclaim the nitrogen, using nitrogen generators. The rest of the waste we'll process it so it can be safely jettisoned into the gulf, there are going to be some mighty happy fish down there before we're through. The gulf has some of the best sea bass around; I hope you like seafood."

"But what about radioactive waste?"

"It's a totally closed system. Both the steam line and the coolant line are self-contained and separated, so there is no radioactivity, just heat transfer. One of its primary functions is really to provide the initial power necessary for the fuel cells; a little piece of technology we borrowed from NASA."

"Is it safe?" It seemed only Dallas was concerned.

"Quite; and it's our only practical solution. Normally you'd use solar cells to power the electrolyzer, but we can't do that, for obvious reasons. Did you know a baseball-sized mass of reactor core material has as much energy potential as one million gallons of gasoline?"

"I can honestly say I didn't know that. How many people will Seahab support?"

"We've got sleeping quarters for twenty-five, but I'm not set on the final count just yet. We'll have the whole team, of course, that's twelve, counting Sam, plus myself, and some support personnel; technicians, cooks, and the like. We still have plenty of time to work out the details and get everything onto the Seahab before we arrive."

"Seems to me," Jon spoke up, "that this sounds a lot like the old Sealab experiments of the 1960s."

"Quite so."

"But if I'm not mistaken, those experiments ended after someone died."

With little extra piece of information, everyone became suddenly silent.

"Well, yes, that's true," began Joshua slowly, "a man did die, of carbon dioxide asphyxiation. It happened in February 1969, off the coast of California. But the work continued, albeit in secret. And, I might add," he added defensively, "it was through human error and not equipment malfunction that the diver died. Someone neglected to prepare the dead man's CO_2 scrubber properly. Those functions are now controlled by computers and sensors; humans are safely out of that equation. I should also point out that the technology has advanced light-years since that accident. It's all perfectly safe."

"Joshua." It was Jorge. "Just how long will we be aboard before we reach the dive site?"

"Oh, I'd say about six weeks, give or take. We'll cruise south toward Brazil. Once south of the equator, we'll cut across the Atlantic to Africa before going down the west coast and around the Cape of Good Hope. We're in no hurry; besides, we'll need all that time to train those of you who will be piloting the individual segments."

"Wouldn't it be better to take the northern route," asked Jorge, "go across the North Atlantic, into the Mediterranean, and through the Suez Canal?"

"No; for two reasons." It was Sam who spoke up. "First, we're currently in the hurricane season in the northern hemisphere, so we should go south; just in case. Second, and, frankly, the major reason is that the ship is too big for the Suez. The canal only handles ships up to 150,000 dead tons; we're double that, not to mention we draw twice as much water as the canal can handle. To put in layman's terms for you, professor, we're too wide, too heavy and ride too low in the water; the canal's not wide enough or deep enough."

"Oh, I see." Jorge was impressed with her knowledge, if not her demeanor.

"Joshua," Dallas whispered as he pushed the wheelchair, "tell me, why are all the women around you so difficult?"

"Are they? I hadn't noticed?" The director smiled as Dallas steered the chair toward the section containing Seahab's living quarters. "Would all of you like to see inside?"

An hour later, Dallas confessed he was impressed, very impressed. Once again everyone's quarters mirrored those both at the museum and aboard the tanker, with one unique difference; windows. Each of the suites and work areas had them; certainly a first in his time with the Guardians. He guessed they weren't afraid of the fish. As he examined the elaborate research facilities he found himself wondering, once again, how they had gotten everything ready so quickly. The design specs alone should have taken months, if not years, to complete. And then there was the construction to consider, modifications to the tanker, the living quarters, the Seahab; none of this could have been constructed within the time he had joined the group.

Dallas took in all these facts and found growing within him his own private fear; that he would not be able to translate the tablets. Despite all his time staring at the cuneiform over the past two months he was no closer to solving their puzzle. He had no idea if he'd made the right choice on the Gulf expedition, and yet they seemed to have no problem committing vast sums of money and quantities of time into making his vision into reality.

When the tour came to an end, Dallas left the others, intending to return to his office, when he felt a tug on his sleeve; it was Miranda.

"Lunch?"

"Huh? Oh, sure. Miranda, do you think this is a fool's errand?"

"Well, it was your idea; so maybe you've answered your own question."

"Very funny."

"Truthfully, I guess we need to start somewhere. If nothing else, it might satisfy your curiosity about us. I mean, if you find a settlement site, then it would have to date to sometime before thirteen thousand years ago, and that would mean we're telling you the truth; and either way it got all of us out of our little cave and actually doing something.."

"Be that as it may, "Dallas mused, "I wouldn't waste the group's resources just to satisfy my personal curiosity. I know we won't find any clay tablets. But if we do find artifacts that survived over thirteen thousand years, then that means we've found something of incredible historic importance; question is, what?"

Miranda sat quietly for a moment before responding. "Dallas, what exactly are we looking for?"

"I honestly don't know. The first hope, obviously, is finding a vault. Perhaps Sam is right; maybe we'll find a spaceship. Even a settlement site would be exciting; it would prove we're on the right track."

"I must admit," Miranda offered, "that even with Graham Hancock's book in front of us, we hadn't given much thought to pursuing underwater sites. And we've never even discussed the Persian Gulf."

"I hope that turns out to be a compliment … "

Later that afternoon, as everyone settled into their separate duties, his mind returned, as it inevitably always did, to the tablets. The need to take the next step continued to rattle around in Dallas's mind, leaving him with the same frustrated feeling one gets when they can't remember the name of the actor in their favorite movie. Like that name, the answer to Dallas's question of how to translate them seemed poised on the tip of his tongue, within sight but just out of reach.

As Dallas walked around the cavernous interior of the converted tanker, he had the eerie sensation that he was still at the headquarters bunker complex. If it weren't for the occasional subtle sensation of movement beneath his feet, he would have sworn he hadn't left. What he saw all around him was a monument to obsessive-compulsive behavior; every corner, every hallway was exactly the same. His current living quarters duplicated those at headquarters, which duplicated his former apartment, now seemingly a lifetime away.

He could only assume Joshua was a fanatic about familiar surroundings. If so, then the boat must have already been in operation. Any modifications must; therefore, have been merely to do with the research portion of the mission. Dallas walked the halls automatically as he analyzed them; an interesting dichotomy. Since the ship had clearly already existed, it only left one question; why it had existed in the first place. That was the same question he'd been asking himself ever since Joshua showed them Seahab.

He wandered absentmindedly through his door and only then realized he had been so lost in thought that he wasn't even conscious of the path he'd taken to get there. Walking into the bathroom he splashed some cold water on his face and looked up to see his reflection in the mirror; then it struck him.

As unexpected as lightning from a clear blue sky a thought hit him. An epiphany; it came from nowhere yet appeared full form. He stared at himself and he had the answer, he why he had thus far been unable to translate the emerald tablets. Grabbing an eight-by-ten inch photo of a tablet segment from his night stand, he ran back into the bathroom. Instantly he saw he was right. Dashing out of his cabin, he sprinted down to Miranda's door, pounded on it, called her name, and then continued on. She stuck her head out into the hallway just in time to see his feet as he turned the corner and quickly followed him. She caught up with him just has he entered the door of his lab.

"Dallas, what is it? What's got you so excited?"

"Miranda, I've got it. I know why I couldn't translate the cuneiform before. It was staring me in the face all this time. It's so simple, it's ingenious."

"What is it? Tell me!" The excitement became contagious.

"It's backwards!" Dallas could barely contain himself as he turned the emerald over and over in his hand. "This text is upside down and backwards. It's so simple."

"Could it be that easy?" Miranda found herself caught up in the moment.

"Miranda," he could hardly catch his breath, "call whoever we need to call to get my light table unpacked, I need it in here now. Then go to the photo lab. Have them print the largest, clearest color transparencies that they can of both tablets; and I mean really huge. While you're doing that, I'll get things organized here. Oh, and please stop off by your father's cabin and tell him we may finally be onto something."

Dallas knew it would still be a formidable task to decipher the artifact, even knowing its little secret, and they didn't have long; just six weeks until they reached the dive site. Even though the symbols were clearly legible, there were still large gaps in his understanding of both the grammar and syntax and some of the symbols. He cautioned himself that his knowledge was still so limited that he might still come up with nothing but useless gibberish.

Fifteen minutes later, Joshua's knock on the door made all such thoughts on the subject moot. The director wheeled in brimming with enthusiasm and encouraging Dallas to begin immediately. For his part, Dallas tried explaining that it could still be some time before the transparencies would be ready; and that while the workshop could get the light table set up, there wasn't much else they could do until everything arrived. Even then, there would no quick fix, no simple solution. There were at least a million potential potholes on the road to a successful and useful translation of the text. All this caution bounced off the back of Joshua's wheelchair as he rolled away to give everyone the exciting news. It was at that exact moment that Dallas promised himself to reveal nothing of what he might decipher until he was absolutely certain.

Six days, twenty-three pots of coffee, and several dozen doughnuts later, Dallas sat, amazed at what he was discovering. While he was not yet even halfway finished, it was clear that this first piece of the pyramid contained nothing less than a history of the ancient empire's last days. He spent the entire sixth day reviewing his notes and translation over and over. Finally, that evening, knowing he could delay them no longer, he brought the team together to read them what he had translated thus far.

The group was no less ready than he to finally discuss what he had found. Joshua in particular had literally worn tire tracks in the carpet outside his door trying unsuccessfully to get some news of the emerald's contents. At last the moment had arrived.

"I would like to apologize," Dallas said solemnly to the assembly, "for my reluctance in discussing this with all of you sooner, but I had to be sure I was on the right track. There are two points I wish to make before I describe what I've found. First, our initial surmise appears to be correct – this particular tablet definitely dates to a time just before the empire's fall. I can't speak to the other ones as yet but I assume this is also true of them as well. Second, as you all know, translation is not an exact science. There may be some subtle errors in my work but I do believe I have the broad strokes essentially correct, however —"

"Get on with it, man," Joshua interrupted, revealing at last a streak of impatience. His enthusiasm brought nervous yet hopeful laugher from those assembled.

"Very well," Dallas replied with a grin. "What I am about to tell you appears to be the final thoughts and testimony of the Emperor En.lil. An, 523rd ruler of the House of Ed.In. The text lists several honorifics and titles, which I will skip for now. At any rate, this is his story."

8

I, EMPEROR EN.LIL.AN, BRING forth these words to the descendants of my people, the great realm of the Anunnaki. I am to be the last of the emperors of the House of Ed.In, the rulers of that realm and I address you now in the gathering twilight of our civilization. As darkness falls around us for this last time, it is my final duty to explain to my people's children how this tragedy could come to be.

For many thousands of years, the House of Ed.In has ruled this sector of the galaxy from our home world of Nibiru. The distant past is now spoken of only as myth and legend, and I am sure this is also how you will one day come to regard me. Believe me when I say that your heritage is vast, your legacy rich, in ways that, to you, may not seem so. But if you are reading my words, then perhaps it has not all been in vain. Perhaps our race has managed to survive this terrible night that is even now befalling us, and perhaps you who are reading this have risen to the dawn of a new day.

I regret that I can leave only this meager record and the tale which I will tell. It is perhaps the supreme irony that a legacy written in the heavens must now be reduced to stone. We have been forced to devise methods that may stand the test of time, incorruptible, and unaffected by the awesome weapons of our enemy.

Our enemy; let me tell you about our enemy. They are a savage race who call themselves the Ha.Sa.Tan, but my people have come to call them Ta.Alal.Azzagh. What little we know of them has been passed down through the ages, since the time of the empire's beginning. Legends say that they are hideous gray creatures, slight in shape with long, slender limbs and fingers, large heads, and enormous egg-shaped eyes as black as death. It is said they have the ability to conceal their true appearance. They voices are said to be like a beautiful melody, but beneath that alluring tune is the devil's voice. They are the corruptors of truth who ensnare the innocent and the weak-minded, turning them toward their own evil purpose. They whisper their lies among our own population, and some believe them. The greater the lie, the softer the whisper. My ancestor, Ed.In the Great, the first emperor of our house, first vanquished them and forced them outside the borders of our realm. There they vanished into the darkness of space; or so we thought.

For uncounted millennia, our house has ruled in peace and prosperity. Our population numbered in the tens, perhaps hundreds, of billions; so large, in fact, that in these final days no one is sure of our number. As a race, we witnessed sunrise on a thousand worlds, lived and died in the darkness of space and stretched forth our hand to touch the works of the creator.

But as we grew and expanded, small groups of these demons hid themselves on newly conquered worlds, they joined with those who did not welcome our ways, who resisted our common destiny, who foolishly wished to cling to the old beliefs that had first been overcome by the Great Ed.In. Among these agitators moved the whispering devils, spreading their lies, inciting the discontented to do what we had prevented the evil ones from doing themselves for so many millennia. They made promises that were impossible to keep, but like sweet honey on the tip of one's tongue, impossible to resist.

They are a notoriously cunning and patient race. Unknown to us, these demons slowly worked their evil magic until the day came when we realized, too late, that they too had grown into a vast army. They had infiltrated into the very empire itself, searching for the proper instrument with which to destroy all that Ed.In and his heirs had created for them.

I foresaw that, should they succeed, it would mean and end to the House of Ed.In and the empire; that success for the dissidents would come at the price of countless lives. Indeed, it would mean an end to the universe as my people have known it. I fear now my worst visions have come to pass; darkness falls on the empire.

Even now, as I prepare these special messages, the enemy is preparing for a final assault on Nibiru. The people are massing to fight a final defense of their homeland but I fear this battle is hopeless. It is my hope that while the battle may be lost; the war might yet be won. I have set into motion a plan for rebirth, a rising from the ashes, but it is an untested plot. Still, my people have sacrificed much to clear my path, and I must attempt it.

This final crisis began almost a hundred years ago, when the Remali, a people in a distant solar system began to organize themselves around an ancient religion; they called themselves Zorians and became zealots for their cause. It is a rigid religious order, strict in its application, unforgiving of anyone who did not follow "The Way." For thousands of years, the Remali had been loyal members of the empire; and suddenly, uprisings were appearing everywhere, without any visible provocation; the Ha.Sa.Tan had found their instrument.

These Zorians began to openly challenge the authority of the empire, assisted by the Ha.Sa.Tan, the black-eyed demons, who now also claimed to follow "The Way," thus asserting a form of kinship. Then the Ha.Sa.Tan secreted themselves on the next world, found that population's political weakness, and declared allegiance with them as well. The Ha.Sa.Tan did not move directly at the empire, preferring to nibble covertly at the fringes, spreading around the outer borders, until after sixty years, we found ourselves encircled by over one hundred, different, suddenly hostile worlds, all claiming some form of kinship with the Ha.Sa.Tan. Only after we were surrounded did we become aware of the return of the Ha.Sa.Tan, but by then it was impossible to convince the rebel planets that they were being sorely used. Still, we tried maintain the peace.

Then the advance began, and again, it moved with the pace of ice in winter. One planet, one civilization, at a time; until, finally, ten years ago, the Alliance, as it now called itself, and numbering two hundred worlds, declared open war against the empire; the first war in one hundred thousand years of recorded history. It was believed that such barbarity had long since vanished from the galaxy, but while we had rested in civilized innocence, the Ha.Sa.Tan had made it a science, perfecting it as no species in the galaxy had ever done. They produced weapons of such terrifying force that another two hundred planets surrendered almost at once.

We were forced to go into the archives and the ancient records to find ways of defending ourselves against them. Our space fleet managed to capture an Alliance warship and was able to copy some of the weapons. These efforts only slowed their advance; it didn't stop it, and it became clear that the empire must sue for peace.

To handle these delicate negotiations, I sent my brother, Crown Prince En.Ki.An, a man renowned throughout the galaxy for his wisdom. It was only after months of supposed dialogue I discovered that he had fallen under the control of the Alliance, seduced by the dark powers of the Ha.Sa.Tan. He planned with them the final destruction of Nibiru, through the unleashing of an ishakku, a weapon of such great force that it is claimed it can destroy the entire planet. While I do not fully believe these claims, I have begun preparations to evacuate both the portal and the royal court to our sister world of Kia, the planet of the blue waters.

Throughout our history, we have used Kia to provide raw materials for Nibiru. The planet had not evolved an enlightened race like ourselves, but instead, was populated by a savage species, pleasing to the eye, but brutish and better-suited to that massive planet than ourselves. My forebears set themselves on a program of creating a hybrid race, taking qualities of that race and ourselves so that we might better use that beautiful blue world. In time, this race spread across the face of Kia.

Now these creatures will have in their midst the noble seed of the House of Ed.In for I have not choice but to send them to this hostile place in order to survive. Under normal conditions I would not consider sending my portal there, but now it is our only hope. I am sure that my people will adapt. If you are reading this now, then perhaps the doorway to hope survived as well.

I have selected the noblest of men, Ziu.Sun.Da.Ra, to lead this desperate journey. They will travel aboard a specially designed craft that can be concealed from the Ha.Sa.Tan ships. Onboard his vessel, Ziu. Sun.Da.Ra will have the seeds of a new life for our people, including my own dear children; but there is much they will not have when they arrive for we have not built cities on this world. They will have no comforts of our former home.

They must live as the primitives live; they must begin again, and wait for the appointed time to rise again from our ashes. It will interesting to see what has come of that planet, your planet, for you who are reading this tablet, whether of the House of Ed.In or those others, are the descendants of all that I have told you. Now, regardless of your ancestry, you are all, in some measure, Anunnaki.

I cannot say more, because even mentioning it entails great risk, but you must know these facts and you must search them out. You must gather together at the sacred place, at the left hand our people, where more will be revealed. Only then, together, can we begin our return to the stars to reclaim our inheritance.

9

"AND THAT," DALLAS SAID finally, "is as far as I have gotten."

The room remained silent, the team hanging on every word. Dallas looked from face to face across the room; all eyes, save Joshua's, were fixed on him, their faces wearing looks ranging from wonder to shock. It was evident to Dallas that while those assembled had been raised to believe in their version of history, this spin on the events of thirteen thousand, five hundred years ago was more than they'd expected. It is one thing to believe, he realized, and quite another to know.

"So," Dallas began again, "does anyone have any thoughts?"

Joshua, whose eyes had been closed in deep concentration, raised his chin off the perch which had been his entwined knuckles. Finally, he opened his eyes and made contact with Dallas's. Only then could Dallas see that tears had begun to form and slip gently down the director's cheek.

"Dallas," Joshua began with an unsteady voice, "today you have fulfilled my faith in you. Today, you are the most important man in the last thirteen thousand, five hundred years of the human race. Today you have fanned the first gentle breeze on the smoldering embers of our ancestors' memory. You have breathed life into the soul of a man dead for thirteen millennia; you have honored his final wish, that the dawn would one day return for his people."

The room erupted in shouts of agreement and cheers at Joshua's emotional words; the uproar louder than one would think is possible for such a small group. Dallas twisted uncomfortably in the eye of this storm. Knowing the significance of what he had just reported, he still felt awkward in hearing it acknowledged aloud.

The team's physician, Dr. Karen Pollard, broke his silence with a simple, direct question. "Dallas, I'm just a simple country doctor, not an archaeologist like most of you, can you place what we've heard just now into some type of context for me. I mean, how did you possibly manage to translate this tablet; could the language have endured for so many thousands of years? And what does Ha.Sa.Tan mean in plain English, or Ta.Alal.Azzagh or Kia for that matter?"

"Well, Karen, as to how the language survived, I have no clue. Perhaps it lived as a purely spoken language, or perhaps it existed in written form and proof of that has not yet been found. In any event, we know that some closely related form did in fact survive and reappeared in the area now known as Sumer. Regardless, what I have discovered thus far is that many of the root words are roughly similar to these same words in Sumerian. There are some slight deviations, but that is to be expected. Let's start with the simplest first. Kia is straightforward Sumerian, and translates to Earth. Now, there is no word or term in Sumerian resembling Ha.Sa.Tan, but if that is what the other race called themselves that might not be surprising. It suggests that by Sumerian times the danger had long passed, or that they never overtly interacted with them; hence they would have formed no word to name them. As to Ta.Alal.Azzagh, my best shot in Sumerian would be Telal Azag, which, in English, translates to ... demon warrior serpents.

"You might be interested to know," Dallas continued, not wanting to dwell on that last translation, "that the term Ha.Sa.Tan did exist in the ancient proto-Hebrew tongue; in fact, it is the etymology of our word Satan. I don't know yet whether it is a coincidence, or whether the Ha.Sa.Tan, as a group, interacted with some of the earlier prehistoric

Semitic tribes. Certainly, Satan is central to man's biblical fall from grace, and in those texts he is depicted as a serpent. While both those facts are consistent with what we now know from the tablet, we cannot prove a connection between the Hebrew legends and the Anunnaki history; at least not yet.

"Among the other mythological similarities, the name of the emperor's nobleman, Ziu.Sun.Da.Ra, is virtually identical to a character in Sumerian myth of Gilgamesh. In that story, a character named Ziu. Su.Dra saves humanity by preserving life on an ark during a great flood. It has even been speculated that he is the basis for the biblical Noah. Of course, Enlil and Enki are central to Sumerian mythology. The 'An' suffix contained in the emerald tablet appears to be an honorific indicating some form of their father's name. This is still a naming practice still common in some cultures even today, Abu in Arabic, for example. To the Sumerians, Enlil was the god of the Earth, and Enki was the god of the sky, and An was their father, the leading god figure. Simply put, it would appear the emperor and his brother passed into legend over the millennia.

"Joshua," Dallas turned to address the leader directly, "it would seem that En.lil.An tells a different version of events than what you first told me. I suppose that could just be an example of the old axiom of history being written by the victors."

"Of course the discrepancy is obvious, and I truthfully have no answer for that as yet," Joshua pondered aloud. "Remember also that the legends tell of the traitors being exiled here as well, so it may well be that the emperor's brother, En.Ki.An, ended up here. He would have been an enemy of those sent to safety by the emperor, so our oral histories may be the result of a conflict between the different Anunnaki groups after their arrival here. That would fit very neatly with certain elements of ancient recorded Sumerian mythology. I suspect we may know more once you complete the translation of that piece and begin on the second one —"

"More importantly," Miranda interrupted, "let's focus on the positive here. For example, we now know conclusively that there are multiple sites, as the legends say."

"But," Jorge spoke up, "I'm curious. How do we know that the Ha.Sa.Tan didn't already find the chambers? In fact, why would the Ha.Sa.Tan spare this world at all? Why exile anyone? They obviously could have just as easily destroyed Earth as well, and left no trace of the Anunnaki anywhere."

"Perhaps," Dr. Graham spoke up, "the Alliance wasn't interested in total destruction, just independence. Perhaps mercy became an option once victory was assured."

"Possibly," interjected Hakeem, "though from En.Lil.An's description of them, I must say I find that unlikely; but even if the Ha.Sa.Tan could have been so restrained, where are they now? Why did they not take over this planet as their own? Whatever the motives of the Alliance, the Ha.Sa.Tan surely had set their sights on the destruction of the House of Ed.In. I would say this translation raises more questions about our mission than it answers."

"Exactly my point," Jorge added. "It would seem logical for the Ha.Sa.Tan to complete their mission by leaving no royal blood flowing; yet clearly both En.Lil.An's heir and his apparently traitorous brother, En.Ki.An, were both on Earth. It seems odd for the Ha.Sa.Tan to simply vanish on the verge of total success."

"Remember," Dallas said, "I still have some work to do. Perhaps the answers to some of these questions are there."

Jorge sat in bemused silence for a moment before asking the unspoken question on everyone's mind. "Unless I'm mistaken about what we just heard – correct me if I'm wrong, was the origin of Satan, the story of Adam and Eve, serpents in Eden, and Noah's Ark.

"Are we here in this room really ready to deal with the impact of this knowledge on all of humanity?"

Joshua looked sympathetically at the physicist, who was obviously more accustomed to the simplicity and honesty of mathematics. "To answer your questions in order," the director said finally, "Yes, this information offers echoes of Genesis – and other even more ancient texts for that matter, and yes, we do realize the impact this information would have, if we were to release it. I have struggled with that very question all of my life."

"Perhaps," added Joshua, thoughtfully, "Hakeem is correct in his pondering why Earth was spared. It may be that through some strange providence, the Ha.Sa.Tan did not think to look here for knowledge such as this tablet describes. Perhaps En.Lil.An's plan was a success after all, and his enemy did not know that chambers were built or people evacuated. Perhaps there is something about this planet that protects us from the final vengeance of the Ha.Sa.Tan. Perhaps all these reasons are to some degree true. Perhaps none of them are. I can almost guarantee that at least some of the reasons may never be fully known. In any case, I believe there are sufficient grounds to keep this information secret, at least for the present."

"But," Jonathan objected, "what we have heard here turns all that we've been taught on its head. We were the victims, not the aggressors. We are not in exile but in hiding. Perhaps, to honor our ancestors, we should use the artifacts we may find not just to discreetly benefit mankind but to restore our civilization as the emperor had hoped and planned."

"Jonathan," Raj joined, in a suspicious tone, "into whose hands would you place that enormous power?"

"Are you implying something?" Jonathan spat back.

The room once again fell silent as the two men glowered at one another. Some clearly agreed with Jonathan, who was approaching the question from a purely analytical point of view: if the basic premise of the Guardians was incorrect, so too would any decision based on that premise. Others, for the equally logical reasons Joshua had already stated, agreed with the need for continued secrecy. As the only true outsider present, Dallas found himself in the unpleasant position of trying to build a bridge between the two groups.

"Guys, guys, relax. First, I haven't finished my work, so let's be good scientists and not jump to any conclusions. And even if the translation were released, can you imagine the reaction if we just announce it? We'd basically be telling all the Christians, Jews, and Muslims that everything they know is wrong. If we're having problems here in this room, imagine how six billion people would handle it."

"Five billion," Raj said with a laugh, "my people wouldn't have a problem; it pretty much goes with Hindu beliefs. Granted, the other planet thing might take some getting used to, but, as for the rest, we could live with it."

"Besides," Miranda joined in, "there's no way to date the emerald. 'Reputable' scientists would call it a hoax. Look what happened with the so-called Jesus estuary. We don't have anything to say, not really, until, and unless, we find at least one of the chambers."

"Excellent point," Dallas added. "So what say we get ourselves back to work and worry at tomorrow's problems tomorrow?"

"Yes," Hakeem agreed, "as my people say, 'let us not get wet before it rains.'"

The statement's absurdity brought a nervous chuckle from everyone as the meeting adjourned. Miranda, Sam and Rocky stayed behind with Dallas and Joshua, hoping to learn if there was more information that Dallas hadn't yet revealed to the group. It didn't take long to find out.

"Joshua," Dallas said softly as the last of the group filed out, "there are some issues we need to discuss."

"Such as?"

"Well," Dallas responded, leaning back against the conference table, "there is one thing I didn't get into with today's translation; he talks about one of the weapons he's hidden here on Earth."

"What?"

"I didn't mention it, because I haven't finished that section yet, and I want to double check my work first, but it appears he tells of some type of device left in hiding. The secret of its location was supposedly to be delivered into the hands of his young son, Ad.Am.En, who he had renamed Adapa, in recognition of his role as the king of the new world; a role he would assume when he came of age."

"Adapa," Joshua mused, "wasn't he the first human created by the gods, according to Sumerian texts?"

"Yep," acknowledged Dallas, "and, according to the tablet, attending Adapa was Ma.Rd.Uk.En, the nephew of the emperor and the son of En.Ki.An. He apparently assumed the name of Marduk in recognition of his role as regent. Clearly, with Marduk, we're beginning to see the entire Sumerian pantheon; amazing, it somehow stayed intact."

"But," Miranda reminded Dallas, "according to Sumerian legend, Marduk was loyal to his father, Enki. Why would Enlil appoint the son of a traitor to guard his own son?"

"Who knows?" Dallas offered, "Perhaps he didn't blame Enlil for the Ha.Sa.Tan's deception. Perhaps they had some strange ability to control people that could not be resisted. I seem to recall that, according to legend, Enki had a Machiavellian reputation; perhaps his son was a chip off the old block. Maybe the emperor will explain it all as I continue with the translation."

"I must admit to a certain curiosity about some of what you said," Miranda sighed.

"Just some?"

"I know the Sumer mythology fairly well, but I don't know what he means by a portal or this 'doorway to hope'."

"I'm not sure; perhaps it's an expression from his time that doesn't translate well into our vernacular. There is still a lot I don't understand and a lot more to translate, but there is one thing I am sure of."

"And that is?" Joshua asked with a concerned tone.

"It's late, and I'm hungry," Dallas said with a grin. "Who wants dinner?"

"But what about the device?" It was Rocky who uncharacteristically spoke up.

"Oh, that! The text isn't specific. I'm guessing it was the empire's version of a planet buster. I'm not sure what good it would be without a spaceship, though."

"Maybe," interrupted Sam, "we aren't without a ship." She was thinking, of course about their dive site. That simple declarative statement thrust the entire assembly into contemplative silence.

The next morning found Dallas hard at work once again on the tablet. It was an amazing document, and the more he worked on it, the more shocking it became. Now his daily routine consisted of waking up, working until he couldn't see straight, going to bed, and then beginning the cycle over again the next day.

At irregular intervals, food appeared in Dallas's lab, brought either by Miranda or a staff member from the galley. Sometimes he ate, but most times he just nibbled as he worked. With each day, with each missed meal, Dallas uncovered yet more about the life and plans of Enlil. It was amazing how much similarity the old legends bore to the stories he was reading. The utter absence of any known written record after these emerald pieces, prior to the Sumerian tablets first discovered in the 1890s, suggested to Dallas that the legends had to have survived orally for almost eight thousand years, a supposition that he refused to accept.

He began thinking of the Hindu belief about the cycles of civilization; perhaps there had been older written records that had been lost during the human culture's last cycle of destruction, just as the Hindu myths claimed. That could, he thought, explain the apparent discrepancy. The legends were not just oral, and were not without meaning; until this last cycle, when the stories themselves had survived, but the meanings were lost. To him, this fact evoked the totally unscientific feeling that fate decreed the past must not be lost. Dallas finally came to the unsatisfying conclusion that such philosophical pondering was distracting and pointless. Still, he couldn't help but wonder.

Dallas was brought out of these musings by a gentle rapping, a tapping on his cabin door. He shook the Edgar Allen Poe out of his brain and called out that the door was unlocked. It seemed as if destiny wished to continue playing its hand, for there, in the doorway, was Raj, with an excited look on his face.

"Dallas," he began, "I've been thinking these past few days about what you told us about En.Lil.An, and well, I think I've got an idea. In Hinduism, the ancient supreme god was Indra. In Vedic times, Indra was the supreme ruler of the gods. He was the god of war and of thunder, the greatest of all warriors, the strongest of all beings, and he was the defender of gods and mankind against the forces of evil. He is also known for wielding the celestial weapon."

"That's fascinating, Raj, but how does that tie in with what I've translated so far?"

"Just this: Indra's most notable exploit was his victorious battle with a mighty serpent that had stolen all the water in the world for itself. The two clashed, and after a long battle, Indra destroyed his powerful enemy. The serpent had kept the Earth in a drought, but when Indra split open the demon, the waters again fell spilled forth, briefly flooding the Earth. Indra became a hero to all the people, and the gods elected him their king for his victory. Perhaps here we have some answers. The demon serpent is one similarity; remember the emperor's reference to the Ta.Alal.Azzagh? The return of the waters suggests a massive flood. Most important, it suggests that someone, or something, rose up to fight the demon and save mankind."

"You know, Raj, I was just thinking about the Hindu belief in the recurring cycles of civilization. Do you think it is possible we're overlooking something?"

"Like what?"

"Well, we've been wondering why the Ha.Sa.Tan didn't use the weapon. What if that premise is wrong; maybe they did?"

"But we're still here."

"Yes, but what if the planet was too big to destroy? What if they used it to do something like … melt the polar ice cap? What if they were the ones that ended the ice age?"

"The return of the waters! The massive flood! Dallas, I think we've hit on it."

"Perhaps, I just wish I were better versed in Vedic mythology."

"Don't worry, Dallas, that's my job. I'll return to my quarters, collect some of my reference materials, and we can see what other connections we can find. Perhaps, in this combination of the two mythologies, we will learn something."

"Excellent idea; get your stuff and come back. You know where to find me."

With that, Dallas returned to his work. As he habitually did, he lost track of the time and it wasn't until almost two hours later, when there came a sound at his door, that he realized Raj had not returned. The knocking had become a pounding before it raised itself to a level that intruded on Dallas's awareness. Mechanically he walked backwards to the door, all the while keeping his gaze locked on the wall-sized transparency of the engraving. Turning the handle, he walked back to his work.

"Come in, Raj," he offered mechanically over his shoulder, not bothering to turn around.

"Dallas." It was not Raj, but Miranda, and her voice was serious and determined.

Her tone commanded his full attention; surprised, he turned to face her. "What's wrong?"

"It's Raj, Dr. Singala, he's dead."

"What? How can that be, he was just here a little while ago."

"He's dead now. One of the crew found him in the Seahab hanger section of the ship, just lying there. Dr. Pollard is on the way there now. My father wanted me to come get you at once."

They rushed to the location of the body, arriving a few minutes after Karen Pollard and Joshua. Rocky and several of his security team stood behind the two in a semicircle. They walked up to find the doctor pulling a cloth up over their colleague. She remained kneeling beside the body, as if lost in thought. Finally, she rose and turned to face the others.

"Well," she said finally, "at first glance, I can find no obvious cause of death, I don't see any obvious external sign of trauma; I'll need to do a thorough examination to be sure."

"Any speculations?" Joshua inquired.

"Not really, except I know his last physical was fine. He was in perfect health; no evidence of heart trouble. He could have died of boredom for all I know right now." She shrugged her shoulders in frustration. "I don't know, possibly he suffered a cerebral hemorrhage —"

"Or poison," Dallas found himself saying aloud.

"Yes, or poison," the doctor replied in a curious tone. "The point is that we won't know until I do a complete autopsy."

"How long until you know something?" Joshua's manner implied his mind was already at work on the issues. "Rocky!"

"Yes, boss?"

"First, have all the team members brought to the conference room. We need to let everyone know what happened; at least as much as we can tell them at this point. Second, we need to implement the intruder security protocols immediately. No one is to be alone at any time. The security personnel will guard all access to team members living quarters at all times, rotating shifts. Third, you need to inspect and secure the food stuffs and water supplies. Have I forgotten anything?"

Rocky pondered for a moment before answering. "No, sir, nothing I can think of at the moment. I'll get the special security command center opened and functioning at once, and issue radios to all security personnel."

"One more thing," Joshua added, "once you've handled those details, I want you to catch up with Dallas and stay with him at all times. He and his work space must receive the tightest possible protection. Oh, and check his quarters inside and out for anything out of the ordinary – poisons, explosives, everything. I want Dallas and his research cosseted around the clock. I'm holding you personally responsible."

"Yes, sir! You two, with me," Rocky said, pointing to the security team, "You three stay with the director." With that, he whirled around and was gone in an instant.

"Dallas," Joshua said softly as he turned to face him, "I'd consider it a personal favor if you'd escort my daughter back to the conference room and wait with her to the rest of the team arrives."

Miranda stared at the older man in disbelief. "Father, I can take care of myself; and frankly, I am better able to look after Dallas than he is of me!"

"I thought I made it abundantly clear I wanted no one on the team – NO ONE – moving alone onboard this ship until we know what happened!" Joshua nearly rose from his chair as if to emphasize the point. "Now, if your ego requires that you escort Dallas, so be it. Either way I would like the two of you to stay as close together as possible. There are only a few people here I can trust: you two, Sam, the doctor here, and Rocky and his security team. Everyone else must still be considered suspect. Those people we can trust must work together; watch each other's back, so to speak."

Turning to the remaining security personnel, Joshua signaled for two of them to assist the doctor and one to come with him, and then he added the obvious. "Doctor, please let me know the moment you find out anything."

"Of course, Joshua. I'll begin the autopsy and toxicology work-ups at once."

"We'll gather at the conference room in fifteen minutes," he called out over his shoulder to the couple. "Don't be late!"

Dallas and Miranda found themselves alone in this distant corner of the ship on the far side of Seahab. It suddenly seemed an ominous, foreboding place, full of long shadows and suspicious nooks. Dallas felt a sudden reflective icy chill run up and down his spine, coupled by an overwhelming desire to return to familiar territory as quickly as possible.

"Why do you think he was here?" Dallas asked, feeling a need to make conversation.

"Don't know," muttered Miranda with a sense of cool, analytical objectivity, "Curious though, that he should be here."

"How so?"

"Well, for one thing, he had no business being here; he didn't have clearance to visit the Seahab alone. In fact, even if he had clearance, he had no need be in this particular area. There are no access points here, nor any equipment that would concern any of us. I can only speculate that he either snuck in, was brought here by someone who does have access, or he died elsewhere, and his body was brought here."

"So he couldn't have just been wandering around aimlessly, gotten past security and just dropped dead."

"Not likely. What would the odds be for an otherwise healthy, relatively young man dropping dead where no one would be liable to immediately find the body?" Miranda's question was rhetorical.

They began making their way back to the conference room in silence, each lost in their own thoughts. For Dallas, this situation was suddenly becoming very real. Like Jorge, Dallas had not, in his core, accepted the deadly drama that Joshua had continually painted. He had certainly been no more believing of the myths than the geologist; and even now, with the translations in hand, Dallas couldn't accept that someone would actually kill over the information. And yet, he reminded himself, he had witnessed the deadly earnestness of the mission in the murder of Dr. Todd; why should this case be any different?

As he pondered these indeterminables round and round, he realized that his feet had brought him back to the familiar surroundings of the team's quarters. A short distance further, and they entered the conference room to find most of the team already assembled; puzzled looks on their faces. Dallas and Miranda exchanged glances, but said nothing to the others, not wanting to discuss the reason behind the suddenly called assembly until Joshua and the others appeared.

While they were quiet, the others were not. Speculation ran the gambit, from supposed news about the spy, to the possibility of some startling new discovery. For his part, Dallas sat in a morbid, almost amused silence listening to all the guessing; mourning the loss of his friend, and wondering when, or even if, they would find out the truth.

"Dallas," inquired Jorge, "surely you and Miranda must know what is going on. Come, my friend, can you not give us a hint?"

"I could, George, but won't. I think it's best to wait for Joshua and the others."

"Very well, but Raj had better hurry, or I will sell his chair," Jorge deadpanned, pointing to the chair on his right.

Dallas could not respond. Instead, he dropped his head and began studying the top of the wooden table, praying for Joshua to roll through the door. He glanced sideways at Miranda, and they held eye contact, as if by looking at one another they would not have to face the others.

He noticed a hush fall over the room, and he raised his head to find Joshua wheeling into the room, with Rocky at his side. Pushing himself up to his usual spot, next to Dallas and Miranda, the director glanced briefly around the table. Only Dr. Pollard's and Raj's chairs were empty.

"Ladies and gentlemen," Joshua began slowly, "I apologize for this unscheduled gathering, but I have some sad news. A short while ago, some members of the ship's company found the body of Dr. Rajeev Singala in a restricted area of the ship. We do not as yet know the cause of Dr. Singala's death or why he was there." He paused to let the news sink in. As they surveyed the faces of those in the room, Dallas, Miranda and Joshua saw signs of grief and watched for signs of guilt.

"Is there nothing more you can tell us?" Jorge asked finally.

"Honestly, Jorge, I've told you all we know. We will, of course, keep all of you informed on any new information as we deem appropriate. Now, at the risk of appearing insensitive, there is a related matter we must discuss."

Joshua paused for a moment, both to let his words settle in, and to segue to his next point.

"While we don't know the cause of death, prudence requires taking every precaution. Therefore, I am implementing the mission security protocols effective immediately. All of us will be paired with two other people: one team member and one security member. The security members will rotate among the groups to allow them to stand guard and rest. You will remain together at all times, except as personal needs require, of course, or in larger groups. With the exception of security personnel you will not vary your assigned groups. Other than meals, which we will now all take together, you are not to accept food or drink from anyone outside your group. Workspace will need to be reallocated so that you can continue your research and preparations as we continue en route. Any other questions?"

"Yes, Dr. Fisher." Jorge's formality was intentional. "Am I to understand that we are all, in effect, under house arrest here? I for one have no desire to be a party to scientific investigations where lives are at risk. Would it not be best to end the expedition now, before other lives are lost?"

"Perhaps, Dr. Carbonara, it is a matter of perspective; I take the safety of everyone on this mission very seriously, and I feel the security steps I have outlined are warranted for your own protection. I choose to be proactive until the doctor provides me with a cause of death. As to lives being at risk, you are absolutely right – they are. I did my best to inform all of you, as I did Dallas here when he first joined us, of the possible dangers when you signed up for this project."

"Jorge," Dallas interceded, "let's relax a little. First of all, if Joshua's right, then our cabins are the safest place you could be right now. Honestly, if Raj was murdered, none of us are safe by ourselves. As to the mission, it is what we signed up for, after all. Besides, whether we go forward or backward, if it is murder, then … that means the murderer is still here."

"Now," Joshua continued, "if there are no further concerns, I would suggest we adjourn. This has been a very stressful time, and I know we all have a lot to do. Dallas, will you handle things here while I go to the infirmary?"

Joshua wheeled about abruptly and left with his security detachment in tow. That left Rocky, Miranda, and Dallas to sort out the grim details with the others. While no one else had spoken up, it was clear that some of the other people at the table felt as Jorge did; if less vocally. With Joshua's departure the murmuring began, led by Dr. Graham, the team anthropologist. Even Hakeem and Dr. Hardy, the team's astronomer, were clearly ill at ease with all that had transpired. This whole adventure had suddenly become very real, and very dangerous, and none of those assembled knew what to do next.

In short order, the group agreed on the new three-person units. For the sake of propriety, they were organized along male-female lines with one notable exception; Dallas and Miranda ended up being the odd ones out, and along with Rocky, formed unit five. It turned out, given the arrangement of the new units, that no one really needed to move their labs or work areas. Rearranging the quarters was also simple, at least for the short-term; although it was clear the security team wasn't happy about standing a rotating twenty-four-hour guard in the hall. Dallas promised everyone he'd check into more practical arrangements, should it prove necessary. Eventually, after an hour of sorting out major and minor details, the group prepared to leave. As they rose from their places, Joshua rolled back into the room, his face grim. The assembly looked at each other, the unspoken fear etched on everyone's expression. Instinctively, they all returned to their seats as Joshua took his accustomed place at the table. The silence was palatable and painful.

"Dr. Pollard has given me the preliminary results." Joshua's voice was steady, but the anger shone through. "Dr. Rajeev Singala was murdered."

10

DALLAS AWOKE IN A sweat, as he had every morning in the three days since the murder. He was not immune to the same emotions that affected the others, though he felt his position required him to conceal the true extent of his anguish. Raj had been a humorous bright spot in a room of sometimes-too-straight PhDs; a man who never took himself or his degrees too seriously.

The team, following what they deemed to be Raj's desires, had held a quiet memorial service in the Hindu tradition. Fortunately, Nancy Graham, being an anthropologist, knew something of the required rituals. She chanted the mantra, according to Vedic texts, and handled all the other preparations. Dallas found it interesting that crying was considered inappropriate, even shameful. The Hindu, Nancy told the group, believe that excessive grieving keeps the soul of the deceased from moving on.

The cremation had been the most difficult part of the process to arrange, but in that, they were eventually aided by modern technology available to a massive oil tanker. The spreading of the ashes over the ocean was more easily accomplished. The group simply waited until the ship's crew had turned in before going topside to deposit the remains and garlands of flowers into the gentle swells far below them.

Tonight was the night of Raj's first memorial, held according to Hindu ritual three days after his death. Tradition required that they gather for a banquet of his favorite foods while a photo of the late professor sat in his normal place, with camphor incense burning in front of the picture. Dallas reminded himself that he had a full day's worth of translating to do before that dinner, and he dragged himself wearily toward his quarter's small shower. He woke up Miranda before entering the shower, so that she would be ready to use it after he exited. They had developed a ritual of their own in sharing these quarters, one that allowed for the most privacy, while insuring the security protocols were followed in the most efficient manner.

He stood in the shower, the too-gentle stream of water washing the cobwebs from his brain, while his mind went back to the day of Raj's murder and the days that followed. Rocky and his team confessed to being completely stumped in their investigation. Dr. Pollard had discovered a particularly effective and not terribly subtle poison in Raj's system; one that required no more than a drop to be fatal. A search of everyone's living quarters found no evidence of either the poison or its precursors; neither had they uncovered any other clues about who might be the spy. There were only negatives: no fingerprints, no witnesses, and no one unaccounted for.

Assuming Rocky's meager results thus far were correct, that suggested to Dallas only two possibilities; either it was someone on the ship's crew or there was a stowaway hiding somewhere on board. Yet Rocky had assured him that the crew was vetted, and all possible hiding places had been investigated. Yet, seventy-two hours later, the same unknowns plagued everyone. Why kill Raj? Who, if anyone, would be next? Finally, the main unasked question surely on everyone's mind, if there was a next one, would it be them?

The team ceased to be a team. Now it was five units, each unit trusting itself and suspicious of the others. Morale was, Dallas thought, lower than the cliché snake's belly in a wagon rut. It would have to get better just to be merely bad. Perhaps he could bring some measure of curiosity back to the group. After the memorial dinner, he planned to offer the assembly the latest installment from the emerald tablet. He knew the group would be intrigued by the story he had to tell; if, he couldn't help thinking, he lived to tell it.

Miranda's pounding on the bathroom door snapped Dallas out of his showery daydream. It was time for the daily morning ritual of musical rooms. Donning his robe, he exited to dress in the bedroom as a robed Miranda entered the bath with her own clothes in tow. It reminded Dallas of his college days and life at the dorm; he hated the dorm. Dallas's two decades as a bachelor had made him accustomed to the welcome privacy commensurate with that status.

He also detested the waiting. It is a truism, he reminded himself, that men can be showered, shaved, and dressed in less than five minutes; it is also a truism that women cannot. Finally, Miranda came out dressed, chipper, and ready to go. Dallas abhorred chipper, at least until he'd had his first cup of coffee. Miranda began each day like a hot rod in a drag race. Dallas was more of an SUV; lots of torque, but slower off the starting line. Her lips seemed to be moving faster than the speed of sound as she rattled off her thoughts and plans for the coming hours. Dallas "uh'ed" at the appropriate moments to indicate his awareness of her dialogue, but he truly hadn't the faintest clue as to what she was talking about; he needed that first cup of coffee, badly.

Upon exiting the bedroom, Dallas glanced sideways at Rocky to his right, as Miranda rambled on to his left. Rocky looked the same as he always looked; like a piece of chiseled granite with legs. He was polite but quiet; strong without being unduly forceful. He seemed to have neither the inclination nor need for idle chatter. Neither did he appear to take any notice of the ongoing dialogue to his far left. Dallas had the feeling that, even if Rocky were listening, he'd never acknowledge or repeat whatever was said.

Thirty minutes and three cups later, Dallas could feel the synapses of his brain beginning to fire. He even began to construct complex sentences, albeit softly.

"Joshua," Dallas whispered, "I'm planning on reading the next installment tonight after the memorial, unless, of course, you'd rather I wait for the next scheduled team meeting."

"I think that'd be an excellent idea, but you don't have to ask me, these translations are your show." Joshua's sentiment was genuine, though Dallas didn't believe him for a moment. He knew exactly whose show it was, and frankly, he was okay with that. He was happy with his place in this grand adventure, especially since his role did not specifically include having to shoulder the burdens of leadership that came with the death of a colleague.

"Okay, well then, I'll be ready for tonight. Anything new on … you know, Raj?"

"No," Joshua frowned, "I must admit, I'm stumped, and so is security. We were even desperate enough to apply Sir Arthur Conan Doyle's first rule, but that yielded nothing."

"Doyle's first rule?" Dallas was puzzled.

"You know, Sherlock Holmes. 'When you have eliminated the impossible, whatever remains, however improbable, must be the truth.'" Joshua said with a sigh. "I must be desperate when I start resorting to using the reasoning of hundred-year-old detective stories."

"Perhaps Rocky just hasn't eliminated all the 'impossible' options," Dallas offered thoughtfully. "Did he completely eliminate the ship's crew, or the possibility of a stowaway?"

"Yes to both. We've gone over the crew list with the captain three times; besides, only the captain and first officer had access to that part of the ship. And we've conducted at least three ship-wide searches that I know of."

"Okay. How about a commando raid? You know, someone sneaks on, kills Raj, then leaves," Dallas offered helpfully.

"We discussed that, briefly, but it suggests a chain of events that we find extremely unlikely. For example, some type of vehicle, a boat or helicopter, would have had make contact with the ship; but the captain reports no such contact. Then there's the matter of needing inside help to locate the Seahab area; not to mention the choice of Raj. Why not others? Why not all of us for that matter? Finally, the person or people responsible would have had to leave the ship afterwards; how was that accomplished? No, that path leaves too many unanswered questions."

"Are you sure you can trust the captain?" replied Dallas slowly. "After all, other than not murdering all of us, his involvement could explain every objection you just raised."

"I know this is beginning to sound like a broken record," said Joshua, "and I know the credibility of this statement might be somewhat strained, but I trust him completely."

"Father, don't be so hard on yourself. You can't plan for every contingency."

"Perhaps not, but one would expect that I should have anticipated something as serious as murder." Joshua's tone was not one of self-pity, but exhaustion. It was only then that Dallas saw the immense burden that this man had been carrying, silently and alone.

"But you did anticipate it," Dallas offered, "you even warned me about it. I'm sure you were equally frank with the others. You said yourself that the Order was as rich and powerful as the Guardians, and that they would stop at nothing. Clearly, from my first experience until now, we have seen this is the case. Remember, you said we can't let them set our schedule. We have no option but to continue our mission as diligently as we can."

"You're right, of course, we must continue; now more than ever. Miranda, if something should happen to me, you will succeed me. You and Dallas must see this mission through, together."

"I understand, father," Miranda replied firmly, her resolve undiminished, "but nothing is going to happen to you." She glanced at Dallas and wondered why now the idea of Dallas sharing the mission with her didn't seem quite so objectionable.

"Let's not get morbid," Dallas interjected. "We've got a lot that has to go wrong before we start talking like that."

"Right you are, Dallas," the director replied. "We mustn't let ourselves get sidetracked. So, my dear doctor, what ancient tales will you have for us tonight?" Raising his voice and turning his chair to face the others eating breakfast, Joshua continued, "Everyone, gather 'round. Dallas is going to give a sneak preview of the further adventures of the emerald tablets."

"Well," Dallas began awkwardly, "I hadn't planned to get into this now, but as long as you're all here, I can tell you this much. There apparently are concealed weapons and technologies somewhere. I can't say yet whether the chambers contain offensive or defensive weapons, but there are definitely things hidden, and ... there's definitely more than one chamber."

"Really? How many? Where?" It was Rocky; and his sudden interest caught Dallas by surprise.

"As to where, that's a riddle with clues thirteen thousand years old. As to how many, I can't say yet with any certainty; though it would appear there are several and they are of different sizes and serve different purposes. That should be enough to whet your appetite." Turning melodramatically to Rocky and Miranda, he continued, "Shall we go?"

"Uh, no," Miranda said with more than a touch of sarcasm, "I'd still like to have breakfast, if that's okay with you."

"Sure, but you've ruined my exit."

Tense as the team was, the room broke into spasms of laughter. Perhaps it was funny, or perhaps those assembled just needed it to be funny; either way, it proved a catharsis, and for a moment, the group seemed like its old self again. The moment quickly passed, however, and the sense of darkness descended once again onto the room. Even Miranda was silent, although in her case, the mushroom omelet in front of her proved at least partly responsible. Dallas sat across from her, his elbows resting on the table, worshipping the cup of coffee cradled between his two hands. He stared in silence as the omelet vanished before his eyes, the different hemispheres of his brain focused on separate tasks. He needed to go over his notes once more, and that gave him pause; but somewhere in his mind lay a certain envy for that omelet and the relish with which it was being devoured. He found himself wishing he were a mushroom within that fluffy dish. The scientist within him suddenly shook his head, as if trying to dislodge that alien thought from his brain.

There was such an internal debate going on that Dallas almost failed to take notice of Rocky reacting to his radio. The security officer reached up with his right hand and pressed his earpiece closer to the side of his head, glancing over to Dallas as he did so. It was only then that Dallas became aware of Rocky's gaze; and he was looking at Dallas in a way that made the archaeologist decidedly uncomfortable.

The head of security leaned over and began whispering into Joshua's ear. Dallas strained to hear what was being said, while trying to conceal his interest. The look on Joshua's face as he suddenly shifted his eyes toward Dallas only confirmed that Dallas was indeed the object of discussion. All the discreet dialogue made him very uncomfortable, as if he'd been caught with his hand in the cookie jar.

"Dallas," Joshua spoke up finally, "Rocky and I need to talk; in private. Give us five minutes, and then come to my office."

"Sure, whatever you say." Turning to Miranda, Dallas started to tell her finish up, only to be cut off by Rocky.

"Miranda," he interrupted, "would you wait here please? We won't be long."

Puzzled, Dallas waited the appropriate five minutes, then rose and followed the other two men's path. Dallas could only assume there was something wrong with the mission. His first thought was another death, but the entire team was present for breakfast. He didn't have time for a second thought before he entered the office. Joshua wheeled himself around as Dallas walked in and started to speak. The door slammed behind him. Joshua began without even raising his eyes to face the scientist, his voice full of frustrated remorse.

"How much did they pay you to betray us? Or are you just a loyal member of the Order?"

"Excuse me?"

"Don't play dumb." Rocky's tone was accusatory, his body language aggressive. "We know about you; we've figured it out."

"What in God's name are you talking about? What is it you think you know?"

"Dallas," Joshua added, "it's no use denying the truth any longer. I … I just don't know what to say. I can't believe you are the one."

"What are you talking about?"

"Do you deny knowing a man named David Moncrief, Dr. David Moncrief?" Rocky's tone was accusatory.

"Monty? Of course I know him, I was his graduate assistant. He was the one who steered me toward dead languages. The man was a genius."

"He was also," Rocky added, "a high ranking member of the Order. We didn't dig deeply enough to catch your relationship on our first security check; that was my fault. I'm making up for that right here, right now."

"Monty … the Order. You must be joking."

"From our vantage point," interrupted Rocky, "the story as we see it now looks something like this: you were recruited into the Order by Dr. Moncrief and trained in what would become your specialty. Afterward, you became a sleeper agent, waiting to be called upon. That call came with the murder of Dr. Todd and the retrieval of his briefcase. The Order killed Dr. Todd and gave you his briefcase to worm your way into our good graces, hoping to learn what new research we might have. When Dr. Fisher offered to let you join us, you jumped at it, thinking you could feed back to the Order whatever information you could get your hands on. When we put you in charge of this mission, you probably felt like you'd hit the jackpot. Then came trouble; Raj somehow found out about you, and you killed him."

"And I take it you're the one who came up with this little tale?" Dallas's tone dripped of bitter sarcasm.

"I didn't put it together," replied Rocky, "until one of my staff back in the States did a more detailed review of your past. When we couldn't find who was responsible for Raj's murder, I had my staff begin researching everyone's past with a fine-tooth comb, cross referencing the locations all known members of the Order with team members. That's when we discovered your relationship with Moncrief. You were the only one of the group to come into daily contact with even one of the enemy. My staff just alerted me to the results of their investigation. These facts also explain a few other things —"

"Such as?" challenged Dallas.

"Such as you not allowing anyone to work with you on the translations. Such as why the police didn't show up at the museum asking for you, even though the professor's death was front-page news, and the museum was the last place you would have been seen. Such as your behavior in appearing at the museum with an empty briefcase, taking the precaution of depositing in a safety deposit box an artifact that you claim you could not even identify or understand. Such as even knowing to come to the museum in the first place, a location that you claim you figured out from one meager diary entry consisting of just six letters. And, lest we forget, you admit being the last person to see Dr. Singala alive."

"This is absurd." Dallas spun to face his would-be mentor. "Joshua, you've said you trust me, trust me now when I say Rocky's 'theory' is insane."

"Call it what you will, Dr. Roark," said Rocky with a tone that hinted at a mixture of anger and regret, "but you'll be placed in the brig until we can turn you over to the appropriate authorities for the murders of Dr. Rajeev Singala and Dr. Montgomery Todd."

"But I didn't do anything," said Dallas, pounding his fist on the desk.

"The evidence, however circumstantial, suggests you did," Rocky shot back.

"What you're talking about is guilt by association. I didn't know anything about Monty's background until just now. I went to the bank first, precisely because I had witnessed the danger firsthand. I didn't need to understand the tablet to know someone had killed for it. Regarding the translations, I simply prefer to work alone. As for the rest, it was just as I explained it, however hard that may be for you to believe. Joshua, say something."

"Dallas … I just don't know what to say," the man said finally, "I know I want to believe you, but Rocky is in charge of security, and I must let him do his job. And I must admit I find it odd that you had contact with Moncrief, albeit many years ago now. That fact alone merits further investigation. Also, I must confess I also find it strange that the police never showed up to question anyone at the museum, even though, as Rocky says, outside that location was the place you were last publicly seen. We simply cannot afford to take any chances."

"But what about the mission?"

"What about it? Right now we don't even know if there is a mission. We have no way of knowing if anything you've told us is true. For all we know, this has been an outrageous case of disinformation and a tremendous waste of resources. Dallas, we are literally and figuratively going in circles. I must insist that for now you do as Rocky says."

"It would appear I have no choice." Dallas's tone was nonetheless defiant. "I can only say you are making a bigger mistake than you realize."

"Perhaps," Joshua whispered, "perhaps. But as I said, you must accompany the guards to the security area."

"And what about the rest of the team? What will you tell them? What will you tell Miranda?"

"For the moment, I will tell them nothing. As for tonight's session," Joshua replied, "I'll tell them you have decided to do some more work before revealing any more of the tablets' contents. Your absence won't likely be missed, as you mostly work alone anyway. Miranda will have to be told; I'll tell her."

"No," Dallas said, "Bring her in now, I'd like to tell her myself."

"I'd have to recommend against that, Dr. Fisher," Rocky said firmly.

"I'm sorry, Rocky," he replied, "call it a father's prerogative, but I'm going to let Dallas handle it."

In the end, it didn't matter who delivered the news; her response was muted, almost disinterested, leaving Dallas to wonder why he thought she'd care. Miranda's focus seemed to be that she'd once again be sleeping in a private room; her only words regarding Dallas being something to the effect that she wasn't really surprised.

Wounded, Dallas's demeanor became more passive. Why did he care, he thought, if these people wanted to play these games? He knew he was innocent, which meant that somewhere on the ship, a murderer was still roaming free.

11

THE FOOD WASN'T BAD in the brig, thought Dallas on the first day, but it definitely lacked even the marginal ambiance of the dining room. After a day and a night, he could honestly say he wasn't impressed with his situation. He had only one lone visitor, a security team member who would serve the food, remove the dishes, and say absolutely nothing.

Rocky had not seen fit to explain what the plan would be now, or who would continue the translations; not that anyone else on the team could even begin to accomplish that task, and of that much, Dallas was sure. He had to remind himself that by now the rest of them probably didn't believe what he'd said anyway. He found himself drifting between fits of anger and boredom, trying to figure out what to do next, and wondering how he'd ever let himself get involved with such crazy people. They'd left him with no books to read or music to listen to in his exile. His only company was the creaking of the ship, which he now discovered, was much noisier than he'd been aware.

His quarters weren't a jail, not in the traditional sense; not a prison cell, but a secured cabin with no closet or chair. Its only accouterments were a toilet, a sink, and a sparse, almost antique, military-style, metal bed, adorned with a mattress that might just as easily have been called a mere pad. His every movement upon the lone piece of furniture registered an annoying, creaking screech. It had the sole attribute of being elevated, and therefore more comfortable than the floor. The walls were a color he had christened seasick green; the floor and ceiling were in the same shades, only slightly darker. The white porcelain of the sink and toilet stood out in stark contrast to their surroundings, and had became the undesired focus of Dallas's attention. The solitary illumination of the room was a bare lightbulb mounted in a circular prison-bar shaped metal housing which cast annoying prison bar shadows on the walls. Dallas amused himself with the thought that the bulb was as much of a prisoner as he.

That first day, he had been too angry to focus on the isolation, but by the afternoon of the second day, he began to long for the sound of a human voice, even Rocky's. He wondered aloud how real criminals withstood prolonged periods of such enforced solitude. The boredom began to creep across the surface of his skin, like a battalion of army ants that, combined with the creaking silence, brought an ever-growing sense of agitation and restlessness.

Finally, several hours after his meager dinner had been silently served on the evening of the second day, Dallas heard footsteps coming down the long hallway that contained his cell. These steps were different, lighter and less sure, than those of the guard who brought his food. He could hear the feet walking from door to door, stopping briefly and then moving on. He strained to hear something else, the ever-so-slight sound of a hand rattling one door after another. It was accompanied by something else, the muffled sound of a voice calling out softly.

Suddenly the footfalls stopped in front of his door. It was then he realized to whom the feet, the hand, and the voice belonged. He was so surprised he hesitated in calling out. The footsteps had begun to move on before he regained the presence of mind and let out a shout. Within moments, the heavy door unbolted and swung wide to reveal a determined and steely-eyed Miranda.

"God, you look awful. It's only been two days."

"What can I do for you?" His tone reflected the residual anger of his incarceration.

"Come on," she retorted, "don't you know a jailbreak when you see one?"

"A jailbreak? You must be kidding. We're on a boat; where would I go?"

"We ... Where would we go?" Miranda corrected. "And I have that all arranged."

"But why are you doing this? Seems like a far cry from the way you acted when I got tossed in here." Dallas maintained a reservoir of suspicion.

"I couldn't afford to react then. Let's just say that whatever I think of you, I don't think you're capable either of such duplicity, or of murder. Unfortunately, policemen are like hunting dogs, they can only point their noses in one direction at a time. Clearly, you are being framed by someone, and if we don't find out who, then no one else will; hell, they're not even looking."

"And that's it; you're risking everything just because you think I'm innocent."

"That's about it."

"I'm not buying it."

"Can we do this dance later? We've got to get out of here, or we'll be roomies again, and not in a good way."

"But where are we going?"

"You'll see."

"Does your father know?"

"That I'm here? No way. Don't worry about him, I can handle him later. Besides, with you gone, it's not likely that anyone else will get murdered. After all, the real murderer can't do anything more, or everyone will know you're innocent. Now, please, let's go. If we can get off the ship without being seen, they won't discover you're gone until tomorrow, when they bring breakfast."

Dallas hesitated a moment longer, and not seeing any good reason to remain, followed Miranda out the door. They moved silently through several corridors, taking a different route than the one that Rocky had brought Dallas down initially. They worked their way toward the ship's stern, going upward as they went. It would have been easier to use the elevators, but Dallas knew they couldn't take the risk. Finally, after what seemed like an eternity, they walked through one last hatch, exiting the ship's interior to find themselves alone on a deck the length of three football fields. Dallas felt puny looking out over the immense open expanse, framed by the limitless vista of the ocean.

"What about the captain and the crew?"

"Most are below decks. The first officer is manning the watch, and I've told him to expect a helicopter; I just neglected to mention the passengers. We have to hurry; look, see it there on the horizon? That's our ticket outta here. We're only two hundred miles or so off the African coast. We'll land in Swakopmund —"

"Land where?" interrupted Dallas.

"Swakopmund, in Namibia, and from there, we'll take a private plane on to Dubai."

"Dubai? Why Dubai?"

"Simple, it's the closest major city to the dive site. Once we get there, we can charter a dive boat and explore the site."

"What's the point? Surely by now no one believes there's anything there."

"That's why we have to go, to prove you were right, and that you were telling the truth. If we can show them that, then they'll have to see that you wouldn't have had any reason to kill Raj."

"Realistically, the validity of the site doesn't necessarily prove my innocence. On top of that, even with the proper equipment, the odds of success are a millions-to-one; and that's being optimistic. Without the Seahab the chances are virtually nil."

"And I suppose you have a better idea?"

Dallas thought a moment before answering. "What about my passport?"

"Got it."

"Money?"

"Got it."

"My research?"

"Got it."

"Common sense?"

"Still workin' on it. Come on, we need to be in position, or the 'copter won't touch down. We'll have just a few seconds to throw our gear and ourselves onboard. Let's move."

"Gear? What gear?"

Miranda didn't bother to answer. The chop-chop-chop of the white, Sikorsky S-92 Helibus became too loud to talk over as it touched down lightly about ten yards away. She began dashing back and forth between the aircraft and a small pile of duffle bags that Dallas hadn't noticed before. At the bottom of the pile was Dallas's backpack, packed full with his personal papers. Dallas had no choice but to follow her, grab the remaining bags, run the remaining distance, and toss them inside the forward door of the Sikorsky. Dallas leapt aboard to discover a nicely appointed commuter craft. He realized Miranda only escaped in style. As he pulled himself off the floor, the helicopter was already making the tanker a distant memory. Dallas looked at Miranda for confirmation.

"This little beauty has a cruising speed of about 150 knots; we'll be in Namibia in a little over an hour."

"What is all that stuff?" Dallas hitchhiked his thumb toward the pile of gear they'd heaved onboard.

"Just a few things I borrowed from Seahab that I thought we might need: deep diving scuba gear, computers, GPS, metal detectors, portable magnetic anomaly detectors, weapons, things like that."

"Weapons? I don't *do* weapons."

"We'll cross that bridge when we get to it."

"How did you arrange all this?"

"You forget I am – I was, number two in the organization; and the Guardians are a worldwide organization. We have operatives everywhere, going about their everyday lives, waiting for 'the call.' All I had to do was make that call."

"But what's to stop your father or Rocky for that matter from countermanding your orders?"

"Nothing, I guess, but I'm not a poor, dependent little daughter. I have allies and a financial base of my own. Besides, if we're lucky, we'll be long gone before they discover the escape, and they won't know where we are. If we had to hold out for the long-term I might lose, but hopefully, we won't need more than a few weeks. I'm counting on finding something by the time the tanker arrives at the site."

"The ship's still headed to the site?"

"Technically, no. Last night, my father finally told the other members of the team that you're under arrest. The group was pretty much split between continuing on and turning back. Sam, Rocky, and I wanted to carry on; Jorge and Dr. Pollard didn't care; and Jon and Dr. Graham wanted to go home. Finally, the captain said that as long as we had the suspect under arrest, he felt compelled to turn the ship around and go back to the States. Later, after almost everyone had turned in, I just decided I had to take matters into my own hands. Once he discovers where we've gone, I'm hoping he'll see no alternative but to follow."

Grabbing his backpack, Dallas started sifting through its contents. He found all his notes on the translations, but not his notebook; it just wasn't there.

"You didn't pick up my journal?"

"Should I have?"

"But I've been keeping a record of everything"

"You want to go back for it?" The question was clearly rhetorical. He didn't bother to reply.

The couple fell into a deep silence for much of the remainder of the flight. Dallas watched the ocean slide by underneath the aircraft as they flew eastward toward the African coast. The gathering night framed the lights of Swakopmund reflecting off the dark ocean waters. In this darkness, Dallas could see beyond the hamlet to the whole of the Skeleton Coast and inland into the Namib Desert. It was a sparse landscape, foreboding, yet expansive.

Swakopmund was, to Dallas, an architectural oddity. Its Bavarian spires and elaborate Germanic architecture, an enduring symbol of its European roots, could still be seen through the perpetual evening mist, a side-effect of being situated on the shores of the icy South Atlantic Ocean waters.

Miranda described the town as an eclectic mixture of Bohemian and Bavarian, and home to an intriguing mix of artists, hippies, straitlaced descendants of German settlers, and stately Bantu women in Victorian dress. In addition, the city counted among its population of thirty thousand; an odd mix of hard-bitten miners, game rangers, safari operators, fishermen, and various soldiers of fortune. He tried to imagine what possible reason the Guardians would have for posting any operative to such an out-of-the-way location only to remind himself that at this moment this was exactly the location he now found himself.

Dallas reviewed the literature aboard the helicopter and laughed out loud when he read the origin and pronunciation of the city's name. Apparently, the natives had originally named the area after the waters of Swakop River that, during times of seasonal flooding, carried masses of mud, sand, pieces of vegetation, and animal corpses. They called the place Tsoakhaub, which translated into excrement opening; he found an undeniable humor in his preparing to enter the Earth's asshole; given the circumstances it felt entirely appropriate.

The sight of the helipad lights coming quickly toward him brought Dallas out of his daydreams. He saw a circle of lights bordering the traditional "H" that was neatly inscribed on a smooth, concrete slab. Beyond, in all directions, was a beautiful, smooth stretch of closely cropped Bermuda grass. Far in the distance hung the lights of the airport's control tower. It stood like an enormous lollipop, glowing ghostly red against the night sky. As the craft's door opened, he turned to face Miranda.

"Okay, now what?"

"We get our stuff loaded into the van and then head over to the hotel. We'll spend the night here and then meet up with the plane tomorrow."

"Spend the night? Do you think that's wise?"

"It's not my first choice, but we don't have many options. The plane I've arranged won't be here until late tonight, and regulations require the pilots have at least eight hours off before continuing on to Dubai. At least everyone back on the ship thinks I'm in bed with the flu; they wouldn't dare disturb me. With any luck, they won't see you're gone until tomorrow morning. You must admit, it's better than spending another night in that room I found you in."

Dallas couldn't argue that point; he was a scientist, not a warrior. He had come to accept he'd have to put his faith in this modern-day Amazon archaeologist; not such a bad thing, all in all, he told himself. They straggled into the front of an ancient, white van that age and the weather had turned a unique shade of beige. The interior was an equally interesting sight, with a wonderfully eclectic mixture of blue faux-leather upholstery and silver gray duct tape.

The vehicle's driver offered an air of seeming indifference to their arrival, final destination, or even their reason for being there. He was a large, wiry black man with silver hair as closely cropped as the grass upon which he stood. He rolled a freshly lit cigarette between his tired fingers, the blue smoke drifting upward to the infinity of the night sky. He revealed neither an interest in discussing himself or their presence. His lone acknowledgment of their very existence came from the guttural grunt he gave the crew when they indicated the van was fully loaded. Despite this air of nonchalance, Dallas had the unmistakable, uncomfortable, and very familiar sensation of being watched.

Miranda told the driver their destination, appropriately named the Swakopmund Hotel, which he accepted without comment or surprise. Dallas knew from the material onboard the helicopter that this was the premier hotel in town, a fact he did not find the least bit surprising.

The dark silence of the van was oppressive, but suspecting the reliability of their chauffeur, the fugitive scientist resisted the urge to break it. For her part, Miranda also said nothing, although he wasn't sure whether to attribute her behavior to intense concentration or a total lack of interest in the polite art of meaningless conversation. The two had hardly spoken since the surprise rescue, and this left Dallas more puzzled than ever as to her motives.

He contented himself with watching the city flow past bathed in the yellow glow of the city's ample streetlights. Breite Street was a broad avenue; build for an amount of traffic that Dallas was sure would not materialize in a hundred years. Miranda had been right about the architecture; the almost gothic, Bavarian structures, combined with the wide streets reminded Dallas of his nights on the avenues of Budapest.

After executing a series of abrupt left and right turns, the van arrived on Bahnhoff Street, coming to a stop in front of the hotel, an historic landmark which had begun its life as a train station. Miranda jumped out to greet a tall, solidly built man with riveting blue eyes and almost white-blond hair; no doubt, thought Dallas, a genetic leftover from Germany's colonial period. She gave the man a firm hug, which he had to bend over to return. The embrace took Dallas by surprise, and he found himself feeling suddenly possessive. He shook his head as if to drive this unexpected sensation from his mind, and exited the car himself.

"So, this is the mysterious Dr. Roark," the tall German said, smiling and extending his massive hand, "welcome to our little village. My name is Hans."

"Yes, it would be, wouldn't it?" Dallas replied sarcastically, staring at the huge paw momentarily before extending his own hand, which seemed puny by comparison, "pleased to meet you, I guess. Miranda, am I pleased to meet him?"

"Yes, you are, and so am I."

"Come, Professor, we have the Presidential Suite already prepared for you and Miranda. I took the liberty of having some fresh clothes delivered to the suite for you to change into; she provided me with your measurements." As Hans spoke, he eyed Dallas's attire curiously. At that moment, the scientist became acutely aware of his own shabby appearance.

"Uh, thanks." Dallas responded, sheepishly and rubbing his chin. "I must look a bit crumpled ... lost my razor."

But no one was listening any longer. The small entourage, consisting of the bellboy, the concierge, Miranda, and Hans, had already moved toward the doorway. Dallas hurried behind, suddenly feeling very exposed in the rapidly cooling night air. Entering the lobby, he glanced back over his shoulder to see the shabby van, now parked in the shadows in front of the hotel.

Upon arriving at the suite, Dallas excused himself for a much-needed shave and shower. Afterward, returning to the bedroom, Dallas opened the closet door and discovered a complete wardrobe hanging neatly within. Everything was perfectly sized and organized in true Teutonic fashion. To the far right hung a formal white dinner jacket, tuxedo pants, shirt, and bowtie. In short order, he donned the entire Bond-esque outfit; and in a moment of private fantasy, wondered where he left his Walther PPK.

The name is Roark – Dallas Roark, he thought, as he adjusted the bowtie in the mirror. It just didn't have the same ring to it, but then they hadn't made twenty movies about Dallas Roark, either.

"Good evening, Mr. Bond."

Dallas spun around sheepishly to find Miranda standing in the doorway, a grin spread from ear to ear.

"Sorry," she laughed, "I just couldn't pass that one up. Isn't that the typical male fantasy when one dons a white dinner jacket?"

"Yeah, pretty much. But it gets better when the Bond girls show up —"

"TMI; too much information," interrupted Miranda. "Let's get going, we're supposed to meet our contact in the Mermaid Casino."

"Casino?" Dallas ran his thumbs up and down the inside of his lapels. "Do they have a Baccarat table?"

"Yes, as a matter of fact, they just added one; it's for the high rollers —"

"High rollers?"

Yep, and you'll find you have a line of credit already established." As if on cue Hans moved a discrete distance away to allow the couple a chance to talk privately.

"Why, Miranda, you've thought of everything." Dallas turned suddenly serious. "What about the rest of the team, will they be okay?"

"I think so. They must be confused, that much is certain, but I have no more knowledge of their condition than you. There was some … discussion; but, no, in the end I think no one really believed you're guilty."

"Thank God for that. Will we be seeing them again?"

"I hope so, after we get to the Persian Gulf and dive on your site. With a maximum cruising speed of 15 knots, they're still 18 days away, but perhaps by the time they arrive, they'll find evidence aboard ship clearing you; that would come in handy for both of us."

Dallas took a step closer to his accomplice, took her shoulders firmly in his hands, and latched his eyes onto hers. "Miranda, I haven't had time to think about your sacrifices in all this; everything you've risked, on my account. I don't know how to thank you."

For the first time since they'd meet that spring day in front of the museum, Miranda blushed. She diverted her eyes before turning away. From across the room Hans took note of her reaction but said nothing, though his heart fell in the face of the obvious.

"Just find the evidence you need to clear your name," she said finally, "and justify my faith in you."

"Deal," he replied, adding, "and speaking of deal, I'm feelin' lucky."

Two hours and hundreds of thousands of dollars later, Dallas knew he'd been right. He couldn't help but let a mysterious smile crack his poker face. He thought back over the past months, of his life before and after that strange, tragic night of Dr. Todd's death. That night, Dallas could now see, his old life had died as well; and he'd been reborn into a new and exciting, and dangerous world. Before, he'd been an observer, a bystander; but no longer. Now he was at the center of the struggle, even if it was a struggle that almost no one knew about. Now his life mattered. Now he was making a difference; if only to himself.

Suddenly, he felt young again; young and vital. He was no longer one of six billion nameless souls going about their lives in hopeless, meaningless, pointless frustration. He was no longer one of those who would be born, live and die in total anonymity with nothing more than a weathered, forgotten tombstone to mark his time on this world. He felt his heart pounding from the adrenaline; his mind was giddy from the possibilities. It was, he thought, truly a lithium moment.

In the next moment, another thought entered his mind. The people of Earth deserved to know their history and heritage; and to know the possibilities of what the future might bring if the gifts of the chambers of the Anunnaki were revealed. All he could do for the moment was ponder these possibilities; that and play another hand.

12

AT LEAST ANOTHER HOUR passed after his revelation before Dallas began to wonder what had become of Miranda. She'd placed him at the table, with a rather sizable line of credit, and left him as one would leave a child at a daycare center; she knew he was in good hands and would be kept busy while she went on about her work. By now, he had amassed several huge piles of chips and several attractive prospective Bond girls. He was definitely feeling good.

He was in the midst of betting another tall stack of chips when Miranda reappeared. She glided across the room with the stealth of a tigress hunting prey, a purposeful expression etched on her face. Dallas had the sinking sensation that playtime was over.

"You need to say good-bye and cash 'em in, '007,' it's time to roll."

"Miranda, I'm on a hot streak." The Bond girls had already taken the hint and silently disappeared.

"You WERE on a hot streak. Now, you'll be able to say you left while you were ahead."

"Killjoy."

"The operative syllable there is 'kill' which is what might just happen to us if we don't get moving."

"I know Rocky will be angry, but he wouldn't dare kill you; me maybe, but not you."

"I'm not worried about Rocky. There are others who will try to stop us, at any cost."

"You mean the Order?" Dallas whispered. "How can they know about any of this?"

"We can't assume they don't. We have to act as if they knew about the ship, and they were close enough to kill Raj. We must assume the worst, and plan accordingly."

"You're starting to sound like your father."

"And?" Miranda raised an eyebrow.

"And that's a good thing," Dallas recovered quickly. "A very good thing."

"Miranda!" Hans appeared suddenly out of nowhere, "Dr. Roark, we really should be going. I have guards posted on the roof, and I will personally man the team outside the suite. The pilot and plane are in place and set for a six a.m. departure."

"Whoa, big fella," interjected Dallas, "I don't know about Miranda here, but I'm looking forward to sleeping in late, having a leisurely breakfast, maybe hitting the tables one last time … "

"Dallas," interrupted Miranda, "You're enjoying this entirely too much. Hans is right; best case, by the time we get airborne, they'll be discovering you've vanished. Remember, if they figure it out before 3:30 a.m. we could have a problem, that's four and a half hours from now. Rocky could get here before we take off; of course, that assumes he'd know where to go. Besides that, it's an eight-hour flight and a three-hour time change, which means we won't arrive until five p.m. local time, and they'll definitely be on our collective tails by then."

"Miranda, will they be able to follow us?"

"Well, we don't have time to keep everything neat and clean. There are only so many cities within range of a helicopter; the ship's crew will report we left on one. Then there's the flight plan, for one thing, and you've been pretty visible here, but what we're really counting on is getting out of here before they arrive. If we can do that, it may take them a day to follow us, and by then we'll be on the dive boat."

"But won't Rocky call ahead?"

"He might want to, but I don't believe my father will let him make my actions public; at least I hope not. Look, it's a little after eleven o'clock now. We can still get in a good five hours sleep and have room service send up breakfast around 4:30; or you can eat on the plane, your choice."

"Both sound good to me."

Hours later, room service arrived promptly on schedule, and Dallas arose to find Hans still guarding the door like a loyal German Shepherd. Somehow, breakfast before sunrise didn't taste as good to Dallas as it had sounded the night before. He searched for that ever-elusive first cup of coffee while Miranda raced around the suite like a greyhound; it almost made Dallas miss his solitary confinement.

"Miranda," he whispered, "there really is something we should talk about."

"Yes, Dallas?"

"I need to tell you the rest of what I've translated so far. Rocky's arresting me kept me from revealing it, but it is essential to our efforts."

"Such as?"

"Well," Dallas began slowly, cradling his coffee, "it's a long story, but the bottom line is this, according to the tablets the emperor concealed something of immense importance; something even more significant than a planet busting super weapon."

"What is it?"

"I'm not exactly sure. He names it but doesn't describe it; in fact he's downright cryptic. He calls it the 'Heart of the People', although I have no idea that means. There is no correlation in Sumerian. He also speaks of the knowledge of their ancestors being upon their minds, beneath their feet, at their left hand and their right hand. Then he says something to the effect that there is one place behind each place which waits; I take that to mean that, for each primary chamber, there is a secondary facility. He ends by saying that among all these points there is this so-called Heart Chamber: 'that place which beats strong, even in this time of darkness.' If there is a central chamber from which these other chambers points radiate, that means we are looking for nine vaults holding the sum of Anunnaki knowledge dating back perhaps a hundred thousand years."

"Dallas, that's incredible! But where are these chambers?"

"I think we can take his symbolism literally. When he speaks of the ancestor's knowledge being at the left and right hands, the feet and so on, I think he's referring to the cardinal points."

"Cardinal points? You mean like a compass?"

"Yes: north, south, east, and west. And when he says there is another set behind the first, I believe the secondary facilities are located relative to the primary: northeast, southeast, southwest, and northwest."

"Fine, that's eight; but where's the ninth?"

"That's the key. He implies that the ninth is the place where the heart of the Anunnaki beats strong; whatever that means. Possibly it's the central point, the nexus."

"Do you think that could be what's at in the bottom of the Persian Gulf; the ninth chamber? And why here instead of some other body of water?"

"That would be the brass ring. Right now, I'm just hoping we at least find a settlement in the area. Remember the language used on the tablets is an extremely ancient ancestor of Sumerian. That much suggests a long history of human occupation in this area. Even the name Semitic name Babylon comes from the Sumerian Ka-dingir-ra, which means the 'gateway of the gods', although by then Enlil would have probably passed into myth. Before my arrest I did run across one other interesting bit of information that may connect this region to the Anunnaki who escaped from Nibiru."

"What?"

"It's something I read in Genesis, chapters seven and eight. Everyone knows the story of Noah, how it rained for forty days and forty nights, but what most people don't know is that the Ark was actually adrift for one hundred and fifty days. I checked Stefan Ostrowski, the team astronomer, and he told me that the travel time from Mars to Earth would be –"

"One hundred and fifty days?"

"Bingo." Dallas yawned and stretched reflexively as the coffee began to fulfill its function.

"Okay, so we know the legends and myths contain a grain of truth; but we already knew that. If it is a chamber, could it have survived intact all these thousands of years?"

A knock on the door punctuated Miranda's question, and the two turned to see Hans entering, speaking quickly. "We must hurry. My men at the airport have alerted me that a helicopter is preparing to land at the helipad; it has a SWAT team on board."

As the two dashed to grab their belongings, Hans continued, "The tower had alerted the jet, allowing them to conceal themselves. My connections at Flight Operations have destroyed the flight plan, so that much is covered, at least for the moment. Come, we must go."

"Hans, put Plan Alpha into effect. Dallas, we'll leave by the back door; now."

"I have already called for Alpha, Miranda. Dallas, good to meet you, and good luck."

With that, Hans slipped back through the door and was gone. Dallas followed Miranda through the fire escape door, to a waiting car. Dallas turned to face Miranda's silhouette as the car dashed through the early morning light. They took a less direct route back to the airport; a time-consuming but necessary precaution to avoid any possible surveillance.

"Plan Alpha?" he queried quietly.

"While you were busy at the gaming tables, Hans and I prepared some contingency plans. Alpha involves having a couple dressed as our doubles leave, very publicly, through the front lobby, timing their departure so that the arriving security team sees them driving off in the opposite direction. It's a simple plan, but hopefully, the distraction will be sufficient."

"Hans said to expect a SWAT team at the airport. What about them?"

"They'll be fast asleep by the time we get there. Hans had some personnel concealed with tranquilizer guns. Fortunately, you did an excellent job of calling attention to yourself, which left Hans and I free to prepare what we needed to prepare; if anyone was watching."

"You had me out there as a sitting duck?"

"A decoy, yes; quack."

"Thanks."

"Look on the bright side, you were very well-paid. I would safely say you set the record for winning at the Mermaid Casino's Baccarat table. How does it feel to be a millionaire?"

"I'll let you know when – if – I get a chance to spend it," Dallas deadpanned, patting the cashier's cheque in his breast pocket, "What about Hans?"

"He can take care of himself."

"Will he reveal our plans?"

"If asked, all he knew was that I showed up with an unidentified VIP, spent the night, and left."

"Do you think Rocky will buy that?"

"Hans can be very convincing; he'll be fine."

The car slowed to a halt next to a darkened hanger on the opposite side of the runway from the terminal. Miranda jumped out of the car, with Dallas following close behind. Two men appeared out of the darkness and pointed toward the end of the building. Dallas turned the corner to see a jet, its lights off, but its engines humming. The group stumbled up the stairs of the Gulfstream G550 and into the plush cabin while some nameless ground crew tossed the last of the pair's belongings and their smuggled gear into the plane's cargo hold. Miranda pointed Dallas toward a seat while the two men, who Dallas now realized were the pilot and copilot, took their respective places in the cockpit immediately after securing the cabin door. Within moments the plane slowly began to taxi out from behind the building and toward the runway.

"Dr. Fisher," the co-pilot called back a split second later, "We've been cleared for takeoff. We'll turn on the cabin lights once we reach altitude." Sitting there in the darkness, it slowly dawned on Dallas that this time the Dr. Fisher in question was Miranda. While Dallas pondered that concept, the plane began to accelerate down the runway, rolling faster and faster, until the pilot rotated the plane, and the Gulfstream's nose pointed sharply upward into the evaporating darkness of the African morning.

Once the plane leveled off and cabin lights came on, Miranda flipped a lever and swiveled her seat to face Dallas.

"We might as well make ourselves comfortable; we'll be in the air for the next eight hours. There's food and drinks in the galley and a DVD player, if you want to watch a movie." Pointing over her shoulder she continued, "The seat reclines, but if you want to go lie down there's a bedroom through that door there."

"Nice little place you've got here. I could get used to this life."

"You keep saying that."

Suddenly, the bedroom door opened. Out stepped a powerful man with black hair and steel-gray eyes. His jaw was strong and square, with only the slightest hint of a double chin suggesting his age.

"Dr. Roark, so good to see you."

"Oh, no!" Miranda spat with an angry glare.

"Miranda, who is this?"

"Please, my dear, the formalities," the man replied, with a cultured European voice that issued through a menacing smile.

"Dallas," Miranda began, trying to maintain her composure, "This is Camile de Fountaine. He's the leader of the Order."

13

"I'M FLATTERED YOU REMEMBER me," Camile offered with a flourish, "it's been years."

"I guess it would be pointless to ask how you got here." Miranda's tone was bitter, yet resigned.

"I don't mind telling you; after all, as you said, we've got eight hours, give or take. Let's just say that anyone in your organization who would betray Joshua just can't be trusted."

"Hans?" Camile's silence was answer enough. "So," she continued, "there was no SWAT team?"

"Of course there was; we had to look realistic, didn't we? I brought them along in case things started to go wrong. Besides, how do you think you could get a helicopter and plane to your location on such short notice? Really, my dear, I know you're supposed take Joshua's position some day; you really mustn't be so naïve."

"I'm sorry," Dallas interrupted, "are you telling me that the leader of our worst enemy is a friend of the family?"

"It's a small community and a long story," she offered in a defensive and somewhat embarrassed tone.

"Well," Dallas muttered, "as our good buddy Camile here says, we have plenty of time."

"Miranda," Camile interrupted, "please, allow me; it's been so long since I've had to explain myself to anyone; I really need the practice. Now, Dallas; may I call you Dallas?"

Dallas said nothing, but merely nodded his head in reply.

"Dallas, I'm sure by now you know the basics, so I won't bore you unnecessarily. As you know, the two exile groups were relatively small. We've always known one another. It's a little like two political parties; while we may disagree, we are more alike than different. We both do, after all, represent the most direct descendants of the Anunnaki. The rest of you are rather like mongrel puppies."

Dallas suppressed the urge to bark. "If that's the case, then why don't you work together?"

"Because, my dear doctor, they wish to abandon our heritage, while we wish to embrace it. We want to return our people to their former greatness; they do not. That difference has existed since the very beginning, when Miranda's people betrayed the empire and sued for peace. We want to find – we need to find – the chambers in order to lead our people back into their rightful place in the galaxy."

"Camile," Dallas began slowly, "who would control the knowledge of the chambers?"

"To the victor goes the spoils," Camile answered with a grin; instantly demonstrating Joshua's motives and touching Dallas's own worst fears.

"Dallas, we are but two sides of the same coin; yin and yang, as it were. Miranda and I, we share the same blood, the same awesome secret, the same ancient knowledge, the same —"

"Seems to me," Dallas interrupted, trying to sound tougher than he felt, "that all you share is some old wives' tales. You people have been at this for, what, thirteen thousand years? And you haven't found squat. You've got bits and pieces, old stories, a few artifacts, nothing more."

"Please, Dr. Roark," Camile began, reverting to the formal, "you of all people know that is not true. True, in terms of physical evidence, we do not have much, but we have enough to know that what we say is the truth. Where we differ is the end result. The Guardians believe we have been spared the fate of our ancestors. The Order, on the other hand, believes that fate has merely been delayed; for what reason we do not know. We believe that, to be ready for that possibility, we need the contents of the chambers."

"I remember," Camile added somewhat whimsically, "when I was a young man, studying archaeology at the university, I came to see that it would be wrong to deny the human race its true past. I sat, day after day, listening to supposedly learned men spouting nonsense about things of which they literally knew next to nothing; enduring year after year of lectures and seminars embellishing the false fabric of history they wove; watching them destroy any serious archaeologist who dared to propose that there might an earlier history than the one they created."

"Let me guess, you settled on specializing in the Hindu culture."

"Clever boy; it was the only one that survives with an acceptance of an earlier time; the only one that allowed for the possibility of what I already knew to be true."

"I just can't believe Hans betrayed us," Miranda muttered, still unable to accept Camile's claim, "I've known him all my life."

"Don't take it so badly. Besides, Hans viewed himself not as a traitor but as a patriot answering to a higher call. There are more and more Guardians who are reaching the same conclusion about the need for a change. We now have many people hidden within all levels of the Guardians' ranks. It was no mystery to follow your path or your purpose."

Dallas shot a glance at Miranda, who could only shake her head in disbelief. It was clear she had no idea what, or who, Camile was talking about.

"Actually, it had not been our intention to kidnap you. We were quite content to monitor your progress; that was the reason I was in South Africa. So, when Hans called me, saying you were looking for a plane, I just couldn't resist flying up here and collecting you two myself. Tell me, my dear Dr. Roark, do you really believe there might be something of value on the floor of the Persian Gulf?"

"How do you know —" Dallas caught himself; it was Hans, of course. He took a different tack. "Look, I watched your goons kill people in cold blood. You can't really believe I'm going to calmly sit here and just chat with you about this."

"You mean Dr. Todd? You must understand I had nothing to do with that horrible crime. In fact, the good doctor was on his way to see me when it happened."

"That's a lie!" Miranda sprang to her feet in anger. "He was coming to see my father."

"Nonsense, child. I was to meet him at the museum. That's why I had men there. They saw you spirit off Dallas, and later I learned about Dr. Todd. I decided then to bide my time and see what might come of your actions. Frankly, I'd assumed that if it wasn't just an unfortunate accident then your people must have killed the good doctor."

Dallas perked up at this exchange. His mind flashed back to the note in the little black diary: CFatAker; was CF shorthand for Camile de Fountaine? Dallas thought then that C stood for see, now he wondered if he'd gotten it right.

"You thought we killed him; that's nonsense. What about Raj's murder?" challenged Miranda.

"Raj?"

"Dr. Rajeev Singala, our team's expert in Hindu myths, legends, religion, and culture. I suppose you're going to tell me you had nothing to do with that."

A look of seemingly genuine surprise, and perhaps, even worry, revealed itself on Camile's face.

"I have no idea what you're talking about. Dr. Singala is dead? That is a great pity; he was a genius in our field. This changes everything."

"You'll forgive me if I have a hard time believing you." This time it was Dallas who questioned what he was hearing. "You tell me you're not responsible for all these things, and yet here I am on your plane, in your custody."

"I do not deny wanting you, but I do deny murder. I have wanted to meet you ever since the reports I received years ago from Dr. Moncrief.

He was most impressed with your abilities. He was encouraging us to recruit you when suddenly you vanished. At the time, I could only assume that Joshua had gotten to you first."

"Jesus, was the entire world keeping tabs on me?"

"Only the parts of the world that truly mattered. I tell you what; I'll trust you first, and you don't have to trust me yet. I want to show you something."

With that, Camile reached into his coat pocket and pulled out a triangular green translucent stone; the third of the four sides of the pyramid. Dallas could not conceal his excitement in seeing the object that Camile turned over and over in his hand. As he handed it to Dallas, Camile continued. "Miranda was wrong about the bedroom. We've converted that area to a mobile lab of sorts. You are welcome to make use of these humble facilities for the next few hours while we make our way to Dubai."

"We're still going on to Dubai?"

"Of course; from what you've told me just now, going there is more important than ever. Tell me, just what are you really hoping to find in the middle of the Persian Gulf?"

"Really big fish?" Dallas's cast for a laugh got no strikes.

"Miranda," Camile said, ignoring the last comment, "You two have a few hours to … kill; why not go back there and take a look at the tablet. I believe, Dallas, you'll find everything you need. We've already enlarged the script photographically; large transparencies on a light table, I believe that's how you like to work. Perhaps, once you've had a chance to review our tablet, you'll be willing to share anything you may have learned from yours. Now, go, I must consider the news you have brought me … and make a few phone calls."

Dallas tried, without complete success, to conceal his surprise at Camile's familiarity with his work habits. Seeing no alternative, the pair rose and moved to the back of the plane. Once behind the closed door, Dallas opened his mouth to speak, only to be silenced by Miranda. She turned on a few pieces of equipment, which generated a soft, continuous background noise, then leaned over and began whispering.

"Are you going to tell him what you've translated?"

"Isn't it curious," Dallas whispered back, "they didn't seem to know anything about that. That would suggest that wherever he's getting his information, it isn't complete. In fact, it suggests that his spy may not even on the ship; remember, I began using photographic transparencies back at the museum complex. I wonder; who is his source? While I'm thinking about it, is there anything, and I mean anything, else I need to know? You have me flying blind here, if you pardon the pun."

"Nope," she responded slowly, "I think Camile just about covers it."

"Are you sure?"

Miranda could only shrug her shoulders in response. "So what do we tell him?" she whispered. Then, changing the subject, she added, "The most important question is: do you believe what he said about not being involved with Raj's murder?"

"Hell, I don't know," mused Dallas, "he certainly seemed surprised. But if the Order didn't kill Raj then —"

"Yeah, then who did?"

"That leaves one of two obvious conclusions; either Raj's murder had absolutely nothing to do with our mission, or —"

"Or," Miranda interrupted again, "there is someone else out there trying to stop us; could that be possible?"

"You tell me!" Dallas retorted. "All I know is that your father suspected me of being a spy for the Order, and suddenly that's who I'm with now. Raj is dead, but nobody seems to know anything about it. We're still headed for Dubai, and it seems to me that before it's all over, we'll all be swimming in the same place. I think we need to figure out how to get everyone on the same page."

"Only two chances of that; slim and none—"

"Yeah, I know," added Dallas, "and Slim left town."

14

IT WAS AN EXTREMELY angry Rocky who awakened Joshua before sunrise as the tanker cruised toward the African coast. His men had gone to check on their prisoner at around six a.m. and found the brig's door wide open. It had not taken them long to discover the rest. Now the security chief had the unpleasant task of telling Joshua that his daughter had betrayed them all. The director's reaction was understandable; shock, dismay, frustration, and anger. He was visibly shaken by Miranda's involvement in the escape. Had she been duped? Had she betrayed everything they'd believed in? Had she been taken by force? All these questions meandered through Joshua's mind, which searched unsuccessfully for answers. Rocky couldn't provide much information; just that the previous evening, she had given instructions to allow a helicopter to land, and that she had boarded it with Dallas.

According to Rocky there had not been anyone else involved. She had not seemed to be a hostage. Indeed, according to the bridge crew on duty, she had even been seen helping load the helicopter with equipment from Seahab; equipment personally signed out by her from a secure area. Though he hated being the messenger, the evidence clearly pointed to Miranda's willing involvement in Dallas's escape. Joshua could not help but wonder if she had also been involved with the murders as well, though he could not reconcile that possibility with her behavior regarding Dallas.

Rocky had already confirmed that no helicopter had landed at any airport within range, except Swakopmund, nor was there any other airport from which the pair could make their escape, assuming of course that they didn't plan to stay in Africa. Rocky calculated that was a safe assumption. Finally, a father's pride won out, and he instructed Rocky to do nothing until they dropped anchor at Swakopmund. Once ashore, they would take a security contingent into the city and see what they could discover.

Hours later, a very nervous and humble Hans delivered his verbal report to the group when they arrived at the city's airport from the docks. By now it was late morning, and the fog was beginning its long march back out to sea. The low-hanging scud of the dissipating cloud was drifting slowly westward. Joshua set up headquarters in a small, plain room to one side of the airport; its sole attribute being its isolation. It was an unimportant space with functional folding medal chairs and a cheap, imitation-wood table. In this secluded setting, Hans faced the leader of his people; the contrast could not have been starker. Though he'd been in Joshua's presence many times before, this time was different. It was a palatable difference; his nervous demeanor betrayed him silently and almost immediately.

"So, Hans," Joshua began with a frustrated staccato brevity, "you're telling me that Miranda contacts you from out of nowhere with a story of some mysterious VIP and had you organize a helicopter and plane on just a few hours notice?"

"Yes sir, that's it exactly."

"And you made all these arrangements?"

"Yes, sir."

"You made them personally; no one else helped you?"

"No sir, no one."

"And you didn't ask where she came from?"

"Yes, sir … I mean, no, sir."

"And does that sound logical to you?"

For this question, Hans had no answer. He simply stared wide-eyed at Joshua, like a schoolboy who'd just got caught cheating.

"Come on, Hans, tell me everything you know."

"I … I am, sir. She didn't tell me much; just that she needed to get to the Persian Gulf."

"Hans, you two have known each other since you were, what, ten years old? I don't believe she'd be that secretive, not with you. Let's start with something simple. Which of our facilities did you bring the plane from? What was its tail number?"

"Tail number?"

"Hans, really, this is getting tiresome. Where did you get the plane from, and what was the tail number?"

"I don't know the tail number; the plane came from Johannesburg."

"The organization doesn't have any planes in Johannesburg," Joshua replied with a sense of resignation. "Whose plane was it?"

Hans glanced at his watch and decided it was no longer necessary to maintain the charade. "Camile de Fountaine's," he said finally.

"Hans, you?"

There was nothing for the younger man to say, he lowered his eyes to the floor in submission, stripped of his Teutonic pride.

"Where are they going?" Joshua spat out between gritted teeth.

"Dubai."

"Did she tell you about our mission? Did she tell you her final destination?"

Hans paused a moment before responding, "Yes."

"Can I assume you reported all this information to Monsieur Fountaine?"

"Yes."

"Rocky —"

"I'm already on it, boss."

With that, Rocky began calling instructions out on his radio, but his gaze remained focused on Hans. The crippled leader turned back to the traitor with a look that belied his silence. Joshua bit hard to restrain himself, lest he reveal the depth of his anger and disappointment. "Hans," he forced the words through his lips, "there is one final thing I want to know; be honest with me. Was Miranda a party to this deception? Has she also betrayed me?"

"Sir, I can promise you this much: she had no idea what I had done or who was on the plane. She was apparently completely convinced of Dr. Roark's innocence regarding what happened aboard the ship. Her actions in that regard were aimed at proving that. Frankly, I imagine she was as angry as you were when she discovered the truth of Mr. Fountaine."

Joshua said simply, "I doubt she was as angry as I."

With that Joshua raised his hands up and clasped them, as if in meditation. Hans just stood there, watching in confused silence, wondering what the ritual meant, and if there would be any further interrogation.

In the midst of this silence, Joshua's face took on an expression of intensity that the younger man had never seen before; and would never see again. In an instant, Joshua turned his palms toward the confused defector. An intense electrical bolt issued forth from his hands, enveloping Hans, and Hans was no more.

Rocky spoke up only to report what little progress he could make. He took no notice of Hans's absence; no explanation was necessary. As to their current situation, it would be several hours before they could get a plane to their location. He had placed a call to Dubai's Minister of Transportation, who controlled the airport; but he had not as yet heard back from him. Rocky had been able to determine from the flight plan filed by Camile's pilot that his plane already had a three-hour head start. By the time they could takeoff in pursuit, Camile would have landed it Dubai. Unless they could stop them at the airport, they risked losing track of them.

"If Hans told Camile everything," Rocky began, "then we know they'll be headed for —"

"Jazireh-ye Forur," Joshua finished the thought, "but only if Miranda told Hans that much; we don't know that for sure."

"Boss, can we afford to take that chance?"

"Rocky how do you interpret this information in terms of whether Dallas is really the spy?"

"Can't say, but innocent men don't run. And no, I don't think Miranda is really a traitor; but I do think she put her emotions before her logic. She obviously believed in Dallas's innocence enough to risk everything."

"Doesn't sound like my daughter, does it?"

"No sir, it doesn't," replied Rocky, "but love makes you do crazy things."

"Love? Do you think she's in love with him?"

"Me? I think so, but I doubt she's come to that conclusion yet."

Joshua allowed himself a slight chuckle at the thought. "God help him when she figures it out; it will piss her off. Anyway, all that puts us back where we started; either he's a spy or he's not. The question now is – what's our next step? Do we chase her down or stay with the tanker and continue on course with to Jazireh-ye Forur?"

"Well," Rocky began, "I've already arranged to charter a Gulfstream; it's not one of ours but at least it should be on the way here by now. I could follow them in the jet, and you could stay with the tanker. Whether Dallas is a spy or not, we know they are both with Camile. We must try to get them back."

"Agreed; but I think I'll be the one to go ahead on the jet. I want you to stay with the team. If Dallas isn't the spy, then the others are still in danger. The ship is too big a prize to leave unguarded."

"But, sir —"

"No," the director interrupted, "I'm going to be firm on this. I'll take Jorge with me to help out. He's a geologist and his knowledge might be useful when we reach the area; and I think I'll take Sam as well. Go back to the ship and have them get packed; tell them nothing. I'll brief them when they get here."

While Joshua was putting his plan into motion, Dallas was throwing his hands up in complete frustration. Without his reference books, the work was going extremely slowly. So far, he'd learned nothing much of use. This tablet had begun with the same honorifics as the first one; it was also from En.Lil.An, and it appeared to continue the story that was begun on the first tablet. This fact alone suggested that this was the second tablet in the sequence. Also, given the notches on this piece, it suggested that Dr. Todd's piece was the third piece of the puzzle. All this information meant that the final part of whatever story the final emperor had chosen to tell was still to be found. Dallas had a feeling that this fourth piece contained the most vital information of the four triangles.

He also pondered the notches once again. They clearly suggested a base on to which the assembled pyramid shape would be placed. That might be the most important clue of all. If this hypothesis was correct, that suggested the tablets served another purpose besides merely being a last will and testament. He wondered if either the choice of material or their crystalline matrix might be a clue; he reminded himself to ask George if he ever got the chance.

Miranda had been studying the actual piece under a microscope while Dallas worked with the photographic enlargements. It was busy work, really, because she was neither a linguist nor a geologist. The pieces did not give up any secrets to her, nor could she achieve any moment of divine inspiration. She just kept turning them round and round.

"Dallas," sighed Miranda finally, "discovered anything yet?"

"No."

"That's succinct."

"What would you have me say?" His tone betrayed his frustration. "It's very difficult to do this type of work without my research notes. I can only guess at some of these symbols; the syntax is much more complicated than Sumerian."

"Shall we go tell him?"

"Why not? I can stare at this thing all the way to Dubai, but it won't change anything. We might as well get it over with. I wonder what they're serving in first class?"

Much to Dallas's surprise, Camile didn't react to the lack of information. Instead, he offered them lunch and a chance to relax. While Dallas settled in, Miranda's anger festered silently. It was aimed in several directions: at Camile, for his forced gallantry; at Dallas, for his seemingly passive acceptance of their predicament; but mostly at herself, for being captured so easily. She concluded that her current situation was what came when you trusted someone, anyone, but yourself.

As she was reaching that decision, Joshua sat waiting in Swakopmund making some decisions of his own. Quickly he brought Samantha and Jorge up to date when they arrived. What mattered most, he told them, was that Dallas and Miranda were in the hands of the enemy, and apparently, headed first for Dubai and then Jazireh-ye Forur. On that fact, all were in agreement. While all this activity had put a serious detour in the group's plans, the director explained that, once they got Dallas and his daughter back, they'd be 'in the neighborhood,' so why not do a little reconnoitering in advance of the main expedition. Both scientists were weary of ship life. That fact alone made the choice between doing some reconnaissance or spending three more weeks on the ship was a simple one.

By the early afternoon, the jet had arrived to collect the trio. As they prepared to depart Namibia, an identical Gulfstream was touching down at Dubai International Airport. Despite the length of the flight, Dallas was not able to offer much of interest to Camile regarding the third tablet. Instead, the pair engaged in polite banter on subjects of no great significance. It only fueled Miranda's continuing anger that Dallas remained so relaxed. She began to question where his loyalty lay, especially after she had risked everything to free him.

The private plane taxied to the far end of the airport and came to a stop, mere feet from a waiting limousine. Dallas stood next the exit, looking through window at the airport ground crew, completely unaware of what was to come when the co-pilot opened the door. As it swung out of the way the summertime climate of Dubai rushed in like an angry blow dryer. The air was thick with jet fuel fumes, sand and pollution, forcing Dallas to stumble back slightly. Recovering, Dallas became amazed at what he saw upon exiting the plane. The facility that spread out before him took him completely by surprise. The facility rivaled any in the world, and the lights of the city's skyscrapers, visible through the brown haze in the distance, spoke to him of the clash between the old and new worlds. He found a certain irony in their mission. If they were correct, then one of the world's most modern cities was sitting less than one hundred miles from one of the world's oldest settlements; and the former knew nothing of the latter.

The ride from the airport to their quarters for the night was even more of an education. Dallas quickly came to realize that he had spent so much time researching the past that the present had become unknown to him. He hadn't realized that such cities as this existed in this part of the world. This conceit, he quickly realized, was the arrogance of his American upbringing. Still, he gazed out the window in awe of what stretched out before him: a vast highway system teeming with cars of every type and description. He chuckled to himself that he should be surprised by this fact.

Eventually, the group arrived at a magnificent structure that bore the appearance of a modern palace. Despite the desert location the grounds were perfectly manicured, with all manner of flowering shrubs and date palms. The grass was thick and deeply green. Surrounding the entire grounds stood a high wall, as is common in this part of the world. The mansion's massive wrought-iron gates clanged shut as the limo pulled to a stop at the base of the marble steps that lead up to the vast, oversized doors.

"Dr. Roark," Camile began as they exited the car, "It's too late to set out tonight. We'll leave tomorrow; there's no rush; the marina is close by. From there it'll be about a four-hour cruise to the dive site. For tonight, I do hope you'll enjoy the accommodations; dinner will be served shortly. If you go inside, the butler will show you to your rooms. We felt that a hotel offered too many … temptations. Oh, and Miranda, the security personnel on the grounds are armed, so please don't attempt another jailbreak. Now run along, I'll join you in the dining room in a few minutes."

"I am sure we shall be most comfortable," offered Dallas with a slight bow. "Come, Miranda, let's get out of the heat." Then, taking her by the elbow, he led her up the stairs. She tried to jerk her arm free, but this action only encouraged him to tighten his grip. Then their eyes met and she saw a determination in his gaze that made her stop resisting. There was tenseness in his jaw that she had never seen before; it surprised her.

Once they were in the house and out of earshot, he spoke plainly for the first time since they'd left Swakopmund.

"Miranda, there's no point in showing any resistance, they'll only watch us more closely."

"You mean all this passivity is a show."

"Well, if we don't resist, maybe they'll let their guard down. We'll just have to wait for our moment. We'll only get one shot at whatever it is we try to do; if that. If we fail, we won't get a second chance."

"I don't know about them letting their guard down with me around, and those security teams have real weapons; but I give you credit for the thought."

"Well, I don't think we'll be able to make any kind of break tonight, maybe not tomorrow or the next day, but once they think we've settled down; that's when we move."

"And in the meantime?"

"Didn't Camile say something about dinner?"

15

WHILE THE HOSTAGES JOINED their captors in the massive dining room for cocktails, Joshua, Jorge, and Samantha were still hours away from Dubai. Back on the ship, Rocky had already arranged for the organization's agent in Dubai to begin surveillance and prepare for the group's arrival. He also arranged for suites at the Burj Al Arab, one of Dubai's most prestigious and outrageous hotels. Built on a manmade island just offshore on the beaches of Dubai, it rose, tall and white; constructed in the shape of the giant billowing sail of a dhow, the traditional Arabic sailing ship.

Joshua accepted word of Rocky's efforts without comment. At any other time, he might have been more interested, but now his focus lay elsewhere. He wondered how he could have let things get so completely out of control. He worried about Miranda, and assuming she was all right, he worried what he would have to do with her once she was safely back with the organization. For their part, Jorge and Samantha kept to themselves. They sensed Joshua's preoccupation, and after the first couple of hours, could not bring themselves to make any further small talk. The group settled into gloomy silence, broken only when the co-pilot came back to serve dinner.

Eventually, just after midnight, the pilot signaled to prepare for a landing. Jorge stared in fascination at the nighttime scene that spread out beneath him. The lights of Dubai illuminated the size of the city, leaving him in absolute amazement. He had no idea the city was so large, or so modern. The road system, lit with rows of massive halogen lights, snaked across the horizon; and either despite the late hour or because of it, there were cars everywhere.

The vectoring of the plane's final approach brought it from the south to the northwest in a sweeping arch, allowing the travelers to get a panoramic view of the expansive vista below them. The lights along the beach road stood out in stark contrast to the blackness of the Gulf that lay beyond. As they continued their final pivot, which carried them out over the dark waters, the pilot announced they had been given clearance to land on runway One-Two Left.

Jorge glanced out the window on his right as they passed back over the land and noticed a huge complex that had the look of a royal palace. It was a massive, cream colored boxy structure, with equally massive, well lit grounds. It was bathed in a brilliant yellow light, revealing a lush, tropical garden, sitting like postage stamp on a sand-colored envelope that faded into black at the far edges. He wondered to himself what sheikh lived within those luxurious confines.

As fate would have it, Dallas, at that same moment, stood on the balcony of his bedroom, facing the Gulf. He was amazed at the temperature which, despite the late hour, was still over a hundred degrees. Hearing the low roar of jet engines pass slowly overhead, he glanced up to see the red lights of a sleek Gulfstream G550 streaking behind the bright yellow lights of the compound. From the faint outline it looked identical to the one he had flown on to Dubai just a few hours before. He wondered idly where it was from and where its passengers were headed.

"Dallas," Miranda called, bringing him out of his trance, "it's late. We might as well go to bed."

"We … bed?" He blurted out before realizing she was calling from her own balcony and not the bedroom.

"Excuse me?" her tone was the verbal equivalent of a raised eyebrow.

"Nothing, I was lost in thought. Why don't you come over to my room; we can talk."

"Okay, I'll be right over." With that, she was gone, leaving Dallas to return to his daydreams.

Meanwhile, Jorge tensed reflexively as the plane touched down on the blacktop. He was taken by the fact that this plane, unlike commercial liners, made landing a much more personal affair; he felt every bump, every seam, and every lose piece of asphalt as they rolled onto the taxiway. Peering out the window, he was struck by the number and sheer size of the global fleet of planes that stretched before him; carriers from all over the world were represented, and his plane could taxi under the wings of almost all of them. Soon, they rolled to a stop in a distant part of the facility, far from the behemoths they had passed. He noticed a black, stretch limo driving up out of the darkness and coming to a stop near the plane's door. Out of it stepped two men: one in uniform, and the other in traditional attire that told Jorge all he needed to know about the climate. On a signal from the copilot, he and Samantha made their way to the front of the plane and prepared to exit. They knew Joshua preferred to transfer himself back to his wheelchair in private, which he did in short order with the unwanted assistance of the copilot.

The pilot flipped the door's long, recessed handle, unlocking the exit way, and allowing Jorge, like Dallas before him, to experience the full-frontal blast of Dubai's heat for the first time. The outside temperature was at least thirty degrees warmer than the plane; this was the oven that was Dubai in summer. The superheated air, mixed with jet-fume exhaust, forced itself into Jorge's lungs, and he struggled to catch his breath. Samantha offered no reaction to the surroundings, and instead bounded down the stairs and into the limo like a playful puppy.

Once the group gathered at the vehicle, Joshua turned his attention to the two greeters. One was the local member of the Guardians, and the other was a customs officer delegated to the task of greeting and processing whatever VIPs happened to arrive. On this day, it was this group and this plane. The local official had been given no further information past the simple instruction that he was to stamp their passports and send them on their way as quickly as possible.

That task accomplished, and once they were alone, the organization's operative explained, rather sheepishly, that he had indeed seen Camile's plane land some six or seven hours earlier but, owing to airport security, over which he had no control, had been prevented him from following them. The operative explained that his usually reliable inside man could only tell him that, this time, he could not help him. And then their car was gone. There had been no way to pick up the trail. He had taken the obvious precaution of having men watch the most likely docks and marinas but, given that there were many possible options between here and the neighboring Emirate of Sharjah, there was simply no way to watch them all.

Joshua let out a grunt of disapproval, but said nothing further until they had arrived at the Burj Al Arab. On any other occasion, he would have allowed himself the indulgence of reveling in the opulent luxury of this place, but this time the hotel represented nothing more than a waypoint in the pursuit of Miranda and Dallas. Moving inside, Jorge marveled at the pair of massive, two-story-tall aquariums that flanked either side of the hotel's escalators.

"Jorge, will you stop staring at the fish." Joshua's admonishment startled the geologist, who fumbled for a reply. The director waved him off apologetically. "There's no way of finding Dallas and Miranda tonight. We all need to get some rest; we'll try heading out to the dive site first thing in the morning. We know where they'll eventually be heading, if they haven't already. I'm betting that's where we'll have to catch up with them."

"And then what?" It was Sam who spoke up; her voice was firm and free of any of the bothersome baggage of compassion.

"And then, we'll see. I intend to take some security people with us, but I don't intend to get into a conflict, unless it is unavoidable."

"I don't see how you can avoid it." Her response was simple and direct. "Even if Camile releases Dallas and Miranda, he'll be onsite. I'm sure they've told him everything —"

"My daughter would not betray the organization."

"Really? I thought that's what brought us here."

"Now, you listen to me —"

"Joshua," interrupted Jorge, "I'm sorry; and Sam may be out of line, but it is prudent to assume that they've said something, either through force, intimidation, drugs, or ... something." He voice tailed off, not knowing how to proceed.

"We're not going to settle that question tonight," he whispered tersely, "forget it. The Dubai Marina is about five miles from here, that's where our transportation is moored. I'll be leaving instructions for a wake-up call at 5:30 a.m. I'd like to get underway by no later than seven a.m. That gives us time for about four and a half hours sleep. I suggest you two make the best of it."

With that Joshua clicked the joystick on his chair, spun around, and vanished behind the elevator doors. Sam didn't bother to look back in Jorge's direction, but went straight to the second elevator; and in a moment, the geologist was standing alone in the massive atrium of the hotel.

Jorge eventually found his room, which had a panoramic view of the Gulf. Looking left and right from the balcony he saw the lights of the various palaces, hotels, and resorts defining the beach line. It was still uncomfortably hot outside, a fact made even more pronounced by the refrigerated state of the suite. Ah, the suite; he couldn't help but be impressed with the suite. It was a two-story affair with a full bar, a kitchen, a dining room with seating for twelve, a sitting room, and a pool room. Upstairs was a massive loft with a computer workstation and a bedroom right out of a sheikh's harem. The entire space was draped in luxurious pastel silks, and the canopy bed was covered with at least a dozen finely woven silk throw-pillows of every imaginable color.

So much had happened within the past twenty-four hours that Jorge was only now beginning to take it in. He still didn't believe Dallas was capable of such betrayal as Rocky thought possible. Miranda's defiantly loyal behavior only seemed to endorse his own opinion, although he found her approach overly melodramatic. Perhaps he was tired, but to him the pieces just didn't add up. He sensed there was some key fact still missing. Clearly, if Dallas was not the killer, then that person was still aboard the ship. That reason alone made Jorge glad he had flown to Dubai.

If the killer were still on board, he thought, wasn't Joshua taking a terrible chance by leaving the ship to pursue his daughter; and what of the rest of the team? For that matter, what of he and Sam? If the murders did continue, then he, Dallas, Miranda, and Sam – not to mention the obvious, Joshua, would be cleared. On the other hand, if there were no further murders, and assuming Dallas and Miranda really weren't involved, then that could leave only Sam and Joshua as suspects; he was certain at least of his own innocence.

Jorge gave up calculating the permutations. It was like trying to play an entire game of chess in one's head; he was a lousy chess player. He threw himself onto the silken bed and drifted to sleep, still trying, against his wishes, to compute the possibilities.

Mornings in Dubai begin early; the sun rises before six a.m. It rises over the desert east of the city, leaving those facing the Gulf in the shadows. Still, once up, whatever cool might be in the desert air is quickly dissipated under the sun's unrelenting gaze. Jorge would have sworn he could see the water literally evaporating into the air around him. The utter lack of clouds, along with the magnifying effects of the haze and the water, made the morning glare almost impossible to bear, even with sunglasses on.

By the time Jorge, Sam, and Joshua reached the marina, the temperature had already increased by ten degrees Fahrenheit, and being near the water only made it worse. The boat captain motioned for the passengers to take their places inside the ship, named *Emirates Pride*, which was pleasantly air conditioned, although the humidity gave everything within a light coating of condensation.

"How long?" Jorge asked as he struggled unsteadily to his seat.

"God, Jorge," chimed Sam, "we haven't even left the dock yet. Where are your sea legs?"

"On the other ship; I don't like small boats."

"Small!" Joshua's reaction was almost extreme. "This vessel is a hundred feet long. That's not small."

"My friend, compared to what we've been on, it's a lifeboat," retorted Jorge. "How long until we get there?"

"It's about eighty nautical miles," Sam replied. "That's about four hours, assuming we have calm seas. Joshua, I'm going down below to check the scuba gear and the other equipment. Is the MAD onboard?"

"MAD?" It was one of the crew joining in as he passed by.

"Magnetic anomaly detector," responded Jorge wearily without missing a beat.

"Better be," added Joshua, replying to Sam's original question, "We don't have time to waste. As it is, we won't be getting to the dive site until lunchtime at this rate. Now, we'll be on board for the next few days, assuming we find Camile and the others out there. I've also made arrangements for several of the local office's security personnel to join us today, but they do not know as yet the full nature of the mission. They've only been told we're pursuing some fellow members who have been abducted and have the yacht equipped to use force, if necessary."

"Force?" Jorge chimed up as Sam went below. "How much force?"

"Jorge," said Joshua calmly, "why don't you let me worry about that. You didn't think our only plan was to just politely ask for Dallas and Miranda's return?"

"I ... I hadn't really thought about it?" Jorge hesitated before continuing, "I thought you said you did not want to use force if you could avoid it?"

"I have to prepare for the unavoidable, just in case it becomes unavoidable. We'll start out polite, but Camile will be on our dive site; and we have to believe he knows the mission. IF they don't cooperate, I don't see that we'll have much choice about using force."

"What if he feels the same way?"

"I guess we'll have a problem. Let's cross that bridge when we come to it, shall we?"

Jorge began rethinking whether it had been such a good idea to come to Dubai after all. He had moved from a possible confrontation aboard the tanker to a definite one now. Still, he knew there was nothing he could do now but quietly scout out a safe place to hide once the shooting started.

"Let's focus on the positive," Joshua offered, sensing the geologist's concern, "why don't you go below and join Sam in checking over the electronics for your part of the mission – I especially want you to get familiar with the MAD, as it may or may not be like ones you've used; and check out your dive gear as well. Remember, this ship isn't anywhere near as well-equipped as the *Habibti*, and she is still over two weeks away from the region. The best we can hope for it to pinpoint the area of greatest magnetic discrepancy for further study."

The vessel moved slowly out of the marina, maneuvered around the granite boulder seawall, and set course for its destination, located eighty-two nautical miles northeast of Dubai; and only twenty nautical miles off the coast of Iran. From his balcony, Dallas could see the ship move past the seawall and off into the distance; though he had no idea who was aboard her, or where she was bound.

"Come, Dr. Roark, it's much too hot to be standing outside staring into space." Camile had entered the suite unannounced with a broad smile stretching across his face; it was a menacing expression.

"And to what do I owe the pleasure of this intrusion?"

"It is almost time we set off."

"But you don't know where we were going, not exactly. I know Miranda didn't tell Hans everything. Frankly, while I appreciate your … hospitality, I'm not disposed to telling you, either."

"Well," Camile retorted with a curious laugh, "if it were any other time, that is a challenge I just might accept, but I haven't the time right now. As to the exact location, I'd have to confess that I haven't the foggiest idea, but I'm working on that at this very minute."

"If you harm Miranda —"

"Relax, Dr. Roark, Miranda is in no danger. In fact, she's downstairs having breakfast. That is why I came to get you. We'll be setting off momentarily, so I'll need you to come downstairs with me. You may have breakfast now or aboard the ship, if you wish."

"But if Miranda hasn't told you, then how can you be working on it?"

"Let's just say we have secured the services of another guide who'll be leading us to our destination."

"Then why do you need us?"

"On that score, my plans have changed." Camile offered nothing further as he turned to escort Dallas to the dining room.

A short time later, they were pulling out of the marina, heading past the breakwater, just as the other ship had done earlier. The small group, consisting of Camile, Miranda, Dallas, and five security guards, sat around the dining room table of *Navigator*, a beautiful and classic private yacht in the old style, with teak decks and covered walkways. It swayed lazily in the current, in stark contrast to the crew that was working feverously to prepare the ship for sea.

Camile had told Dallas she was one hundred and fifty feet long, but she looked bigger, with several spacious staterooms, a formal dining room, a sitting room with a large number of chaise lounges, and according to their host, a colorful history more expansive than the ship herself. He couldn't imagine a more beautiful ship less suited to the task at hand. Dallas couldn't help but wonder if any of these people – Guardian and Order alike – could ever comprehend living in cramped confines of the real world. He laughed at that thought; whose real world was he referring to anyway?

"So, Camile," Dallas asked finally, unable to hold back any longer, "just who is guiding you to our supposed location?"

"Why, Dr. Roark, I would have thought that was obvious; Dr. Joshua Fisher."

"Excuse me?"

"Of course. It was he who you watched getting underway from your balcony. He believes we already know the location and is racing to confront us. Hans's instructions were to initially resist, then give them impression that Miranda had revealed your plan to him, and that he, in turn, passed that information on to us. Knowing Joshua, I thought it best to lay back, let him charge off to the rescue, and see where he'd head. He pulled out this morning, just as I expected, with a couple of your colleagues in tow."

Miranda was absolutely aghast. "Surely they'll see you following them."

"Oh no, my dear, we'll take a circuitous route, so as not to attract attention. Of course, they might figure it out once they get to the desired location and we're not there, but I'm betting they'll count themselves lucky." Once again, Camile's smile presented itself, and this time Dallas wished he could slap it off that face; or at least he wished he could try.

"All right," conceded Dallas, "So you follow them to the general location – what you think is the location; then what?"

"Then we talk."

"Talk?" Miranda let out with a bitter laugh, "you expect my father to just talk?"

"Oh yes, I do. I don't think he'll want any harm to come to you, no matter how much you may have disappointed him."

"I was under the impression you didn't condone such behavior," interrupted Dallas.

"Oh, I don't, but for the moment, let's hope Joshua doesn't know that. Besides, once we have the site, we'll stay on your people like glue. Then you will have to work with us."

"Work *with* us?" Miranda's tone moved to a near ballistic level. "You're insane!"

"We'll see how insane I am after I've spoken with Joshua."

Seeing there was no further point in this conversation, Dallas stood up and strolled around the massive rectangular table. The room was elegantly appointed, with objects more suited to the Hearst Castle than to a yacht in the Gulf. There were all manner of pitchers, silver and gold bowls, and other assorted bric-a-brac; all resting on beautifully polished built-in sideboards of mahogany inlaid with intricate patterns comprising assorted exotic woods.

"Mind if I go out on deck?" His tone hinted a sense of resignation. He knew there was nothing he could do; a feeling he'd become very familiar with ever since Rocky had thrown him in the brig. How long ago had that been? A mere five days, he reminded himself, and his life had been turned upside down once again.

Hearing no objection, Dallas moved toward the stairs leading up to the observation deck. He took with him an overwhelming sense that he had become a puppet whose strings were being pulled in opposite directions. Fueled by exhaustion, feelings of utter helplessness swept over him like a tidal wave. Reflectively, he gasped for air, his heart raced and his chest tightened. Just then he felt Miranda's gentle touch on his right arm. He turned to face her and marveled at the determined expression chiseled on her delicate face.

"Okay, we're alone;" she began earnestly, "what's the plan?"

"Well, I thought I'd start by getting a breath of fresh air. Then I figured I'd kick back and enjoy the ride."

"What? But you said you were just waiting for the right moment." Miranda's shock was palatable.

"I'm still waiting. Hell, we need to accept the possibility that we may not get a chance."

"Then we'll have to make one!"

"Listen, my little Rambo, I don't like this any more than you, but what can we do out here, miles from shore, and under guard?" The question was rhetorical; they stared at each other in silence, neither knowing what to do or say next as the yacht droned onward toward the rapidly rising sun.

After several hours of staring off into the horizon, watching the shadows shorten, and pondering nothing of particular importance, Dallas came out of his daydreams to spot another the speck of ship's stern in the distance ahead. No sooner did the thought occur to him that it must be Joshua than that fact was confirmed by the crew. His own vessel suddenly came to life as the seaman hurried about, preparing no doubt for the coming confrontation.

For his part, Dallas wondered what role he would play in the soon-to-unfold drama. Did Rocky still think he was guilty? For that matter, did Joshua? Dallas was sure of only one thing, his own innocence. That brought him to the most important question, who was the real murderer? Miranda wandered up to the ship's rail next to him, with that same steely expression in her eyes. This time Dallas was ready.

"I've been thinking," he whispered. "Once we get close, we could just jump in the water and swim for your father's boat. I don't think Camile would really shoot us."

"You don't think? I don't find that choice of words particularly reassuring."

"Sorry, I'm fresh out of better ideas; but if you think about it, harming us wouldn't make much sense. He wants an audience. I can't see how it would make any sense to harm us."

"My father will never negotiate with him."

"All the more reason to jump ship now."

"Strange," Miranda mused, looking out over the water, "surely his crew has spotted us by now. I wonder why my father hasn't reacted. His boat is just floating there."

"Do you think something's wrong?"

"Something is up," she muttered, "but I don't know what."

"Maybe they've already got a dive team in the water."

"I doubt it; I don't see any dive flags or markers out."

Camile wandered up just as the two finished talking, and he seemed every bit as puzzled as his two captives.

"What is your father up to?" His question was simple and direct.

"Funny, we were just asking ourselves the same question."

"As you can see," Camile retorted with a gesture toward his face, "I am not amused."

"No, I suppose not," replied Miranda, "but I really don't have a clue. I'll be happy to board their vessel and find out, if you'd like." The mere thought of that suggestion was laughable, though no one did.

Camile had his ship move up slowly toward the anchored yacht. His crew stood ready, their side arms bulging conspicuously from their hips. As they closed to within a hundred yards Joshua's stationary vessel suddenly roared to life. It executed a one-hundred-eighty-degree pivot on its anchor chain to face Camile's approach. At that moment, Dallas and Miranda noticed the eighty millimeter machine gun that Joshua's security team had mounted on the foredeck of his yacht, its barrel pointed directly at Camile's pilot house. Just then, the bridge's VHF radio suddenly crackled to life.

"Camile," a voice boomed, "you can hold it right there."

Dallas and Miranda stared at one another, not knowing exactly how to react. They could think of nothing to say, either to each other or to their captor. Both of them fixed their gaze on Camile as he stepped inside the pilot house and reached for the microphone.

"Hello, Joshua." His pleasant tone revealed an unspoken dichotomy, "it's so good of you to wait for me."

"Let's dispense with the pleasantries, shall we? You've taken two members of my team; I want them back."

"Yes, I have been entertaining your two 'team members,' and of course I'll return them, but first, we need to talk."

"We could have done that anywhere. Clearly, you have a purpose in all this intrigue; what is it?"

"Well, I must confess to wanting to know what you're up to. It's so hard to come by information since you set sail."

"Hasn't your spy told you everything?"

"My spy? Why, my dear Joshua, you're even more paranoid than when we last met, in Paris. I haven't the faintest idea what you're talking about."

"As if you'd tell me the truth ... Let me speak with my daughter!"

"But of course." Turning toward Miranda, he extended the microphone with a smile. "Indulge yourself."

"Hello, Father."

"Miranda, are you all right?"

"I'm fine."

"Then how's Dallas? What in God's name were you thinking?"

"I did what I did because I believe he is innocent. Whatever has been going on, it wasn't his doing." Her voice was firm.

"We'll discuss that later." Joshua's voice hinted at mixture of doubt, disappointment, and hope. Miranda could ask for nothing more and defiantly thrust the microphone back at Camile.

"So, my friend, what do you say? Would you do me the honor of joining us aboard our humble vessel?"

The airwaves were silent for what seemed like an eternity before Joshua finally responded. "A gracious offer, but I'm sure you'll understand if I prefer the comforts that 'my' humble vessel has to offer. Besides, as a practical matter, I'm sure you'd agree it would be much simpler for you to come aboard my ship than vice versa."

Joshua's simple statement brought forth from Camile a genuine look of concern; even, Dallas observed, a sense of compassion that seemed wrinkled up within his kidnapper's furled brow.

"I bow," Camile said finally, "to the regrettable logic of your request. We will be aboard momentarily; out."

Without instruction, his minions immediately began preparations to lower the yacht's tender into the calm, gulf waters. As this activity hovered around them, the leader tapped his fingers on the radio and stared off into space, clearly pondering his next move. Finally, he turned to his subordinates. "You two," he said, pointing, "are with me. Leave your weapons here; we do not go there seeking a confrontation."

Dallas was becoming more confused by the minute. From what Joshua had told him, these people represented the enemy. They were the ones who, for centuries, had supposedly stopped at nothing to destroy the Guardians, and yet, in this moment, when Camile seemingly held all the cards, he was choosing to parlay. He could just as easily launch a preemptive attack, to which Joshua, cannon or no cannon, would be reluctant to respond given that his daughter was here. Camile, sensing the scientist's puzzlement, could only repeat what he had said before.

"I do not seek conflict; the fate of the world is at stake. From what Miranda and Dallas have told me, I believe this crisis has grown beyond our philosophical differences. All of our futures may well rest on what happens here: today, now. We must put aside our differences, or we will surely all perish."

"I wish," Miranda responded wearily, "that I could believe you."

"Soon, you may find you have no other choice."

16

LESS THAN AN HOUR later, Joshua found himself repeating Camile's words for emphasis. "So you are telling me you are not responsible for attack on my team, the death of Dr. Singala, or the hit-and-run death of Dr. Todd."

"That is precisely what I'm telling you; what I've been trying to tell you since I came aboard."

"And Dallas is not working for the Order?"

"No, although I would be honored to have a man of his caliber. He is not, nor has he ever been, our agent, or spy, if you prefer. Monty was quite fond of the lad." Camile's expressive wave of his right hand drove that point home with emphasis; perhaps a little too much so for Dallas's taste.

"So, according to you, some common enemy lurks here, waiting to eliminate the rest of us."

"Oui, Joshua. What other answer could it be? If the Guardians have had its men murdered, and if it wasn't us – on that you have my oath – then who was it? And, of more pressing concern, why? Why would they kill Dr. Todd? Why would they kill your Dr. Singala? How could they know about the tablets? For that matter, how could they know enough about your organization to infiltrate it and gain access to your research ship?"

"How do you know about our ship?"

"Who do you think awarded you the government contract to build the sister ship? But let's not go there right now. If you agree for us to work together, then we'll have plenty of time for such conversations. My point is simply this: in my opinion there must be another group, one that knows what we know and, until now at least, had the advantage of complete secrecy."

"Well," Joshua replied slowly, "I must confess that recent events suggested as much. But we are nothing any other race would be concerned about, nor do we possess anything that another race might covet. Near as I can see, we have become the flotsam of the universe. Why would these mysterious beings be after us?"

The assembled group fell silent, staring at one another, searching for answers to the questions posited by this new reality. It was Dallas who blurted out the obvious.

"The Ha.Sa.Tan?"

"Dallas! That's enough!" If he could have, Joshua would have come out of his chair.

"Who?" Camile was suddenly alert, leaning forward like a cat trying to catch some tasty morsel.

"He said, 'the Ha.Sa.Tan.'" This time it was Miranda who spoke up. "Father, we don't have time for this nonsense. This common enemy which you suspect exists, they are called the Ha.Sa.Tan, or at least they were. If it wasn't us and it isn't you, then it must be them. Now, Monsieur Fointaine, that's our show of good faith. Let's have yours."

"Very well, Miranda. Dr. Todd; you say he was coming to see you. In point of fact he was coming to meet with me —"

"I refuse to accept that," interrupted Miranda. "He was a trusted member of the Guardians."

"And so he was, but he must have come across something in his research that brought him to the same conclusion that Dallas just voiced. He never had the chance to tell me what he'd found; he said would he would only discuss it face-to-face. That is why I was to meet him.

He was the one who wanted to arrange a truce and arrange a meeting

thought was a manuscript for a book on Mayan culture. Do you remember that I originally put everything in the safety deposit box that
morning? It was with the things that Rocky and I retrieved. Everyone
was so interested in the tablet that I guess I just forgot it. The Maya are
not my area of expertise, so I just put it aside; it's with the rest of my
papers."

"Let's get back to that in a moment," said Camile, "tell me, Joshua,
did Dr. Todd say where he found the tablet?"

"He was rather cryptic about that, but that was not surprising given
the importance of the news; prying eyes, you know the type. All we
know was that he had been on a dig in the central Yucatan area. He
had been a sabbatical of sorts, rather burned out from our primary mission; so we gave him a year off to work on a pet project of his. We were
surprised to hear from him, but we understood the significance of his
unexpected find, which was why we thought he'd returned."

"This is all beginning to make sense," intoned Dallas. "Don't you see,
Joshua? Your Dr. Todd was researching Mayan culture when he found
tablet in a New World archaeological site. Clearly, he must have also
discovered something else; and it's probably what got him killed."

"And," said Joshua, picking up the thought, "if you're not the spy,
and if it's not Camile's people, then the murderer is back on the *Habibti*
with the others, and with this paper you mentioned."

"Not necessarily. I can only assume the murderer is still aboard the
ship because it's not me. As to the paper, I believe Miranda had the good
fortune to collect it with my research when she broke me out of the brig.
I had tossed it in my folder marked 'unresolved,' with copies of the tablet
segments still to be translated. It should still be there."

"And where is 'there?'" asked Joshua.

"In what I assume," responded Dallas, "is Camile's little palace by
the Gulf."

Camile smiled modestly, "I call it home. It is not nearly as elaborate
as your facilities, I'm sure, but it should suffice as a temporary headquarters until your ship arrives."

"I haven't said yes, yet," Joshua replied. "Tell me, how would this proposed partnership work?"

"We'll pool our knowledge and resources, work toward a common resolution and cover one another's back. With any luck we'll find these Ha.Sa.Tan of yours who have been killing your people and solve the riddle of the tablets."

"Then what?"

"I could say," Camile smiled, "let us cross that bridge when we come to it, but for the sake of conversation, let's say we put it to the people, our people. For that matter, I'm willing to put it to a vote of just your people. That's how sure I am. I believe even the Guardians would want to tell the world what we know, if we tell them everything we know. If they say no, then we'll do it your way; we'll conceal our past forever."

"And we should trust your word on that?"

"For God's sake," Camile fumed, "how much more reasonable can I be? You speak of trust, but was it not your ancestors who were the betrayers? You are the descendents of traitors; it is we, the heirs of the loyal few, who should question whether we can finally trust you."

Joshua stared at his counterpart with an anger no longer concealed. Dallas turned to face him, to try and calm the situation, when he noticed the man's eyes begin to glow a deep, crimson red. They shone like a pair of evil beacons, and Dallas drew back in shock. Joshua raised up his hand, with his glowing palm facing outward, preparing to strike out at Camile with the very force of his mind, when Miranda reached out and pushed his hand back down to the tabletop which sat between he and his nemesis.

"You needn't worry, Miranda," said Camile in a steady voice, "your father is powerful, but he cannot hurt me. I am also as those of the beginning time."

"My apologizes," said Joshua finally, after he regained his composure. "Dallas, we — Camile and I — are throwbacks of a sort. As I told you when we first met, occasionally someone is born with a fraction of the powers of our ancestors. Those who are the most powerful among us, it is our mission to lead. So it is for Camile and I; we, who are the two most powerful of our generation."

Dallas glanced at Miranda, who seemed to blush in response. "Don't look at me. My talents mostly amount to parlor tricks. Unlike most other things, our powers develop with age. I am far too young to shoot lightning bolts from my finger tips."

"Even then," added Joshua, "it is extremely exhausting for us. It is not a thing to be used lightly; like opening locked doors on ships."

"Guilty as charged," conceded Miranda, "that's about all it's good for, right now."

"Is that how you broke me out?" asked Dallas. No one bothered to respond to the obvious.

"Still," offered Camile, "I feel it is good for you to practice. It will make you stronger."

"We don't believe in developing these powers for frivolous purposes," countered Joshua, "and if we are going to be working together, then I must ask you to respect our beliefs."

Camile leaned back in his chair with a look of genuine joy and relief stretching across his chiseled face. He extended his hand across the table to seal the deal; it was a gesture not immediately reciprocated.

"Circumstances have brought us together," said Joshua, "but let us not kid ourselves. For the moment, we share a common enemy; that is all we share."

Drawing his hand back, Camile could only offer, "We shall see."

It took another two hours before the logistics and nuance of their new alliance was finalized. Joshua thanked Camile for his offer of accommodations, but felt it better to maintain independent lodgings. He also felt that it would be best to bring the rest of the team to Dubai at once; they could interface with a selected number of Camile's people and prepare for the research ship's arrival, still weeks away. While there were other housekeeping issues to settle, they both decided it would be best to leave them for later.

With little fanfare, Camile returned to his vessel with the backup anomaly detector from Joshua's ship. Once his crew had the device ready the two ships began an agreed-upon standard search pattern, each using their MADs in a coordinated effort to locate the area of maximum anomaly. While the reading appeared onboard the ships, the actual torpedo-shaped device was dragged behind each craft on long stretches of cable. Even in these calm waters, it took steady, careful seamanship to maintain their grid search without fouling one another's lines or otherwise colliding with the other's MAD.

The balance of the afternoon was spent in a futile attempt to locate the anomaly annotated on the charts. As darkness stretched out across the Gulf, the two leaders had to concede that, charts aside, it was a larger body of water and a smaller anomaly than they realized. In the end, they could only annotate their charts, note the coordinates of their failures, drop anchor and prepare for the next day's work.

And so it went, for several days, searching for the anomaly. Dallas was beginning to feel uncomfortable with the various turns of events; it was he, after all, who had proposed this particular body of water in the first place. He tried to remind himself that the anomaly had not been his idea, but that thought gave him no real comfort. It was, Dallas kept telling them defensively, like trying to find one specific grain of sand on the beach. The cliché needle in the haystack became the combined groups' motto. Sam remained defiantly optimistic in the face of continuing failure. For her it was simple; her charts said it was there, so it must be there.

The two ships remained for a further three days of what proved to be fruitless searching. Finally, it was agreed that the boats would return to Dubai, restock their supplies, and return in two days' time to continue the hunt. When they eventually docked at the Dubai marina, it was well after dark, but the horizon was bathed one again in a halogen-induced yellow haze. Dallas disembarked dejectedly behind an overjoyed Jorge, who almost threw himself to the ground in gratitude for dry land. His animated enthusiasm was the sole point of humor for the assembled passengers of the two vessels.

The four full days on the water had given everyone a fresh coat of color, and it became clear to all of them that the months of mole-like behavior, both beneath the museum and aboard the tanker, had rendered them all unacceptably pale. Under the unrelenting desert sun, the white was replaced with various shades of red, from light pink to crimson. All had raccoon eyes where their sunglasses had been, and Dallas found himself battling the urge to scratch, an act that brought with it the realization that the coming effects of full-fledged sunburn were not far behind.

After all those hours of hunting together, the two groups had already begun to develop a certain bond, a shared desire and curiosity to actually locate what everyone had naively assumed would be so easy to find. For the moment, however, exhaustion trumped desire. The only aspiration shared by the two groups was clean sheets and a bed that didn't rock slowly back and forth. Camile took his people back to the mansion, while Joshua headed back to the Burj el Arab, this time with Dallas and Miranda in tow.

It was the following morning, when Jorge, Samantha, Dallas, Miranda, and Joshua assembled in Joshua's suite before anyone felt like addressing the coming need for the division of labor. After devouring a delicious breakfast of eggs benedict, juice, coffee, and assorted pastries, they finally began to concentrate on the necessary issues. It was clear that Dallas had work to do, work that need not be done onboard either of the two ships. For his part, Jorge was quite content to remain on dry land, and he made those sentiments plainly known, in at least two languages. Dallas couldn't help but be amused by Jorge's attitude. He wondered what the geologist would do when the time came to don a wetsuit.

Samantha, as the lone underwater archaeologist, knew that she was vital to continuing the search. Joshua and Miranda were torn about what each of them should do; they both agreed that they couldn't both be in the same place. If one went out into the Gulf, then the other should remain behind. In the end, Joshua conceded it would be simpler for him to remain behind; his disappointment at this realization was both visible and understandable. Jorge promised to use Miranda's two days on land to train her in the use of the equipment; and he reminded her that, if there were a problem, he was only a radio call away. She could only offer a feigned smile of gratitude in reply.

With that matter settled, Joshua informed the small assembly that he had made arrangements with the American University in Dubai to base the research operations on that campus; apparently, he had made them an offer they couldn't refuse. The campus presented two main advantages for the displaced group: it was near the marina, and it's engineering school offered ample lab space and computer access. Jorge's eyes lit up at the possibility of being back in a geology lab again, although at the moment he couldn't imagine what he'd do in it.

While Jorge pondered that question, Joshua informed them that the balance of the team was busy making preparations to be flown in from the *Habibti* and should arrive before Miranda and Samantha set out again. The ship would continue on at flank speed, and it would arrive in the region within 12 days or so. It was only then that it occurred to Dallas to ask the suddenly obvious question; "Have there been any further incidents aboard the *Habibti*?"

"No," Joshua sighed, "Rocky reports that all is quiet; boring, in fact, as you were the one leading the research. It seems everyone's tired of rechecking their equipment."

"That doesn't make me look innocent in Rocky's eyes, does it?" Dallas asked.

"As a practical matter, it proves nothing," offered Joshua, "the real murderer would be forced to lie low, if only to keep you implicated and keep anyone from looking elsewhere."

"And that means we still have a murderer in our midst," said Miranda without emotion. "What precautions shall we take?"

Joshua thought a moment longer before responding, "For the time being, everyone is safe enough. The killer won't dare strike again until the entire team is together again. There's clearly only one choice; the only thing we can do at present is to keep the eye of suspicion focused clearly on Dallas. Perhaps we can use that distraction to our advantage."

"Excuse me?" Dallas had the unmistakable sensation of being a Judas goat.

"Think about, my boy, if the killer thinks we still suspect you, and if he – or she – thinks you are locked away, then they won't dare take any action for fear of showing themselves. No, you'll have to masquerade as the suspect until we get a real lead to follow."

"You're not really going to lock me up, are you?" Thoughts of his short time in the brig flashed uncomfortably through Dallas's mind.

"No, of course not, but we'll have to keep you out of sight. It's best that I arrange quarters for you over at the university. This way you can work undisturbed, have access to research, come and go as you please, and no one will be the wiser."

"Who will we let in on this plan? Even Rocky's security teams can't be above suspicion at this point. The fewer people that know about it the better."

"Yes," said Joshua slowly, "I see your point, though I don't like it much. It means we'll need to keep it from everyone aboard the ship, even security; that makes me uncomfortable, but I agree we have little choice."

"And that gives me something to do," interjected Jorge, "I can come and go from the university also; so can I, what is the expression, run interference for Dallas?"

"I'll be glad for the company, and, George, I'm grateful you feel safe with me."

"Si, but, my friend, if I am to be your sidekick, I must ask one favor."

"You've got it, whatever it is, just name it."

"My name," Jorge said softly, "it isn't George; it's Jorge. Please."

17

DALLAS ROSE EARLY ONCE again and stared out across the grounds of the university. As an academic, he found it comforting to be back on a campus once again; it satisfied something deep within his soul. Perhaps, he thought, when the all this excitement had passed, Joshua could arrange a teaching or research position for him.

From his window, Dallas could see across the length of the campus, from the soccer field and athletic facilities in the foreground, to the main academic buildings farther off. In the distance, across the massive interstate style highway, sat the golf course, which annually hosted the Dubai Desert Classic. He couldn't help but marvel at how the local population had so changed the landscape; truly creating a paradise out of the sand.

Had their distant ancestors attempted the same; creating a new world for themselves after the fall of the Anunnaki Empire? It was a question that Dallas could not answer yet, but it was enough to know that it was a possibility.

Today, he would once again tackle the tablets. It had been nine long days since he had first arrived in Dubai, and he had yet to see much of the city. George – Jorge, he had to remind himself – had been nice enough to smuggle Dallas out of his campus confinement twice in the last three days. Mostly, these trips became shopping expeditions to the city's many malls; each excursion carefully planned to insure that they didn't run into the other members of the team, who were still functioning under the impression that Dallas was under house arrest.

He had seen Miranda briefly the two days before, just as she and Samantha were preparing to set out for the second session of anomaly hunting. The two ship's companies had used their respite from cruising in circles to huddle together and determine their next underwater target. In the end, it was Samantha who once again proposed the next search area; a portion of the gulf slightly to the west-northwest of their original location. The bathyspheric data indicated a slight channel branching off the ancient lake bed and wrapping around the western side of the island. The available charts on the area were frustratingly vague, referencing the anomaly, but giving no specific location.

The rest of the team had arrived from the *Habibti* just as the two smaller vessels were to leave, allowed everyone to be brought up to speed on the search before the ships set out once again. It also gave the team's anthropologist another opportunity to complain endlessly about the many failings of the mission and of Joshua's leadership. For Dallas, the sole saving grace of his faux imprisonment was that he did not have to endure Nancy Graham's incessant whining. It was this thought that filled his mind as he heard the sound of anxious knocking at his dormitory door. Opening it, he found an equally anxious Jorge.

"Dallas," the geologist began earnestly, "where were you last night?"

"Good morning, Jorge, I'm fine. Thanks for asking," he replied, smiling sarcastically.

"Good morning," repeated Jorge, "where were you?"

"Last night … depends on the time. I was working in the engineering building until very late. I came back to the room around one a.m. Why? What's happened?"

"It's Dr. Graham … she's dead."

"What?!"

"I rushed over here as quickly as I could. Rocky's got to be right behind me. Did anyone see you moving around on campus last night?"

"Quite right, Jorge." Rocky's voice could be heard from around the hallway corner, "and I would also like an answer to that same question."

"Look, this is silly." Dallas's tone was unrepentant at the sight of the security chief. "This little charade has gone on long enough. Joshua has cleared me. As for my whereabouts; I worked late, I came to bed. I was working alone and I saw no one. I didn't go out the gate and security didn't come to the building, so I guess I have no alibi. Check with Joshua, he'll fill you in."

"What, you think he didn't tell me? Look, I've got to admit I'm having second thoughts about your guilt; but you know this will be investigated. I'll do my best with the local authorities; we'll get to the bottom of all this." With that, Rocky spun on his heels and was gone.

"Dallas, I am sorry. I was supposed to be your alibi, and I let you down."

"Don't be silly, Jorge. You can't just sit around and watch me translate a tablet. It would be easier to watch grass grow."

"Why would I want to watch grass grow?"

"Just an expression. Look, we should get over to Joshua. There isn't much point in me staying cooped up here anymore."

"Okay," Jorge replied, "he's at his office on campus with Jonathan, we can walk there."

Within minutes, they were the four men were seated in Joshua's office with the rest of the team considering the next move. Joshua had already sent word to Miranda, who immediately turned the ship around. He told the group she expected to be back in the marina by noon. Just then, Rocky strode into the room.

"Joshua," Rocky began, taking absolutely no notice of the others in the room, "I must object involving the police until we are sure of the case of death —"

Joshua cut him off; an act which seemingly required great effort and caused him great pain. "Rocky, we've had this conversation, we have a legal responsibility. Now, you may either join us in our discussion, or go on with your investigation; either way, we must proceed with our meeting."

Rocky locked his eyes on Joshua, but he bowed his head only slightly in submission. "Circumstances require my presence elsewhere." Then he turned and was gone.

The momentary confrontation focused everyone's thoughts on the tragedy of the anthropologist's death and increased their own determination to succeed. According to Jorge, her final conversation with him involved a stated desire to reread some apocryphal texts; she had an idea she wished to present at the next meeting. All that was known, Joshua said wearily, was that she had missed that meeting after checking into the hotel. No one thought much of it at first, writing off her tardiness to jet lag stemming from their early and somewhat complicated departure from the tanker. It was only later, after she'd also missed breakfast, that they grew concerned. It was Rocky who first questioned her absence and sent his team to investigate; they found her dead, in bed. Like Raj, Rocky reported no outward signs of struggle. She was dressed for bed, and to the casual observer, it appeared to be natural causes. Now all that remained was to receive the lab results.

"Realistically," intoned Joshua, trying at last to change the subject, "it is a matter for the police, and, Rocky's objections not withstanding, the police here in Dubai are most efficient. Now, Dallas, have you made any progress in your translations? We have lost valuable time with your internment, and Sam and Miranda's efforts aside, we need to get back on focus."

"Well, yes," Dallas replied, "I have more to read to you, and whoever else cares to listen. Do you want to invite Camile to —"

"Camile?" asked Jonathan suspiciously. "You've met Camile de Fountaine?"

"Joshua, haven't you told them yet?" Dallas sat, puzzled by the omission.

"No," the leader replied tersely, "seeing as that conversation was part of your planned seclusion, it seemed difficult to go into one subject without the other. No matter; I guess now is as good a time as any to bring everyone up to speed."

A few minutes later, the room was filled with gasping mouths and the sounds of silence. None of those assembled could believe that their oldest enemies were now their newest allies; a group they had all been raised to mistrust, if not outright hate. Given the spate of deaths and homicides, the thought of working with them seemed unimaginable. A belief that Joshua had to concede that he still held, given the most recent death, and despite Camile's continuing assurances that the Order was not responsible.

"How do we know," questioned Jonathan, "that they didn't kill Dr. Graham just to play on our fears?"

"Because," said Dallas, "they could have done the same with either Miranda or myself at any time. In fact, as far as I can tell, they have gone out of their way not to hurt anyone."

Turning to face Joshua, he added, changing the subject, "I would like to suggest we reconvene when Miranda returns. I think she'll want to hear what I have translated."

Three hours later, the group reassembled with Miranda and Samantha present. The group waited patiently, first for Rocky, and then for Camile to appear in the meeting room. As they waited, Joshua briefed them on what little further information they had on Nancy Graham's death. He was finishing just as his counterpart entered with a new member of the team: Dr. Khalid Al Rafeeri.

Dr. Al Rafeeri, according to Camile, was an underwater archaeologist with a background in both Mayan and Hindu cultures. He was the most qualified person Camile could bring into the operation on such short notice; the scientist's first impression did not inspire confidence.

Khalid stampeded into the room with the grace of an elephant. He was a short, bulky man with salt-and-pepper hair and beard who wore a traditional white dishdasha. Despite his appearance he spoke eloquently with a properly clipped British accent; the product of many years spent at either Oxford or Cambridge. His personality seemed passive in the extreme, and it came coupled with an annoying habit of being obsequious where Camile was concerned. This type of personality, Dallas thought, would not survive for long with the strong willed, independent minded group that Joshua had assembled. Then, he reminded himself, survival was not looking good for anyone in the group right this minute.

After some discussion, however, Dallas became acutely aware of Khalid's powerful intellect, made even more forceful by the man's soft-spoken approach. Dallas wondered if Khalid's behavior was merely an affectation designed to increase the apparent forcefulness of his arguments. Whether natural or forced, it was a technique that proved effective.

"First, I apologize for my delay in joining you," Khalid began softly, "but Camile felt it best become familiar with your project. Now, my dear professor Roark, I have read the translations of the first tablet which you so kindly provided; thank you very much, by the way. It was a most wonderful piece of linguistic work. Anyway, as I was saying, the Ta.Alal.Azzagh, the Ha.Sa.Tan, as you call them, have you any further thoughts on them?"

"No ... I really haven't given them any more attention," responded Dallas carefully, "I just took them for what the text said. I mean, the extension of the serpent concept as a racial memory brought into Judeo-Christian tradition is fairly obvious and elementary; I'm sure you know that. Of course you know that; why do you ask?"

"Tell me," pressed Khalid, "did Dr. Singala discuss that particular aspect of the translation with you?"

"No," Dallas paused in thought, adding finally, "but he did mention something about someone named Shiva, Siva, something like that, battling serpents —"

"Right, in the Rig-Veda, the Hindu bible, the story of the past cycles of civilization," interrupted Khalid, "then what?"

"Well, we were talking about the flood, and I suggested that maybe the Ha.Sa.Tan had in fact fired on the planet, and that action, in turn, could have melted the polar ice caps, causing the Great Flood, and he goes, 'That's it, you've hit on it,' he mentions this Siva person and heads off to get some research he wanted to bring back to show me. That was the last time I saw him alive."

"Don't you see, our Ta.Alal.Azzagh, his story of Siva, it is all part of a universal memory reduced to myth. In ancient Egypt, the evil serpent that attempts to destroy the daylight is called Apep, in Sumerian – as you know—Azag means both serpent and demon, and is pictured with wings. Ningishzida was the Sumerian Lord of the Underworld, the darkness; as was symbolized by a horned, winged serpent."

"All that's very interesting," offered Dallas, still puzzled, "but what has that —"

"Consider this," interrupted Khalid, "in Mayan history – the culture Dr. Todd had been researching before his death – the ancient mythical ruler of the Toltec was Quetzalcoatl – a name that means winged serpent. He is well known in the Aztec and Mayan cultures as well. It was he who supposedly invented the Mayan calendar, along with teaching the Maya about science, the arts, and agriculture."

"But," interjected Samantha, "wasn't Quetzalcoatl supposed to be a 'good guy,' the god of civilization and all that?" Looking around at the others, who were visibly surprised by her grasp of the subject, she could only add, "What? You think I spend all my time underwater?"

"Quite right," responded Khalid, not getting the joke. "He is traditionally considered the god of light and good. His counterpart was known, is known, as Tezcatlipoca, and was considered the god of night and the stars. But in another version of the story, Quetzalcoatl and Tezcatlipoca came together as allies to defeat Tlatecuhtli, another god; the god of the waters, who existed in the form of a great reptile, a caiman, or a crocodile. They transformed themselves into giant serpents and descended to the waters where Tlatecuhtli dwelled. When they found Tlatecuhtli, each serpent grabbed a hand and a foot. They pulled in opposite directions, tearing the great reptile apart. This dismemberment of Tlatecuhtli supposedly resulted in the Earth's creation."

"Wait a minute," Dallas said excitedly, "this fits in perfectly with my latest translation. Frankly it was making damn little sense; it had no context. Now I can see how that fits with this Mayan legend, but I am beginning to wonder if we're in the right hemisphere. These Mayan legends, Dr. Todd's research —"

"Do not forget," Khalid interrupted, "the tablets are in the ancient tongue that would become Sumerian. I, for one, feel your instincts are quite correct. Clearly, the tablet's information hints at a connection with Quetzalcoatl and the Mayan culture, which, as Camile says, must be significant."

"All that is well and good," a frustrated Rocky spoke up, "but what about Dr. Graham? Her area of expertise had nothing to do with any of this nonsense. Why would someone kill her?"

"Of that, I cannot be sure," replied Khalid. "Perhaps she reasoned it out, just we have done, and it raised a question in her mind, or perhaps she had some thought regarding the murder. For that matter, she may have been killed because she determined the murderer's identity. That would be sufficient grounds for the killer to strike again. We cannot be sure at this point if she was murdered. Her death, however oddly timed, might be a macabre coincidence"

"Sounds more like you want my job," Rocky muttered defensively.

"Not at all, and I mean no disrespect. What I have said comes from the advantage of hindsight. We simply know more now. Now, let us return to the tablet; its presence in the Yucatan does pose some interesting questions. How did a tablet get to there in the first place? Was Quetzalcoatl a member of the Ha.Sa.Tan, or was he Anunnaki? Was he a spy for the empire? Were the Ha.Sa.Tan here on Earth?"

"It certainly sounds that way," interjected Dallas, "either that, or there was at least a battle here. More importantly, given the recent deaths, it is time we address what Camile and Joshua discussed when they first met, but that we have not discussed with you until now: are the Ha.Sa.Tan here still?"

That last thought left the room to silence and, while he'd mentioned it last, it began to seem like the most important issue facing them at this moment. It was a question that none of them had thought to ask, much less consider; yet now it seemed not only possible but painfully obvious.

"But the Ha.Sa.Tan?" questioned Hakeem finally, "how could they still be here? Why would they still be here?"

Dallas explained the rational. "Let's assume that the Ha.Sa.Tan did occupy the planet after the empire's fall. After several thousand years, they appear to leave; only they don't. That would explain why culture suddenly began to reappear; and why the written word would reappear. Both features returned after the people thought the enemy had departed. But what if some of the Ha.Sa.Tan stayed behind to watch the Guardians and the Order?"

"It is really so hard to believe, my friends?" It was Jorge with his own observation. "We've all read the stories: alien abductions, UFOs, Area 51, Roswell, Kecksburg, and Rendlesham Forest. But it must beg the question: if they are still here, why are they still here? And if they are spying on us, then what do we have that they could want; could it be the tablets. That, in turn, supposes both that they know we have at least one tablet, and that they have a reliable inside source telling them what we are doing. These tablets must contain some information to defeat them, or at least something that scares them —"

"Not necessarily," interrupted Miranda. "Perhaps they contain knowledge that will give them even greater power."

"Or both," Dallas added.

"The chambers!" the assembly spoke as one.

"And now," replied Joshua, "you know why their location and the knowledge they contain must be kept hidden for all time. That is why we Guardians have worked so hard, for so long, to keep our past hidden."

"But," countered Camile, "we cannot be as ostriches, keeping our heads buried in the sand, hoping the danger just passes us by. Clearly, hiding is no longer working. It is precisely for that reason we must find the chambers; their contents may represent the only hope for mankind against annihilation."

"Or," countered Joshua, "their contents could be the cause of mankind's annihilation."

"I believe that brings us full circle," said Dallas. "I've found some things in the tablets that may explain all that; the makings of a bold plan to preserve the very essence of the empire from their enemy. Let me read the latest bit for you."

18

"I, EMPEROR EN.LIL.AN, BRING FORTH these words to the descendants of my people, the Anunnaki. We have battled the Ha.Sa.Tan for many years now, and despite everything, they continue to grow in strength. They had knowledge of things for which knowledge should be impossible. How can one know the unknowable? For years, we had asked our scientists and advisors this very question. Our greatest philosophers have also been asked, but to no avail.

"Some, in fear, had said that perhaps the enemy is the tool of the One, the creator of all things, who is angered by us, his chosen people, for turning our backs on the ancient ways. These fearful ones believe we have somehow brought this moment of darkness upon ourselves.

"They claim that the Ha.Sa.Tan are the visible hand of Alla Xul, the Evil One, who had been sent away eons ago after the final victory of the One. There are prophecies that, in the final battle, Alla Xul did not die but was simply cast out; that he would rest for time and then, rising again from his tomb, bring forth his vengeance like a swarm of locusts against the chosen of the One. They long claimed that one day he would stretch forth his hand and raise up plagues against the chosen ones. These people now believe that the Ha.Sa.Tan are this plague.

"I believe none of these things. I believe that all civilizations, in the fullness of time, rise and prosper, thrive and grow, and then, like people in the middle of their years, grow comfortable and lazy in their success and achievements. I believe that, for all peoples, at all times, there comes a moment when they turn their faces from tomorrow and look back on yesterday; to times when their glory was clear and their achievements were stunning. But in looking backward, they fail to see the dangers that each new day brings. We, in our folly, had come to believe that the sun would never set on the empire, and in so doing our people stopped looking toward the challenges brought by each new sunrise. The price of this terrible mistake will be visited for eons on the peoples of the empire, and it seems there is now nothing we can do to prevent that from happening. Now, I have a plan, a daring plan, that will allow us to view a new sunrise, to rise up and defeat the enemy when they, too, have grown too comfortable and secure. We have discovered too late a secret weapon with which to fight the Ha.Sa.Tan. It is too late to stem the tide of the battle, but not too late have the final victory.

"Soon, with the help of the One, we will return to our most secret places where, armed with our most loyal Etlu, our warriors, we will rise up, and then we shall become the Lalartu, the Phantoms, who haunt the evil ones. We will pour forth from our hidden places to retake what once was ours and to establish on Kia a new world – Earth – as the center of the reborn empire of the Anunnaki.

"But heed carefully to my words; upon you and those who come after will come the great burden of preparing our path. You who read this are the gatekeepers, the Guardians of the Way; you must teach those who are to come that they must remember our words if final victory is to be ours."

At this point, Dallas ended his narration by presenting the final piece of text in both its original form, and his translation of it. It was a tongue-twisting and torturous process, through which he proceeded slowly.

"Alaku Edin Na Zu Du Erset La Tari (*Go into the desert! Go into the Land of No Return*) **Ruqu Ultu Shin'ar** (*far from the Land of the Watchers.*) **Lequ Ana Harrani Sa Alaktasa La Tarat** (*Take the road whose course does not turn back,*) **Anna Ina Apsu** (*unto the Place of the Deep Water.*) **Alaku Anna Saquutu Badgaldingir** (*Go to the fortified place of the gods,*) **Ina Ina Kimah**

Ina Dirga Ina Dimtu (*in the tomb of the glowing tower,*) **Su'Ati Nibruki Ina Shulim** (*that place which emits the light of the four regions.*) **Nuru Il Immaru Ina Utukagaba** (*See the light they cannot find, the light at the Gate of the Waters,*) **Asar Anna Peta Daltu Anna Ensi** (*where you open the door for the righteous leader.*) **Panu Sakanu Ana Adannu** (*At the appointed time proceed;*) **Peta Daltu Anna Sarrum** (*open the door for the king.*) **Wabalu Ina Baraggal** (*Carry the Holy of Holies,*) **Ma Ina Rebu Nisiqtu Edubba Abnu** (*and the four precious tablet stones*) **Ina Mul Magan Ziusudra** (*from the celestial metal ship of his life-days prolonged,*) **Ma Peta Kadingir** (*and open the gateway of the gods.*)"

Dallas repeated the passage once more, straight through, in English, "Go into the desert! Go into the Land of No Return, far from the Land of the Watchers. Take the road whose course does not turn back, unto the Place of the Deep Water. Go to the fortified place of the gods, in the tomb of the Glowing Tower, that place which emits the light of the four regions. See the light they cannot find, the light at the Gate of the Waters, where you open the door for the righteous leader. At the appointed time proceed; open the door for the king. Carry the Holy of Holies, the four precious tablet stones from the celestial metal ship of his life-days prolonged, and open the gateway of the gods."

"Frankly," Dallas added, as he finished, "I read that in the original language, because it almost sounded like a chant, something that could have been passed down. I thought it might have some meaning for one group or the other, or both for that matter. Of course, I worked with Sumerian and took it backwards eight millennia; I'm stretching some of the syntax like a rubber band. For all I know, it could just as easily be a recipe for chocolate cake. Does any of that last part have any meaning for either of you?"

"Well, Joshua, I must say you have outdone yourself finding Dallas," said Camile with a broad smile on his face. "Unfortunately, other than the obvious, it means almost nothing to me; but I must admit, Dallas, to being thoroughly impressed with your work. Tell me, Joshua, what do you think it means?"

"It begins clearly enough, Camile, I'm sure you'd agree. The Land of the Watchers - Shin'ar, which would be Sumer. 'Take the road whose course does not turn back,' that sounds like a river to me —"

"Could be the Tigris or Euphrates," added Miranda, "but whatever river it is, it sounds like you're supposed to go down it. You take the river southward through a great desert and to a great body of water, perhaps a sea or ocean, where you'll find a fortress. Apparently whatever we're looking for is there; wherever 'there' is."

"But what about he rest of it?" Jorge asked. "What is all that about opening a door for the gods?"

"Not a door, a gateway; and god only knows," said Dallas, adding, "no pun intended. I did find it interesting, the apparent reference to the space ark of Ziu.Sun.Da.Ra. I have no idea what the Holy of Holies are but he also speaks of precious tablet stones. Are the Holy of Holies somehow related to the emerald tablets; certainly sounds that way."

"Well," Sam offered, "whatever this Holy of Holies thing is, one thing is clear. This text makes it plain that there is, or at least were, tablets aboard the space ship. If that anomaly is the ship, then the final tablet could still be down there. This brings us to our little update." Sam smiled at Miranda as she spoke. "We believe we should have the center of the anomaly pinpointed by tomorrow. We'd like one more day to map it out, but I definitely think we're got it located, at least generally, right now."

That announcement brought a round of cheers and applause; sounds which faded rapidly as everyone remembered the original reason they had been summoned. While Dr. Graham had not be a popular member of the team, she had, nevertheless, been a member, and her death served to remind those assembled from the Guardians that once again one of their own had died. It was also on their minds, though not spoken aloud, that perhaps they could be next. For Camile, Khalid, and the few members of the Order in attendance, it was becoming clear that this alliance was bringing with it an unknown and unanticipated risk.

Camile seized that moment to bring the two groups together. "At the risk of spoiling the moment, I, on behalf of all those of the Order, would like to express our deepest sympathy for the loss of Dr. Graham. While I had not met her, please know that we feel your loss. We find ourselves standing shoulder to shoulder, once again, just as our ancestors did when they prepared to begin their final battle. Now the Anunnaki are once again united against our common foe. We have all lost a comrade here today, and she, along with Drs. Todd and Singala, will earn their rightful place in the history of our people. Now we must move forward, to insure that their sacrifice was not in vain, and that they will not be forgotten. We must find this place of our ancestors and fulfill the destiny that the emperor has called on each and every one of us to fulfill."

The others could feel the electricity of the moment, a moment that Joshua feared would also signify the slipping away of the mission of the Guardians, of the millennia they had served their task, and of the many thousands who had lived and died in honorable service to that quite different mission. Their sacrifices, he promised himself, must also not be forgotten; their deaths must also not be in vain. This was not the moment to speak these thoughts. That time would come when the tide could be turned. For now he did all he could do; he cheered with the others and then endorsed Camile's hopeful words.

After the formal session broke up, Dallas and Miranda went outside and wandered around the campus in the hot, afternoon sun. It had seemed like a good idea at first, but within a few minutes they were reconsidering. They decided to sit under the sparse shade of a small tree, one not native to the area, and surviving only by the grace of God and a functioning sprinkler system. The grass was warm to the touch, and the ground was even harder and less inviting than it had appeared. Still, they sat, silently at first, wondering just exactly what to do next.

"Miranda," Dallas asked finally, "is Camile right? Can the animosity between the two groups be so simply and easily set aside?" He stared at her intently, watching the warm breeze ruffle her beautiful blonde hair, grown longer in the months since they'd first met. She reached up, brushed it to one side, and then caught him watching her. She locked her gaze on his, and for the first time, he noticed her deep blue eyes.

He wondered how he had ever missed them before. Miranda looked up into the cloudless sky, averting his gaze.

"Dallas, I honestly wish I knew. They say the enemy of my enemy is my friend —"

"But," he interrupted, "what side would that logic put the Order on, ours or our enemy's?"

"That's what I've been asking myself." She let her frustration slip. "All my life I've been raised to beware those in the Order; to never trust them, even if you had to talk to them. And while it might be true they haven't killed one another lately, I can assure you, despite what Camile might say, that there was a time, many years ago, when we would not have been in the same room without a weapon in our hands and an ally at our backs. They were not to be trusted, ever. It's hard to overcome that level of doubt just because of one pep talk, no matter how well-delivered."

"I know I suggested it, but can the Ha.Sa.Tan still be here, among us, spying on us? The more I think of it, the harder it is to believe. Judging by the emperor's description, it seems like they'd have a hard time just blending in."

"True," countered Miranda, "but the description he gives definitely resembles those given by people claiming to be abducted by aliens, and it is possible they did their own genetic manipulation —"

"What? They created their own humans?" Dallas was stunned.

"Could be; or perhaps they have the mental power to manipulate how we see them." Miranda offered. "Perhaps it's simpler than that; maybe they recruited followers here on Earth."

"Too much 'perhaps-ing' for my taste," Dallas said, shaking his head. "Can't we go back to the casino?"

"Sorry, Mr. Bond," she said with a smile, "besides, James never had a mission like this. Okay, let's get serious for a minute."

"I think I can handle that." Dallas stretched out on the warm grass and closed his eyes.

"Can we identify these people somehow; you know, using DNA or something?"

"I don't know how; any tests are an extremely long shot at best. Of course, if they are aliens, one would assume that they have a different DNA sequence or chromosome count from hominins. On the other hand, if they have human followers as spies, then no test would be effective. And, forgetting all that, if they do, in fact, have the ability to manipulate our minds, then they could easily keep us from seeing the true test results."

"Here's a thought," Miranda began, twirling her finger in the grass. "Obviously the spy is among our team, and if everything else we're speculating is correct, then that may mean the only ones we can trust to help us are Camile and his people; Jesus, I never thought I'd hear myself say that."

"How'd it sound?" Dallas asked finally.

"Weird," replied Miranda. "Very, very weird; kinda leaves a bad aftertaste."

"Well, Miranda, I think you better get used to the idea. Mind if I join you?" It was Camile de Fountaine.

"It's a big yard." Miranda's answer was curt. Despite everything, she just couldn't help herself.

"I see we have some work to do on our attitudes." His voice had the unmistakable edge of condescension to it. "At any rate," began Camile, taking a seat on the ground beside them, "you were right; we are the only ones you can trust."

"I guess I deserved that," Miranda said contritely. "Pardon me if it takes me some time to adjust."

"So, what did you want to do so badly that you need us?"

They briefly outlined their thoughts, filling in the holes as they went along. It almost became laughable, trying to figure out how they could secretly collect everyone's DNA. Camile finally dismissed it with a wave of his considerable hand.

"It is an interesting concept, but it's problematic at this point. Even if we could organize everyone and get DNA samples, we couldn't get the results back before we go to the tanker. Besides, if we do have Ha.Sa.

Tan in our midst it's not likely they'd just stick out their arms and let us take a sample."

"Not unless they're also human."

"Perhaps," Camile conceded, "but if that were the case then we wouldn't learn anything of use. Let's just keep our eyes open while we try to come up with some other way to identify them. I'll ring you in a couple of days." With this parting piece of advice, Camile strode off toward the parking lot and his waiting Mercedes limo, leaving the pair to sweat under the increasingly hot sun and warm grass.

"Okay," began Dallas, as Camile drove away, "Let's make this simple; you watch the girls, and I'll watch the boys, except for your father. You watch him."

"My father!"

"Do you know another way?" interrupted Dallas. "I don't. If the Ha.Sa.Tan do have the ability to control minds, then you'd never know if that person is, in fact, your father."

It was an odd thought. With all that had transpired it was the one thing that had never occurred to her; the possibility that her father might actually have been replaced by an impostor. While it may, at one time, have seemed too farfetched to consider, she now had to admit it was not beyond the realm of reason.

"Granted," she finally conceded, "but this whole conversation has a certain paranoid feel to it. Aren't we playing right into the murderer's hands, doubting one another?"

"Hopefully not; but we must find a way to spot them. We must know whether or not it's not the Ha.Sa.Tan after us; or if they are, but have human followers."

"This brings us back to where we started. A thought just came to me; want to hear it?"

"Shoot."

"How do we know that Camile isn't also a Ha.Sa.Tan spy? I mean, the Order has been looking for the chambers for centuries; wouldn't they be the obvious ones for the Ha.Sa.Tan to infiltrate."

"I'm getting a headache." Dallas teased her, rubbing his temples; only partly in humor.

19

TRUE TO HIS WORD, two days later Camile called Dallas's cell phone. By now it was late in the afternoon, and for hours, Dallas's mood had alternated from frustration to anxiety and back again. He had felt that way ever since he'd received the phone call earlier from Joshua concerning Nancy Graham; he confirmed that she had also been poisoned.

Apparently, just like Raj, she suffered cardiac arrest after ingesting a rather exotic, and potent, type of alkaloid poison, Pyrrolizidine, which occurs on the skin of the Dendrobates Pumilio, or poison-dart frog. This proved interesting, primarily because this species is native to Central America. Could this, as Joshua had posed to Dallas, be another link with Dr. Todd, whose research on the Maya had taken him to this particular region? Dallas's only contribution to that thought was that she had kissed the wrong toad; a joke that fell miserably flat.

He walked across the campus carrying his backpack, and stood just outside the security gate. Loitering aimlessly in front of the uniformed guards, Dallas could not shake the feeling that he was making a drug drop for a Colombian drug lord.

The horizon was being swallowed by the coming darkness; yet beneath the jet black sky, the nighttime glowed yellow-orange from the street lights that seemed to illuminate everything beneath them. Finally,

Dallas could see Camile driving toward the appointed location, just out of earshot of the main security gate of the university. Owing to the university's location at the end of a street and just past the local Hard Rock Cafe, it was clear that when any vehicle appeared, it was there for a reason. The campus was truly on the road to nowhere; and any car that got with eyeshot of the gate had no choice but to proceed on until it arrived at that point. And at this moment, nowhere is exactly where Dallas felt like he was; either that or the Twilight Zone.

Moments later, a large, stretch-Mercedes pulled to a stop in front of him. The windows were so heavily tinted that there was no hint of its occupants, but he knew it was Camile, if for no other reason that no one could hide in plain sight quite like Camile de Fountaine. His musings were cut short by the barely audible sound of a window lowering followed by a hand waving for him to come inside.

"Hello, Camile," Dallas said as he slid his six-foot-five-inch frame in beside him. "Joshua called me right after you did. Two things: it seems Nancy Graham was poisoned with the same alkaloid poison that killed Raj. It's a poison native to an unusual type of Central American frog. Also, the *Habibti* will be entering the Gulf of Oman in tomorrow night. We'll be taking the copter out to the ship sometime Monday so we still have time to find the murderer."

"Hmmmm, interesting bits of news. Still, even if we somehow determine the killer's identity before we depart for your research vessel, I would suggest we not tip our hand until after we get back aboard."

"Why?"

"Because once on board, we'll be in a closed and controlled environment. If we hold off, perhaps we can learn something of value."

"Perhaps," Dallas muttered, "but it would be hard to feign ignorance of the killer's identity merely for a tactical advantage."

"I understand, and if I had been through what you'd been through, I'd probably feel the same way."

Dallas could think of no response to that, and the two rode in silence for a while.

"Dinner?" Camile offered finally as a formality, and with only slight enthusiasm.

To Dallas the tone of Camile's voice suggested that politely declining would be preferred. "Thank you, but no. I really should check in with the others over at the Burj el Arab; I do hope you understand."

"Absolutely, my boy, absolutely." The relief in Camile's voice was self evident. "I'll have the driver run you over there, and then I think I shall go back to the villa and turn in, this jet lag is still with me; I'm not as young as I used to be, you know."

To tell the truth, that thought had not occurred to Dallas before. He had no idea of Camile's age. His only assumption was that the leader was older than him. Upon reflection, he had to concede that his assumption was based as much on Camile's position of authority as anything outwardly visible. For all Dallas knew, Camile could be a tired fifty or a youthful seventy; there was a large margin for error where this man was concerned. In truth, he carried the thought further; the same could be said of Joshua. Were it not for the wheelchair, there would be no preconception of age.

When the limo deposited Dallas at the hotel he bid Camile good-night and went immediately to Miranda's room. He arrived to find her very agitated, pacing around the room like a hungry lioness waiting for steak to be pushed under the door.

"What's wrong?" Dallas called out to her back, after she'd turned away from the just opened door.

"I can't believe it," she kept muttering to herself, "I just can't believe it."

"What? You can't believe what?"

"My father! He's planning on arresting Camile and his people once they get aboard the *Habibti.*"

"That's kidnapping."

"Thank you! That's what I said to him. I told him, 'you can't just arrest someone. You can't slap them in irons like common thieves.'"

"And he said?"

"'Watch me!'"

"Is there any point in my talking with him?"

"How the hell would I know? I feel like I'm talking to a brick wall. You can talk to a wall as easily as I can."

"Come on, let's go try again."

"Don't bother," came a voice from behind them, "I'm not changing my mind."

The pair wheeled around to find Joshua in the doorway, with Rocky behind him. Sliding the joystick forward, he rolled into the suite. His security chief walked purposefully across the room, taking up a flanking position.

"Father, how long have you been there?"

"Long enough; brick wall, am I?"

"Joshua," Dallas began, trying to play the role of mediator, "surely we can't just confine Camile and Khalid aboard the *Habibti*. We agreed we had to work together. There must be another alternative."

"I only agreed to those terms to keep him and his people in view until the ship arrived; that happens tomorrow. Do you think for a moment that I believed that song and dance about Mayan legends and Dr. Todd? Hogwash. We don't have to look any further than the Order to find the cause of our troubles. Just like always, they are our enemy. Do you remember when we first met; we talked about Occam's Razor?"

"Yes ... "

"Well, which is easier to believe, that the Order is our enemy; or that we have all been infiltrated by evil alien midgets with big heads and big black eyes?"

"How do you know they are midgets?"

"I was speaking figuratively, for Christ's sake. Dallas, I know Camile's kind, they are killers; we can't trust them, never."

"You say you know they are evil; that they've killed. But how are we different? Has our side ever killed?"

"Tea?" The director wheeled his chair into the suite's kitchen with Dallas in tow, leaving Rocky and Miranda in the sitting room.

"Joshua, I need to know."

"You really should try it; it's very relaxing."

"JOSHUA."

"My dear Dallas, what would you have me tell you? Can I say the innocent haven't been caught in the crossfire? I can't. Should I tell you that all those who died deserved it? I wouldn't, although I'm sure most did. Should I claim their sacrifice was all for the greater good? Well, perhaps that's true, although I don't think they'd agree with me.

"The fact is that we – both the Order and the Guardians, are trying to steer the entire planet in particular directions, different directions. We are both attempting to direct the social and cultural evolution of billions of people toward different, specific points. Accomplishing that task has put us on various sides of various conflicts at various times. Millennia ago, we advocated and promoted the divine right of kings, and when the time came, we engineered their downfall. Through the centuries we've aided all sides because we had to produce a particular outcome. We have aided fascists, communists, and democratic governments; not because our agenda has changed, but rather because it has not. Each, in turn, served a specific need at a specific time, to produce a specific result. We have not set out to injure anyone or any group out of any sadistic desire. What we have done had to be done. The alternative was —"

"The alternative," interrupted Dallas, "could have been to let mankind develop in its own way, in its own time. Perhaps we would have surprised you."

"Or perhaps we would all have been destroyed; or perhaps we'd be living the same destitute and primitive existence as your primitive ancestors were thirteen thousand years ago, living on roots and killing stray animals just to survive. Never, and I mean never, underestimate the bloodthirsty nature of your fellow human. No, Dallas, we had to direct that negative impulse, channel it, toward a greater good. The dictators, the power hungry, the freedom fighter – each got what he thought he wanted, but collectively, their vision was myopic. We do not plan by the leader or by the decade, but by the century and the millennium. We manage on a macro level; we steer big events and leave the little ones to themselves. Imagine the human race as pieces of flotsam in a stream

— to direct that flotsam you don't need to control each piece, you just need to control the stream.

"Then how are you different from the Order?"

"In actions, not at all. In motives we are worlds apart."

"So the end justifies the means."

"Pseudo-intellectual double talk. We are in a war, not one of our choosing but a war nevertheless. We are two Goliaths doing battle in the midst of an unsuspecting rabble. We have no choice but to fight with the same finality, the same brutality, as our enemy; because that is what war is. There is no easy way to kill, no good way to die. The only solution is to fight the war to win the peace."

"What does peace mean for you?"

"We must lift humanity to a higher level of existence, of understanding, of—"

"And," Dallas exploded, "how big a pile of dead bodies will it take to lift up the living?"

"It is time you stopped to consider how many dead bodies there might be if we hadn't been doing what we've been doing all these centuries."

"But what of your promise to Camile. Don't we all suffer if we sacrifice honesty on the altar of victory?"

"Sacrifice honesty on the altar of victory? God, what nonsense; you sound ridiculous. Let me tell you my view: honesty is so rare and valuable that it must be dispensed sparingly and with great care lest it be wasted."

"Nig-ge-na-da a-ba in-da-di nam-ti ì-ù-tu," Dallas stared squarely at Joshua as he quoted from the tablets, first in Sumerian and then in English, "Whoever has walked with truth generates life."

"Father, Dallas is right! We must not sacrifice who we are." Miranda had caught only the end of the debate, but what little she heard disturbed her greatly. She did not recognize this man who seemed to be her father in appearance only. Ever quiet, Rocky hung in the shadows behind her.

"This discussion is pointless. As I said when I came in, my mind is made up. You two have only one decision to make. Will you support me or not?"

Both nodded reluctantly but neither offered a verbal endorsement. They sensed the futility of their effort and the need not to alienate him any further.

While Joshua sipped quietly on a hot cup of tea, Dallas and Miranda exchanged crossways glances. She seemed to understand Dallas's passive acceptance of her father's harsh attitude; in fact, she understood Dallas's position better than her own father's. After a period of time, the fire went out in Joshua's eyes and be began behaving more like the father she remembered.

The outburst seemed to tire him and soon Joshua excused Rocky and himself, saying that they had to work on preparations for the coming transfer back to the ship. There would be a meeting in the morning, not too early; about nine a.m., over breakfast. With that last bit of news, he left, with his watchdog in tow.

"What was that all about?" she muttered rhetorically.

"Have you ever known your father to take such a harsh position, on anything?"

"No, never. I mean it sounded like him, but not him; almost an exaggeration of himself. I've never heard him define our mission so cynically. He's had his moments, but all that crap about doing whatever it takes to get the job done; Jesus. Sure, we're concerned about the big picture, but I'm not aware we ever helped any group just to advance our cause; that would go against everything we believe in."

"Perhaps you haven't been told everything yet."

"Something like that would be a little hard to hide, don't ya think? Still, if it isn't my father, it's an incredible performance. I'd swear it was him."

"Well then? Is he a fake, and do we tell Camile?" His tone was decidedly rhetorical.

"I gather you have an opinion on that."

"Yes, yes I do; at least on the second point. Camile wouldn't want us to show our hand until we were back aboard ship. I doubt telling him would change that fact. On the other hand, if your father is correct, then we risk protecting Raj's and Nancy's murderer. For now all we can do is keep our eyes open and try to stay in your father's good graces. The last thing I want is to end up in the brig again."

"Agreed. In the meantime, I'm going to try and discreetly trace my father's travel since he left the ship. If he has somehow been affected, then whatever happened must have happened after that point. I'm sure he was himself when we were all aboard the *Habibti*."

"I'm sorry." Dallas's tone took a markedly humbled tone.

"For what?"

"All these troubles started when you broke me out. It might have been better to have left me there."

"Nonsense. Raj was already dead. Clearly, Nancy Graham's death proves the killer would have eventually struck again, whether we were onboard or not. If anything, the timing suggests attempting to use you as a patsy."

"But your father … " Dallas's voice trailed off. He didn't want to utter the obvious, unspoken possibility.

"Really, Dr. Roark, I'm tougher than that." Her use of his formal *nom de titre* told Dallas more than her words; he let the subject drop.

"All right, what do you want me to do while you're backtracking your father's movements?"

"You stick to what you are best at: keep translating those tablets."

20

HOURS LATER MIRANDA STOOD at her glass balcony door staring out over the Gulf, pondering her next move. In lass than a day they would all take a Sikorsky Helibus back to the *Habibti*, and she was fresh out of ideas. In the time since Dallas left she had tried every possible source and backchannel to quietly check on her father and his activities. She had found out absolutely nothing. There had been no further discussions with either her father or Rocky regarding Camile's arrest and everything seemed, on the surface, to be perfectly normal. Dallas had been as supportive as possible, but for her, that seemed odd and unfamiliar territory.

Perhaps her father was right, at least in so far as her inability to allow for entanglements. Relationships were, to her, a needless complication; a distraction which could at any moment jeopardize whatever mission she might be on. Now, on the most important mission of her life, when clear thinking was crucial, not only to her but to the entire human race, she found her mind wandering inconveniently down winding paths that always seemed to lead to Dallas. Reflexively she shook her head, as if trying to physically dislodge an offending thought. It was only partially effective.

To top it all off, she hadn't been able to reach Hans, and no one seemed to know where he'd gone. Why had Hans vanished? What had become of the rest of his station's personnel? What about their agents at the airport? What was Dallas doing right now? She shook her head; there was that thought again. In a fit of resignation, she reached for the phone only to have it ring as her hand drew near. It was Dallas, insisting she come to the university at once. He would tell her nothing else, except that he had something to tell her of the utmost importance. Ten minutes later, she was walking into his makeshift lab at the university's engineering building, wondering involuntarily whether Dallas closed his eyes when he kissed someone. Her mind was still wandering down that particular path when she entered his lab to find him, deep in thought, staring at a billboard-sized image of all the tablets. She couldn't help but admire his intensity, the depth of his intellect, and his magnificently shaggy salt and pepper hair.

"Dallas?"

"Oh, good, you're here."

"Why the rush; what's the urgency?"

"Miranda, do you remember the first time we met?"

"Oh yes; I wanted to kick your ass." She couldn't help but smile at the memory.

"Well, I need to ask you something … tell you something … and when I do, you may feel that same way again."

"Oh." She was suddenly serious. She couldn't image what he could say that would make her feel that way, and her inability concerned her. What, she wondered, could he possibly say?

"Miranda … I was thinking about what Jorge said, remember … about Nancy's last words being about re-reading some apocryphal texts? That started me thinking about the night Dr. Todd died; he said, 'they are watching.' Anyway, Jorge got me thinking about Biblical texts, which really wasn't my academic specialty. Finally, I remembered where I'd heard of the Watchers."

"I'm not following you. There's no mystery about The Watchers; you know, Sumer, Shin'ar – Land of the Watchers. Even your most recent translations make that plain."

"Quite; but I mean aside from the Sumerian inference. Are you familiar with the Hebrew apocryphal text the 'Book of Enoch'?"

"Enoch?"

"Enoch; great-grandfather of Noah. The book is a collection of stories about a group called Watchers and divine judgment. Apparently, the early Christian Church rejected the Book of Enoch and tried to destroy it; only two complete ancient copies survived. The first copy was rediscovered in Ethiopia in the 1770s by a Scottish adventurer named James Bruce. Anyway, the first Book of Enoch is referred to as the 'Book of the Watchers.'"

"All that's extremely fascinating, I'm sure, but—"

"Bear with me a moment," Dallas interrupted. "In that book, the Watchers are referred to as the Holy Watchers. It describes the rebellion of angels. The fallen angels are also called Watchers; they had sex with human women, who then give birth to a race of wicked demonic giants; the Nephilim."

"That's silly; we're the Nephilim; that is, the Nephilim were the Anunnaki descendents on Earth."

"Exactly my point, but don't get ahead of me. Anyway, Enoch tells how the fallen angels came to him, bringing culture and civilization. They told Enoch they were fugitives from the Watchers, and they would be punished if they returned home. Enoch attempted, in vain, to intercede on their behalf."

"I still don't see—"

"Miranda, it's as plain as ... . . Look, if the Watchers are in fact related to the Anunnaki, then Enoch's fugitives from the Watchers could be the first Guardians. Joshua suggested as much the very first day we met. But the Enochian texts also clearly state that the Nephilim, the descendants of these fugitive Watchers, became the demons of Satan – or Ha.Sa.Tan, a term that exists also in the proto-Hebrew tongue. The bottom line: the Anunnaki on Earth and the Ha.Sa.Tan are somehow related."

She said nothing, she just stared; not an angry evil glare but one of puzzlement. Was it, Dallas wondered, an expression of genuine surprise, or of surprise in his realizing the truth. Was she wondering what to do next, or wondering what to do next with him?

"That is absurd," she whispered finally, not convincing even herself. "These apocryphal texts are separated by many millennia. There's no telling how much that text may have evolved in over thousands of years."

"You believe in your many oral traditions, and they've lasted for many more millennia."

"But how could we be related to the Ha.Sa.Tan? We are not even of the same species."

"Aren't you? Perhaps there is another interpretation. Perhaps it is suggesting that the Ha.Sa.Tan infiltrated those Anunnaki on Earth. That could be, since we know the Ha.Sa.Tan existed before the Watchers of Enoch's time."

"But the Ha.Sa.Tan are little gray men with big black eyes, just as the emperor said. We look nothing like them, we are nothing like them. For that matter, we don't even know for sure if the Ha.Sa.Tan even still exist. You've been working alone too long."

"Perhaps, but the emperor says that his knowledge of the Ha.Sa.Tan was mere legend; clearly he'd never seen one. Think about the implication when he talks about how the Ha.Sa.Tan infiltrated the worlds of the Empire. Little four foot tall aliens couldn't have done that. No, whatever else you say about them, they must be, or be able to assume, human form. We cannot be sure of their actual physical appearance."

"If you are right, why tell me? How did you know I wasn't Ha.Sa. Tan? How did you know I wouldn't strike you down?"

"I know. I know because you wake up with a smile on your face … because you can be frustratingly chipper before your first cup of coffee … because you take forever to get ready in the morning … because you love mushroom omelets … because you have a sarcastic streak even wider than mine … and because when you believe in something, or someone – like me – you believe completely … . In short, Dr. Miranda Fisher, I know you. You may be tough, but you couldn't be evil if you tried. You try to hide it, but you are too kind, too caring, and too loyal for that."

That was not the answer she expected; she locked her gaze on his, but said nothing. For the moment, there was nothing she was ready to say.

"Let me put it another way," she began finally, "what I hear you saying is that there is a spy among us, but we already know that. So, even assuming you're right, how does this little insight help us?"

"I … I don't know for sure. What I'm seeing, if this is correct, is not just a rogue spy but an infiltration that may have begun thirteen thousand years ago and continues to this day. Remember, Dr. Todd said, 'are watching'; not were. We could be confronting another whole layer within the Guardians and the Order, a layer you know nothing about; one that's watching what we do, waiting for us to find whatever it is we find."

"And you suspect my father?"

"No … . No, I don't. If he were Ha.Sa.Tan, then there would be no need for the murders, he could have just waited to see what we might find. No, it's someone else; someone involved with what's going on, but not in complete control of it. Whoever it is, I don't believe they originally intended to kill Raj and Nancy. After all, if they've kept a low profile for so long, why change now; unless something forced their hand. It's my guess the spy was found out and felt he had to silence those two."

"What about Dr. Todd?"

"The simplest answer is that whatever he discovered in the Maya tomb may have revealed the true nature of the Ha.Sa.Tan infiltration. Maybe it was his stated desire to bring the two groups together; that would be the last thing the Ha.Sa.Tan would want. In fact, they've probably responsible for the continuing animosity between the two groups. Of course, if your father felt betrayed he has demonstrated he is clearly capable of retribution. Finally, there is the possibility, however remote, that Todd's death is not even related to the other two."

"So, what? Now, we could have two murderers?"

"Look, I'm not head of security. I'm just telling you what I see. First, the MO is different: two poisonings, one hit and run; two with no witnesses, one with a witness; two inside, one in public —"

"I get the point. Did you know you talk almost entirely in complex sentences?"

"Oh."

"Better, much better."

"Very funny."

"So, what have we got – two murderers and the Anunnaki are really the Ha.Sa.Tan? Does that just about cover it?"

"Pretty much."

"And what do we do about all this information?"

"We watch … we listen … but most of all, we have to be ready to act, and we have to know we're watching each other's back."

"Wouldn't you rather watch my front?" Miranda cringed and looked away the moment she said that. "Forget I just said that. So let me tell you what I've been up to. I've been going nuts trying to contact Hans. I can't raise him, it's like he just vanished."

"Try the casino?"

"Very funny; and yes, I did."

"Airport?"

"Everywhere. I called everyone I can think of and no luck; done a lot of catching up though. I hope I never see another telephone. My fingertips are sore from punching buttons."

"Ah, do you want me to kiss them and make it better?"

"Rain check." She blushed, and cursed herself for it. "How's the translating going?"

"Truly amazing. Look at this," Dallas gestured toward the billboard-sized tablet enlargements behind him, "I am literally rewriting human history with every pictograph I translate, and you know what I just found out?"

"No," a voice from behind them said, "what did you just find out?"

"Hello, father," said Miranda without turning around, "what brings you here at this time of night?"

"Exactly my question, my dear."

"Dallas asked me to stop by." She pivoted to face her father when Rocky appeared from around the corner.

"I'm jealous," said Joshua mockingly, "there was a time when you'd only come running when I called."

"Oh, please. I didn't 'come running.' We're supposed to be a team, all of us. We used to be, what happened to that?" Looking at her father's escort, she added, "Rocky would you excuse us for a moment please? You can wait in the hall."

The security chief wavered for a moment, as if waiting for Joshua to intercede. Then he abruptly spun on his heels and walked out. "I'll be right outside the door, Dr. Fisher, if you need me."

Dallas looked back at Joshua just as the older man shook his head, and sagged in his chair as if waking from a dream.

"Joshua, you okay?"

"Yes, Dallas, just tired, I guess. The strain of all this is getting to me." His voice seemed softer, gentler somehow.

"Father, what's going on? You've seemed so different lately."

"I know, Miranda, I know; but I don't know why. Sometimes it seems like it's someone else speaking. I know it's me, but it's not me. I guess I'm just getting old; this wheelchair must be getting to me. I'm so tired ... so tired."

"So," Dallas spoke up, filling the void, "would you like to hear the latest?"

"This may surprise you, but I think I can wait until tomorrow, when you tell the rest of the group. Really, I just came by because Rocky wanted to check on Dallas. I'm going to get him to take me back to the hotel."

"Daddy?" Suddenly Miranda was a little girl again, in spite of herself. "Do you want us to go with you? Maybe we should call Karen, have her check you out."

"No, let's leave Dr. Pollard out of this, at least for now. I think I just need a good night's sleep. We've got a lot to do tomorrow: hearing Dallas latest work, transporting everyone out to the *Habibti* ... so much to do." Then, in a louder voice, "Rocky, I'm ready, let's head back to the hotel."

Rocky said nothing, but he strode back into the lab. As he moved closer to Joshua, the Guardian leader began to sit more erect, and the look of fatigue faded from his face.

"Let's not have anymore of these clandestine, late night meeting, is that clear?" Joshua's voice was clear and strong, and his tone slightly menacing, "Let's go, Rocky. Remember, you two, meeting tomorrow at the hotel; 9:30 a.m., be on time."

The two watched in silence and confusion as Joshua and Rocky disappeared. Dallas started to speak, but Miranda signaled for silence while she moved slowly toward the door. Cautiously, she peeked around the doorway to make sure that the pair had truly departed the building. Convinced that they were once again alone, Miranda returned to Dallas.

"Okay, I know he's your father ... but that was weird."

"Yep. That's exactly the scientific term I would use – weird, very weird."

"One minute he's tired and gentle. The next he's almost paranoidly suspicious."

"'Paranoidly'? Is that a word?"

"You understood my meaning. What's all that about clandestine, late-night meetings. Since when did he care if we met alone? For god's sake, we are a team, after all."

"A good one, I think." Miranda grinned, in spite of herself.

"Me, too. It's almost like he had multiple personality disorder; no offense."

"No, I agree with you."

"And what was that about being on time? He adopted an almost imperial demeanor. That just didn't seem like Joshua."

"I don't know what to say ... .Perhaps it really is just the strain."

"Miranda ... has it occurred to you that you might have to be ready to 'assume command' of the Guardians?"

"A coup? You expect me to betray my own father?"

"I'm not encouraging you to betray anyone, but the day may be coming when you have to choose between your father and your duty."

"And you say you know me? How would I choose?" But her denial was hollow because she knew Dallas was right, and because she, too, realized that success might require she make that choice.

21

DALLAS ROLLED OVER AND glanced out the dormitory window as the sun began to break the horizon. Finally, the day arrived when he could leave campus and return to the ship. He had a plan in mind for what he had learned from the balance of the tablets; a plan he had shared with no one but Miranda.

They had worked late into the night on their scheme, and it would be risky, but they reasoned there was no other choice. They also agreed that Camile and Khalid must not be locked up aboard ship, although the solution to that problem was more elusive than what to do with the translations.

It was finally Dallas who hit on the leverage point they could use – could they really afford to leave those two on the surface while Joshua and Rocky were on the seabed. Given the depth, they would face a two-hour decompression period before they could return to the ship; meaning that should anything transpire aboard ship, the Order would have a twelve-hour head start. No, Dallas had told Miranda rhetorically, this was a prime example of the old cliché about keeping your friends close and your enemies closer. Only keeping them on the sea floor with them could keep other members of the Order at bay.

Dallas's thoughts wandered back to the present. He rolled slowly out of bed and stumbled toward the shower; it would be another terrible coffee-free morning. At the appointed time, he and the other remnants of the original group, with Camile and Khalid in tow, gathered at the Burj el Arab. They were gathered in one of the hotel's meeting rooms, with a pile of baggage thrown haphazardly to one side.

As he double-clutched a hot, soothing mug of strong coffee, Dallas marveled at how so much baggage could be acquired by so few people in so short a time in one city. Obviously, while he had been working, the others had found the time to conquer every souk and bazaar in Dubai. For his part, Dallas's final moments before gathering had not been shopping, but in thanking the members of the university's staff for their hospitality during his all-too-brief stay. He volunteered to return and teach someday; an offer greeted by nervous laughter and awkward glances, which left Dallas feeling very uncomfortable. He began to regret not spending more time filling suitcases as his colleagues had done.

As the group gathered, one of Rocky's minions walked around, handing out both an itinerary of the meeting and a schedule for the group's exodus to the *Habibti*; documents which left an unconsulted and perplexed Dallas wondering about his current status. He didn't have long to ponder such thoughts. Joshua called the room to order and invited everyone to sit in the chairs arranged in front of the small presentation board residing at the far end of the room. According to the schedule, Rocky would first review organizational and security issues, then have everyone cleared by the local customs official – a mere formality – and, finally, when the meeting was over, organize everyone for the flight back from the marina's heliport to the ship.

Karen Pollard followed Rocky with a briefing on diving and living at depth aboard the Seahab. As Joshua had told them weeks before, they would be breathing a mixture called TriOx, composed of varying amounts of oxygen, helium, and nitrogen both on Seahab and while diving. Dallas knew from the team's earlier scuba instruction that diving with normal air for long periods below depths of one hundred feet could bring on a condition called nitrogen narcosis, similar in effect to alcohol intoxication. Using pure oxygen was not an option, as increasing oxygen consumption at such pressures was potentially fatal. This meant that the only other choice was using a combination of gases.

As a precaution, she announced two main medical protocols: the first, and most disappointing to the group, was the she wanted everyone totally saturated to depth before the first dive. She planned to introduce the TriOx atmosphere gradually so that the first dive could not take place until they had been in place on the sea floor for three days. Second, she announced her intention to limit the amount of diving that would be allowed until she could assess the effects of the atmosphere and general stress of all those aboard Seahab.

"Doctor," Dallas asked finally, "what effect will all this have on the need for decompression?"

"Well, decompression requirements are a function of the time it takes to safely expel the nitrogen that has been absorbed into the body's tissues under pressure. Unlike oxygen, nitrogen is not metabolized by the body, and so it builds up in the tissues. The longer the diver is at depth, the more nitrogen is absorbed. Also, gas compresses with depth, so if the diver returns to the surface too quickly the nitrogen can expand faster than the body can handle it. In this case, it separates from the blood and forms bubbles. These nitrogen bubbles, in turn, can cause a variety of problems, some temporary, others permanent. In more serious cases I've seen—"

"But what about us?" interrupted Dallas.

"Well, as we will be living on the Seahab for many days, the decompression time would be the maximum: twelve hours regardless."

"Why twelve hours?" It was Jorge, who was suddenly uncomfortable with the entire subject.

"The simple answer, Jorge, is that all bodies reach a point of saturation, where no more nitrogen can be absorbed at the given depth; liking filling a glass with water. Once it's full, it's full. Once you reach that point, the decompression time is twelve hours; it doesn't matter if you're down there a day, a week, or a year it would still take twelve hours to decompress from saturation. The only thing that matters, with regard to Seahab, is any dives to a much greater depth than the station. Once you are all acclimated to that depth, any decompression requirements will be figured relative to that depth —"

"Which means," interrupted Sam, "that, assuming the Seahab is based at a hundred and sixty feet, we can dive down one atmosphere from that depth – thirty-three feet – and not require decompression time. So, basically, our normal working range will be from one hundred and sixty to a hundred and ninety-five feet."

"Now, as we all know, Samantha is the most qualified diver here," Joshua began, before catching himself, "along with Dr. Al Rafeeri, of course. As such she will be serving as the team's dive master, as well as working with Dallas in coordinating the dive site and the 'dig'."

"Will I be working with Dr. Layne?" Khalid spoke up, politely, from the back of the room.

"Ah, yes, Dr. Al Rafeeri, don't worry; you have not been forgotten." His sideways glance to Rocky was barely noticeable, except to Miranda and Dallas, who winced, but said nothing. Turning his attention to Dallas, Joshua offered a perfunctory, "Do you have anything to add?"

"Not at the moment," he replied, "except for the obvious. When we get back onboard … how long will we have?"

"How long would you want?" The reply was almost a challenge.

"We'll have at least a day," interjected Sam calmly. "Proper dive protocols require at least twenty-four hours at sea level prior to diving. As we will be flying to the ship via helicopter, we shouldn't begin the Seahab operation for at least a day. That shouldn't present a problem, as we'll be rejoining the ship with she's still the Gulf of Oman; we're at least a day from our goal anyway."

"Okay," Dallas began, feeling the need to reassert his authority, "say a full day after we get back onboard, we'll have a day to go down our individual checklists and our equipment lists, etc. In short, we'll have one day to get done what should have taken a week, including getting whatever research or personal belongings we are allowed to bring."

The room went silent for a moment. Everyone shifted uncomfortably in their seats, unsure of how to respond.

"Dallas." It was Hakeem who finally spoke. "While you were ... gone ... we did get a lot of that done, however, I have no doubt we need to double-check everything. Also, we did get all the gear and most of our personal items on our assigned sections of Seahab. You'll need to get your things together; I'm sure you'll want your own research."

"Right ... thanks." Dallas felt suddenly humbled by the realization that their world hadn't stopped just because he'd stepped off it. "Anyway, I do have to finish translating the final bit of the tablets, but that can wait until later. I'd like to get back to the ship as quickly as possible. Miranda, do you have anything to add?"

"Nope. Notta thing ... boss." Her obvious show of support did not go unnoticed by anyone in the room.

"Very well, then." Joshua conceded the moment, "I must agree with Dallas. We need to get to the ship right away. Oh, Camile, my apologies, do *you* have anything you wish to say?"

"No ... yes. I would like to wish all of us Godspeed and blessings on this mission. And, I would like to say how wonderful I think it is that our two groups, separated by millennia of distrust, have come together to rediscover our common destiny."

A wave of "hear, hear" washed across the room, joined in reluctantly by Joshua and Rocky.

The group's transportation to the marina wasn't nearly as dramatic the first time they had departed for the ship. This time, a swarm of bellboys hustled the luggage into a series of large, white, Ford Econoline vans, organized for precisely that purpose. The four vans sat a short distance away, glistening in sunlight, which was already uncomfortably bright in the morning haze. The drivers wandered around aimlessly, waving their arms and giving loading directions to no one in particular.

In the distance, one of the drivers stood apart from the rest; a large, wiry black man with closely cropped silver hair who appeared to be watching the proceedings with supreme disinterest. The man leaned idly against one of the vans, his fingers rolling a freshly lit cigarette back and forth, its blue smoke drifting upward. Dallas glanced in the man's direction and experienced an uncomfortable sense of familiarity.

Suddenly, he noticed his luggage being moved in the wrong direction, and he ran off to retrieve it; in the process forgetting his momentary distraction. Dallas, perhaps more than the others, was anxious to get on with the research; he was relieved when all the transfers and loading went as planned. It took two helicopters to ferry the assembled group, which numbered in excess of twenty when one counted the security personnel. In addition, there was the luggage for the entourage as well as the equipment that Miranda had brought originally, all of which required its own helicopter. It was a two-hour flight from Dubai to the tanker's position, some fifty miles north of Muscat, Oman, and the team had nothing better to do than watch first the desert and then the waters of the Gulf of Oman slide by underneath them. Some tried to read, and others to write. Samantha busied herself reviewing dive procedures and equipment lists; which the others decided was about as exciting as watching inch-worms race. Miranda simply stared out the window, watching the hazy brown of the horizon. She said nothing. He knew she was worried for her father, for her people, and perhaps even for Dallas himself; but her instinctive response was to center her mind even more intensely on the mission. It must, he thought, make for a very lonely existence.

It was a loneliness he understood well, having lived his own private version of it for many years. It had begun after his self-imposed professional exile years before, and had really only ended in the moments after Dr. Todd's death. The reality of that isolation was still palpable, and the mere thought of those times sent twinges of regret running up and down his spine. He wished he could do something, anything, to rescue her from her personal hell. There was nothing he could do, and that realization caused him physical pain.

Almost at once, he reprimanded himself for not recognizing this characteristic in her before now. She had always seemed so involved – so central to everything his world had become, that it had simply not dawned on him, until this moment, that she shared with him this sense of detachment. He saw their separate reactions were driven by a common trait. In spite of himself, he chuckled at such irony; that, in the midst of his almost complete isolation from the human race, he should find himself with her. She glanced toward the sound with a puzzled look on her fact. He promised himself that one day he would share the joke with her.

None too soon, they were all safely ensconced in their own quarters. Dallas had to admit that, after all that had transpired these past weeks, it felt good to get back to familiar surroundings. Quickly, he opened his nightstand drawer and found his journal sitting right where he'd left it. Relieved, he threw himself headfirst onto his bed and sank into its comforting confines. For a few seconds, he allowed himself the luxury of thinking about nothing of any importance. It was a moment he would have wished could last forever, if Miranda had given him enough time to make a wish; her knocking began almost immediately after he laid down. Wearily, he rolled to one side, threw his feet over the edge and stood up.

"Dallas, you in there?"

"Yep," his response was made superfluous with Miranda's opening of the door.

"So ... are you getting settled in?" Her demeanor seemed tentative, almost awkward.

"I never thought I'd say this, but I missed my room. It feels good to be back."

"Yes, it does."

"I am missing one thing, though."

"Oh, what's that?"

"It's a little lonely in here. I miss my roommate."

"Oh."

They just stared at one another, neither knowing exactly what to do or say next. He started to take a step toward her as their gazes locked on one another, when the ship's intercom buzzed to life. It was Joshua, summoning everyone to a meeting in the conference room.

"Oh," she began again as they began their walk to the meeting, "I was able to talk to my father alone after we landed, and now he agrees with us about Camile and Khalid making the trip on Seahab with us.

"That's a relief. How did Rocky take the news?"

"Don't know. He wasn't with us at the time. I don't know if my father has even told him yet. It was strange, father acted as if it were obvious that they would be coming; like he had totally forgotten about arresting them."

"That's curious. I wonder how Rocky will react when he finds out?"

Miranda felt the need to change the subject. "Have you finished making the room assignments for Seahab?"

"Yes, it's being typed up now. They'll be distributed along with the seat assignments for each of the four sections. According to Sam, I'm piloting section one, you're doing the second, Rocky is doing the third and she's piloting the reactor section. I must confess I'd like one more shot at the simulator before we launch. Do you think we'll have time?"

"For something that important, you find the time."

"How about you? Do you want another practice run?"

"Sure, why not?" Miranda knew she didn't really need it, but saw no reason to make that point.

As they walked to the training center, Dallas filled her in the Seahab assignments they'd worked out so far. Joining him on the command bridge would be Jorge, who had vowed if he was going to drown during the descent, it would not be in his bedroom, and Jon Hardy, who felt likewise. Miranda's team included her father, Karen Pollard, and Camile. While Dallas had voiced concern over the leadership of both groups riding together, the two men had been adamant. Rocky's section contained his security team, who would also double as assistants on the various dive teams. Sam's section would carry the five technicians who would complete the final assembly once the four parts were in place on the bottom. They would double as station personnel once on the seabed.

Before their day was done, the entire group had worked twelve hours straight getting ready for next day's launch. It was only when people started falling asleep with clipboards in their hands that they called it quits. Wearily, everyone slowly wandered off in their separate directions, with barely a wave of farewell.

Before returning to his own quarters, Dallas met quickly with Joshua and Miranda. The time had come to take the mission from thought to action, and no amount of double-checking or triple-checking could delay that eventuality any longer. It was now time to test their theory, their equipment, and themselves; a realization that gave the three a burst of nervous energy, not to mention a cold chill.

Later, once he was alone, Dallas ran through his mental check list yet again. There were such mundane things as clothes and such critical things as his latest translations. There were boxes and cylinders; books and papers; pots and pans; linens and towels; and all manner of sundries. On top of all that they had to double check the system's computer core, as well its multiple redundant backups. Not to mention an incredible array of electrical spare parts.

With their lives literally on the line in Seahab, they all knew there was no such thing as too safe or too cautious. Their facility would be resting somewhere between a hundred and sixty and a hundred and ninety feet beneath the usually calm surface; little more than half a football field. Dallas had to continue reminding himself that the potential danger was real and must be treated with great respect. Still, it was only about sixty yards; they could swim to the surface if needed, and they had emergency subs. To top it all of, they'd only be a few miles offshore from Jazireh-ye Forur. So why, Dallas asked himself, in the face of all those comforting facts, was he so nervous?

Hell, he told himself, you'll be living with twenty other people in a couple of cigar tubes at the bottom of the ocean for god only knows how long, with no easy way out, and one of them was most probably a murderer.

"Now why should I worry about that?" he muttered sarcastically.

22

DALLAS SAT IN THE command seat of section one, waiting nervously for his turn in the "poop shoot," a not-so-glamorous term coined by the crew for the Seahab's method of departure from the *Habibti*. While expression might not have been pretty, it was a fairly accurate description of what was about to happen to him. He had watched both Aquarius vehicles, as well as sections three and four, literally be flushed from the bowels of the massive tanker in a most unceremonious fashion and now, with Miranda's section preparing to descend into the Gulf, he sat in silent anticipation with Jon and Jorge. He had initially been happy to command section one, cryptically dubbed *Opus X* by the cigar-smoking Jorge, thinking that he would be first in the water. It wasn't until later that Dallas discovered they would be launching reverse order. This turn of events brought to Dallas's mind the old Biblical injunctive that those who are last shall be first, and those who are first shall be last. Finally, the crackle of the radio and the technician calling his name told him that his time had come.

"*Opus X, Opus X*, this is control. How do you read, over?"

"Control, read you loud and clear."

"Very good. Section two has cleared the shoot. In a moment you'll notice the slight sensation as we move your section into place. It's nothing to worry about. Once you're in place the chamber doors will close.

It will be completely dark except for your interior lighting; suggest you turn on interior and exterior lights at this time. Over."

"Roger, lights." Suddenly, *Opus X* jerked violently, leaving the three scientists grabbing at the armrests of their captain's chairs and distracting Dallas as he reached for the lighting controls. "Whoa, control, what was that?"

"We're just moving you into position."

"I thought you said 'slightly'?"

Dallas's sarcasm met only silence.

"*Opus X*, control, we're are commencing launch sequence; five minutes, on my mark … mark."

Dallas looked at the other two men, both of whom wore the same helpless expression as he was sure that he himself wore at that instant. The universal shrugging of shoulders indicated that none of the men understood the need for a time hack. Suddenly a complete and utter darkness enveloped the trio, leaving Dallas fumbling around the console for the light switch. Flipping them, the men were comforted by the warm, soft, yellow diffuse glow of the bridge lights. This allowed Dallas to find the fore and aft external light switches. It was only then that the men saw the confines into which they had been hermetically sealed.

"*Opus X*, control, launch in four minutes, thirty seconds. Please insure you are powered up and prepared to descend. You should bring your engines on line by T minus two minutes but remember not to initiate forward drive until cleared by control; do you copy?"

"Roger, copy that," muttered Dallas defensively. The three men looked at each other with embarrassed smirks. Now they knew why the hack; an epiphany framed by the seemingly distant rumble of rushing water. Jorge rose up slightly from his seat to look down the side of the *Opus X* and could see the rising water in the form of shimmering reflections bouncing off the chamber walls.

"Gee, it's filling up quickly," whispered Jorge. "Dallas, are sure you know how to handle this thing?"

"George," kidded Dallas, with a big grin, breaking his promise, "you doubt me?"

"Hail Mary, full of grace … "

"Funny, very funny."

"*Opus X*, chamber ninety percent full, prepare for launch. Repeat, prepare for launch in T-minus thirty seconds."

"Roger, thirty seconds to launch." Now Dallas was focused. After all the hours in Joshua's simulator, Dallas was under control. He felt an almost detached calm as he prepared to execute the often rehearsed maneuvers.

"*Opus X*, chamber full, bay doors open. Prepare for release in five … four … three … two … one —"

With that, the clamps holding *Opus X* released, and the section slid smoothly backward, through the trap doors, off the chamber's ramp, then sank like a stone into the waters of the Gulf. Although they had been warned, the sudden drop caught them by surprise. Dallas at least had the controls to occupy him, but Jorge and Jon were left to hold onto their shoulder straps, contemplating their nausea.

"Uh, Dallas, can we wait just a moment?"

"Wait, Jon, why?"

"I'm sure I left my stomach back there somewhere. I'd like to give it a chance to catch up."

"*Opus X*, control, you are clear and free to navigate, good hunting."

"Roger that and thanks. Miranda, do you copy?"

"This is *Guardian One*," Miranda chirped; "jump in, Dallas, the water's fine."

As Dallas gained control over *Opus X* and leveled her off, he could see the other cigar-shaped sections holding position about fifty yards ahead of him, and about twenty feet deeper, leaving them some forty feet above the sea floor. They were arrayed side by side, with about thirty yards separating each of them. Farther ahead and deeper down still, Dallas could see the ghostly outlines of the two Aquarius mini subs, their bright halogen lights searching for a likely area to set up Seahab.

"All right everyone, listen up." It was Sam, whose section, dubbed *Treasure Hunter*, was designated as the command module for the trip down. As the most experienced underwater member of the team next to Khalid, she would be in command of the journey to the seabed and the assembly of the undersea laboratory. "Everyone, let's do a radio check."

"*Opus*, do you copy?"

"Loud and clear."

"*Guardian One?*"

"Read you five by five."

"*Security?*"

"Copy."

"*Aquarius One?*"

"Read you, *Treasure Hunter*."

"*Aquarius Two?*"

"Loud and clear."

"Okay, everyone, one more time, here's the plan. Aquarius One and Two, begin your final area survey. Once you identify the best location for Seahab, mark it, then take a position about fifty yards to the east of that marker and await instructions." With that, the two vehicles pulled slowly away, as Sam continued, "*Opus X*, *Guardian One* and *Security*, you will follow my lead. Once we identify a suitable location near the anomaly, I will take position on the sea floor. *Security*, you will then land parallel to me on the port side. Remember to turn over the final sequence to the computer; it will use the bow and stern thrusters to settle in the proper position and distance from *Treasure Hunter*. *Guardian One*, you'll be next. You'll need to pilot to the sea floor and position yourself perpendicular to us, at our bows. The guidance computer will take over final coupling but you'll have to set the initial position yourself manually. *Opus X*, the same goes for you. Once *Guardian One* is leveled and secured, you'll repeat the procedure at our stern ports. Now, *Guardian One* and *Opus X*, your command bridge is sitting midway between the docking ports on your sections, so you should have good line of sight for your maneuvers. Finally, remember we all have manual overrides. If something doesn't look right, it is better to abort than make a mistake.

That said, let's try and do this right the first time because we'll be stirring up the bottom and we don't want it too turbid. Everyone copy?"

Upon receiving everyone's acknowledgment, Sam moved *Treasure Hunter* off toward the *Aquarius One* and *Two*, now just tiny blips on the radar screen. The remaining sections followed in turn, at a discrete distance. Given that the top speed of an Aquarius was about three knots this was a slow process. During Sam and Miranda's initial surveys of the area before the *Habibti's* arrival, they had charted and logged several potential sites deserving of closer examination. Khalid and Hakeem, having been the first to launch, had already considered several of those locations by the time all the Seahab's sections had joined them. Now they were down to the last two sites, and Dallas was secretly wishing they'd make up their collective mind.

In the meanwhile, Jon, Jorge, and Dallas amused themselves by trying to harass the various aquatic life forms that swam by the command dome. There actions were clearly visible to the other sections; a point brought home when Miranda called to remind them that once they were diving, the bigger fish might have the last word. It was only then that the concept of sharks crossed Jon's mind. Much to his chagrin, Sam quickly pointed out that, yes, there were sharks in the Gulf. She sadistically neglected to tell him they weren't particularly aggressive.

After what seemed like an eternity, the pair of Aquarius subs reported success, directing the other vehicles to the chosen spot. For Dallas, what happened next could best be described as an hour of boredom and five minutes of high anxiety. The boredom came from watching the other sections settle, ever-so-slowly into their appointed positions. Sam's effort was in most ways the easiest as she had only to choose the first spot. In truth, that was more difficult than it appeared to Dallas, as she had to gauge the terrain not just for her section but also for the others as well. Next, Rocky settled into place, the computers aided by sonar positioning his segment in the appropriate location. Then, gently and gradually, Miranda followed.

Finally it was Dallas's turn. The bottom was now completely turbid, the fine silt and sand drifted and swirled in the water like a thick,

London fog. It was simple enough to steer toward the other three sections, now securely joined together with their lights glowing in the watery haze. It was quite another thing to work the section sideways in the gentle current, watching as the sterns of the first two pieces inching closer and closer. Automatically, as *Opus X* glided into position, its hydraulic supported extended with a hum from beneath its belly. They would finish full extension only when the section was properly positioned. Even with the computer at the helm, Dallas maintained contact with the controls, just in case. Everyone was silent as *Opus X* covered the final millimeters before softly butting up to its opposite numbers.

There was a distant sound, and gentle nudge as it slid into place. On cue, Dallas's control panel's hatch lights blinked from red to green. A cheer went up from the other sections as they flashed the thumbs-up sign to one another from their separate command bridges. Proudly, Sam called to the *Habibti,* reporting, with a "the-Eagle-has-landed" tone, that Seahab was operational on the ocean floor. Looking upward, Dallas could see the bottom of the massive ship's hull hovering above them like a massive storm cloud, blocking out the sun. He knew the massive ship would soon continue on to port, leaving them alone on the seafloor.

With the undersea research facility in place, command of the mission was passed back to Dallas, a fact momentarily lost on the three men of *Opus X* as they stared in fascination at the abundance of life swimming around them. Miranda's radio call shook Dallas from his daydreams, as she reminded everyone that Dallas had scheduled a staff meeting to commence in fifteen minutes. Silently, he thanked her for reminding him as well.

Jon and Jorge preceded Dallas down the ladder connecting the command bridge with the rest of *Opus X.* As they descended, the technicians from *Treasure Hunter* were already busy checking the electrical connections, seals, and bolts on their new home. Seahab was still operating at sea-level air pressure, but with their arrival on the sea floor, the process of pressurizing it and converting to TriOx would soon begin. Until they were nitrogen saturated, there would be no diving. That meant until Dr.

Pollard gave her okay, they couldn't don their dry suits and begin their work. It did not mean, however, that the two Aquarius subs couldn't look around; a thought Dallas filed away for the first opportunity.

In short order, the research team filed into Security section, site of the Seahab's conference room. They were soon joined by Khalid and Hakeem, who had to wait until everything was in place before they could dock their vehicles and board Seahab. As Dallas watched the assistants and technicians straggle into the room he became overwhelmed by a strange feeling of déjà vu. There, in the back of the line among the security personnel, was a large, wiry black man with closely cropped silver hair who seemed to be trying a little too hard to be inconspicuous. There was something about him that Dallas recognized, yet not quite; something was different. He couldn't place it, but the man was somehow familiar. It was a thin strand of a thought, a mere thread that snapped when Miranda walked up to him, wearing a smile that lit up the room. She congratulated him on his piloting, and he gave her a brotherly, for-public-consumption hug; brotherhood was most decidedly not on his mind.

The group agreed that Khalid and Hakeem had chosen a spectacular location for Seahab; resting on what appeared to be an antediluvian shoreline, about fifty yards from a massive cliff. While the entire seabed was strewn with coral, loose rocks and debris, the chosen site held something different. To their trained eyes, the rubble held a certain symmetry – lines and rows, squares and spaces – all of which suggested to Khalid and Hakeem fallen walls, rooms, and ancient passageways. Perhaps they were right, or perhaps it was wishful thinking; but to Dallas, the patterns, if they even existed, were subtle indeed.

Three days later, after spending the better part of that time taking many short journeys in the mini-sub with Hakeem, he could still only barely make out what his pilot swore was plainly in front of his face. True, the rocks seemed denser in some areas, rising higher at certain points, but did that really constitute an archaeological site? Tomorrow, he reminded himself, they would finally get to put on the dry suits, and maybe discover for themselves. They were all past being anxious, and they were ready to begin the next phase of the operation.

He brought himself back to the present and directed Hakeem to move the vessel in a different direction. *Aquarius One* had a maximum rated depth of one thousand feet, making the ancient lake bed, another hundred and thirty feet further down, easily accessible to the pair. They ventured down the side of the cliff, into these darker depths, and found nothing unique about the seabed there. The total randomness of the debris pattern here allowed Dallas to finally see what Hakeem had been trying to show him earlier. It was on their gradual ascent up the side of the cliff, however, that Dallas noticed something distinctly odd. At first, he thought it was merely a shadow caused by the bright halogen lights mounted on the exterior of the sub above their heads. Dallas gestured for Hakeem to turn to the right and slow down.

"Look, what's that?"

"What?"

"That," Dallas said, pointing excitedly. "That dark spot right there, between those two boulders."

"Just looks like a hollow between the rocks —"

"No, it's a small opening."

"Maybe." Hakeem pondered for a moment. "Surprising though; remember Jorge's briefing about the geology of the area? These are coral encrusted islands, a lot of sand; cave formations would be most unusual. Well, mark its position on the chart. Maybe we'll get back to it later. We're still ten to fifteen feet below the old shoreline so I'd have to give it a low priority for the time being."

"Maybe, so; I'd like to check it out later."

"You just want to drive around in the Aquarius."

"And your point?"

"You are, as your people are so fond of saying, the boss. You may indulge yourself, but remember, we have to get back to Seahab; doctor's orders."

"I sure am sick of this particular doctor's orders."

"Look at the bright side, the wait is almost over."

Dr. Pollard had been insistent on gradually increasing the pressure and introducing the TriOx mixture. To that end she had instituted the seventy-two-hour rule that lay at the heart of Dallas's frustration. The introduction of the helium had occurred so gradually that none of them noticed the changes in their voices; although now they all sounded something like attendees at a Mickey Mouse convention. Of course, that also meant limiting the length of each excursion on both Aquarius subs so that their occupants didn't get too out of sync with the slowly changing pressure of the base. Now, after three days, they had finally reached total saturation and the necessary pressure to allow for work to begin. Owing to the time of day, however, it was agreed that they would begin the following morning.

Dallas returned to the Seahab to find Miranda hard at work, preparing the airlifts for their initial tests under actual conditions. The airlifts were nothing more than enormous vacuum cleaners that the team would use to suck up the sand and other small debris from the supposed rock foundations identified by Khalid. Usually, such devices would be based and supported by a surface research vessel. However, given their depth, it was decided that *Aquarius One* and *Two* would pilot the huge hoses into position and support their mass, allowing the divers to maneuver the ends with little effort. The giant vacuums would be used in a sledgehammer approach in dredging the sea bottom. The use of such devices would not allow an archaeologist to consider any potential finds *in situ*, but it would allow them quickly to clear away large amounts of sand and debris. Their hope was that in removing the sand, building foundations would be easier to identify.

While the sand was being moved, however, it would not being completely disregarded. The security-guards-turned-divers were to monitor the sifters where the sand was to be deposited on the off-chance that some small artifact appeared among the rubble. This was not being worked as an archaeological site in the traditional sense, but they planned on taking the time to collect any pottery shards or loose coins.

Dallas and Miranda already knew the biggest debate at the evening meal would be who would get to handle the airlifts. That job would be the most exciting job on site; with everyone else out there working only in support positions. Only Jorge, with an interest only in geology, had no expressed interest holding the "big suckers", as the vacuums had become known. For all the archaeologists, that experience was shaping up to be the highlight of the expedition, at least until they found something more interesting.

The drysuits were decidedly less popular. Not only were the suits tricky to get put on, but insuring the *O*-rings for the hands and feet were correctly sealed was problematic at best. Of greater concern for the nouveau divers was learning to manage their buoyancy in these suits. Unlike the wetsuits they had all learned in, these suits were more similar to swimming inside a tight-fitting balloon. While they had all tried a drysuit in a pool, they had no experienced them at depths greater than one atmosphere. Since air compressed with depth, the reverse was also true; it expanded as a diver moved toward the surface. If one of them weren't careful, they might wander up a little and find themselves rising faster and faster toward the surface; a potentially fatal possibility if they didn't decompress properly first.

The suits had the benefit, as the name implies, of keeping the diver dry. Unlike a traditional wetsuit, drysuits literally seal the diver in a watertight envelope of air heated by their own bodies. While the more well-known wetsuits worked fine near the surface, or for extremely short duration deep dives, they would not provide them with sufficient warmth for this depth or dive duration, where the water temperature remained a relatively constant four degrees Celsius. Given the length of time they wished to work, the concern over hypothermia was as great as that of nitrogen narcosis.

All this information served to make the group tentative, and more than just a little cautious. Now everyone understood why Hakeem had been so willing to volunteer to pilot *Aquarius Two*. He only grinned sheepishly at that suggestion.

Eventually, everyone made it into their suits and stood in a broad semicircle on one side of the dive platform; a huge, open circle in the center of the floor. On the other side of the platform stood Sam and Khalid. With the assembly anxious to begin their mission, Sam reluctantly agreed to use this last orientation dive as the group's first exploratory dive. It would be the assembly's first time in drysuits in salt water, so she reviewed with them one last time on the suit's operation and dive protocols. Then, pausing momentarily to don her swim fins, she stepped off the platform and into the ice cold water. In prearranged sequence, they all took the same last step.

As each person entered the water Sam motioned to them to swim clear of the entrance so that the next diver could enter. In a few minutes, the entire group was floating silently in a large circle, staring at one another. Dallas had to admit that this was a much more exhilarating sensation than he'd felt while learning in the pool. Though only mere months ago, those training sessions now seemed a lifetime away, and so much different from what he was experiencing now.

His body slowly adjusted to the slight chill of the water, still barely noticeable through the dry suit. The full-face diving mask was wired for sound, making all the complex sign language he had learned in the pool totally superfluous. He heard the excitement in Miranda's voice crisp and clear in his left ear.

"Isn't it incredible?" Her enthusiasm was contagious, and the others all joined in a chorus of admiration. Finally, it fell to Sam to focus the group's attention on the mission.

"Listen, everyone," she interjected in the squeaky voice that everyone had grown accustomed to, "the greater our excitement, the faster we use up our air. Let's keep the conversation to a minimum. Everyone has a dive partner. Let's get paired up; and remember to stay with your partner at all times. Also, let's don't have any pairs swimming off out of the sight of at least one other team. Now, this is supposed to be both an orientation dive and an exploratory dive. We can swim around the site for about thirty minutes; that's about all this tank of air should last. Let's try to get some ideas for where to begin the serious work on the next dive. Okay, Khalid, let's move them out. I'll bring up the rear."

"Right." Khalid motioned to Dallas as he began to swim. "Dallas, this was your idea, why don't you and Miranda take, what is the expression, 'the point'?"

"Thanks," Dallas blurted awkwardly. He was sure he was blushing beneath his dive mask. "Miranda, ladies first."

With one quick scissor-kick, the pair moved out into the infinite horizon. Beneath them lay boulders, sand, rubble, coral, and an abundance of marine life. Schools of brightly colored fish darted this way and that, changing directions seemingly on a whim, with no obvious reason and little regard for whatever other fish happened to be in their vicinity. Dallas was captivated by the diversity of life they had intruded upon, and which now engulfed them. Unlike land creatures, there was no reaction of fear or surprise from the local population. The divers were treated like any other large fish and simply given a wide berth. It was an observation that Dallas took to heart, should he encounter any creature larger than he.

The entire assembly stretched out to form a straight line, with Dallas and Miranda at the epicenter. He looked left and right, taking in the sights and feeling contentment, unlike any he had ever known; consumed with a sense of purpose that left him almost giddy. It was only Sam's voice over the earphone, reminding everyone to check their tank pressure, that brought him back to reality of their mission. By prior agreement and standard diving practice, they would begin their return to Seahab at half-pressure-plus-two-hundred-fifty psi. Since they had all begun with three thousand psi, this meant they would turn back at one thousand, seven hundred fifty psi; a point they were rapidly approaching. Dallas was amazed at how quickly they had reached that point. He had not expected such a temporal distortion, but the time had literally swum by. When Sam asked where he thought they should begin using the airlifters, Dallas admitted, somewhat sheepishly, that he had gotten so distracted by the sea life that he hadn't taken much notice. He was somewhat relieved to hear everyone else confess to virtually the same thing.

Sam's reaction was, to Dallas, almost as surprising; she actually laughed. "Don't worry, that's the most common reaction in the world. Now you know why I love it so. But this is a world you must respect, or it will kill you. Khalid and I were looking for some sites to begin working, and we can discuss them over lunch." As they approached the dive platform, she added, "First in, front out. I'll be waiting up top to help everyone with their equipment. Okay, let's go."

They made four more dives that day, slowly working up their tolerances to those that are required for operating equipment at that, or any, depth. They discovered all too well that physical exertion caused them to suck up air at an incredible rate. Because of the sensation of weightlessness, Dallas didn't realize how much he energy he was using with each dive, and by the end of the day he was starving and exhausted; he was not alone. By the time Dallas had showered and made his way to the galley, the entire group, except for Miranda, had left. Only one other person, a solitary technician, sat on the other side of the galley, seemingly oblivious to anything around him.

Miranda barely waved at Dallas as he entered the room. She managed a weak smile and slight downward motion of her eyes, the only gesture Dallas needed to know she was inviting him to join her. As he sat, Dallas had the weary feeling that sitting would be far easier than rising again. He crossed his arms as they rested on the table and lowered his head on this makeshift pillow.

"Tired?" She could barely whisper the question.

"Hmsotird."

"You're mumbling."

Turning his head, Dallas tried again, "I'm soooo tired. Can you believe people do this for fun?"

"Poor baby," Miranda teased sarcastically as she slowly stroked his head. "Of course, they aren't usually setting up huge vacuum cleaners on the sea floor."

"I think I liked it better when you hated me."

"Who says I've stopped?" The twinkle in her eye hinted at an entirely different opinion. Dallas was too tired to show much reaction, save a soft, guttural growl.

Joshua wheeled up to the pair with a frustrated expression on his face. He had become restless with the slow pace, and it appeared to Miranda if that impatience was about to find voice; she was right.

"Miranda ... Dallas, you two having fun?" It was also clear he wasn't happy with their growing closeness. Dallas put the behavior down to cabin fever and a slight case of claustrophobia.

"Hello, Joshua. Fun is not what I'd call it. Miranda here was just reminding me she still hates me."

"Dallas, we need to regain our focus. Everyone is just lying around in their quarters."

"Joshua, we're mostly scientists. We're mostly middle-aged, and not one of us is a physical-fitness fanatic, except maybe Sam. We're lying around because we are exhausted. We've spent the last four-plus hours in the water getting our bearings and setting up equipment and grids. Pushing them harder won't make them go any faster or any more effective. In fact, I'd wager the opposite."

"Very well then, when will we begin serious work?"

"I'm sorry," Dallas felt his temper rising, "I thought I just said we had already started 'serious' work."

"Boys, boys," Miranda interjected, "we're all anxious and tired. Father, we're really working as fast as we can. Tomorrow we'll continue dredging the sea floor and then we'll see. I think if you talk to the doctor, you'll see we've done everything we could, as quickly as we could."

"I know, I know." Joshua shook his head wearily. "I don't know what's wrong with me lately, it's like I have two voices in my head. I find myself saying things, doing things, and it's like I'm on the outside, looking in; listening to myself."

"Maybe you're just tired," Dallas offered sympathetically.

Joshua shot an angry glance toward the younger scientist that stopped him cold. It was replaced by a look of confusion, then one of inner struggle. All this transpired in barely a moment, ending with Joshua drawing a deep breath. An air of exhaustion seemed to surround the suddenly fragile-looking leader. Without a word, Joshua flicked the joystick on his wheelchair, spun around, and left the galley.

Miranda started to go after him but Dallas grabbed her elbow, holding her firm.

"I think we need to have Doc Pollard examine him, and right away."

"What are you saying?"

"Miranda, you just saw that display. There is something seriously … troubling him."

"He's just exhausted; and who are you to say, anyway? You were nothing before he brought you into the group; just a small-time professor at a no name school. How can you possibly judge him?"

He loosened his grip on her arm, turned, and started to walk away. He stopped and turned back for a moment, locking his gaze on her with a barely containable anger, the likes of which he'd never felt before.

"Who am I? I'm the guy who only a few months ago your father said was the most important man in the last thirteen millennia. I'm also the guy your father put in charge of this little operation. And, until a moment ago, I was the guy who thought he was falling in love with you … .I guess two out of three ain't bad."

With that he spun around again and left leaving a speechless Miranda in his wake. The entire exchange was witnessed by the anonymous technician who sat across the room; a large, wiry black man with closely cropped silver hair who appeared to be watching the proceedings with an air of supreme disinterest.

23

DALLAS DIDN'T REGAIN HIS composure until he reached the junction of *Security* and *Opus* and began climbing the stairs to the second level and his quarters. He was left with equal measures of confusion and angst, and unsure of how to proceed. It seemed that it was becoming harder and harder to trust anyone on this expedition. As he reached his door, he also reached a decision; he would talk to Camile. It wasn't his first choice, but he was out of first choices. Something was going seriously wrong, and he didn't know who else he could turn to now.

After hesitating a moment, he continued on down the corridor and knocked on Camile's door.

"Enter." The command had been simple and direct. Dallas did as he was told.

"Hello, Dallas. I was wondering when you'd come to see me."

"Really, why?"

"Now, you needn't be so suspicious. It's just that it's been days since we've spoken. Anyway, I just had a feeling you'd eventually feel the need to talk to me."

"Well, if you know that much, then what do I want to talk to you about?"

"Very well," Camile became deadly serious, "I sense a presence on board the Seahab. Powerful minds are reaching out, trying to manipulate the other individuals aboard. Not everyone, mind you, but key ones; and they are frustrated that there are some minds that they cannot control, at least not yet. I am one, you are another. They are reaching out for my mind, but have not yet found me; I have mastered techniques which allow me to conceal myself. Nor have I identified these minds yet."

"They?"

"Yes, they. They sense we are close to something they want, and have infiltrated the group to get it, whatever it is. I also sense they are extremely frustrated by their inability to control your mind; they don't understand it, and it angers them, although they won't reveal that anger. I have no earthly idea what protects you."

"Well, if you don't know, you can bet I don't; but who are 'they'?"

"There are two answers to that, of course. As to their specific identities; for the moment, I have no clue. But as to who they are, in general, it is as we suspected, the Ha.Sa.Tan are here."

Dallas collapsed into a nearby chair. Then it was true: they are alive, and they are here. It was his greatest fear; it suggested he'd been right about the *Book of Enoch* and the Watchers.

"But we're all humans."

"Perhaps that is true. That would, of course, mean the Ha.Sa.Tan must have infiltrated us, despite the ancient legends."

"So what do we do?"

"For the moment, nothing. There isn't much we can do. They have the advantage over us at present. All I can tell you is that there are at least two."

"But how do you know that, are you telepathic?"

"No, more empathic really. I can't sense specific thoughts, just feelings, emotions. I can sense their presence, their anger, and frustration, but nothing more."

"But why can they gain control of Joshua or Miranda, but they can't control me?"

"As I said, I don't know, neither do they. That may be their biggest weakness. You are an unknown quantity to them. Perhaps it's just fate, or perhaps some rare, unique genetic mutation; who knows? My mental training allows me to keep below their radar, so to speak, but they really couldn't care less about me at this point. It is you they are focusing on. It would appear you have what they want, or you know how to get what they want. Apparently, they want you to help them get it."

"This is crazy. I don't know anything."

"Really? Nothing that you haven't told anyone else?"

"Hell, you're like a damn lie detector. There is one thing, but I've not discussed it with anyone yet … except Miranda. I don't know who to trust anymore. They've got almost everyone under their spell."

"I see. As to a spell, it's not quite that. They can't control completely, and they can't control everyone at once. Besides, they don't need that much control. It isn't necessary that they control everyone, just the key moments; the key events."

"They just need to control the stream … "

"Excuse me?"

"Something Joshua told me not so long ago; that the Guardians didn't try to control people, just the flow of major events. You know, like a stream. If you control the stream, then you control everything in it."

"And Joshua told you this?"

"Yes … what a minute, you're not suggesting that he's—"

"No, but it does suggest that his mind has been touched by them. That would be bad news, depending on the level of access they have established."

"And what about Miranda … She's just started acting strangely too?"

"This is very bad. Tell me exactly what you've observed."

For the next hour, Dallas reviewed all the strange, disjointed conversations; how Joshua would be alternately angry, then kind; hostile, then friendly; determined, then exhausted. Camile sat quietly, taking it all in, and prodding Dallas only slightly when he sensed something was being left out. Finally, with a wave of his hand, he signaled he'd heard enough.

"At least now we've identified one of them. From what you say, I believe Rocky could be a Ha.Sa.Tan."

"Rocky?"

"It all fits. He would be perfectly placed to lead the investigation against you, and you are the key target for them. As the lead investigator, he would be above suspicion and could manipulate the evidence. Also, he remains constantly at Joshua's side. That puts him in a perfect position to 'control the stream,' as you put it."

"But when he was trying to frame me that would have stopped the mission completely. Now you say you feel they want me to complete it."

"Either he received new instructions, or something happened that required him to change his tactics. Or perhaps he was controlling events to push you in a certain direction; he may have been the reason Miranda freed you in the first place. He may have engineered all those events. In any case, we know they are the killers you're looking for; they murdered Raj and Dr. Graham, and they could have done it right in front of you and make you think it was necessary. Our sole advantage seems to be that each of them can only control one mind at a time. You cannot be affected, so you put trust only in yourself; myself second and Miranda, if you must, third."

"What about Joshua. Don't we tell him what you suspect?"

"No, it's not likely he'd believe you, especially if he's been under Rocky's control for any length of time. We don't know for sure if it has a cumulative effect."

"You agree that I can tell Miranda?"

"Risky, still, I don't have any other idea at this point. Rocky couldn't be manipulating her, not if he's handling Joshua; that's one reason I say 'they.' You need to get her alone, and I mean completely alone, and tell her everything. Again, based on what you've said, I suspect their mental powers have a finite range; let's hope that's the case."

"Then what?"

"We'll have to figure out a way to arrest and hold both Rocky and the other Ha.Sa.Tan. Frankly, I'm not sure how to accomplish that."

"They're murderers; why not just put them out the airlock?"

"I understand the temptation, but we may need them; we'll certainly want to question them. At any rate, we can't show our hand until we are sure we have them all. Remember, I'm only guessing there are two. I can sense multiple minds, but as Rocky is head of security, who knows how many others have been infiltrated. They may have the same mental ability to hide themselves that I do."

"There must be a way."

"Have you found anything on the tablets that can help us?"

"Nothing comes to mind. I'll reread everything."

"Okay, now go figure out how to tell Miranda. I must meditate further on all that we have discussed."

Leaving Camile, Dallas returned to the galley, but Miranda was not there. He tried her quarters with no luck before finally finding her in the lab, staring absentmindedly at some totally meaningless artifacts. She turned at the sound of his voice, her eyes red and puffy.

"Dallas, I'm so, so sorry. I can't believe I said those things to you. I don't know what came over me; it was like hearing someone else speaking with my voice."

"Tears," he said cautiously, "that isn't like you."

"No, I suppose not, but it isn't often someone tells you they love you and really means it."

"Oh, that. Yes, well ... look, we need to talk, privately, now; and I mean right now. I think I can explain what you experienced, but we need to be alone."

"But, Dallas, we're alone."

"No, I mean completely alone." Then, in a fit of inspiration, he added, "How about a little spin on *Aquarius One*?"

"Sure." Her voice reflected confidence, but she wore an expression of total confusion. Without further discussion, she followed him to the docking port for the mini-sub. They climbed inside and sealed the hatch. Taking the controls, Dallas released the clamps holding the sub in place, and only then, as it dropped slowly away from Seahab, did he power the vehicle and shift into forward thrust. With that action, the radio crackled to life.

"*Aquarius One*, this is Command."

"Go ahead, Command."

"Dallas, what are you doing?" It was Hakeem. Dallas breathed a sigh of relief, but immediately motioned for Miranda to remain silent.

"Well, I don't have anything to do right now, so I thought I'd go take another look at the site; see if we've missed anything."

"But the paperwork —"

"Hakeem, I don't pull rank often. I just approved my paperwork, okay?" Dallas heard a chuckle from the other end.

"I get your point. Have fun; and since you're in charge, when you get back, I want to talk about this duty roster. I'm a scientist, not a policeman."

"Right. That would come under Sam's duties, and you know how tough she can be ... but I'll see what I can do. *Aquarius One*, out."

"Roger, *Aquarius One*. Now, remember to check in at fifteen-minute intervals; I think those were YOUR standing orders. Command out."

With that, Dallas turned off the radio completely to ensure they would not be overheard.

"Dallas, what is this cloak and dagger all about?"

"I was talking to Camile, and we – he and I – believe we know what's going on."

"What?"

"You're little outburst in the galley earlier, your father's mood swings, Raj's murder—"

"Dallas, just tell me."

"The Ha.Sa.Tan are here, aboard Seahab."

"You're not saying my father is —"

"No, of course not, but he is being influenced by them. He's fighting it, but I don't think he even realizes what's going on himself. For all I know, he may just think he's losing his mind. That's why he keeps shifting back and forth, not remembering wanting to arrest Camile, and looking so fatigued. The battle must be unbearable."

"Well, who then?"

"Rocky."

"Rocky?!" Miranda's reaction was in the extreme. "He's been with us for as long as I can remember; it can't be. You must be wrong."

"It's the only answer that makes sense. He's constantly at your father's side. And whenever he isn't, then your father is entirely different."

She let that thought sink in and also began to see the pattern. "Still," she added finally, "he wasn't in the galley when I acted so strangely. For that matter, why me and not you? You're more like a mongrel puppy than the Anunnaki; no offense."

"None taken. Camile believes there are at least two Ha.Sa.Tan on Seahab, possibly more. He thinks that if we're right about Rocky, then probably the whole security team might be compromised. As to me, perhaps it was the genetic alterations made by the Anunnaki that made us mongrels immune. Perhaps that was the real reason we were bred, to give the empire an army that the enemy couldn't influence."

"Oh my God!"

"Exactly; and that's why all the cloak and dagger."

"But what if Camile is only telling you part of the truth? What if he's also a Ha.Sa.Tan and he's using Rocky as a decoy? And why tell me? Based on what happened earlier, you'd have to think I'm vulnerable."

"I thought about all that. As to Camile, if he is Ha.Sa.Tan, he would have been better served to have not raised my suspicions at all."

"I see your point."

"As to telling you … what can I say? … I love you. I'm willing to take that chance … because if you're the enemy then I'm switching sides."

She took his hand and squeezed it tightly, letting her touch say what her lips wished to utter. Staring into his eyes, she said the only thing she could say, "Dallas, I AM Ha.Sa.Tan."

"NO!"

She burst out laughing, unable to keep a straight face any longer. "No, I'm not, but I just couldn't resist; it was just too tempting."

"Oh, you are evil. I'll have to give you a good spanking when we get back."

"Promise?"

He looked askance at her, and she began laughing again. "You'll learn to love my sense of humor," she added lightheartedly. Dallas looked at her radiant smile and wondered whatever happened to that stern, no-nonsense woman who had confronted him on the park bench so many months ago. He pictured her then, in his mind's eye. He could still see the scene. The sky had been a deep blue, dotted with cotton-ball clouds. It had been a beautiful spring day with only a slight breeze to remind him that winter had not completely surrendered its grip. She had stood in front of him with her navy trench coat fluttering in the breeze and ... Dallas suddenly jerked the mini-sub's controls to a stop, leaving them to drift with the current.

"That's it!"

"What's it?"

"I was just remembering the day we first met —"

"You mean the day I threatened to kill you," she interrupted.

"Yes. Do you remember that day? I was sitting there, frankly feeling very foolish, and looking around —"

"And?"

"And I saw him, even back then."

"Saw who?"

"One of the technicians on the Seahab crew. Back on the day you and I met, he was there, watching me from the line of trees next to the street on the other side of the museum. It was him, I'm sure of it; and that's not all. Now that I think of it, I believe he was there the night Dr. Todd was killed, dressed as a policeman. I'm sure he was the taxi driver in Namibia, and then again in Dubai where he was one of the charter boat crew. Now he's down here with us. He was the only person in the galley when you 'reacted.' He's been following me from the very beginning."

"Are you sure?"

"Absolutely. I remember staring at him the day we landed Seahab on the bottom, trying to place where I'd seen him before. It was him, I'd bet my life on it."

"So, my first instinct was right; I should have killed you."

"Not funny. Besides, if he is working with Rocky, then he may have been following you at first, not me. But that confirms Camile's hunch."

"Why did we come all the way out here for this little conversation?"

"We – Camile and I – are thinking that their ability to influence minds is limited both by distance and numbers. At least that's what we're hoping. I thought by bringing you out here we could have a completely private conversation."

"Better turn the radio back on; it's time for us to check in."

"Oh, right. Thanks." Dallas picked up the microphone. "Hakeem, this is *Aquarius One* checking in."

"Roger, *Aquarius One*," mumbled a very bored Hakeem. "Anything remotely interesting out there?"

"Nope, just fish. Next check in fifteen minutes. *Aquarius One*, out."

"Command out."

"Now," he said, turning the craft toward the cliff, "as long as we're here, let's examine that cave I saw yesterday."

24

DALLAS TURNED THE MINI-SUB around and pointed it toward the cliff where he had seen the outcrop of rocks. It was now nighttime on the surface and one hundred sixty feet down the area outside the range of the sub's floodlights was pitch black. Cautiously, he pushed the Aquarius over the edge and down the side, until he came alongside the same gap in the rocks he'd noticed before; the opening was even more pronounced in the intense illumination. Miranda stared at the opening in complete disbelief.

"This opening shouldn't be here."

"I know. Hakeem didn't take much notice of it, he called it a hollow; but I found it curious, to say the least."

"No. I mean it really shouldn't be here. Look, those rocks there, the ones covering the opening, they look like basalt; I've seen such stone at digs in Egypt. They don't belong with the rest of the formation. It's almost as if they were placed there to conceal the opening. Look at the size and shape of the entrance; it's easily ten feet high and at least as wide, if you move those boulders. Dallas, I believe this opening is manmade."

"That's exactly what I thought when I first saw it."

"Aquarius is equipped with a lighted camera boom. Let's extend the camera into the opening and see if there's anything inside."

"All right."

With the flip of a few switches, the interior video monitor sparkled to life. Miranda took charge of the video boom joystick and inched the camera toward the opening. The screen flickered momentarily as the camera adjusted to the increased light, and even then everything appeared a slightly dull, greenish hue.

At first, the opening revealed nothing of particular importance. Then the narrow entry broadened quickly into a massive chamber that extended so far that the light failed to illuminate the far side. The floor fell away with a series of what could only be called steps; the space beyond quickly opened to the size of a small chapel. Despite the scattering of debris and overgrown sea life, it was clearly an artificially constructed space. Every so often, a small fish would swim nonchalantly past the camera; each time distracting Dallas from the sights beyond the fins.

Rebuking himself from the loss of focus, he stared past the fish into the gray-black darkness at the edge of the light's reach. He could see the ghostly outline of the far end of the room. He could make out the faint signs of the walls and floors coming together at right angles. The walls were rough hewn and beige, giving the appearance of limestone, but the floor looked basaltic, like the cover stone. Both were overgrown and cluttered with sand and debris, yet revealing hints that they had been both polished and artificially shaped.

Dallas's reaction was immediate and extreme; he wanted to go through the hatch and swim into the chamber. It was only Miranda's quick reflexes and clear thinking that keep him from flooding the Aquarius.

"Dallas," she shouted, protecting the emergency escape latch. "We can't just go for a swim, we're not equipped."

"But this could be the clue we're looking for! This could justify the entire mission!"

"True; but you can't just swim out there. We're part of a team, the rest of which is sitting over at Seahab, right this moment, wondering where to dig."

"Aren't we forgetting something?"

"What?"

"Rocky and our nameless technician; if we're right, that they're both Ha.Sa.Tan, then anything we take back there will be instantly revealed to our worst enemies."

"And you're sure we can trust Camile?"

"I believe so," Dallas said upon reflection, "I truly do. As to the Ha.Sa.Tan, if we're right about not reading minds, then we may have a chance."

"Yes; we could select a small group and attempt to work covertly and never let ourselves be alone. We also need a way to counteract their powers. There must be some way to disrupt them."

"If it's brain control, it must have an electrical component —"

"I didn't know you were a biologist, too," Miranda interrupted, "I thought you were just a fair-to-middling archaeologist."

"Fair-to-middling? Well, I don't need to be a rocket scientist to know we're all basically electrical. Anyway, maybe Jonathan can create something. We could put him to work on that."

"You've been watching too many bad sci-fi movies."

"You have a better idea; now's the time."

"We'll come back to that. What about Jorge?"

"George? Sure, he'd love to get a look at this cavern."

"What about Samantha? And Khalid?"

"It's a coin toss; after all, your father was under Rocky's influence when he sent for her."

"I suppose you don't intend to include my father."

"Miranda … "

"Don't say it; I guess I'd have to agree with you, at least until we can figure a way to counteract the Ha.Sa.Tan's effect.

"If that's even possible —"

"And what if it isn't?"

"Their power must have some limitations, or we wouldn't be having this conversation."

"True. What about the others?"

"It's going to be difficult to move too many people and keep it secret. So far we've got you, me, and Camile. If we count adding Jon, George, and either Sam or Khalid that would be six; it's too many to keep things secret. We'd never be able to move all those people out here without attracting attention."

"But how do we organize ourselves to fight back?"

"Okay," offered Dallas finally, "how about this: we tell Jon about the mind control problem, but not the cavern. We bring Jorge out here, but don't tell him that we've included Jon. Basically, we keep everyone in the dark. We'll leave Khalid and Samantha out for the moment; that gives us Camile, Jon, George, you, and me. Camile can keep track of things on the station while the rest of us do what we need to do. Only you and I will know everything. For everyone else, everything is strictly on a need-to-know basis."

"Sounds good to me," she said supportively, adding as she looked at her watch, "It's time for another radio check with Seahab."

As much as it pained him to leave the cavern entrance, it was time to head back to the Seahab. Although Hakeem hadn't specifically insisted upon their return, Dallas got the sense that his fellow scientist was both bored and curious, a combination lethal to the newly hatched conspiracy.

The ride back took only a few minutes, unlike the tedious and painfully slow process of docking up with Seahab. Finally, a frustrated Dallas turned over the controls to Miranda, who promptly parked the mini-sub. She tried, barely, to conceal her pride, while he could only shrug his shoulders in concession to her obviously superior piloting skill.

It was Hakeem who greeted them with a sly smile as he opened the watertight hatch.

"I bet you two thought you were pulling one over on me, smuggling Miranda out there like that; I know what you were up to."

"What ... what were we up to?" Dallas asked cautiously.

"Come on, I know about you two, sneaking out in the sub for a little 'private time.'"

"Oh, that," Miranda jumped in quickly, flashing a coy smile. "I guess we can't fool you, Hakeem. Please, do us a favor and keep this to yourself, at least for now. It might get a little awkward for us, with everyone living so close together and all." Turning to Dallas, she winked agreement at the neatly provided alibi and stretched out her hand, "come on, darling."

"Yes ... Muffin." Dallas choked back a laugh; an effort in restraint made harder by the raised eyebrow that greeted his response.

As they walked down the corridor and past the bulkhead doors into the next watertight compartment, Dallas could hear two things; the fading laughter of Hakeem behind them, and Miranda muttering, "Muffin!" over and over to herself.

They caught up with Jon in his lab, where he was amusing himself with some abstract and supposedly unproven theorem. After a few moments of painfully dull small talk, Dallas moved cautiously to the half-open door, glanced outside, and then gently shut it. He turned to see a puzzled look on Jon's face and motioned to the scientist not to speak until he had checked all the doors in the lab. As Dallas did this, Miranda walked across the room and turned on the small, portable stereo that sat on the bookcase. Instantly, the room filled with the sounds of Mozart.

"Serenade Number Thirteen in G major?" asked Miranda, adding, "the fourth movement, I think."

Jon smiled approvingly, "I see you know your classical music."

"It's one of my favorites, and certainly one of his better-known pieces."

Dallas's expression was a study; revealing both his desire to question her statement and an open acknowledgment that he wouldn't have the faintest clue about whether any answer she might give would be correct.

She read his look and added with utterly false humility, "Eine Kleine Nachtmusik – A Little Night Music."

"Dallas, surely you two didn't come hear to listen to music. What's this all about?"

A half-hour later, they departed, having told Jon as much as they dared, which appeared about as much as he could handle as well. He agreed to work on his part of the plan, although he freely acknowledged that he had no clue where to begin. Their next stop was Jorge, who was busy relaxing in the facility's only hot tub, with a tall glass of champagne in his right hand and his ghetto blaster sitting tub side, cranked up to earthshaking. Dallas reached for the volume control, lowering the music to merely deafening. Miranda stood discreetly on the opposite end of the room, unsure of what Jorge was wearing beneath the Jacuzzi's bubbles.

"Come, sit over here, my dear," motioned Jorge. "Do not worry; I am – how would you put it – decent." Turning to Dallas, he continued, "So, my friend, how may I help you?"

"George, I think we've found something that just might capture your attention. Can you have a cave formation of limestone and basalt embedded in a coral reef?"

He pondered the question a moment, sipped his drink, and stared intently at the tiny bubbles for a moment more before answering.

"Strictly speaking, limestone caverns – we geologists call them solution caves – and coral reefs are born of the same basic environment. A solution cave is formed by acidic water eating the limestone. Usually, this all takes place below the water line. Once the water – how would you say it – drains out, you get secondary formations, stalagmites and such. Clearly, these formations require the cave to be above the water line. Now, it is possible for the cave, once formed, to become filled once more with water. If conditions are right, then yes, you could have coral formations grow in the area of such a cave. As to basalt being a structural component of the same cave in this part of the world, I would say no; never."

"Why?"

"Because, my friend, they are the oil and water of rocks. Basalt is an extrusive igneous rock, and limestone is sedimentary. They are formed by two very different processes. Basalt is the most common rock in the Earth's crust and, for that matter, the sea floor. It forms when lava rapidly cools. There are certainly caves formed through volcanism, lava tubes and such, as well as sea caves carved at the water line into basalt; but to have these types in the same formation with limestone at such shallow depths; perhaps you might find something similar at the bottom of the ocean, near the Mid-Atlantic Ridge, but not here in the Gulf, no. But, Dallas, why ask me what I'm sure you already know?"

Dallas looked at Miranda for a moment. "George," he began, "what would you say if I told you that we – Miranda and I – just found such a cave?"

Jorge leaned forward, his bushy eyebrow cocked in anticipation. "Then I would say you found something that shouldn't exist."

"Interested?"

"*Si*, of course, but what about the others? Why are we discussing this in private? We must tell the others."

"That," replied Dallas frowning, "will require a lot more explanation."

Once again, Dallas told only as much as he and Miranda agreed about Rocky and the Ha.Sa.Tan, but keeping Jon's and Camile's names out of the tale. Dallas could honestly say he had discussed the cave with no one else; thought the ease with which he delivered that white lie bothered him.

Leaving Jorge, the pair continued on their covert mission. They quickly located Camile in the dining room, quietly sipping a cup of coffee. Their furtive glances would have told anyone who cared to notice that there was something amiss; fortunately, no one noticed. Camile's pretense of nonchalance was also wafer-thin and the three found themselves tripping over contrived small talk.

"So," Camile spoke up finally, once the room emptied, "did you tell her everything?"

"Yes, but we've also discovered something; something incredible," Dallas whispered excitedly, "it's a huge cavern; manmade. We couldn't tell much from the sub; we've got to figure a way to get to the cave without being missed."

"Really; manmade! Still, it'll be difficult to do much completely unannounced. What's your plan?"

"We're working on some things, but it is best that we keep it need-to-know. What we want you to do is keep your eyes on things, cover for us until we're able to determine what, if anything, is in that cave."

"Who else are you going to tell?"

"We've decided it best to keep that information to ourselves at present. I'm sure you understand."

Camile sat in silence for a moment. He wasn't used to being kept in the dark; still he could offer no other alternative. He nodded his agreement, reluctantly.

"Dallas, I have no choice, but remember, you and Miranda hold any chance for success in your hands. You must not fail."

"Gee, no pressure."

25

A FTER TWO WEEKS – two painfully slow weeks – Dallas, Jorge, and Miranda had still not devised a plan for covertly exploring the interior of the cave. Jorge had discreetly wandered over to the cave site with Dallas and quickly examined the exterior geology, and in so doing, confirmed his initial assessment. They had been unable to accomplish more.

On each dive during those two weeks, they would have to swim in frustrated silence past their hidden site en route to the antiquated foundations and ruins the rest of the team had found. Everything about that time had been frustrating, not just ignoring the cave. Dallas and Miranda decided it best to maintain the appearance of a purely professional, even icy, relationship, Hakeem's lone observation notwithstanding. This pretense meant keeping a public distance, and in Seahab there was no private. They even staged several very loud and very visible arguments in an attempt to convince the spies that their effort to separate them had succeeded. What private contact they did allow themselves, encrypted messages using the station's computer network, was circumspect and vague.

While both their private personal goals went unattended, the mission of the team had begun to yield tantalizing tidbits almost from the first full day of work. What began as a trace or fragment soon turned into a virtual torrent of history-making artifacts. Beneath the sand and grit, buried with the dead shells and coral rubble, they had unearthed what the rest of the world would have thought impossible– a small ancient settlement. It was amazingly complete, with bronze implements, pottery shards, and assorted unidentified animal bones. What they had uncovered during those weeks was fascinating, historic, yet almost totally useless for their greater quest.

The one surprising exception was stone carvings on bits of basalt in the now familiar proto-Sumerian cuneiform. Dallas admitted being intrigued by the inscriptions, but he already knew it did not date to the time of the emerald tablets. It was clearly older than any other known writing anywhere in the world; at least twice as old as the oldest known specimen, making it twelve thousand years old. Ancient as that was, however, he felt it was still at least a thousand years separated from the date of the empire's last stand. Even allowing for life spans of biblical proportions, he knew that still meant a spread of maybe twenty generations.

Dallas's work with the emerald tablets made the translation of these carvings a relatively simple affair. As near as he could determine, the stone was, among other things, a maker identifying the village they had discovered; BI.TAN.ZU, which, as Dallas told the others, meant "House of He Who Knows the Heavens." In traditional archaeology this could have meant either a temple or the home of the temple priest. At any other time in his life, the discovery of this stone and its translation would have represented the pinnacle of a life's career, but for Dallas, now jaded by his months of work on the tablets, that part represented little more than a minor distraction.

For all his privately blasé attitude over the find, the rest of the team was ecstatic. For them, it confirmed their beliefs and extended known human history by six thousand years. Dallas did his best to mirror their enthusiasm, but always, in the back of his mind, was the cave. What did excite him was the second line of the translations, an oblique reference that he did not share with the others, save one; Miranda. That reference – "AL.HAL.SU HU.RSA.GMU" – was chiseled beneath the site's name; it meant "Fortification of the Sky-Chambers." To him, this reference could only mean one thing; that the site was not just a village, but the ruins of the fortress intended to protect the sky chamber mentioned in the emerald tablet.

It became clear to him that the basalt boulder at the cavern's opening was intended as a capstone; a capstone that had shifted – or had been moved. Its position, beneath the waterline of the ancient lake, suggested to Dallas its concealment, even in ancient times. Its location would also have made vandalism unlikely. Given the length of time between the fall of the empire and the carving on the stone, Dallas wondered if those who lived there even understood the significance of what the marker said. Perhaps, he mused, they could no longer even decipher the true meaning of the writing on the sign. Perhaps its presence was a mystery to them, a symbolic expression whose meaning had passed from fact into myth.

Miranda winced noticeably when he shared this secret with her. She was clearly troubled by the thought of concealing something so central to the mission.

"Dallas, what if the cavern really is the entrance to the vault? Assuming your translation is correct, how will you explain that you withheld this information from the others?"

"It will be easy to explain, when we make our move; once we know who we can trust. Those we can trust will understand. I thought you were with me on this." Dallas eyed her suspiciously.

"I am, I'm just don't like doing nothing. We need to take action."

"I know, I'm frustrated, too, but until Jon comes up with some way to fight the control of the Ha.Sa.Tan, there's simply no way to insure we have control of the station. There's been no trouble, we've laid low. Realistically, we can't confront them without some advantage, there may be too many of them."

"But we don't know that; not for sure. The only ones we know about for sure is Rocky and the technician. Hell, they may be the only two. We've got to take a chance."

"Rocky was head of security. That means his team must be suspect."

"Even so, that's only four men —"

"Four armed men."

"Granted; but sooner or later we'll need to confront them."

"And then there's the technician. If there's one infiltrator in that group there could be more."

"Okay, so there are five of them. Assuming all of them are Ha.Sa. Tan, that means ten enemies are on the station. That still means we are at least evenly matched."

"Assuming that none of the others are corrupted; but what are you suggesting? We get into a fire fight on the ocean floor? Besides, we don't even know the extent of their powers, if provoked. The only thing we do know is they are capable of murder."

"We must do something."

"This brings us back to the where we started."

Both of them threw their arms up in defeat. At that instant, they were startled by a knock on the door. They looked at one another anxiously. Had they been found out? Had someone been listening to them? The knock sounded again, seemingly more urgent. It was followed by a whisper. "Dallas? Are you there?" It was Jon.

Dallas rushed to open the door, and Jon bolted through quickly, carrying a small bag.

"I've got it! I've found a way to counter the effect of Ha.Sa.Tan; and, I think, the device will reveal them as well. Here," he said, reaching into the bag, "wear these medallions. They work like the noise-canceling headphones you wear on airplanes. They react to specific brainwave patterns by setting up sympathetic waves of opposite frequencies; negating their effect. It creates a sort of invisible shield around each wearer. And if I'm right, then the closer you get, the more uncomfortable they'll get. Get within one foot, and it should cause them great pain, perhaps even making them unconscious. Either way we'll know who they are."

"How," interrupted Miranda, "did you figure it out?"

"Well, you told me Rocky was one, so I built some extremely sensitive sensors and hid around my lab, then asked him and some of his team to come see me on some silly security question – I wanted to get a letter to the folks, you know. Anyway, while talking, I got them to move around the room, near each of the sensors. Each piece of equipment registered a set of brain wave frequencies in a unique bandwidth not common to us Homo Sapiens, so I used that as a guide and built these things to block that range of frequencies."

"How did you test it?"

"Test it?"

"So ... you haven't tested it?"

"Doing so would have tipped our hand."

"I see your point," replied Dallas, "So how many of those little medallions have you made?"

"I've got enough for everyone down here, plus a few spares. Now, here's the trick," Jon turned one over in his hand as he spoke. "You press here to activate it. Once on, you can't turn it off."

"Okay," Dallas replied, "here's the plan. First, let's put these things on. Next, I'm going to call a meeting for everyone in the dining room. Miranda, get a staff list and make sure everyone is present. Also, you two get a couple of stun guns from the armory for back-up; no bullets. We can't risk it; and keep them concealed. Once we're all there, you two will shut the doors, and I'll begin the meeting. I'll need to have something to talk about, perhaps some more of the translation. As I'm doing that, I'll walk around the room with this bag and we'll see what happens. Jon, if you're right, then I'll stand next to Rocky; if it works, we should at least see some physical reaction from him."

"But what if Jon's medallions don't work?"

"Well then, Miranda, I better have something important to say, or I'll look mighty foolish."

There was much Dallas could add, but it was unnecessary. They all knew they were down to their shot; their first, last and only shot. He sent Jon on his way with the understanding they would rendezvous within the next fifteen minutes. Once they were alone, Dallas turned to Miranda.

"We need to go to Jorge first and give him his medallion, in advance, just in case."

"And Camile?"

"Yes, and Camile. That at least gives us five some level of protection. But we must try to avoid getting too near anyone before we're ready. If they can sense these devices, we're busted."

"We'll have to get to the conference room first then," Miranda added, moving toward the intercom. She announced the meeting over the station's loudspeakers in fifteen minutes time then took his hand and moved toward the door.

After making their two stops, the couple moved on to the dining room ahead of most of the crowd. Dallas remained standing as the balance of Seahab's contingent wandered in while Miranda slid quietly into a seat next to her father's wheelchair. Rocky entered and took his normal place on Joshua's opposite side. The room soon reverberated with the gentle buzzing of ten different conversations going on at once. They seemed to take little notice of Dallas standing there at the front of the room. He looked first to Miranda, who silently confirmed everyone's presence, and then over to Jon and signaled for him to shut the door and take up his position, his hand resting in his white lab coat pocket.

"I suppose you are wondering why I've asked everyone to come here this evening." He panned his gaze across the room as he spoke, trying to take the measure of those in the room that he wasn't sure he could trust. His eyes came to Camile, whose expression of support gave Dallas the strength to continue.

"I was going to tell everyone the last bit of translation from the village signpost we discovered the other day, but first I have an important announcement to make."

"Is it about you and Miranda?" Hakeem chirped up, grinning broadly.

"What about you and Miranda?" It was Joshua.

"No, no. That isn't what I was going to say." He waited for the room to quiet down before continuing. "As you all know, we've been down here together for some time now. Before I get into the latest translation I think it's important to acknowledge how well all of us have worked as a team."

As he made small talk, he worked his way around the room, with his left hand in his pocket, the medallion clutched between his thumb and fingers. Coming to a stop next to Rocky, he pressed the device, activating it. Watching the suddenly fidgety security chief's growing sense of unease gave Dallas the confirmation and the confidence for what would come next.

"However, Miranda and I have come across some very disturbing information. I feel now is the time to take action." Dallas took a long, deep breath before dropping his bomb. "We have been infiltrated by the Ha.Sa.Tan. They are here on Earth, here in this room, right now."

The room froze for a moment. No one said anything, but everyone's heads were turning this way and that, waiting for someone else to react. Suddenly, Rocky jumped to his feet, lunging for Dallas. The security chief immediately doubled over and tumbled unconscious onto the floor. The rest of the security team rose to their feet, and then stopped, unsure of what to do. Jon pulled a stun gun from his lab coat pocket and motioned for the men to return to their seats.

"Jon, my compliments," Dallas offered, smiling, as he raised his left hand in the air. "All right, everyone, we have something to give each of you. In a moment, we'll know who the rest of the traitors are. See this medallion, it will protect those of us who belong here and hurt those of you who don't. I suggest, for your sake, you identify yourselves, NOW."

Slowly, first one, and then another of the interlopers rose to their feet. All the security team and the technicians stood up silently. Then, Khalid rose slowly to his feet, joining the other intruders. Camile's first reaction to this betrayal was shock; followed almost at once by seething anger. Camile promised himself that Khalid would pay most dearly. Dallas instantly realized that the Ha.Sa.Tan equaled the combined members of the Guardians and the Order; an observation not lost on anyone else in the room. Only the medallions kept them from being completely overrun. As Dallas stepped away from Rocky, the security chief regained consciousness and stumbled to his feet.

By now, Camile, Miranda, and Jorge had drawn their stun guns as well. Quickly, Dallas activated medallions and gave them to Hakeem, Dr. Pollard, and Joshua, all of whom were stunned by the sudden turn of events.

"Will someone kindly tell me what the hell is going on?" Joshua began; Miranda cut him off.

"In a minute, father, but first, we need to put these people away for safekeeping."

As Miranda turned back to address the infiltrators, one anonymous technician – a large, wiry black man with closely cropped silver hair – rose from his chair and moved to pull his hand from his pocket. Before the man could raise his arm, Camile fired his stun gun squarely into the man's back. He collapsed to the floor; his mind literally short-circuited by the jolt from the stun gun. Rocky's eyes glowed crimson red as he stared at the body, but he held his ground.

"Jon, give your stun gun to Camile. You and Miranda," Dallas spoke up, "disarm the others. Jorge, get that rope I asked you to bring and start tying these 'people' up —"

"Dallas?" This time it was Hakeem. "What is going on?"

"In good time, Hakeem. Let us get them situated first, and then we'll talk."

"You have no idea what you've done," Rocky growled, "none at all."

"Oh, I don't know. I think I've got a good idea. For one thing, I think we're caught our murderer —"

"You are all fools."

"Really, we're the ones with the guns. What does that make you?"

"So, Camile, what should we do with this crowd?"

"I vote for the airlock," Jon interjected, "for Raj."

"Me, too!" This time it was Jorge.

"No, my friends," said Camile slowly, "we cannot be better than them if we act like them. Besides, we may have use for them later, once we explore the cave."

"You mean you've found it!" Rocky's tone became angrier. "You must take me to it."

Dallas turned to Joshua, whose mind seemed to be clearing under the protection of the medallion. "Well, boss, what do you think?"

"I think … Camile is right, though I have no problem executing them if – or when – it is necessary. I think we should confine them under guard; for the moment."

"But I must go to the chamber."

"Relax, Rocky, you're not going anywhere."

"No, it is the vault; THE vault. Fate decreed you would find it, and I must go with you."

"Never gonna happen. Jorge, finish tying everyone up and then we'll take them to their quarters. Everyone else wait here, we'll be right back."

Soon, Dallas and Miranda returned, but only after ensuring that each of the Ha.Sa.Tan was securely locked away. They returned to find everyone sitting around the dining room's center table, drinking coffee and waiting anxiously to hear more of this cavern that Rocky seemed so insistent on seeing.

"So, my dear Dallas, tell us what you've been up to?" It was Joshua, but a Joshua that Dallas hadn't seen in weeks. Once more, the elder leader had that glimmer in his eyes; Dallas breathed a sigh of relief that they had chosen the correct course.

"First, let me say that without Jon's skill, we wouldn't be here now having this conversation. We now know why the Guardians and the Order have been kept at odds for so long; you have had a serpent in your midst, probably from the moment the Emperor sent you here. At any rate, as I said earlier, there was an additional inscription on the sign we found – 'AL.HAL.SU.HU.RSA.GMU.' I've translated that to mean 'the fortification of the Sky-Chambers.' I believe it ties in with something Miranda and I found two weeks ago —"

"You mean you two weren't out —" began Hakeem, before being interrupted by Dallas and Miranda in unison.

"NO!"

"But your dirty mind did give us a cover story," Dallas added. "Anyway, we found what appears to be a manmade chamber, under the ancient waterline. But we couldn't explore it or even reveal it to everyone – except Jorge – until we had dealt with the Ha.Sa.Tan."

"Jorge knew?" questioned Jon, whose facial expression at not being trusted with that information revealed how this new revelation wounded him.

"Don't feel so bad," said Camile, "I didn't know about either you or Jorge until today, although I knew that these two suspected Rocky and the others. I'm sure the need for secrecy is obvious to all of us."

"All this is well and good," interjected Joshua, "but what exactly have we found?"

"Well, if we're right, we've found the first step toward what we're looking for. This site is not just a simple village, but a fortress; a fortress built to protect a sky chamber."

"And what exactly is that?"

"Not a clue; but we think it's high time we found out, don't you?"

"But how can we go and leave those spies behind?"

"I've double-locked each cabin and hung devices outside on every door. They're not coming out. We can leave a couple of people here as guards, just in case."

"We could drug them," Dr. Pollard said finally. "You know, Diazepam, or perhaps Sodium Pentothal." It was a suggestion that caught the others completely by surprise.

"Truth serum?"

"Yes, Dallas, but it's mainly a sedative. It isn't much of a truth serum, that's a myth. Given the proper dose, people under its effect will talk; you just can't trust what they tell you."

"What the other drug you said, that 'daisy pam' stuff?"

"Diazepam. You'd know it better as Valium. In liquid form, injected directly into the bloodstream, it can be very effective, but my first choice would probably be pentothal. We can get them all hooked up to IVs, and then I can keep an eye on them while you guys are swimming around out there."

"We saw how the stun gun effected one of them; how can we be sure the drugs won't kill them?"

"We don't know for sure if it was alien physiology or just a weak heart. That is one reason I prefer Pentothal; it's much easier to control reactions."

"Okay, we'll pick someone to stay behind with you. No one works alone from now on; not until we've finished what we started."

"Dallas?" It was Joshua. "Given what you have discovered, I think we must consider the possibility that the *Habibti's* crew has been compromised. We must assume the Ha.Sa.Tan control that vessel, especially since I made the crew assignments while under Rocky's control." There was more than a touch of self recrimination regret in his voice.

"Don't be so hard on yourself," Camile said slowly, "after all, this is a race that toppled a galactic empire; and you had no way of knowing they even still existed. There was nothing you could do to defend yourself. Their power is indeed formidable."

"Coffee?" It was Miranda, who had vanished, and then reappeared with a freshly brewed pot.

"Umm, thanks … dear." Dallas winked.

"It seems to me," interjected Jon, "that we have several questions to answer on that score. Such as: why aren't you and Dallas affected? Why did they allow both groups to exist; and the entire population for that matter? What are they looking for that they needed us to be down here? After all, they could have simply stopped Joshua from proceeding with the mission, but they did not. Why?"

"All excellent questions," conceded Dallas as he absentminded tapped his fingers on the table, "and my bet is only Rocky knows the answers to those questions; but, doctor, you said truth drugs don't make people talk. Are you sure?"

"Like I said, they'll make people talk. Hell, you can't get them to shut up, but it doesn't mean they're saying anything even remotely resembling the truth. It's more like a bad acid trip; they could just as easily be describing their dreams, fantasies, nightmares, or whatever. There is no way of separating fact from fiction."

"Then we must not drug Rocky, not until we've had a chance to question him."

Miranda joined in the discussion, stating the obvious. "Dallas, there's no way of knowing he'll tell the truth, with or without the drug. And, besides, he's a murderer."

"True, and I have no illusions on either score, but he knows more than we do, and perhaps we can offer him an incentive."

"How so?"

"Clearly, he desperately wanted to come with us to the cavern. He said it as if it were preordained, 'fate,' he called it. He's obviously feels a need to go. That's our lever."

"So," Joshua asked finally, "what's your plan?"

"Well, it's too late to do any diving tonight. The earliest would be in, what, eight hours or so, if we start at first light. For tonight, we need to keep guard. Now, there are nine of us and ten of them; but I won't ask Joshua to stand guard, so that leaves eight of us; which means four two-man shifts of two hours."

"I'll get the sedatives ready for the others; that'll take about fifteen minutes or so," interrupted the doctor. "We'll have to restrain them on the beds and sedate them. They should be manageable."

"Thanks, Karen." It was one of the few times Dallas had used her given name, and despite the group's time together, she blushed slightly upon hearing it. "Get started; Hakeem, please go with her." Dallas handed him a two-way radio, adding, "Keep in touch at all times. The same goes for the rest of you. I know Rocky and his guys are locked behind metal doors, but we can't afford to make a mistake."

26

SOON KAREN AND HAKEEM returned with a crate full of medical supplies. Each hypo and IV was labeled with dose and patient name, along with a makeshift log so she could keep track of them properly. While she had no problem sedating them, she had no intention of harming them. Dallas quietly admired her dedication to her medical oath, especially in light of the knowledge that the Ha.Sa. Tan had killed two of her colleagues.

Jon waited with Joshua, Camile, and Miranda while Dallas joined the doctor, Samantha, Jorge, and Hakeem in sedating the prisoners. The process was slow and methodical, and hampered by resistance from the Ha.Sa.Tan. In the end, only Rocky was still conscious, and he remained supremely defiant in spite of the weapons pointed at him. He did not retreat or cower from the four, but instead, squared his shoulders and glared at them in silence. While he said nothing, he yielded to the logic of his situation and moved in the direction that Dallas gestured to with the flick of his wrist. There was little else Rocky could do; the remainder of his people were strapped either to beds or gurneys with slow drips of sodium pentothal coursing into their veins.

The group entered the dining hall to find the others sitting quietly, nursing their cups of coffee. They shifted in their chairs to let the armed escort move to the center of the room where Dallas motioned for Rocky to take a seat. He remained standing.

"Take a seat!"

"Or what? Are you man enough to make me?"

"I'm assuming you don't want to die."

"I'm prepared for it."

"Oh, really? I don't think so. You want to see the cavern as much as we do."

Rocky sized up Dallas for a moment, thinking back to the first day they'd met. "You've changed," he said finally, taking a seat.

"I'll take that as a compliment."

"As you wish. You mentioned seeing the cavern?"

"Tell us why we should let you? What do you know that we don't?"

"Just about everything."

"Very funny," Joshua deadpanned, lifting up his hand. "You remember this?"

It was the small, pewter-colored pistol-like device Dallas had first seen back on the very first day.

"You should," he continued, "it occurs to me that you were the one who taught me how to use it."

"You won't kill me."

"No, I won't; but I've come to realize one of its settings was designed for people such as you. I'm betting it won't kill you like these primitive human stun guns, but it will make you wish you were dead. I suspect it is indescribably painful."

"Your kind hasn't changed; not in the thousand millennia before your fall, nor the thirteen millennia since."

"Ah," Joshua replied, "our kind?"

"You decrepit spawn of the Anunnaki; your ancestors were the cock-roaches of the galaxy. They had no respect for 'The Way,' no respect for the need to hold to the natural order. They would come, lay waste to entire star systems, and move on. They cared neither for what they found, nor for what the left behind; and you, you are no better. You think of yourselves as the pinnacle of evolution. You are nothing but insects, even less than insects."

"Okay, fine. So why didn't you just destroy us completely all those millennia ago?"

"Because the doorway was opened!" In his rage Rocky blurted out the kernel of truth that lay at the center of his mission.

"The doorway?" Joshua raised his eyebrow as he locked his eyes on their antagonist.

"Yes," Rocky spat out, realizing the pointlessness of not speaking out, "the doorway. When we conquered Nibiru all those thousands of years ago, our forces fought their way through the emperor's defenses until we had him cornered within his palace. We discovered too late that he had been sending ships to Kia for many months before he sent Ziu. Sun.Da.Ra, and onboard one of them was the doorway. That meant we had to reach him before he could escape through it. Just as our forces reached him, the doorway was activated, and he stepped through it; a short time later, the entire palace was destroyed. Since then, we could only wait until the day finally arrived when the Kia doorway was found. Only then could we hope to find him and finally put an end to all this."

"But," puzzled Dallas, "you said the doorway was on the ship. If he was still on the planet, then how could he step through the doorway?"

'The doorway was one of a pair, fool."

"A time portal?" asked Jon finally. "Can you tell me how it works; I mean, how is time travel possible?"

"Your mind, your grasp of science, is too primitive to understand. Besides, we wouldn't trust you with such knowledge, even if you could comprehend it."

"The truth is," Joshua observed, "is that you don't comprehend it either; isn't that it?"

"What?" whispered Dallas, "is a time portal?"

"Don't you see," Jon replied, "the pair must function as a time portal. Think about it; what is the biggest problem with time travel?" It was a rhetorical question; the others just stared, waiting helplessly for the answer.

"The biggest practical problem with fourth dimensional travel, assuming it is even possible," he explained, "is that one doesn't know what will be occupying any future space; one might materialize inside a tree, a boulder or even another living being. It isn't like driving down a road where you can see danger ahead. The only way to solve that problem is to have both a predefined entry point and a predefined exit point."

"But if he sent it away on the ship, how could it be activated back in on Mars – Nibiru, whatever. Wouldn't he have been dead by the time it was activated?"

"You're not thinking fourth dimensionally. If it connects with the past, then it would appear to be a contemporaneous, even instantaneous, event —"

"I hate time travel," interrupted Dallas.

"Now," continued Jon, "since the doorway 'opened' that could only mean that the doorway had been successfully hidden away and activated at some point in the future to reach back into the past. Hence, they couldn't destroy Earth, because the very fact that the doorway opened told them that they had not done so, and they couldn't change history, even future history. All they could do is watch and wait. Am I right?"

"Yes, you are; and in all the thousands of years since the fall of the empire, this is the first time anyone has come so close to finding that doorway."

"But," countered Jon, "I don't understand. Why didn't you just use another set of doorways to travel back and change the past?"

"The emperor's doorway was the only pair in existence, and our history says it was found by Dr. Roark —"

"By me?" Interrupted Dallas, "how could your history possibly know about me?"

"In the minutes between the emperor's escape and the destruction of the palace we learned your name. You should be thankful, for that fact is all that kept you alive. But since our history says you find it; that is why I must be there – to kill the emperor when he steps through."

"And … you expect us to just let you kill someone?" Dallas realized immediately the naivety of that question, given that Rocky had in fact already killed twice before; a thought that prompted his next question. "Why did you kill Raj?"

"He discovered our existence, he confronted me; it was a simple as that."

"But I don't understand; if I'm so important why frame me?'

"I had to provide a suspect; Dr. Moncrief being a member of the Order was a fortunate coincidence. I figured I could get the ship to continue on to Dubai and clear you on the way. When the captain insisted on turning around I planted the breakout idea in Miranda's mind; given how she already felt that wasn't terribly difficult –"

"You mean that wasn't my idea?" Miranda gasped.

"Sorry, my dear but no it wasn't," Rocky responded cynically, "though I have no doubt you would have gotten around to it in time. I just couldn't wait for you."

"And Dr. Graham?" Dallas brought the interrogation back into focus.

"Come, Dr. Roark, tell the truth; you didn't even like the woman. Can you truly say you are sad she's gone?"

"That … that's not the point."

"Isn't it? At any rate, she realized the truth behind the Watchers; that it meant the Ha.Sa.Tan had infiltrated the Guardians, and she wanted to warn Joshua. She came to me in all innocence, not realizing who I really was."

"This is getting us nowhere," interrupted Miranda, "Dallas it's time for Rocky to take a nap."

"No, you must not. I must go with you."

"We've covered this, you're not killing anybody."

"No, you need me for another reason; I know the secret of how to enter the vault … "

"How can you know so much and still need us to find it?"

"Because we knew it existed, but we didn't know where it was hidden; and we knew we didn't find it, because we would never have activated it."

"So you had to wait for us to do your dirty work for you?"

"Works for me!" Rocky couldn't resist the dig.

Dallas glanced over Rocky's shoulder at Dr. Pollard, who stood silently ready. He nodded slightly, and instantly a hypodermic entered Rocky's bicep. He jumped to his feet, only to collapse a moment later, all the while protesting that he must go.

"Jon," Dallas added as he lowered the unconscious man to the floor, "take sleeping beauty here back to his 'room' and make sure he's secured. Hakeem, will you please accompany Jon and the doctor?"

"Dallas," asked Miranda as the others removed the body, "do you think he's telling the truth?"

"Doesn't much matter. If he is, then we can always come back and get him, but I'd rather try without him first; agreed?"

Everyone nodded their assent. Dallas couldn't help but wonder about the histrionics of it all; the Ha.Sa.Tan had been waiting thirteen thousand years for him to appear. Had they been watching over him all his life? Had the events on the night of Dr. Todd's death all been coordinated because they knew he must become involved? Did they kill that man just so Dallas could fulfill his destiny? The burden of that thought was almost too much to bear: that another man had to die because of him.

Miranda seemed to read his mind and moved to comfort him.

"Dallas, everything happened the way did because it had to, you couldn't change anything."

"Don't tell me, let me guess – it was fate."

"For lack of a better word, yes. Somehow, they learned about you, and that seems to have set everything in motion."

"Doesn't that thought make you dizzy? I mean, they learned about me ... they will learn about me ... and it sets the whole thing in motion again. Once that doorway opens, the clock resets to thirteen thousand years ago, and it begins again; countless lives, generations living and dying, until our own time. Then we are born and they know the time has come, again. How many times has this sorry story played itself out? What would happen if, this time, we just pack up and go home?"

"How do you know Rocky's telling the truth? How do you know that isn't exactly what he wants you to do, to walk away?"

"Let's just kill him, like he killed the others. Wouldn't that change history?"

"Don't know, but I don't believe you're the type to kill Rocky in cold blood, no matter how much he may deserve it."

"I agree." It was Joshua. "When, or if, that needs to happen, we would not expect you to face that choice alone. We owe you that much."

"Thanks, Joshua, but you don't owe me anything. You told me months ago that I had to make a choice; I did."

"That's a decision for another day," Camile interjected. "I think it best to take advantage of our relative security and get some rest. Tomorrow will be a busy, and exhausting, day."

The others agreed; all of them suddenly weary as the adrenaline rush from the earlier confrontation wore off. They each moved off quietly toward their individual assignments, whether it was guard duty or a sleep, there wasn't much left to say; and even if there were, no one had the energy to say it.

A few hours later, Dallas stretched lazily, rolled over, and reburied his head into his feather pillow. It was a thought process in slow motion that gradually reminded him of all that transpired. His eyes went wide as he began to remember the night before. His first passing thought was that it had all been a dream, a notion that he laid to rest when his eyes focused on the head of blonde hair sleeping on the pillow beside him. It had not been a night of passion; just two bodies collapsing into the same bed. Still, he found it comforting to see her lying there. Gently, he shook her shoulder and was rewarded with a slight smile as she began her own frenzied procession toward consciousness.

By agreement the night before, the doctor had not kept Rocky on heavy sedation. Though none liked the idea, no one wanted to gamble against the chance that Rocky might just be telling the truth; that his presence would eventually be required at the dive site. So, while Dallas and Miranda were rousing, Rocky laid on a gurney, mumbling to himself in a semiconscious stupor as he slowly recovered from the sodium pentothal of the night before.

Dallas and Miranda dressed silently and moved off to meet the others for a brief breakfast and to map out their plan for exploring the cave. They could not all go at the same time, so the privilege of being first fell to Dallas, Miranda, Camile, and Samantha.

Only Hakeem was truly frustrated with the selection. Doctor Pollard knew she had to remain with the prisoners, Joshua conceded he couldn't be of much help, and both Jorge and Jon were quite content to listen to the exploits over the radio. Of course, they all knew that, in the end, if they did truly discover something, then they would all have to go over. Anticipating that possibility, they prepared the prisoner's section of Seahab to be completely isolated from the others, locked from the outside, and totally disabled; dependent on the other sections for life support.

Finally, the time came for the four to depart. Given the equipment they would be taking with them, they decided to use the sea scooters for the journey to the cavern. In almost no time, they covered the distance between the Seahab and the massive basalt boulders concealing the opening.

"I think," Samantha said finally after examining the entrance, "we can squeeze through the opening, if we remove our tanks and bring them through behind us. I'll go first; pass me the flashlight." She quickly removed her tanks before the others could object.

She worked her way through the narrow opening and then, using the torch, shined the light around the nearby walls, ceiling, and floor of the entrance. Only after that act was accomplished did she turn back to pull her tank through. Dallas passed the equipment through to Samantha, and then followed after it. The others entered behind him as he stood watch over the darkness facing them. Once everyone was inside, they swam perhaps a hundred feet and moved downward perhaps another twenty feet before the passageway opened into the cavern that the

camera had revealed earlier. Floating in the center of the room, the four
shined their lights randomly, not quite sure what they were looking for.
They separated and drifted off in different directions, examining the
floor and walls.

"Dallas, come here," Samantha called out minutes later, waving her
light frantically, "I've found something!"

The entire chamber turned out to be the size of a good-sized church,
and, Samantha observed, in the same familiar cross-shaped pattern of
the grand cathedrals. Following a hunch, she moved in the direction she
imagined an altar would be, and at that point found a massive, rectangular block, about one-and-a-half meters high, one meter wide and two
meters long. Unlike the other pieces of rock, this one was completely
smooth and unblemished, its edges sharp and clear. The center of the
block was notched in a peculiar pattern that appeared familiar to her.
Dallas and the others reached her at the same time, and all of them
marveled at the huge altar stone.

"What do you think it is?" Miranda asked, drifting above its
center.

"Can't say." muttered Sam. "If this were a church the answer would
be obvious, but here … I just can't say. That 'U' shaped pattern of
notches —"

"I know what you mean," said Miranda, "They look so familiar—"

"It's the emerald tablets," Dallas cried out excitedly. "God knows I've
stared at them enough to recognize the pattern. Remember the bottoms
of those tablets, I'd bet anything they fit into that pattern. It's a pity
there are no instructions —"

"What?" interrupted Camile. "Don't the tablets tell you?"

Dallas began again. "There are no instructions in the tablets, not
even oblique ones. And there's not a single mark on this … this …
whatever it is; it's totally smooth. It looks like it could have been put
here yesterday. Jorge, how is it that this – thing – can be so clean?"

"There's no geological reason that I can think of." Samantha mused.
"Perhaps we should have brought Jorge after all,"

"He'll be thrilled to hear that."

"Actually, I'm not the least bit thrilled." It was Jorge who had been monitoring the team via their radio link with Seahab. Jon jumped in, "Miranda, use the detector I gave you; see if there any electrical fields in there."

"Electrical fields?"

"Yes, Dallas, that's the only thing I can think of that might keep plant life from taking hold."

"You mean, like a force field?"

"A repulsive electrical field, yes. But I'm betting it's something more. Perhaps a combination of things. Has anyone tried to touch it yet?"

"No."

"Don't; there's no telling what effect any field might have on humans. It sounds to me like we need to get the three emerald tablets in there with you."

"Okay, Jorge," said Dallas, "suit up and bring 'em with you."

"But, Dallas, I don't think —"

"No 'buts,' Jorge; we don't have time to waste. You can get here twice as fast as we can get there and back. Trust me; it's completely safe in here."

"I don't think so." It was Joshua. "Dallas, I'm with Jorge on this one. I think we need to do this by the book. Let's set up the monitoring equipment, take a full battery of photos, thermographs, the works; and then we can talk about taking the tablets out there. They're just too important for us to jump the gun."

"Joshua, don't misunderstand my next question. Jon, how is Joshua's medallion working?"

"Just fine. We're all in good shape here."

The entire team drifted above the megalith in silence, waiting for Dallas's next move. He stared over at Miranda, searching her eyes for the right answer. They had only thirty minutes of air left before they had to return to Seahab, which left little time for further discussion. This fact also helped Dallas make up his mind.

"Okay, Joshua, we'll start making our way back once we've go the equipment in place." Dallas glanced back at Miranda, who winked in silent reply.

Quietly, the team set to work. While the others set about the task of assembling the lights and cameras, Dallas used the still camera to take high-resolution photos of the entire visible surface of the block. It was tediously slow and frustrating work that was made all the more diffi-cult by the currents and eddies of the cavern. Camile worked the ther-mal-imaging video camera, while Samantha and Miranda assembled a myriad of scientific devices for measuring everything from temperature to light beyond the visible spectrum.

Finally, with everything in place, and after insuring that Seahab was receiving the equipment's radio signal, they exited as they had entered and made their way back to their base. The trip back to Seahab was uneventful, as was the next two hours. A rest period dictated by Samantha's dive protocols. While no one knew what to expect from the remote sensors, everyone did expect something; so far everyone but Jon was disappointed.

"That … thing … is definitely putting out an electrical charge. It's incredible! If it's been down here for thousands of years and still able to generate that level of an electrical field, then it must be nuclear powered; but we're getting absolutely no hint of radioactivity."

"That whole cavern must be blanketed in an electrical field," replied Samantha. "We had to run the antenna cable all the way outside the entrance before you got a clear signal."

"Who knows, could be powered by something we haven't discov-ered yet? Do you think there's any danger?" Dallas asked as he drained another coffee cup.

"No … at least I don't think so; neither does Karen. Sam's right; the electrical field is respectable, but not dangerous in itself. And, as I said, there's no radioactivity that I can measure."

"And the thermographic scans?" asked Camile.

"Absolutely clean, it's almost like it's not there; which is surprising, since any energy source would give off a heat signature."

"So where does that leave us?" Miranda joined in the discussion in earnest.

"I'll tell you where," countered Dallas, "absolutely nowhere. I thought that perhaps the photographs would tell us something, but I can't find any evidence of anything, just a continuous smooth surface. No seams, no cracks, no joints, no marks of any kind."

"I hate to say this, Dallas, but —"

"Don't say it, Jon, don't —"

"But I've got to; maybe we should talk with Rocky, see what he has to say."

"He's gonna say he has to go with us, and we don't know if we can control him or what he'll do." Dallas's frustration was clear.

"Dallas," interrupted Miranda, "Jon's right. Rocky says he knows what to do; unless someone has a better idea, I don't see we have any choice."

"Joshua? Camile?"

The two leaders stared at one another for a moment. Finally, Camile gave a slight nod and deferred to Joshua.

"Much as it pains me, Dallas, I am forced to agree with Jon and Miranda. We'll just have to take a chance."

The others agreed, leaving Dallas with little choice but to have Rocky brought to the dining hall. He was fully conscious and more than a little smug at having been summoned; he knew it could only mean one thing, and it was a moment he intended to savor.

"So, Dr. Roark," said Rocky with an evil grin as he sat, cradling a small bag he had been allowed to retrieve from his cabin on his way to the dining room, "how may I help you?"

"You know perfectly well, Rocky."

"Yes … yes, I do. And I am completely willing to join you in this cavern of yours."

"First, answer my questions."

"Sure, why not?"

"Tell me everything you know about this doorway."

'Such as?"

"Such as why weren't your people able to destroy it in the first place?"

"Well, that's an interesting story. The abbreviated history version is that he sent it into hiding before we ever got to Nibiru. At that point we didn't know that he even possessed it. We had intelligence that they possible, at least in theory. It wasn't until we reached his inner sanctum and actually found one that we realized they were real. Shortly after it activated strange things happened. First, the vile emperor made good his escape. Our people sent word of that much, and other things, when, a short time later, the entire building exploded. We could only assume he had booby trapped it. However, in those few moments we somehow learned about you, Dr. Roark, and your involvement in the project; about how you opened the doorway. At that moment, we knew we would have to wait thousands of years; and we knew there was nothing we could do about it."

"You mentioned 'fate' decreed you must be present. How do you know that?"

"Our history doesn't mention me specifically, just you, but it does say that 'we' were ... will be ... present. Since you are here, and I am here, I assume it is to be me."

"But why you? Why not send one of your security guards?"

"Two reasons. First, because I'm the only one of us who has this ... " With a dramatic flare he reached into his small bag and pulled forth an object wrapped in suede. He wrapped the object with great reverence and placed it on the table. Instantly everyone was shocked into silence. There, on the table, was the fourth emerald tablet!

"You've had that all along?" Joshua's tone was at once angry and incredulous.

"Oh, yes. It was actually quite humorous watching all of you chasing around, looking for it. This is my ticket for admission into the chamber, and to the altar stone."

"How do you know about the altar stone?"

"Really, are you going to make me repeat myself? Just accept that what I know, I know."

"Very well, so what do we do with this fourth piece of emerald tablet?"

"We take it, and the three pieces you've already got, and position them into the pattern on the stone."

"That's it?" Dallas sounded more than a little skeptical.

"That's it! Oh, and you have to know how to activate it."

"And we do that … how?" asked Dallas.

"That would be the second reason as to why it would be me. It is also my secret; and my insurance that I get to the cavern."

"Joshua? Camile?" Dallas's question was almost rhetorical, but he still wanted confirmation of the obvious. It was Camile who spoke this time.

"Like you, I don't like it, but I see no alternative. However, I will say this much, and it is a promise, Rocky, if you make one single false step, one single wrong move, and I will kill you myself; Joshua?"

"I couldn't have said it better myself. Rocky, I don't care what you think you know of history, do not make the mistake of thinking we care whether you live or die."

"Funny," replied Rocky, "I was just thinking the same about you two. Yes, I think the Ha.Sa.Tan will do well in your era."

27

I N DUE COURSE, THE first team, plus Jon, Joshua, and Rocky had reentered in the cavern, and floated in a circle once more above the massive altar. Carefully, Rocky began assembling the emerald tablets in the proper order. Its assembly served as a combination lock, he told the assembly, with the pieces needing to be positioned in the proper sequence. How he knew the sequence, or if he was just guessing, no one knew. Whatever the case, he seemed well-satisfied with his work, and in seconds, the emeralds were assembled into the shape of a pyramid. It looked to everyone like the miniature of the Great Pyramid on the Giza Plateau. After he put the final piece in place, Rocky floated back with the others and waited; nothing happened.

"Okay, now what?" Even over the scuba communication system, Dallas's tone dripped with obnoxious sarcasm.

"I … I don't know. That should have worked. I'm sure I placed them in the correct order."

"Tell us again about destiny —" Dallas's comment was cut off by his sudden realization that the emeralds had begun to glow; faintly at first, but the intensity of the light quickly increased to fill the entire space with a soft green hue. Everyone seemed to notice at the same time, and they all began talking excitedly over one another.

"Oh my God!"

"Look!"

"Is someone taking measurements?"

"Incredible."

It took Dallas a moment to put the comments in order: Miranda, Camile, Joshua and Samantha. He couldn't help but be amused that only Joshua was concerned with scientific study.

They were all so focused on the light that none noticed the entrance had closed. A solid wall of perfectly clean metal had dropped quietly into place, as if out of nowhere, and sealed the cavern tight. They also didn't notice the water level lowering – slowly, almost imperceptibly, as it was draining out of the chamber. Then, what was imperceptible became obvious, and everyone realized the water was vanishing from the room. As the levels dropped, the walls changed. The thirteen thousand years of encrustation simply vanished, leaving behind smooth surfaces, exactly like the altar. Within minutes, they found themselves standing in the middle of a massive rectangular space bathed in a soft greenish glow. The air should have smelled of rotten sea life; instead it was fresh and clean.

"The water —" Miranda kept repeating.

Rocky ripped off his mask and dropped his weights, clearly not surprised by what had just happened. Joshua collapsed, his useless legs further burdened by the sheer weight of the scuba gear. Everyone began stripping, beginning with their weight belts. Miranda helped her father shed his equipment, and with Camile's help, shifted him into a more comfortable position leaning against the altar. Dallas was mindful enough, even with the shock of what had just happened, to have everyone keep their gear accessible, just in case the water should return as quickly as it had left. He grabbed the backpack he had brought with him inside his dry suit and withdrew his journal. As the others wandered around the chamber in awe, Dallas took a moment to sketch the placement of the emerald tablets, thus insuring their independence from Rocky. As he did that he realized he'd written nothing since his prison break from the tanker. He made a mental note to update it upon his return to Seahab will all that had happened. With the sketch completed he returned the small book to his bag and tossed the whole thing over one shoulder. He then turned his attention to their prisoner.

"Okay, now what?"

"I cannot say for sure. I knew how to activate the device; I can only assume the next step will be obvious."

"Well, I don't see a next step."

"Give it a minute."

As if on cue, the wall opposite the entrance slid noiselessly to one side, revealing an arched opening about six feet wide and ten feet high. Beyond that opening, a growing illumination of green light enticed them to enter. They could see a long tunnel that sloped steeply downward, winding to the right as it declined. It went such a distance that they could not distinguish what lay beyond. Dallas looked around, trying to gauge what to do next. He felt compelled to move forward, if only because this is what they came for, but he didn't want to leave Joshua behind.

Without needing to say so, everyone felt the same way; they couldn't have gotten to this point without Joshua's drive and dedication. They had no intention of leaving him only feet from their goal. Despite his protests, Jon and Camile lifted him up from either side and, carrying him, followed Dallas into the tunnel. The green light preceded him, illuminating the way as he went. Miranda moved next to Dallas, and the couple led the way forward. Only Samantha remained. She motioned for Rocky to precede her, mindful that this spy still had a mission to complete. She was determined not to let that happen. They emerged from the tunnel minutes later, entering a large vault; Jon couldn't help but marvel at the obvious level of technology.

"Do you realize, Dallas, that whatever is powering this facility has been waiting for thousands of years, and yet it functions as if it were brand new. It's fantastic."

"Yes, it is; and humbling. What must our ancestors have been like to have had such knowledge?"

"They were monsters, demons," Rocky hissed. "They pressed their boot heel to the throat of a thousand different races, forcing them to bend to their will —"

Miranda twirled around to confront the enemy. "And if that is true then how are they are different from the Ha.Sa.Tan?"

"Fanaticism in the pursuit of truth is not evil."

"Oh, please." Miranda turned away. She could see that further confrontation was pointless.

Joshua gestured for his porters to loosen their grip slightly, and then he reached into his dive suit, pulling from it the same oddly shaped object he had shown Dallas when they first met so long ago.

"I brought the Baphomet amulet along," said Joshua, handing it to Dallas. "Remember? I said we'd need it."

Dallas stared at it for a moment, turning the triangular object over and over in his hand. Aside from engraved images, there were no other marks; at least none visible to the naked eye. Absentmindedly, he dropped the piece in his pants pocket. The entire group wandered around the vault, which was as cluttered as the cavern had been empty. The space was the size of an airplane hanger, and was filled with all manner of items, artifacts and treasures, both literal and scientific. In the exact center, elevated above everything else, were two massive columns centered on a large landing, with steps that lead up to it from the floor.

"Whoa, will you look at that," said Dallas breathlessly.

"I've died and gone to heaven." It was Jon, his eyes were darting around the room like a junkie on speed and his mouth was drooling over the prospect of studying everything in the room. "I may never go back to the surface."

"I can help you with that," said Rocky, sarcastically. "Rest assured the Ha.Sa.Tan will put these weapons to good use, I promise you."

"Why?" asked Miranda. "You've defeated the empire, what else is there?"

He hesitated a moment before responding, and his answer stunned them. "The empire lives."

"WHAT!" The team spoke as one.

"Yes, barely, its forces exist as rebels and bandits, hiding on a few isolated worlds; they are disconnected and defiant, but still they hang on, clinging to pathetic fantasies. To them the ancient emperor has become a god. They believe that he will one day reappear and lead them to victory."

"I finally see," Dallas spoke up. "You're afraid I'll do something to save the emperor by opening the doorway, and that he will then rejoin his forces and overthrow your sorry bunch."

"And if you do so, you'll be condemning the galaxy to countless more years of warfare and the deaths of billions, beginning with your own planet."

"As if," Camile added, "you don't already intend this planet's destruction, regardless of what Dallas does."

"Excuse me?" Dallas muttered, turning to face Camile.

"Of course, it is obvious. They couldn't do anything to you or this planet until you fulfilled their expectation of the future. Once having done so, there will be no further reason to spare or us. We must bring the emperor through and hope he is able to defend this planet."

"Or," countered Miranda, "not activate it yet and continue to keep that possibility hanging over the heads of the Ha.Sa.Tan. Remember – we're safe until that doorway is opened, then all bets are off."

"And this brings us back to our original conflict, if I am not mistaken." It was Joshua, who couldn't help but chuckle at the irony. "This must be the origin of our conflict with the Order; why they wanted to find the vaults and why the Guardians didn't. In our own ways, we were both trying to protect the planet from destruction. Now it all becomes clear."

"I could use a little help here," said Dallas. "Do we look for the doorway or not?"

"If Rocky is correct," replied Camile, "then we already know what you do."

"But why can't I just turn around and walk out of here?"

"We're locked in, where would you go?" This time is was Samantha. "More to the point, history tells us you don't."

"I'll go with my original thought – I hate time travel. Look, since we all seem to know what I'm going to do, why don't we just find the 'on' switch or button, or whatever it is, and get this thing over with."

"But we can't," Miranda challenged. "Once we do that then we will doom ourselves."

"How? Will somebody please tell me how? I mean, how will the Ha.Sa.Tan know that it was today that I turned it on, or tomorrow, or next year for that matter? They already know it happens, and that it is apparently me, they just don't know when. Let's face it; it could be a great grandson – with the same name – that does the deed. We're just not that sure of our facts. For all we know, I become the new high priest and father a line of Roarks, all named Dallas. For all we know Roark could the newest form of Caesar."

No one could argue that point, because no one knew for sure, not even Rocky. It was a possibility that had not occurred to anyone until Dallas said it; they couldn't be sure that he was THE Dallas Roark who would activate the doorway.

"For God's sake," fumed Camile, somewhat uncharacteristically, "can we stop talking nonsense and start exploring? We don't even know how to identify the doorway, much less activate it. Let's start looking around and cross that bridge when we get to it."

"I'm just guessing," Dallas replied, "but I'll bet that the doorway has something to do with those two columns over there on that platform. What say, Rocky, is that it?"

The absence of a response only served to confirm Dallas's statement.

"Okay, let's go check it out." Dallas moved toward the steps, followed by the rest of the group. Climbing the steps, they began to get a true sense of the scale involved. They had moved downward almost fifty feet, a thought that began to concern Miranda. That represented almost two atmospheres of depth greater than the depth of Seahab; requiring a prolonged decompression stop upon departing for Seahab. On the other hand, if the vault was pressurized to sea level, then they had the opposite problem; one that could prove deadly. If it had been above water in ancient times, then the pressure would have been unimportant to anyone entering it. Now, however, their bodies had become adjusted to the Seahab's depth of five atmospheres. This meant the bends were imminent. Without her dive gear, she had no way of measuring the pressure, or of even knowing what the exact air pressure was in the vault. Still, they had been out of the water and walking around for some time and she felt no ill effects. She pondered the possibility that the enclosure had some form of technology that allowed it to measure their physiological conditions and adjust the environment as necessary.

They reached the top of the platform and moved to the base of the closer column. It rose twenty feet in the air and bore a faint resemblance to the Greco-Roman style. The pair stood approximately fifteen feet apart, and despite their appearance, they were not, according to Samantha, made of marble. On the sides facing one another, a one-foot metal plate ran up the entire length of the column.

"Jon, what do you make of this?" asked Dallas.

"Looks like strip of metal."

"Funny, very funny."

"Honestly, I don't know. I don't know what type of metal it is. I don't even know what these bloody columns are made of."

"Could this be the doorway?"

"Sure; don't know what else it could be; but beats me how it could possibility do anything. Personally, I want to start examining the stuff on the shelves; my God, it goes on for thousands of square feet."

"Put me down," said Joshua, "while you people look around. I have a good view from here. I just wish the light were better."

Surprisingly, the chamber obeyed his command. The green illumination gave way gradually to a brilliant yellow-white light. The group looked at one another in continued amazement.

"Does this place understand us?" Dallas said, as much to himself as to the others.

"It must be brainwaves that it's reacting to; thought patterns," responded Jon. "Even if it were a super computer, it couldn't know English; the language didn't exist when this place was built."

"Incredible!" Camile was almost giddy, staring upward and trying unsuccessfully to locate the source of the light. At that moment, Rocky made his move. He shoved Samantha to the floor and threw himself over the side of the landing. Before anyone could react, Rocky had vanished into the rows and rows of artifacts. The stacks were piled high and ran in all directions.

"Rocky! Give it up," Dallas screamed in no direction in particular. "You can't get out of here."

"I'm not trying to. Sooner or later, you'll open that doorway, and I'll fulfill my function. Either that, or I'll figure out how to use one of these weapons to destroy the entire vault."

"You can't do that," interrupted Jon, "that would cause a temporal paradox that might destroy everything."

"Okay, fine. Then tell Dallas to open the doorway."

"We can't do that, we don't know that this is the time."

"We don't know that it isn't." With that came a bolt of blue light, like cracked like thunder as it past over the heads of the team. "You have the doorway; I have the arsenal. Activate it, NOW!"

"Don't fire those weapons." It was Joshua. "You don't know what damage you might do."

"Do you think I care? Do you think I care if I destroy everything, including this stinking planet? I would be a martyr among my people."

"But don't you understand?" interrupted Jon, "if you attempt to alter the past, you could undo everything. For all you know, destroying the doorway might also destroy the Ha.Sa.Tan."

"You don't really believe that; and neither do I."

"My point is we don't know. We can't be sure."

While this exchange was taking place, Camile crawled over to Dallas, who was doing his best to become one with the floor.

"Dallas," he whispered, "we must stop him. You must activate the gate now, before it is too late."

"You're overlooking one important fact; I don't know how. Everyone thinks I know what I'm doing but—"

"Dallas," added Joshua, "Camile is right. You must find a way to open the doorway."

"Joshua?"

"I know what I said before, but it's clear now that Earth was only safe all this time because it was what *THEY* wanted; not because of anything we've done. You must do it!"

"Maybe so, but for the moment, our problem is Rocky. Even if I knew how to do as you say, he'd still kill whoever came through. Then he could still kill us later, or destroy the world with what may be hidden in here. We have to lure him up here; we'd be sitting ducks trying to get down to floor level." In a louder voice, Dallas called out to Rocky, "Okay, what do you want?"

"Open the doorway, now, or you die." He punctuated his command by firing again. Another blue lightning bolt illuminated the room, this one aimed directly at the columns. The electric charge found its mark, but nothing happened. The column simply absorbed the charge without any physical effect.

"Rocky," Dallas called out again, "look, I'll be honest with you. I could care less about any of this. I'm an archaeologist; civilizations only interest me once they're dead. This battle between the empire and the Ha.Sa.Tan ended thousands of years ago. Earth is no threat to anyone now."

"Your point?"

"I'll give you the key, you do your thing. You let us live and leave Earth alone."

"And you'd take my word if I agreed?"

Dallas looked at the others. There was universal agreement that no one believed him; still he had no choice to at least pretend. "Sure, why not?"

"You don't lie well."

"Let me try put it another way. Now, you may succeed in destroying the doorway; but that may – correction, will – change the past and thus the future. The only alternative is to come, get the key, open the door, and then do what you have to do."

"You forget, history says you open the doorway."

"Okay then, you come up here, and I'll open the door. You know we're not armed. Bring your ray gun. We just want to get out of here alive, is that too much to ask?"

Rocky's response came in the form of a third blue bolt. Like the last, this one also found its mark; this time the other column. The results were no different; the two tall columns silently held their ground.

"All right," Rocky called out. "I give you my word; you can leave here alive; just open the doorway." After a moment's pause, he added, "I'm coming up; remember … I'm armed."

The others spread out along the landing on either side of the columns as Rocky approached from below. Slowly, he climbed the stairs, a rifle-like device held level in front of him. Dallas stood as he approached, while the others remained on the floor.

"Let's get this over with," Dallas said to his approaching enemy.

"Most reasonable of you, Dr. Roark. Now, let's figure out how to open the door."

Dallas reached into his pocket and withdrew the amulet that Joshua had given him. The face of Baphomet stared back at him. What, he asked himself, could it be saying to him from across the ages? He took his eyes from the amulet and began examining the area around the columns. He realized for the first time that the area of the landing around the columns was covered with metal tiles of similar shape with markings like the talisman. He studied the seemingly random symbols for what felt like forever, when he suddenly realized what he was looking for was on the floor. It wasn't the symbols on the amulet he should have been looking for, but the shape of the piece itself.

With Rocky watching him in puzzlement, Dallas dropped to the floor and began running his fingers across the tiles, looking for a blank, recessed space in the same shape. The floor was like a puzzle and he held in his hand the final piece. The diffused lighting made the search more difficult than Dallas had expected. In fact, he was beginning to think he was on the wrong track, when his fingers wandered across a matching triangular shape. He looked up momentarily to signal to Rocky that he'd found the spot. He also glanced over to Miranda, locking eyes with her to let her also know, silently, that he was ready for whatever move she might have in mind. All that was transmitted in an instant, and then his gaze returned once again to the amulet. He turned it over once again in his hand, wondering which way should face up. With no further fanfare, he reached his hand out and placed the metal piece in the triangular space on the floor. It seemed to lock into place as if it were magnetic.

"Well, Rocky," Dallas said, "that's the best I can do. If that doesn't work, I don't know what else to do."

"Okay, Dr. Roark, I believe you." With that he leveled the weapon at Dallas's chest. "You are of no further use to me."

As he was about to open fire on the surprised scientist, the columns began to glow. It was an unearthly blue glow that seemed to get slowly darker in the center, almost to jet-black. The area of blackness was utterly opaque, yet had absolutely no depth. The group froze, too fascinated by what was happening even to react to Rocky's imminent betrayal. A visible electrical field began to radiate from the metal strips running up the columns. Rocky seemed to grasp the significance, and quickly stepping backward and moving to his left, he centered himself between the pillars. He no longer had his attention on the present; now his reflexes were focused on things transpiring thirteen thousand years ago. He waited for that moment when past and present would meet, and he would fulfill his destiny. It was at this instant that Miranda struck, springing from her kneeling position and planting her shoulder squarely on Rocky's chest.

So complete was Rocky's surprise at the attack that he stumbled backwards, the weapon dropping from his hand. Executing a perfect shoulder roll, Miranda sprang to her feet, pulled her diving knife from her ankle sheath and flung its five-inch blade; sinking it deep into the center of Rocky's back. Dallas had also lunged at Rocky, missed, and fell to the floor, totally off-balance.

Anger glowed in Rocky's eyes as he regained his footing and stood over the fallen scientist with his bleeding back to the doorway. Dallas looked up; the advantage of surprise now lost, and prepared himself for the beating that was to come. Suddenly his eyes grew wide in awe.

"Is that a look of fear? Excellent!" Rocky taunted as he reached behind his back to withdraw the knife. "Now I will give you the slow, painful death you so richly deserve," Turning the red-stained blade in his right hand, he reached down with his left hand and grabbed Dallas by his backpack. The archaeologist turned in his shoulders, and spun away, leaving the enemy holding the bag. He raised his arm up to toss the pack to one side when a massive hand grabbed hold of his wrist. Rocky spun around and found himself face to face with a stranger; it could only be the Emperor – En.Lil.An.

"What are you doing, Ha.Sa.Tan?" Everyone could hear him clearly, yet his lips did not move. He was a tall man, if he could truly be called a man, with pale skin and hair so blonde it bordered on white. He stood over seven-feet tall, well-muscled and powerful; not at all the type of physical specimen Dallas had expected. Rocky tried to resist, but was held powerless. "Answer me!" En.Lil.An's 'voice' rang out again.

"You are the enemy of all living things. It is my mission to kill you before you can rise again."

"Wrong, puny one, you have failed. I throw you back to your kind; they await you in Hell, on the other side of the doorway." With that, En.Lil.An gave a simple flick of his wrist, and Rocky, still clutching Dallas's backpack, with his journal still inside, disappeared into the blue-black emptiness from which the emperor himself had stepped moments before.

Turning back to face the assembly, the emperor stared, and his voice erupted in their minds. "He was not properly prepared. He died the moment he exited the doorway. Who are you?"

"We are the Order —" began Camile.

"And the Guardians," interrupted Joshua.

"And I," added Dallas, "just came along for the ride."

"The Order? The Guardians? I must know more, quickly. Give your minds to me." The emperor closed his eyes and remained silent, and he absorbed everyone's thoughts. After a few moments he began again, this time speaking aloud and in English.

"Has it really been so long? I had no idea so much time would pass."

"Much was lost, My Lord," Camile offered apologetically, "and the tablets were scattered. We have not done well in fulfilling your vision. Our people know nothing of the empire, much less the galactic struggle our people have faced."

"Still," En.Lil.An offered consolingly, "you have given us hope, and for that, I am grateful. You have given the empire a chance to throw off the yoke of the evil serpents that threaten to destroy us all." Looking at Joshua lying on the ground, En.Lil.An knelt down and spoke gently, "And you; were you injured in my service?"

"Yes ... no. I was injured in pursuing the truth of our people; the path that led us to this time and place. We did not know of your existence until recently, when Dallas translated the tablets."

"Still, you have honored our race." With that, the emperor extended his hand over Joshua's body. A brilliant, radiant light enveloped Joshua for an instant and then it was gone. "Arise, my friend, for the empire still has need of your services." Joshua shifted slowly, and then rose gingerly to his feet. Miranda hugged her father, with tears running down her cheeks. Camile grinned and slapped him on the back. Turning to Dallas, En.Lil.An continued, "So, you are responsible for our salvation?"

"I ... I had help ... Your ... Excellency," Dallas stammered, unsure of exactly how to address this being. "Miranda gave me strength."

"Ahh, I see. Still, you are a person of singular skill. Now, your world has need of your skill as well."

"But ... Sir, this world doesn't know that you ... or the empire ... ever existed. We are a petty, divided world with hundreds of little nations."

"From what you say, it is clear that the time has not yet come for my return. Kia … your Earth, must be educated; it must be prepared if we are to move forth and defeat the evil that fills our galaxy. This is the mission I task you with: prepare them for what is to come. You must make ready the path for my final return. From what I saw in your minds, the serpents are here on your world. Do not underestimate the enemy; they pose a great danger. This vault has much that will help you. The others have still more. The technology of our people is on this world. The history of our people is here. All that you need to complete your mission is here."

"My mission? But I am an archaeologist; not a leader of men. I cannot unify an entire world."

"I have faith in you; you must have faith in me. You are my choice. Hear my words – you who call yourselves the Order and the Guardians, the time for your differences is now past. You have both fulfilled your ancient mission. Now, you both must come together; and you, Dallas Roark, shall lead them. Miranda Fisher, I sense your desire to stand at his side and be his strength; let it be so. You and your descendants shall lead the people in the name of the House of Ed.In. When all is ready, you must return to this place and once again activate the doorway. On that day, we shall go forth together and return to the stars."

"But I thought you needed two doorways."

"No, though it is what we let the Ha.Sa.Tan believe. You need two fixed points, yes; but they can be points in time as well as space —"

"Never mind … Sire," interrupted Dallas, "as long as Jon gets it. Time travel isn't my strong suit. But how will we know when we've succeeded? Or even if we've succeeded?"

"By your reckoning, what is the time?"

Looking at his watch, Dallas replied simply, "16:44, local time."

"Very well, when the day comes to once again activate the gate, set its coordinates for 16:45 on this date. And, if you succeed, then —" He turned to face the doorway and waited.

As if on cue, the columns powered up once again. A broad smile flashed across En.Lil.An's face. "To answer your second question, you appear to have succeeded; take comfort in that. As to when, that I cannot say. It might be you, or it might be a distant descendant a thousand years from now; but let history show that it will one day come to pass."

"But where are the other chambers?"

"The tablets hold as much information as I dared say. They are at your hands and feet; but above all you must find the heart of our people if we are to achieve final victory."

"The heart of our people, you mean this chamber is not the heart?"

"No, it is not."

And with that, the emperor stepped into the darkness and was gone.

"You know, Lord Dallas," Jon chuckled, "you still have a couple of issues to contend with, like the Ha.Sa.Tan back at Seahab —"

"And maybe onboard the tanker," added Camile.

"Not to worry. The doorway opened, so we know it all turns out for the best."

"I hate to say this,'" said Joshua slowly, "but how do we know the Ha.Sa.Tan don't defeat us, somehow steal the date and activate the doorway themselves?"

Everyone went silent, staring at one another for a long time, and wondering what the future really held.

"Come on, everyone," Dallas said finally, "There's only one way to be sure. We have work to do!"

THE END

Printed in the United States
85716LV00005B/29/A

9 781425 930165